Praise for *King Kong Theory*

'Despentes argues compellingly about
power and the way that both are still
after the supposed triumph of fem
Independent

'A gloriously aggressive and fearless writer' Lisa Hilton, *TLS*

'A manifesto... part memoir, part political pamphlet, it is a furious condemnation of the "servility" of enforced femininity and was a bestseller in France – the title refers to her contention that she is "more King Kong than Kate Moss"' Elizabeth Day, *Observer*

'*King Kong Theory* is a free-ranging feminist manifesto... her writing has an undeniable edge and urgency' Lesley McDowell, *Independent on Sunday*

APOCALYPSE BABY

VIRGINIE DESPENTES

TRANSLATED BY SIÂN REYNOLDS

Culture

This project has been funded with support from the European Commission. This publication reflects the views only of the author, and the Commission cannot be held responsible for any use which may be made of the information contained therein.

A complete catalogue record for this book can be obtained from the British Library on request

First published as *Apocalypse bébé* in 2010 by Grasset, Paris

First published in this translation in 2013 by Serpent's Tail, an imprint of Profile Books Ltd
3A Exmouth House
Pine Street
London EC1R 0JH
website: www.serpentstail.com

ISBN 978 1 84668 842 3
eISBN 978 1 84765 790 9

Designed and typeset by sue@lambledesign.demon.co.uk
Printed and bound by CPI Group (UK) Ltd, Croydon, CR0 4YY

10 9 8 7 6 5 4 3 2 1

MIX
Paper from
responsible sources
FSC® C020471

'... como dos vampiros dormiremos sobre tu tumba,
calentaremos tus huesos, como dos vampiros vendremos a saciar
tu sed de sexo, de sangre y de testosterona'

Testo Yonqui

To B.P.

PARIS

NOT SO LONG AGO, I WAS STILL THIRTY. ANYTHING could happen. You just had to make the right choice at the right moment. I often changed jobs, my short-term contracts weren't renewed, I had no time to get bored. I didn't complain about my standard of living. I rarely lived alone. The seasons followed one another like packets of sweets: easy to swallow and differently coloured. I don't know quite when it was that life stopped smiling on me.

Today I have the same pay as ten years ago. Back then, I thought I was doing all right. Once I passed thirty, the spring went out of things, the impetus that carried me along seemed to ebb away. And I know that next time I find myself on the job market, I'll be a mature woman, without any qualifications. That's why I'm clinging on for dear life to the work I have now.

This particular morning, I arrive late. Agathe, the young receptionist, taps her watch with her finger and frowns. She's wearing fluorescent yellow tights and pink heart-shaped earrings. Easily ten years younger than me. I ought to take no notice of her impatient little sigh when she thinks I'm taking too long to take my coat off, instead of which I mutter an indecipherable apology, head straight for the boss's door, and raise my hand to knock on it. From inside his office comes the sound of hoarse screaming. I step back, alarmed. I look at Agathe questioningly, she pulls a face and whispers, 'It's Madame Galtan, she was waiting for you outside, before we opened this morning. Deucené's been getting it in the neck for twenty minutes now. Go in, go in now, it'll calm her down.' I'm tempted to turn on my heel and rush downstairs, without a word of explanation. But I knock at the door, and they hear me.

For once, Deucené doesn't need to glance down at the files strewn across his desk to remember my name.

'Ah, this is Lucie Toledo, you've already met, she was just...'

He doesn't get to the end of the sentence. The client interrupts him with a shout. 'So where were *you*, you stupid cow?'

She gives me two seconds to digest the verbal assault, then carries on, turning up the volume. 'You know how much I pay you not to let her out of your sight? And then she dis-app-ears? In the metro! In the MET-RO, I don't believe it, you managed to lose her in the metro! Then you wait half the day before leaving me a message. The *school* let me know before you did. That seem normal to you? Could it be you think you've been doing your job properly?'

This woman is possessed by the devil. I can't have reacted enough in her view, she loses interest in me, and turns back on Deucené. 'So why was this gormless halfwit the one you had following Valentine? You didn't have anyone brighter on your books?'

The boss looks daunted. Up against the wall, he covers for

me. 'Let me assure you that Lucie is one of our best agents, she's got plenty of experience on the ground and...'

'You think it's *normal* to lose a girl of fifteen, on the journey she does every morning?'

I had met Jacqueline Galtan when we opened the file, ten days or so earlier. Impeccable blonde bob, stiletto heels with red soles, she was a cold woman, well-preserved for her age, very precise with her instructions. I hadn't guessed that as soon as she was crossed, she'd develop Tourette's syndrome. In her anger, lines start to appear on her forehead. The Botox is fighting a losing battle. A drop of white froth appears at the corner of her lips. She's marching round the office now, her bony shoulders shaking with rage.

'So just HOW did you lose her, you bloody idiot, in the METRO???'

The word seems to excite her. Facing her, Deucené cowers in his chair. I feel pleasure watching him shrink back, since he never loses a chance to act the hard man in company. Jacqueline Galtan improvises a monologue, delivered at machine-gun speed: it's directed at my ugly mug, my scruffy clothes, my total inability to do my job, which heaven knows is not very difficult, and the lack of intelligence that marks every damn thing I do. I concentrate on Deucené's bald head, speckled with obscene brown spots. Short and paunchy, the boss isn't very sure of himself, which tends to make him ruthless towards his subordinates. Right now, he's paralysed with panic. I push forward a chair and sit down at the side of his desk.

The client stops to draw breath, and I seize the chance to join in the conversation.

'It happened so fast... I had no idea Valentine was likely to disappear. You think she's run away?'

'Ah, how helpful, now we're actually talking about it! It's precisely because I'd like to know the answer that I'm paying you.'

Deucené has spread out a number of photographs and reports on his desk. Jacqueline Galtan picks up a page of a report at random, between two fingers, as if it were a dead insect, glances quickly at it and drops it again. Her nails are impeccable too, bright red polish.

I try to justify myself. 'You asked me to *follow* Valentine, to report on where she went. Who she met, what she was up to... But I wasn't at all expecting anything would happen to her. It's not the same kind of assignment, do you see what I mean?'

Now she bursts into tears. That's all we needed to put us totally at ease.

'It's just so awful, not knowing where she is.'

Deucené, looking apologetic, avoids her eyes, and stammers, 'We'll do everything we can to help you find her... But I'm sure the police...'

'The police! You think the police give a damn? All they're interested in is getting the media involved. They just have one idea – talk to the press. You really think Valentine needs that sort of publicity? Think that's a good way to begin her life?'

Deucené turns to me. He'd like me to invent some line of enquiry. But I was the first to be surprised that morning, when I didn't find her sitting in the café opposite the school. The client is off again.

'Right, I'll pay. We'll do it my way, a special contract. Five thousand euros bonus if you bring her back in two weeks. But the other side of the bargain is, if you *don't* find her, I'll make your life a hell on earth. We have connections, and I imagine an agency like yours doesn't want to have a lot of, let's say, *unwelcome* inspections. Not to mention the bad publicity.'

As she utters the last words, she raises her eyes to look straight at Deucené, quite slowly, a very elegant movement, like in a black and white film. She must have been practising that gesture all her life. She looks again at the page from the report. The files on the table are all mine. Not just the ones I put together all day and all evening yesterday, but ones they must have gone to fetch themselves from my computer. They can do what they like to someone like me: obviously they've been checking to see I've brought everything out, and haven't forgotten or hidden anything. I spent hours selecting the most important documents and sorted them into categories, and they've made a total mess of it, of course everything's out there now: from the bill at the café where I waited to the least interesting photo I took of her, including ones where all you can see is a bit of her arm... It's their way of telling me that even if I spend twenty-four hours on a dossier making sure it's cast iron when it's asked for, I'm deemed incapable of judging what's important and what isn't. Why should they be deprived of the pleasure of being sadistic to someone, when I'm right there, available, at the bottom of the food chain? She's right to call me a halfwit, the old hag. If it makes her feel better. Yes, I'm the halfwit, who gets paid peanuts, and has just been on duty for almost a fortnight trailing a nymphomaniac teenager, who's hyperactive and coked up to the eyeballs. Just for a change. I've been working almost two years for Reldanch, and that's the only kind of assignment I ever get: snooping on teenagers. I was doing it as efficiently as anyone else, up to the moment Valentine disappeared.

That particular morning, yesterday, I was a few steps behind her, in the corridor of the metro. It wasn't difficult to pass unnoticed in the crowd of commuters, because the kid hardly ever took her eyes off her iPod. As I made for the exit, an older woman, heavily-built, suddenly collapsed in front of me. And my reflex was to stretch out my arms as she fell backwards. Then, instead of just lowering her to the ground and hurrying on, so as not to lose my quarry, I stayed with her for a minute until some other people arrived. I'd been trailing Valentine for most of two weeks. I was sure I'd find her in the café next to this crammer she attended, stuffing her face with muffins and Coca-Cola, like she did every morning, with some of the other kids from the school, but sitting a little back from them, calmly keeping her distance. Except *that* day, Valentine disappeared. It's always possible something has happened to her. Obviously, I wondered whether she'd spotted me and taken advantage of the accident to lose me. But I'd never felt she was suspicious. Still, after long experience of trailing after teenagers, I'm beginning to understand what makes them tick.

Jacqueline Galtan looks down at the photos on the desk. Valentine giving a boy a blowjob, on a park bench, hidden from passers-by by a waist-high shrub. Valentine snorting a line from her exercise book at 8 a.m. Valentine, having done a bunk, jumping on the back of a scooter ridden by a perfect stranger she'd stopped at a traffic light, late at night... I didn't have a colleague working with me on this job. So because of budgetary constraints, I'd been teamed up with a notorious crack addict, who'd work for any rate at all, as long as he was paid in cash every night. I suppose his dealer had let him down, but anyway he'd never turned up to relieve me, and his voicemail was full, I couldn't reach him. Nobody thought it was a matter of urgency to replace him. You had to be under the kid's window, in case she did a runner, and at the school gates next morning as well. In fact, it was lucky I was actually there when she disappeared. Most of the time, I had no idea what she was up to.

At the beginning of the assignment, I'd used classic tactics: I'd got another kid who helps us out sometimes to offer her an irresistible smartphone for a very good price, so-called 'fallen off a lorry'. Mostly when we're dealing with teenagers, we just tell their parents how to fix their child's mobile. But Valentine didn't have a mobile, and she didn't deign to switch on the one I'd sent her way. That didn't help. I don't often have to track a teenager without a good GPS installed.

The ancestor lines up the photos, looking thoughtful, then swivels her gaze on to me. 'And you wrote these reports, did you?' she says quite affably, as if we'd had plenty of time to digest her tirade. I stammer out a few words, she isn't listening. 'And you took the photos too? Well, you did a good job before you screwed up.' Blowing hot and cold, the way of all manipulative people: first the insult then the compliment, and *I'll* be the judge of the tone of our exchanges, thank you very much. It works too; her recriminations were so unpleasant that the compliment is like a shot of morphine on an open wound. If I dared, I'd roll over and let her scratch my stomach. She lights a cigarette. Deucené hasn't the courage to tell her it isn't allowed, and his eyes dart around looking for something to offer her as an ashtray.

'I assume you will take *personal* charge of finding her.'

Yippee, brilliant: she's just using me as a punchball. I wait for Deucené to tell me the name of the agent who will take over the case. I've never done missing persons, no experience. But he turns to me.

'You're already familiar with the file.'

The client approves, she's smiling again now. The boss gives me a conspiratorial wink. He looks relieved, pathetic jerk.

An insect crawls along the top pane of the window in the broom cupboard I have to use as an office. It has huge antennae.

I take out my card index. I don't store much on my computer. If I'm shot dead tomorrow and they come and search through my things, and find my notes, they'll probably think I've invented a system of coded language that would make Enigma look like child's play. The truth is that when I try to read it over myself, I wonder what I meant to say. Luckily, I've got a good memory, and I usually end up remembering what I intended to note down, more or less. I have this set of index cards covered with weird signs, sometimes mathematical (as if I know anything about algebra).

Since I've been working here, I've got really fed up at being assigned these teenagers. A kid can't smoke a joint in peace without me personally being right up behind him. The first year, I never had to follow anyone under fifteen. Nowadays, it doesn't surprise me to be asked to work in the primary-school sector. The life of their children belongs to adults of my generation, who don't want to let their youth get away from them twice. I can't exactly say I hate what I'm doing, but fixing little kids' mobiles is neither glorious nor exciting. I ought to be feeling pleased at getting a bit of variety in my work, except that I haven't the faintest idea what I should do. Deucené dismissed me from his office without asking me if I needed any help.

I try typing in Valentine Galtan's name on the internet. And draw a blank. No surprises there. She's the first kid I've been tailing that I've never seen send a text message. And yet even youngsters high on crack take the time to post a video of themselves looking totally spaced out on YouTube.

Her father, François Galtan, is a novelist. I met him briefly, the day the grandmother came to hire us. He didn't say a word throughout the conversation. His Wikipedia page is typical of those insecure people who write their own entry – any sense of decency's gone out of the window. Who he sat next to at school, where he went to school, what books influenced him, what the weather was like the day he wrote his first poem, his super-important lectures in improbable seminars, and so on. On the photos accompanying the press reports devoted to him, you can see he's very proud of not going bald, his hair's combed back in a great wavy mane. I suppose the first thing I should do is contact him.

Valentine's mother abandoned the child soon after her birth. The family claims to have no idea where she could be today. I'll have to find her, of course. The scale of the task overwhelms me. I consider resigning. But it would be better if they sacked me for incompetence, if I want to claim unemployment benefit. I've reached the stage of wondering whether I should look again at the TV shows about private investigators that used to make us laugh so much, to get some inspiration, when Jean-Marc knocks at my door – I know it's him without seeing him, he bends two fingers and taps the panel gently, his way of flexing his wrist is elegant, sexy. He puts his head round the door to see if I'm alone, then goes over to the window looking on to the street. I make some coffee. He hums 'J'aime tes genoux', a Henry Salvador song, beating time with his shoulders and hips, not bothering to take his hands out of his pockets. He's tall, thin, but strong-looking, with a powerful frame and a way of standing up straight, occupying a lot of space. His features are irregular, he has deepset eyes, a rather thick nose and a bulging brow. The kind of craggy face girls often like, but the ones it really turns on are his male colleagues. They think he's a god. Jean-Marc is the only one on the team who dresses well. The rest of us look like sales reps from the provinces. We're not doing a job where it pays to look conspicuous. He always wears a black tie and an impeccably white shirt, and tells anyone who'll listen that by not wearing ties, men have lost their virility. Stop wearing a suit, according to him, and you stop representing the law. He rarely visits me, unless he needs to contact some kid who might be useful to him. I have a helpful network of youngsters willing to run errands on the cheap. Today he's come to see me because I've been given this difficult case. Agathe must have filled him in. From her desk, she can hear and follow everything that goes on in the boss's office. The Reldanch agency premises are a former blood testing lab, and the walls haven't been soundproofed. I'd like it if Jean-Marc were to suggest working together with me on this enquiry. But he thinks I can handle it on my own.

'Where are you going to start?'

'That's just what I'm wondering. This kid is half-crazy. I've no idea what's happened to her. And the grandmother is so scary that I can't lean on her about it. Honestly, I don't know. Her biological mother, I suppose.'

He looks at me without saying anything. I think he is waiting for me to outline my plan of attack.

I ask, '*You*'ve done missing persons, haven't you? Aren't you sometimes afraid you'll find something grim?' I'm trying to sound casual, but just pronouncing these words opens up a hollow in my chest. I hadn't realized how scared I was.

'Well, five thousand euros reward, what can I say? I don't ask myself if I'm afraid of what I'll find, I ask myself how I'm going to track down this kid. If you can't see how to handle it yourself, just delegate. Everyone else does. You can share the bonus. Do you need some contacts?'

'I thought about that. I'm going to put a proposal to the Hyena. She knows the ropes.'

It's the first name that comes into my head that might impress him. I let it drop in the tone of voice of a girl who calls up the Hyena every time she loses her house keys. It's true that I know this guy who knows her, but actually, I've never set eyes on her.

Jean-Marc utters a slightly choked laugh. He doesn't look anxious and concerned any more, he looks distant. The

Hyena has a reputation. Declaring I could work with her is tantamount to saying I have clandestine activities. I'm already regretting the lie, but I go ahead with my yarn.

'I often meet people in this bar where she hangs out. The barman's a pal of mine, and he's a big friend of hers.'

'So one way and another, you've got to know her.'

I don't answer. Jean-Marc blows on his coffee then says, thoughtfully, 'You know, Lucie, it's just a matter of luck and perseverance. It may look impossible at first, but somehow or other a lead opens up, and then it's just a matter of sweating it out.'

I agree, as if I could see what he means.

Jean-Marc has long been the star of our outfit, not just because he composes his reports in such a dazzling style that even when he fails on a case, by the time you reach the end you would think he had succeeded. He was the right-hand man of our old boss, and everyone thought he'd be the official number two, and go off to direct a big branch. Then Deucené was appointed director, and Jean-Marc made him ill at ease. Too tall, probably.

Jean-Marc closes the door quietly behind him. I look for the index card for Cro-Mag. I'll call him from a cabin when I go down to lunch in a while. I don't trust the phone lines in the office, they're all tapped, although I can't think who'd have the time to listen to our conversations. It's a professional reflex, I only use my mobile to text birthday greetings and I avoid sending emails altogether. I know what they can cost you if there's an enquiry or a lawsuit. And I know they can be hacked by anyone who's nosy. I still often send letters by snail mail. To guess the contents of an envelope is a skill most agents don't have nowadays. I've never had anything important to conceal, but in this job you develop a degree of paranoia.

Cro-Mag doesn't burst out laughing when I tell him I want to contact the Hyena. I'm grateful to him for that. He tells me to call back later. I head for Valentine's school, to have a coffee in the bar where the kids go every lunchtime. This little private school doesn't have a canteen or a playground, it wasn't designed for the children's needs. I don't try to talk to them, I just eavesdrop on their conversations. Nobody mentions Valentine. They don't know she's missing, which means the police haven't been called in yet. Though I'd have been willing to bet that the Galtans are well-connected enough to get the police to give this case more priority than they would for some ordinary missing person. The kids go back in to class. They're empty-headed, noisy and over-excited. Interchangeable profiles. I'm not interested in them. It's mutual, I haven't registered on their field of vision. That's my strength: I'm dispensable. I stay there most of the afternoon, reading every word of a newspaper a customer has left on a table, and ordering more coffees. Guilt at hanging about instead of starting the enquiry nags at me a bit, but not enough to prevent my enjoying the afternoon off.

On the pavement outside the bar where Cro-Mag works, a group of Goths are smoking, and laughing a lot, which seems contrary to their philosophy to me, but then I'm no specialist. None of them takes any notice as I push through the throng to go in.

Cro-Mag welcomes me warmly. Given his lifestyle – alcohol, hard drugs, up all night, surviving on kebabs and fags – he's looking good. He still has the kind of loopy energy most people lose after thirty, and in him it doesn't look forced. His ear lobes are deformed by the huge earrings he wears, his teeth are nicotine orange but at least he's got them all, that's something. He leans across the counter to whisper that she'll be along soon. From a distance, it must look as if I've come in looking for drugs and he's telling me where to find a dealer. Scratching his chin, and tipping back his head in a virile but unattractive movement, he adds, 'These days, she's sniffing around this girl who comes in often. It wasn't hard to get her to drop by.'

I order a beer at the counter, I'd have preferred a hot chocolate because it's cold outside, but I've got a date with the Hyena and I don't want her to think I'm a wimp. I don't often touch alcohol in bars, it gives me a headache and I don't like losing control. You never know what you might be capable of once you lose your inhibitions.

I've known Cro-Mag a long time. Over one winter, about fifteen years ago, we slept together. I'd thought him rather ugly, but after we'd had a lot to drink, he'd insisted so much that we should go home together that it was tempting. Then one day he turned up with a girlfriend in tow, from some distant province, dark-haired and pretty enough not to be ashamed to be seen with a type like him. Cro-Mag avoided me for a while after that, feeling guilty and afraid I'd ask for explanations or make a scene. But I'd stayed calm, so he'd become affectionate towards me, and could always be counted on to call and ask me to go for a coffee if he was in my neighbourhood, or to invite me if he threw a party. It was via him, two years ago, that I'd heard they were looking for staff at the Reldanch agency.

He tips out some peanuts, puts one saucer down beside me, gives me a friendly wink and goes back to filling glasses behind the bar. He's only too willing to talk about the Hyena: he loves describing their adventures. They used to work together. They even started off in partnership. Debt collecting. Their first customer was a so-called textile merchant, in tiny premises in the 12th arrondissement, who'd 'forgotten' to pay a supplier. Their job was to suggest that he paid this long-standing bill off as soon as possible. Before they went there, the Hyena proposed to Cro-Mag that she'd be the bad cop and he could be the good cop, and he'd felt insulted. 'Have you seen what I look like?' A reasonable response: Cro-Mag is built like a colossus and with his small, dark, close-set eyes, his expression veers between a scary stupidity and bestiality. Being more impressed by his mission than he wanted to admit, he'd given the guy a brutal shaking, counting on his energy to make up for his lack of experience. The guy was whining, but you could see that he was playacting just to get them to stop. The Hyena had stayed in the background, not saying a word. Then just as they were leaving, she had wheeled round, grabbed the man by the scruff of the neck, smiled and snapped her teeth three times in his ear. 'If we have to come back here, you turd, I will personally bite your cock off with my teeth, got that?'

The way Cro-Mag tells it, it was like coming into contact with the Incredible Hulk, only not green: she'd mutated into a monster, anyone would have run a mile from her. And yet afterwards, she was depressed, and thought it hadn't worked. 'Couldn't smell fear on him. Smells like fucking ammonia, it's so gross if you smell it on someone, makes you want to hit them at once.' Cro-Mag had been even more worried than during the confrontation itself: 'You're sick,' he said, 'you're really sick.' The moment she'd grabbed the man by the neck, he'd felt as if something had splashed on to him. He called it 'the urge to kill, naked, something you can't fake'. The man had paid up that same evening. Gradually, they'd found their rhythm: he'd make the first approach, she'd go in to underline the message. A sort of alchemy surrounded them, so they made excellent persuaders. He liked to recall that it was him who'd given her the nickname: 'if you'd seen her in action, in those days, you couldn't think of anything else. A hyena; the more vicious and sadistic she was, the more she enjoyed it.' Cro-Mag was full of theories about that period in his life, and I guess he'd worked them out by talking to her. 'Fear's something animal, it's beyond language, even if some words spark it off more than others... you have to feel your way, it's like with a girl, you're on a date but you don't know her, you move your hands around in the dark until the precise moment when it starts to work, all you have to do then is hold it there and you can reel her in. So whether you've got someone who's dumb but obstinate, or someone who's imaginative and nervy, you have to make them get the message loud and clear: next time we'll go for the jugular, you won't get away, and you know that.' He'd loved working with her, he boasted about it willingly to the kids who hung around his bar as if he was giving them important lessons for life: 'We made a good team, we were agreed on the basics, such as:

take long breaks often, the job works better if you're feeling relaxed; always accept a bribe if it's substantial, and, above all, when in serious danger, running away is not harmful to your health. We talked a lot about girls too. It's important to have interests in common. You can't talk about the job all the time, too stressful.' And then one rainy morning, in the 13th arrondissement, they were going after a Russian – Russians had started arriving in Paris, this was a long time ago – and Cro-Mag had complained about his stomach ulcer. The Hyena had asked him, 'Are you fed up with this job?' and it had been like a light bulb going on: yes, he was fed up of getting up every morning not knowing who he was going to threaten next, whether there would be many of them, whether he'd be frightened or, worst of all, whether he'd feel sorry for them and ashamed of what he was doing. He was fed up with clenching his buttocks every night when he put the key in his front door, with a hollow in his stomach at the thought of finding some men waiting for him in the sitting room, or his girlfriend's body lying mutilated in the kitchen, or being pinned to the ground by a squad of cops. Yes, he was fed up with living in constant terror, without earning enough to move out of his thirty square metres in Belleville. The only reason he was hanging on was to work with her. She had said, 'If you give it up, yes, I'll miss you. But you're capable of doing something else. I'm not. I can't stand being crossed. Whereas you can adapt, it's a shame for you to wear your health out doing a job you hate.' Cro-Mag says that made him want to cry, because he realized at that moment he *was* going to give it up and that it was over, being a team with her. But also because he knew she was telling the truth:

she was beyond saving, unfit for normal life. The difference between the truly tough and those who opt for redemption is that some people have the choice, others don't. Every time he reached this part of their story, he got emotional, spontaneously, as if he'd abandoned an injured teammate on top of a mountain, knowing he couldn't last long, and was now feeling guilty at being able to escape on his own two legs and get back to normal life. 'The Hyena, she's pure tragedy, when you get close to her, you really understand what it is to be lonely, sad, and unfit for the world.' When he went on like this, it was obvious that he loved her. Not 'loved' as in I want to eat your pussy, but like when someone's whole attitude is dear to you and every memory you share is covered with a fine golden sheen. Well. In the two years I've been doing my present job, I've had many occasions to hear things about her, and I've learnt that she has inspired the same feelings in many people, so don't try to tell me she suffers from loneliness...

They'd carried on meeting, in the usual Cro-Mag way, for a coffee from time to time. This guy must spend a crazy amount of energy keeping up with old friends. Over the years, the Hyena had become a star among private investigators: there aren't many of those in the trade, outside crime novels. Her speciality was missing persons. Since then, the stories told about her have evolved into various, contradictory versions, some of them pure fiction. Everyone has their own tale to tell, lawyers, informers, special branch, the cops, other PIs, journalists, hairdressers, hotel staff and prostitutes... anyone who's involved in our little world has their own story about what she's up to, where, how, and who with. She provides drugs for government ministries, with cover from the secret service, she recruits call girls for officials, she has ultrasecret information about ex-French Africa, she speaks Russian fluently and gets on fine with Putin, she's on a mission to rescue hostages in Turkestan, she's trafficking on behalf of South American countries, she's spying on the Scientologists, she's involved with synthetic medicines imported from Asia, the big agro-industrial firms have hired her to defend their interests, nuclear power holds no secrets for her, she's protected by radical Islamists, she's got a house in Switzerland, she often travels to Israel… But the stories all agree on one point: she's never been sentenced in any court, because her files are too explosive for her not to be covered in any circumstances. And it's a fact that over the past five years, when lawsuits and trials have mushroomed, no legal practice has boasted of having her as a client. She hasn't worked for any single outfit for a long time now, but her name crops up – occasioning scorn, admiration, anger or amusement – whenever people are looking for something vaguely sensational to talk about.

I watch the door out of the corner of my eye, with growing nervousness. I repeat over and over the sentences of introduction that I've prepared. I keep telling myself for reassurance that she can't have done a tenth of the things people say, and that in times of economic crisis, five thousand euros cash bonus is a sum worth discussing. At regular intervals, Cro-Mag asks me if I want anything else, I refuse, and he shuts his eyes and nods several times, a mysterious smile floating across his face, all meaning, I presume, that she'll be along soon, you have to be patient, she's no doubt on some top-level mission. The bar has filled up, a hoarse-voiced male singer is croaking something out of the speakers, I'll never understand the appeal of that kind of music, you'd think you were on a building site. Suddenly Cro-Mag's face lights up, and the Hyena is right beside me. Very tall, hollow cheeks, Ray-Bans, men's style, a figure-hugging white leather jacket, she must think she's a film star. Cro-Mag points towards me, and she holds out her hand.

'Lucie? You wanted to see me?' She doesn't take the glasses off, doesn't smile, and doesn't give me time to say anything. 'Five minutes if you don't mind? I've got to say hello to some friends, then I'll be back.'

Seen close up, she doesn't look at all like the mythical person I've heard so much about. I wait, while conscientiously sipping my half-glass of beer, clench my teeth, and tell myself that even if this is a ridiculous attempt, it won't kill me to have made the effort.

'Shall we sit down over there? It'll be quieter to talk.'

She goes ahead of me, confident and casual, her legs are long and slender in her tight-fitting white jeans, she's fashionably slim, a body that tends to vanish and carries clothes well. I feel like I'm short and fat, my jumper is damp with nervous sweat, I realize my hands are shaking, and I reckon I'm lucky not to fall on my face as we go over there. She sits down facing me, arms draped over the back of her chair, legs apart, as if she's trying to take up the maximum of space with the minimum of body mass. I collect my wits and wonder how to begin. She takes her shades off at last, and gives me a long cool look up and down. She has very big dark eyes and an expressive face, lined like an old Indian woman's.

'I work for the Reldanch agency.'

'Yeah, Cro-Mag told me.'

'I've sort of specialized in checking up on minors.'

'On to a good thing there, I gather.'

'Yes, it's one of our best lines. I've been tailing this girl, she's fifteen, and I lost her, in the metro, the morning before yesterday on her way to school. She didn't come home, she hasn't been in touch. Her grandmother's offered five thousand euros if we can get her back in a fortnight. And…'

'Five thousand euros, alive or dead?'

I suppose that's the kind of question I ought to have thought of asking.

'I hope we'll find her alive.'

'What do you think, runaway or kidnap?'

'No idea.'

'What kind of girl?'

'Difficult, sex-mad, off the rails.'

'What's the family like?'

'The father's a writer, with a private income, from the family pharmaceutical company somewhere near Lyon. He brought the kid up on his own, with the grandmother being around a lot. The mother took off when Valentine was two years old, doesn't see her, and nobody seems to know at the moment where she is.'

I open my backpack and bring out a photo of the kid. The Hyena hesitates to take it.

'I don't really see how I can help you…' She glances down at the picture, and seems to think for a while as she observes it. She hesitates. I feel reassured.

'And how much will you give me if I work with you?'

'The five thousand euros bonus. It'll be in cash. And if

there's no result... we'll have to work out how to divide up my pay.'

'At that kind of rate, I wouldn't want to put myself out too much.'

She smiles as she puts the glasses back on. I can't tell if I amuse her or annoy her.

She has started calling me 'tu' now. 'So you let me keep the money, young Lucie, but are you going to work on it too, or do sweet FA?'

'I... I'd prefer to have someone working with me, in the sense that...'

'That you have absolutely no idea where to start. Well, at least that's clear. Did you bring the file from when you tailed her?'

'It's all on my laptop.'

I bend down to take it out, but she stops me with a click of her fingers. 'Can you put it on a USB?'

The Hyena has put Valentine's photo in the middle of the table facing her. 'Teenagers aren't really my thing. They usually have good reasons to clear off, don't they?'

'She might have been kidnapped.'

She puts her head on one side and seems lost in contemplation of the photo. She has beautiful hands, pale with long fingers, I notice that the nails are bitten down to the quick. She wears an enormous ring with a death's head on it, a bit pathetic in my view, who does she think she is, the Keith Richards of the shit-stirrers? She concentrates for a moment on the portrait of Valentine, who is smiling into the camera, three-quarter angle, bright eyes, pretty dimples, glossy hair. Slightly plump. Like all girls of her age, in family photos they just look like nice kids. Then the Hyena fixes her eyes on me pensively, there's something disquieting about the insistence of her gaze.

'Little girls with puppy fat are trying to cover up for their father's lies.'

Brilliant. I thought I was working with James Bond, and now I'm dealing with a family therapist. I don't know how to answer in a way that doesn't seem disagreeable, so I opt for being pragmatic.

'Teenagers go in for a lot of sugary drinks.'

'And why did the family take the step of having her watched?'

'I think they thought Valentine was... putting herself in danger.'

'What kind of danger?'

'You'd need to look at the other photos in the file, she...'

'Later. So what do they think *they're* going to do, to protect her?'

'I haven't had a chance to discuss that with them...'

'But all the time you've been doing this job, you must have some idea what the clients want, don't you?'

'I don't know. No. I don't have anything to do with what they get up to, once the tailing's over.'

'OK. I want the five thousand euros in exchange for the kid, you can tell the clients to get it ready. And you can also tell them that there'll be expenses. They're rolling in it, you said?'

'Yes, but I'm in no position to bargain, because I lost sight of her...'

'You lost nothing of the sort. You know exactly when she

went missing and where. If she decided to make a break for it, you weren't being paid to stop her. If she was kidnapped, you weren't being paid to act as her bodyguard, you were simply following her. What can you possibly blame yourself for? Pull yourself together, and tell her father it's going to cost him plenty.'

'It's the grandmother I see for everything. She's not an easy client to deal with, very aggressive, I don't know whether...'

'Perfectly normal. She wants the job done on the cheap, we'd do exactly the same in her place. But two can play at that game: just because she has a nice try doesn't mean to say she gets away with it. Do you want me to call her for you? What's your last name again?'

At once, I'd like to go and get myself a mechanical shovel, dig a hole in the ground, bury myself there and let time pass. The Hyena takes out her mobile, asks me for the personal number of the client. She looks as if she's enjoying herself. I'm not, on the whole. Madame Galtan answers at once. The Hyena adopts a firm and suave voice.

'Madame Galtan? This is Louise Bizer, lawyer at the Paris bar, I'm working with Mademoiselle Toledo, and please forgive me for troubling you so late, but we... Thanks for being so understanding. We have a little problem with the assignment, because Mademoiselle Toledo tells me that there has been no agreement about expenses... Of course, Madame Galtan, I quite see that, but you'll understand that we can't embark on a matter of such importance, and with such a short deadline, without running up a certain number of expenses, and it could have an unfortunate impact on the results if we

had to take the metro all the time, or send you a justifica-
tion ten pages long, before feeling entitled to take a plane...
But Madame Galtan, I'm sorry to tell you that the contract
you have with the Reldanch agency doesn't cover a missing
person search... No, I don't know what Monsieur Deucené
saw fit to assure you, but what I have in front of me is a signed
and sealed contract, which only covers a report on *watching*
your granddaughter... Yes, I have been informed about the
reward, and if you are aware of the standard procedures in
these cases, you will know that it's the absolute minimum for
this kind of thing... Oh yes, I assure you. No, it's not negli-
gible, but it's certainly well below the usual rate...'

She stands up, takes her empty glass to the counter, and
signs to Cro-Mag to get her another Coke. An amused smile
playing round her lips, she winks at me from a distance. The
old bat must be putting up sturdy opposition, but the Hyena
looks as blissful as if she's pulling on a really good joint. After
a further ten minutes' argument, she ends the call and comes
back to me looking highly pleased.

'A good sort in the end, our Jacqueline. She's agreed,
she'll cover any expenses. And she's given way on the ridiculous deadline of a fortnight. We need to take a bit of time
over this, or we'll look like total idiots.'

'I'd never have believed she could be persuaded...'

'Don't bother, the magic word was lawyer. Rich people
always try to get away without shelling out, but at heart they
believe you have to pay serious money, otherwise you'll only
get poor service, and vice versa. Why wasn't it the father who
asked to have the girl followed?'

'Monsieur Galtan wasn't too keen on the idea. I gather

that it's the grandmother who's mostly been concerned with the kid.'

'You don't take a whole lot of interest in what you do, eh?'

'I'm not used to working on this kind of case.'

'In future, try and *listen* to the client when they come to tell you about their case. For one thing it makes them trust you, if they get the impression you're interested. But above all, if you listen properly, eight times out of ten, it'll tell you where to start. This truth they've come looking for, if it didn't hurt them so much in the first place, they wouldn't need our services to hear it. And you'll see, when you bring along your conclusions, even with photos under their noses, people will refuse to admit what they're seeing.'

I can see this is going to be a whole lot of fun: if she's going to lecture me like this the first evening, what'll it be like in a week's time? She takes a USB from her pocket.

'Put everything you've got on here, OK? And when you've finished, come and find me at the counter. I need to see someone.'

I've had my fifteen minutes. She dumps me there and then, not without patting my shoulder as she goes past. Looking round discreetly, I see that it's a girl, a little brunette with short hair and thick glasses, nothing special to look at, who now has all her attention. The Hyena has her Ray-Bans back on, and she's listening without moving a muscle. Once the memory stick has loaded up, I go over to give it her, and she barely registers me. Even through the dark glasses, you can tell she's eating up this girl with her eyes. I thank Cro-Mag and get away as soon as I can. At the door, I turn round and see the Hyena lean slowly towards the girl, interrupting her in mid-sentence to kiss her. It's just her head that's moved closer to the other woman's, her arms and hands haven't budged. Then she returns to her initial position. She still isn't smiling, it doesn't seem to be part of her repertoire.

FRANÇOIS

SHOWER. SHAMPOO. MOISTURIZER. IN HIS
bathroom, standing in front of the mirror over the basin,
he practises breathing through his nose, slowly. He regrets
having agreed to this interview, his diary's already overbooked.
There are dark circles under his eyes, he's drunk too much
these last few days. He thinks his complexion looks greenish.
The sleeping pills probably. He can't get used to greying
at the temples. At least he's not losing his hair, it could be
worse. But seeing himself in the mirror is still an unpleasant
shock. He can't get used to being this middle-aged man. On
the radio, a minister is talking about locking up paedophiles
who might reoffend. Three psychiatrists have been invited
along with him, to oppose the decision. François is irritated
at their cautious tone. Are they afraid the paedophile might
get bored in the end? The previous day, François recorded a
TV broadcast at 9 a.m., with the minister of labour, who had
just finished doing a radio show. He arrived accompanied by
a team of four advisers. You wouldn't have thought he was
so well-briefed though, seeing him on set. While they were
doing the makeup, someone came to tell François Galtan
that he must never reply directly to the minister, he must
address all his comments through the presenter. It was a bit

annoying, as if they were afraid he wouldn't know how to behave. In any case, he could have jumped on the minister's lap and given him a kiss and it wouldn't have mattered, nobody watches the show. The places he gets asked when he's just published a novel have about as much public exposure as the sandpit down in the garden. *Le Figaro* has still not published anything about his latest book. He calls his press agent, a bimbo who thinks she's charming. She has big thighs and thick ankles, he can't think where she gets her confidence from. She's not there, of course. No doubt accompanying some author who's further up the best-seller list. He asks her to call back, knowing full well she'll forget to. He can't get used to the polite indifference that greets his books when they come out – three vaguely favourable reviews, two minor TV shows, three provincial radio stations, and that's it. He can't complain about being besieged by autograph hunters. Yet he believes in the book sincerely every time. A huge success, his comeback on the literary scene. He affects a dignified indifference to the pointlessness of his efforts, but in a few weeks he realizes it's true, his novel has made no impact. Once more, he feels he's going through hell.

His first novel had been well reviewed by François Nourissier. His enthusiasm hadn't surprised Galtan, he considered recognition no more than he deserved. You didn't write novels like his without people noticing. He'd been invited on to the TV book show *Apostrophes* when the second one had come out: *Rain*. It had meant something in those days. You didn't get on TV as easily as all that, and certainly not to do some chitchat about anything other than your writings. Some good reviews, a reputation for brilliance. Even Pierre

Frank, in a short paragraph at the end of one of his articles, had mentioned François's book. He'd had a few successes, nothing vulgar, nothing over the top. He'd been noticed, but he hadn't won any prizes. He was still under thirty then, and convinced that one day he'd get the Prix Goncourt. He didn't have any doubts. And he didn't suspect anything. He counted the potential jury votes as he wrote his books. He had a prominent publisher, Le Seuil, and he'd been shortlisted three times. Never won, though. Always an also-ran. People told him it wasn't good to get it too young. He took it nonchalantly. He didn't know that he'd already had his moment of glory, that this was *it*. A promising beginning. Followed by not very much. He didn't have the right contacts, he wasn't well-enough connected. No hook to make an impression. Nothing but his books. A bit late in the day, he'd discovered this wasn't going to be enough. He would have liked to be able to console himself by concentrating on posterity, on the generations of young Japanese readers who would be moved to tears when they discovered him too late, and who'd write many biographies, indignant at the vulgar indifference that had greeted his publications during his lifetime. But the more years went by, the less likely that seemed. He didn't lose confidence in his work, but he had his doubts about the world of the future. He'd published the early novels convinced that one day there'd be a Pléiade edition of his collected works, that his oeuvre would be looked at as a whole: readers would admire its coherence, its stability of purpose, with its clear progression, its willingness to take risks and its striking intuitions. He hadn't imagined what would happen in the early 1990s. That was the first sign of decline. The scruffy, uneducated, journalistic writers who'd become the best-sellers for their generation. He was ashamed, in retrospect, that he hadn't anticipated what publishing would turn into: an industry as stupid as any other. A resentful and antiquated streetwalker. Mincing about in tattered robes. Dependent on television and trendy magazines. Enemies whose nuisance value he hadn't spotted. Neither left- nor right-wing. Neither classic nor modern. TV personalities. Celebrities of the day. Pitching a line, always on the lookout for fresh flesh, greedy for readership figures. At first, he had decided to laugh them off. And he wasn't the only one. He remembers, with bitterness today, a dinner party at which an eloquent publisher had kept them in stitches talking about the current best-sellers, forecasting that the way things were going one day people would want to read novels by young girls going into detail about their haemorrhoids. How they had laughed. No, he hadn't seen it coming. Authors who wrote about their eating disorders, or getting raped by their fathers, writers who were illiterate sluts, writers who boasted of screwing teenage girls in Thailand, or of being high on coke. He hadn't seen it coming at all. Not to mention that the 1990s, compared with what followed, were in the end quite tame. He could have adjusted. But then along came the internet. Nowadays, he had to make a constant effort not to spend all day long searching the web, haggard and depressed. Reading the comments. The anonymous load of crap. The litany of non-stop insults delivered by the incompetent. As soon as he discovered them, he realized he had entered the tenth circle of hell. Parallel little comments, deaf to each other, all in the same format, laconic and sickeningly hostile.

Mediocrity had found its voice. The comments on the internet. He wasn't even being insulted. He would have liked to be able to rage and complain about the way he was treated. But he wasn't even interesting enough for these sick fashionistas to launch campaigns against him. He was reduced to writing under a pseudonym, a few words of subtly critical praise for himself on the literary forums and blogs. He did have a few loyal readers, but they didn't feel any pressing need to discuss his work on the internet. Still, he didn't throw in the towel. For his latest novel, *The Great Paris Pyramid*, he'd tried to adapt. Without betraying himself. People were talking about the return of the great French novel; he thought his moment had come at last. Times had changed but he wouldn't. This might finally do the trick. A bit of Egyptian history, which he was knowledgeable about, a romantic plot, young characters who listened to music on their mobiles and talked about sex with no holds barred. But it didn't seem to be taking off. And yet writing it had been a real pleasure, such as he hadn't felt for a long time. He'd taken it for a sign. He'd been drafting the first few pages while suffering with terrible toothache. The dentist had prescribed Solupred pills, which would reduce the abscess enough for the tooth to be extracted. Never having taken them before, he didn't realize he was particularly sensitive to the effects of cortisone. He finished the packet, after the tooth had been pulled, and asked a doctor friend to prescribe some more, then more again, and so on until the book was finished. He wrote for twelve hours at a stretch, smiling over his keyboard. He'd completed it in five weeks, a record for him, since usually every page called for scrupulous rereading, second thoughts, and searching criticism. Fear of being untrue to himself had surfaced briefly, but the siren hopes of making a huge literary comeback were growing inside him, the warm welcome he'd get when he visited his publisher's office, the endless invitations to prestigious dinners, the voicemail full of requests for interviews. It would be worth cheating on his talent if it succeeded. He went on taking cortisone while reading the proofs, and the effects didn't wear off. When he wasn't writing, he was talking, talking to anyone and everyone, he who was usually so reserved. It had been a sparkling season. He would probably never have stopped if he hadn't one evening watched the transmission of a pre-recorded music programme made in the ministry of culture, in which he'd taken part alongside the minister. He'd spoken well, brightly and incisively in the short interview he'd had, so he wasn't worried as he waited to see himself. On the wide TV screen, he'd wondered with amusement who that great fat whale was in his tight grey suit, fidgeting nervously alongside the other guests. And then he'd recognized himself. His wife and daughter, the first gently, the second rudely, had pointed out to him that he'd been putting on weight these last few weeks. But seeing himself every day in the mirror, carried along on a wave of euphoria and creative energy, he hadn't realized it. Until that evening, watching TV, he hadn't taken in how much he'd changed. And then he had seen himself, flopping about, sweating like a pig, his red face reduced to a pair of obscenely joyous cheeks, and talking non-stop, nobody being able to curb his logorrhoea. That very night, the packets of cortisone, hitherto carefully kept in the bathroom, went into the bin. Thereafter, he was to regret not having listened to the advice of the doctor friend who had warned him, as he bent over the precription pad, that he was renewing the pills for the seventh time in three months, and that he should be aware of the risk of stopping them suddenly. He hadn't taken him by the scruff of the neck, put him up against a wall and shouted 'Watch out what happens if you stop taking the meds,' which would at least have been clear. The doctor friend, whom he called Dr Drug during his season on Solupred, was rather easy-going, and like many in his profession, insensitive to other people's pain. He had merely said in a gloomy tone, 'You'll have to come off these sometime, so let me know before you do and I'll tell you how to handle it.' But when François had seen himself looking so grotesque, he had felt he should give up the pills at once. He regarded himself proudly as a strong-willed character, his book was written, that was enough, no more foolishness. The first day, he'd thought it an interesting experience, if he'd had the strength he'd have taken notes, since he had never suffered so much pain. No corner of his anatomy escaped the disaster. By the end of the first week, he told himself he wanted to die, that he was an imposter, his friends were useless, his wife old and ugly, his daughter a fat little fool, he'd never have any literary reputation, his books wouldn't survive him, everyone despised him, he'd never written a good sentence in his life. These moments of lucidity exhausted him. He came to think that suicide was the only strategy that would validate his work. Tortured by fearful hunger and early-morning cramps in all his muscles, he began the second week in a state of complete collapse. It was at that point that Claire had packed him off to see her osteopath, a woman of immense strength who had set about trying to break every bone in his body before putting him on to a vitamin diet of such complexity that simply adhering to it had monopolized all his energy: Spirulin, fermented beetroot juice and fresh almonds... he endured such delights as these, plus an hour's jogging every day. By the eighth day of this regime, which he followed religiously, the depression began to lift and leave him in peace; he no longer had the strength to feel any emotion. Progressively, he was regaining something like the physical appearance he'd had before the cortisone, and the mental capacity to pass a whole day without looking up at the ceiling of every room planning where to fix the sheets he intended to hang himself with. But just as he had kept a bit of a paunch, he had retained a vague sensation of unease. And a solid addiction to vitamin B6. And then, four weeks after the publication of the novel of which she *knew* he was expecting so much, his daughter Valentine had disappeared.

Valentine. The gap left by her absence. The guilty feeling of relief that followed from it. Valentine has never been easy. He has no illusions about that. It doesn't stop him loving her, knowing that she's the woman of his life, the only one he has cherished and protected so much, the only one who's made him laugh such a lot. But it's never been easy. Children are women's work really. He can see that with Claire and her two daughters, quite different. It's all so upfront. Claire's perfectly happy to see to the older girl's dental brace, to check the younger girl's dancing classes, their school grades interest her, she gets on well with their teachers. Even what they have to eat for tea can be a subject of conversation. He loves his daughter. But the high maintenance he's had to do alone really pisses him off. It gets in the way of writing, going out, listening to a record in peace, reading a book in the morning, having some private time with Claire. Constant annoyance. Children are a rope round your neck, anything else is manageable. And even so, when Valentine was little, it was quite sweet, the Aristocats slippers, showing her Buster Keaton films, getting her a Cosette costume for the school fête. There'd been the odd hassle, but there'd been fun as well. But these last years she's exhausted all the concern of which he was capable. And she knows it. He's had enough of Valentine's escapades. The phone calls from school, when she was caught 'up to no good' with boys in the toilets. What kind of 'no good', how many boys, he had taken good care not to find out. Five schools in two years. The same scenario every time. An astronomical sum spent on psychologists who hadn't the slightest idea what was the matter with her. It wasn't rocket science, she just wanted to make as much trouble for him as possible. She wanted him to ditch Claire, like he'd ditched his other women. Valentine's unlucky, she's turned out to look like him. He recognizes himself in her face, her figure. She might have inherited her mother's looks, but the older she gets, the clearer it is that she takes after him. OK in a man. But for a woman… He understands why she's unhappy. When she wears short little dresses like other girls her age, she looks like a rugby player. But that's hardly enough reason to make him suffer as she does. She's full of energy. Naturally, in their teens, they don't tire easily. And she employs it full time to get on his nerves. It's never been easy. When her mother walked out, the little girl was like a poisoned souvenir of how things had been between them. Vanessa. Vanessa had been called Louisa when he met her. She'd decided to change her name one day. Vanessa liked change. The clear memory of the years spent with her. Fourteen years later, and it seems like yesterday. The cruel illusion, when he wakes up, that she's beside him, still tortures him with piercing sharpness. And Valentine is the living proof of that failure, of his great love story. Having been abandoned by the same woman, they were tied together for ever, and by the same token separated. And Valentine had become the ideal pretext for his mother to invade their lives. Just what he needed. His mother, every day or almost, in the house. His mother who never says anything openly pejorative, never asks indiscreet questions, but who looks disparagingly on everything he does. His mother is too fond of him to admit that he's a failure, living off her money. But at heart that's what she thinks. A silent comparison between his father and himself. The businessman and the writer. For example, his mother cuts out every article she can find about the digital future of the book, brings it to him, and if he doesn't read it at once, summarizes it for him. This is her way of letting him understand he's made a mess of everything in his life. A life dedicated to books, when books will soon have vanished from the face of the earth. The same way she has just hired a private detective to find the child. The point of this is to make him see he hasn't stirred himself enough. As if it isn't obvious where the kid is. What's he supposed to do? Go down there and beg her to come back? What's the point? As if he didn't beg hard enough fourteen years ago?

From the other end of the corridor, the cleaner calls that she's finished the ironing and is going home. He glances at his watch, twenty to twelve. Of course, she'll count it as a full hour. The timid treasure who came to work for them two years ago has changed a lot. The Italian journalist is late. And already he's not that bothered to meet her. But his books haven't been translated into Italian for a good while now, and a favourable interview for *La Repubblica* might bring him into the public eye. She's developing a project on the French literary landscape, he's flattered that she has contacted him. But it's annoying that she's late. He wonders whether she'll be pretty, her voice on the phone sounded nice, slightly husky. And then there was the Italian accent. Because Italian women don't just know how to dress. Anna used to slide her finger up his ass every time she gave him a blowjob, just the end of her finger and slide it. Without ever referring to it when the sheets were back in place. As soon as he hears that accent, he gets a hard-on. Her sophisticated Italian look when he took her out, her way of wrapping herself up so that you could only see her dark eyes, the curve of a shapely lip. The nonchalant way she let him open doors, or would give him a parcel to carry. Her regal manner, but without the irritating arrogance of Parisian women. Never trying to be a brilliant conversationalist when they were out for the evening, too beautiful for that. And when they broke up, a fury. Magnificently feminine, when she was shouting insults at him and throwing his clothes out of the door. Then she had hammered him with a series of rapid and vicious little blows with her clenched fists, fists so delicate he would have sworn they could do no damage, but when used like that in repeated regular fashion, they had left a constellation of bruises on his chest and back. He had had to resort to various subterfuges for a fortnight so as not to undress in front of Clothilde, his official wife at the time, with whom he was still living. That was his second marriage. Two divorces, three marriages, a respectable average as he approached fifty. Clothilde had never wished to acknowledge that he was cheating on her. He hadn't bothered to hide it from her any more than from the others. But she chose not to know about it. She had invented an extremely flattering portrait of him, as being not the kind of man to cheat on his wife. She maintained it, come hell or high water. So he could say he was getting back after playing poker with his friends all night, that he was doing research in bars for his novel, that he'd had a late-night discussion with his publisher. He had only to take the trouble to invent an excuse for her to choose to believe it. Her trust had at first bothered him with remorse. A woman so affectionate and upright that she couldn't even imagine he would lie to her. He felt guilty, but unable to stop himself being turned on by a new acquaintance, a presence, a way of moving, of standing in a room, a smile or a voice. He couldn't not do it. He had felt guilty for months, before he realized that Clothilde's lack of jealousy was entirely founded on the deeply condescending idea she had of him. She put up with him because his small-scale fame gave her some kudos, but at heart she found him insignificant, lacking breeding or sophistication, slow-witted and uncharismatic. She viewed him as so far below her that he was reassuring: a little frog like him could only adore a princess like her, and be grateful that she had raised him to her level. It had taken him a while to work out how this functioned, but once he had decoded it, he began to hate her. She had come into his life only a short while after Vanessa had left him. The wound was still too raw for him to forgive Clothilde for making him feel useless and unimportant all over again. He had left her in the lousiest way possible, taking care to make plans for a holiday with friends before walking out one July morning without a word of explanation, to join another woman. Clothilde had wept for months, telling all their friends about it, exhibiting her pain as proof of his ingratitude and dangerous nature. By so doing, she had rendered him extremely desirable to all her female acquaintances. What a stroke of luck. Clothilde hadn't made him happy, but thanks to her he had felt good, being labelled as a bastard, a seducer and a breaker of hearts. Anything was better than the taste in his mouth of the humiliation that Vanessa had forced on him. A little boy, abused and at risk.

'So sorry to be late, it was hard to find a parking place.'

Slight disappointment: she must be in her forties. But the excitement comes back once she takes off her coat: she's taken trouble with her outfit, sure of herself, flirtatious without being vulgar, available for games of seduction without looking as if she's already conquered. Better than pretty. 'Shall we do the photos first? Liam's got another photo-shoot after this.' François agrees with enthusiasm, he too would prefer to be left alone with her. The press agent had warned him there'd be photos, to which he'd replied that he'd prefer to do both together, the interview and the portrait, he's taken care to wash his hair to destroy the ridiculous blow-dry the TV makeup man had inflicted on him the previous day, in spite of his protests. The photographer accompanying the Italian woman is an ape. On the pretext of finding 'a good spot', with the right light, one that would inspire him, he was preparing to roll around on François's bed, a move from which he had to be dissuaded practically by force. Occupied in making the acquaintance of the journalist, François has had no time to stop the photographer rushing into his bedroom, 'to check what it's like'. He keeps flashing around a black box, a light meter, he's here, there and everywhere, standing up against the windows, looking through every room with the air of a madman, muttering comments that are incomprehensible but not necessarily complimentary about the décor. A little ape let loose in the house, you feel like taking him by the scruff of the neck to shake him, as you would a kitten that's peeing everywhere. Photographers are capable of anything. Earlier that week, a young idiot with acne had spent ten minutes insisting François be shouting, with his mouth wide open. Because 'I only do that kind of shot'. 'Glad to hear it, but I don't shout on my photographs.' The young man had sulked, apparently convinced that anyone his magazine sent him to photograph was duty-bound to satisfy the slightest wishes of an untalented child. A year or two back, another one had wanted him to jump in the air in front of the Pyramid of the Louvre. 'We need some movement, you see, otherwise it's too static,' he'd explained in the tone of voice you might use to get a senile old man to go back to his rest home. 'We need the shot to look interesting, you see. I can't take you sitting in a chair with your chin in your hands, we'd lose all our readers.' François couldn't decently jump about in front of the Louvre, with all the people going past. He usually manages to hold out, but sometimes they cancel the article and his press agent scolds him. 'It seems you wouldn't play ball when it came to the photos.' He tries to check the lunatic galloping round the house.

'We usually do the photos in my office or in the library.'

'Yeah, that's just it,' says the imbecile, as he darts into the kitchen. 'I'd like to find a fresh angle, more everyday, more human.'

François wants to shout, 'I write books, you fucking moron, why should I have my picture taken in the kitchen? I'm not going to appear in *La Repubblica* cooking a cassoulet.' The journalist realizes the situation is getting grotesque, so she tries to mediate, succeeding fairly well. She seems taller than she is, just coming up to his shoulder, although she looks long and willowy. She smiles as she tells him about her project, he hardly listens to the list of authors she hopes to include in the series, he presses a cup of coffee on her, unable to concentrate on what she's saying while the photographer is scampering around the 250 square metres of the apartment. He hears him opening the french doors on to the balcony and joins him, feeling infuriated. The idiot is leaning over the guard rail. 'If you don't mind, I'd prefer we stick to the library. I don't like photo-shoots and I want to get it over with.' The photographer turns round, holding the camera, and twisting himself into a ridiculous attitude, takes a picture, 'from life', while repeating, 'Yeah, yeah, super, got it all, the light, need some light, turn your face a bit to the right, chin down a bit, no lower, like that, look at the camera, that's super, face the light, yeah, yeah, got it, perfect, in the can!' All over in a minute, leaving François with the bittersweet impression that he's being treated like some bimbo. 'What do you mean, it's in the can?' he asks, leaning across to the camera to see the result for himself. It's all very well not liking photo-shoots, he knows from experience that it normally takes longer than this. The degenerate ape shrugs: 'I don't do digital, it's all about getting the atmosphere and the definition, sorry, can't show you now, but I've got an eye for it, I felt it here, we've got it.' Conman. Italian. Halfwit. François's sure he'll end up looking like an idiot, surprised by the cretin waving his arms about on the balcony. Well, too bad, after all he isn't there to look like a film star, he'll concentrate on being brilliant in the interview. Just before leaving, the imbecile points to one of his bags. 'You got WiFi? Can I just check my email before I go?' François can't suppress an irritable sigh. 'I do have WiFi, but it's a bit of a nuisance to go and look for the code.' 'No problem, I've got my own dongle, it's just that it's easier here than on my scooter.' François indicates the Mies van der Rohe chair in the vestibule – 'OK, you can sit here if you like' – and shakes hands, thanking him, in a manner that says don't bother telling me when you've finished. He goes back to join the journalist in his study. She is calm, leaning forward slightly on her chair, with a carefully judged décolletage, just enough to be exciting, but too demure for one not to want to see more. He sits down opposite her. 'At last we can start.'

'Photos all right?'

In a tone of maternal concern, the so-and-so. He tries to calculate how much genuine kindness there is as opposed to professionalism, and what his chances are of getting a dinner date with her.

For some time now, many things have ceased to interest him. A veil of depression has come between him and the world. He's plain exhausted. His daughter's flight has proved that to him. She's abandoned him, and in the end, he couldn't care less. Even his inability to feel anything doesn't bother him any more. He has the feeling he's lived thirteen lives and no longer has the slightest energy for the one he's living at the moment. He feels defeated on all fronts. Only women can still rouse his full consciousness, from time to time, like delightful sirens binding him to the pleasures of life. He's gone past the age of feeling remorse at cheating on his wife. It's part of life, Claire knows it, they don't need to talk about it. Women, a few glasses of wine, certain evenings in good company, the kind of thing that happens less and less often. He gives his answers while looking deep into the journalist's eyes, affecting the air of condescending tranquillity, with occasional flashes of friendliness, which he knows women adore.

SINCE I'VE BEEN WORKING FOR RELDANCH, I'VE always been careful not to take any interest in the kids I've been tailing. In our profession, you call the person you're following, 'the mark', and the quicker you can forget their first name, the better it works. I have a mobile phone with a Carl Zeiss lens, panoramic viewfinder and digital zoom, HD camcorder and ultra-sensitive microphone. I'm more interested in the state of the batteries for my gadgets or scratches on the lens than in the person I'm following. Asking me what Valentine's like isn't part of how I've learnt to do the job. In fact that kind of thing seems unnatural.

My mobile rings just before midday, and I haven't budged from the sofa where I collapsed after my morning coffee. When I sit up to reply, I realize I've got a crick in my back, I must have been lying too long in an awkward position, listening to the radio. I say 'Uh, yeah, hello,' in a harassed tone, intended to make the caller think they've interrupted me in the middle of a task that needs all my concentration.

'Hi, it's the Hyena, where are you, kid?'

As if we'd been hanging out together every day for years. I'm already sorry I ever asked her for anything, I'm realizing that it would be wise not to succeed in our search, instead we should just wait calmly for the inevitable ghastly fallout. I continue to act evasively. 'Oh, hi, yeah, um, I'm going here and there, places I saw Valentine… hoping something'll come back to me.'

'You think you're Inspector Maigret? Want me to bring you beer and sandwiches?'

I don't really get her sense of humour and her cheerfulness sounds too loud. I wonder whether she slept with that girl yesterday. I reply more sharply: 'I was just going to call her father and try to see him as soon as possible, I think he can help me locate her mother.'

'I'd rather you put the father off till tomorrow. I've got someone round there today. I'll explain. Can we meet?'

This woman's a loser. Just wants someone to spend the day with. Her reputation must be even more exaggerated than I thought, she's so much at a loose end that she hasn't had work for months, so she's pounced on my case like a tiger on a monkey. Just my luck.

'Well, I was going to…'

'Because I called her school, and I've got an appointment with the headmistress at two o'clock. The kids eat outside the school, don't they? I'm going to go round there when classes finish, to try and question a couple of them.'

I feel like reminding her that I arranged with her to do the things I *can't* do, not the ones I can carry out perfectly well. I pretend to be immensely busy, checking the diary to see when I've got a spare moment.

'And you want me to come with you, is that it? I was going to…'

'But you're at home, aren't you?'

'No, I already said.'

'Because I'm not far away from Pyrénées metro. If you're ready, I can be downstairs from you in ten minutes, I'm in my car.'

'Look, I'm not at home. I just said. I can get to Belleville metro in, ooh, let's say fifteen minutes?'

I get there a little late. (It's one stop from Pyrénées.) I look at all the drivers halting at the lights before I see her, watching me, sitting still, on the terrace of the Folies café. When she sees me coming over, she consents to get up and join me. She holds out her hand to greet me, I wonder whether she thinks I'm going to give her some infectious disease or whether at her age she doesn't know that these days between girls we kiss. Or else just say hi. She's double-parked her car, with a doctor's permit slipped under the windscreen, but that isn't the oddest thing: she's driving an old red Mercedes, must date from before I was born. Perfect for a private eye, eh? Nobody would ever notice a car like that, would they?

'I usually take the metro; the traffic's so awful in Paris.' That's all I find to say, to sound a bit sulky, to show that I'm not the sort of girl who's going to be mollified by the luxuriously shabby beige leather of the seats. Cigarette in mouth, she pulls away without a word, stops at the lights, and smiles at two little African girls with cornrows who are holding hands to cross the road. They have identical white socks pulled up tight over their calves. The Hyena looks happy. I wonder if she's on Prozac. That's what I tell myself about anyone I find a bit too dynamic. A GPS is clamped to the windscreen but it's not switched on.

I can't manage to stay silent for long, we don't know each other well enough to sit side by side without speaking.

'You don't bother looking for a parking place then.'

'There are plenty of car parks, we can put it on expenses.'

'As a freelance, do you get lots of expenses?'

'Why?'

'I dunno. Just that I'm on a wage, and they check things carefully.'

She charitably chooses not to point out that we're not operating in the same league. 'I'm hungry. We'll stop and have a bite near the school, I know a good Italian place round there.'

We've left the Chinese quarter, and drive past the tower blocks of Télégraphe. The district is poorer, less commercial.

'You said you'd prefer me to wait before seeing her father?'

'Yep. I've got a contact going in there today. She's going to call me, she had an appointment with him for late morning. I saw that there was a WiFi code mentioned in the file but that you hadn't copied Valentine's hard disk. I thought it could interest us though. I asked for the hard disks of the whole family.'

'You've got someone who can get into their building and hack their systems?'

'Look, we have the code, we go in, we don't hack anyone. I also asked for photos of the whole apartment. So I won't need to go with you. I want to see what it looks like.'

'What do we do about the interviews at the school?'

'Don't worry, I'll take care of everything. But I'd like you to be there, you never know…'

'As your assistant? Great.'

'Look, kid, chill out, can't you? You haven't got the slightest idea how to run an enquiry, so just be a good girl, follow my lead and do what I say. If you don't like it, you can get out right now, and deal with your own problems. OK? This cheapskate enquiry of yours, all right, I'll do it. But if you've got self-esteem issues, just sort them out yourself.'

She says all this without getting cross. I think she's even hiding a smile by the end, seeing the look on my face. We're blocked by a delivery truck that's created a small traffic jam. I sulk and look out of the window. Some morons are hooting their horns behind us. Three young girls cross the road. Parisian style on the cheap. Slim, long-legged, fashionable little furry boots, big busts and big tote bags with fringes. Cut-price copies of authentically rich sluts from the Marais, the kind that put on a tarty look but make you think of ads for perfume, not of little working-class girls from sink estates.

The Hyena leans out of her window. She gives an admiring wolf whistle. The girls turn round, looking blasé, but they can't conceal a movement of surprise – or shock – when they see it comes from our car. The Hyena gives them a thumbs up, to show she thinks they look good, and also sees fit to insist, yelling, 'Hiya girls! Love the look!'

They hurry on and don't burst into nervous giggles until they're about a hundred metres away. The Hyena adjusts her dark glasses in the mirror, shrugs and notes, with magnanimity, 'They weren't that marvellous, but hey, it cheers them up, doesn't it?'

'They were very young, was what struck me.'

As if that was the problem.

'I like girls. I like girls too much. Of course I prefer dykes, but I like all girls.'

'Don't you think they might feel insulted getting whistled at in the street?'

'Insulted? No, they're hets, they're used to being treated like dogs, they think it's normal. But it's a nice change to hear it from a superb specimen like me. Even if they don't realize it, it lights up a tiny utopian candle in their poor little heads, after being smothered by heterocentrist macho awfulness.'

'How do you know they're straight? Is it written on their faces or what?'

'Of course. I can spot a dyke from behind at five hundred metres. I've got radar. We all do. How do you think we'd ever find someone to have sex with if we didn't have a sixth sense to spot each other?'

'Sorry. I didn't know you needed a sixth sense for sexual orientation.'

Finally we get past the delivery van, and she glances rapidly at me before pronouncing, still with a smile, 'Jeez, it must be really tough being you.'

The minute you get inside the door of Valentine's posh school, you're caught in the throat by that typical atmosphere of factories for turning out kids. A mixture of boredom and rebelliousness. I've got used to waiting outside school gates, but I've never before had occasion to go inside. The headmistress comes to fetch us, and we go along the main corridor, where the classroom doors are still open. The sight of all the tables lined up, the blackboards, and the maps hanging on the walls suddenly makes me want to cry. The only memory

I have of my school is looking at my watch. How long till the end of the lesson, how long till the end of the day. Even my work, which often bores me, has never made me feel so cooped up. And yet I'm pierced with nostalgia, with that sadistic and seductive pull that is so typical of it. I'd be hard put to find a rational explanation: there's nothing about my high school years that I miss. I was an average pupil, I didn't have any close friendships, I didn't have a crush on any teacher. Blank years, of deep boredom. So who knows why tears come to my eyes when I see that they're still writing in chalk on a big blackboard.

The headmistress is obese, affable and competent. She's wearing a black and orange outfit and makes the fabric ripple every time she moves. The Hyena has put on a denim jacket to cover up the tattoos on her arms, but doesn't take off her dark glasses during the interview. She has introduced herself as my assistant, which doesn't stop the headmistress addressing all her remarks to her. She's taller, thinner, more beautiful and more confident: so she's the one people want to talk to. I generally inspire a slight revulsion in people, I think it's because I'm so ill at ease that they prefer not to look me in the face if they can avoid it. I'm fascinated by the vast size of the headmistress. She really takes up a lot of room. The Hyena has sat down as usual, legs apart, chin up, and is asking a series of precise questions, taking down notes on a little pad, in her tiny close-packed writing. I wonder what this lady thinks about the huge death's head rings.

'... yes, often absent, which is a real problem for us. Apart from the last fortnight, when she's attended all her lessons, we've had trouble getting her to come regularly. She doesn't turn up for detentions either... I discussed her a lot with her teachers before the police came round. She didn't confide in any of them in particular. She had good grade averages on the whole. This is a private school, and we specialize in helping pupils who haven't performed well elsewhere. That's not exactly her problem. Valentine wasn't outstanding, but she didn't have any trouble with her school work.'

'Was she good at any subjects in particular?'

I ask myself what criteria the Hyena has in the questions she asks. As if the head is going to tell us that she was good at maths and, Eureka, we'd go and look for her in a chess tournament. The thing is, she puts her questions with such aplomb, and this ingratiating air of being serious and concerned, that the person facing her offers answers without realizing the absurdity of the conversation.

'No, there are some assignments she hands in, and gets reasonable grades for' – the head is turning over the records so that the Hyena can see them, she's completely eliminated me from her field of vision – 'and there are some tests or assignments she doesn't deign to do at all. That's why her average has gone down, you see: she has zeroes in every subject somewhere, but the grades she does get are around ten out of twenty. Which is quite good, for these pupils.'

The Hyena has more shock questions up her sleeve. If she carries on like this we'll be here all afternoon. I try not to fall asleep.

'And how did she get on with her classmates?'

'Well, again I asked her teachers, before talking to the police... but I didn't gather much, I'm afraid. She's never been told off for cheek or fighting, she wasn't a chatterbox. I saw her apparently getting on with the other pupils when she was here, but I've never noticed her making particular friends with any group or individual. Let's say that she mostly turned up because she'd been told to, and we do insist on that, and because her grandmother kept tabs on her, but we never sensed any enthusiasm. The possibility of expelling her had come up several times, because we can't accept a child who makes the others think school is optional, but we never took that step, because it's equally hard to expel a child who has never caused any discipline problems.'

Blah blah blah, I've already noted the fees: at three thousand five hundred euros a term, I imagine that pupils who are expelled from this school must at the very least have tried to massacre the others with a chainsaw.

The head accompanies us to the main door, repeating to the Hyena that no, the police don't seem to know at all what's happened. I wait for her to go back in.

'Lucky we came, eh? Fantastically interesting. She told us piles of things she didn't think of telling the police, so we're way ahead of them.'

'Do you ever get fed up of being so negative?'

'I'm not being negative. I could have told you about her grades without us having to sit and sweat in this bell jar: if you've read the file, everything's in there. The grandmother had told me about them. And that she bunked off school, same thing, mega scoop. That's why I was hired in the first place.'

'And it doesn't strike you as interesting that precisely for the fortnight you've been following her, she's been coming to school every day?'

'Yes of course it has. And it pisses me off, believe me.'

I said that for no special reason, just to say something back, but you would think I'd made the gag of the year, the Hyena bursts out laughing and looks at me almost with affection. I think perhaps she's flirting with me, but at the same time what do I know?

'Show me where the kids eat lunch.'

The school is on the banks of the Seine, in one of those districts full of office blocks and fancy apartments where it doesn't seem possible that anyone needs to go out for a loaf of bread or a litre of milk. Car sales, hi-fi equipment, computer shops. But nothing much that's convivial, bars, restaurants or little boutiques. I've never understood why there are never any practical shops or nice coffee bars in the areas where the very rich live. Is it such poor taste to eat out? So the kids have the choice between a brasserie which is very expensive and a long way off, and a tiny bar that sells little plates of sushi and three kinds of sandwich on white bread. That was a problem for me: passing unnoticed in such a small place was difficult. Luckily, the young don't usually bother looking at people my age. I point out to the Hyena a table where I recognize some pupils from Valentine's class. She's taken off her jacket now, and slung it over her shoulder, revealing the Japanese-sailor-type tattoos that crawl all over her arms. She goes up to the biggest of them, by instinct, he has the face of a mischievous child on the body of a lumberjack.

'I work for a firm of private investigators. Valentine's parents have called us in to back up the police effort.'

A small curly-headed youth with freckled cheeks, wearing a hoodie and wide trousers, sees fit to reply. 'Yeah, they're right, the police do fuck all, look at the traffic chaos everywhere.'

Chorus:

'The police didn't even come to talk to us.'

'There wasn't anything on the TV news, was there? So what did they care?'

'Yeah, that's right, there was this girl last summer and she'd been gone a week, and people recognized her from the photo, so how are people going to know she's missing?'

The Hyena hasn't sat down yet, she's listening to them seriously and casting an amused look over them. I'm two paces behind, and not too surprised that not one of them says, 'Hey, you're always round here.' My talent is being invisible.

'Did you know her well? Did she have many friends in school?'

'No, she wasn't all that friendly with people in school.'

'Yeah, she could be, she sometimes ate her lunch with us. But mostly she went off on her own with her iPod.'

'Mostly she didn't come back either.'

'She was a bit snobbish with us, if you want to know. If you said something, she'd put on this superior air and say the opposite. She was more friendly at the beginning of the year, I thought...'

'She's not friends with any of us on Facebook, is she?'

'We don't even know if she has a Facepuke page, actually...'

'But did she have problems with anyone at school?'

'Nah, not even. Perhaps she thought she shouldn't be here at all. Dunno.'

'And none of you saw her outside school?'

'Yeah, I did, but it was a long time ago, oh, about three months ago. But we had words.' This is a dark-haired girl with very pale skin speaking: she looks intelligent, but so languid that you feel like shaking her to see if she'll switch on.

'What happened?'

The girl who'd said this purses her lips and looks at the ceiling, not sure how to reply. The other kids burst out laughing.

The curly-haired one, who didn't think the police were doing their job, intervenes. 'Valentine's a bit weird. Kind of OK, but weird. Very hot. Especially when she's had a few.'

'She ought to be in the ads against binge drinking for teenagers. You really wouldn't want to be her when she's drunk.'

The brunette takes up her story again. She talks like a little girl, in an unpleasant whiny voice. 'She can be funny if it's just the two of you, she's fine. She's nice. But if you go out somewhere, she can be a real drag. She binge-drinks. She knocks it back till she can't stand up straight, and if you're at a party, no prizes for guessing you'll have no fun, you'll end up carrying her out to the taxi, and then she'll be sick all over it, and then you'll have to help her get up the stairs at home. See what I mean? A drag.'

The Hyena is nodding her head all this time, looking round at them in turn, then suddenly asks, 'And what about boys, what's she like with them?'

A tall gangling youth with a long, horsey face replies.

'She can come on to you just like that, saying "Wanna

blowjob? If you want one, just tell me." Well, that's what she used to do, when she first got here. Boys she liked, she'd go up to them and, pow! just like that, she'd come out with it. But she calmed down. In fact lately, she didn't seem to bother with us.'

The brunette takes up the story again. 'Say you go out in the evening with a few guys, well honestly, you feel ashamed for her. When she drinks, she'll do anything with anyone. But I think in the school she was in before, the girls were all like that. Or so she said.'

'So you got fed up going out with her, that it?'

'Yeah… and she can be pretty wild too. She comes out with really mega awful stuff.'

'Like what?'

'Oh anything, if it can upset someone. If you're a blonde, it's something bad about dumb blondes, if you're Jewish, it's anti-Israel, if you're black, she'll talk about banana trees, if you're gay it's about AIDS, and so on. Valentine's always got an insult for everyone. And in the end you can't take it any more, you just want a quiet evening.'

There are few reactions round the table. Their apathy hasn't been disturbed. A girl who was kind of OK, not too many problems. Nothing out of the ordinary. The more I see of this generation, the more I imagine how they'll be as adults and the less I want to make old bones.

'Still, she isn't the local clown. When she's sober, she's even rather quiet… And she's good at lessons. When she got here, we were well impressed by her level.'

'She's good at everything, she reads books and all. But she's good at maths too. And chemistry. Yeah, everything really.'

'The teachers like her fine. But she misses too much school. That's why she was sent here. She's been chucked out of all her other schools.'

'She bunks off school.'

'Valentine doesn't care about grades, her dad's this writer. When she wants to work, he'll pull strings for her, that's all, that's how it goes.'

Three of them are doing the talking, the brunette and the two boys. The two other girls are holding back, laughing at the right moments, but saying nothing for now. The Hyena asks, 'But the boys she *was* interested in, where did they come from, then?'

'When we were still friends, she liked heavy metal. She didn't miss any concert by PUY, she was very in with them... Well, you know what I mean... she was a groupie. I didn't want to go with her to see them, it was around the time she was giving me too much grief with all this acting like a slapper.'

'PUY?' The Hyena gets out her notebook.

Amandine confirms: 'Panic Up Yours, hard rock, heavy metal. I don't know, it's not my scene really.'

'I think I'll remember the name.'

'I don't know if she was still hanging round them, because she changed, Valentine did, over the year.'

'Did she talk about her parents? Her home, at all?'

'Not a lot, no.'

'I know she adores her father.'

'But the stepmother not so much, normal, isn't it? She doesn't have to sleep with her.'

'What did you think, when you heard the news she'd disappeared?'

'We flipped, we were worried for her.'

A blonde girl, with a nose so tiny that you wondered how she got enough oxygen, dressed like a Roma but every garment must have cost a fortune in the Marais, speaks up for the first time. 'We thought something horrible had happened, of course. When a girl goes missing, you're always afraid they're going to find her dead in a ditch, beaten up.'

'None of you thought she might have run away?'

This option shocks them more than the dead-in-a-ditch version. 'Run away?' Leaving behind the PlayStation3, the fridge full of food, the domestic help, Daddy's credit card...

'Yeah. Could be, of course. She'd changed a lot lately. She changed the way she looked, she wasn't so much fun, more distant... She could have been planning something. You could tell, couldn't you?'

The girl who said this was drop-dead gorgeous: all the time we've been sitting in the bar her face has been so radiant that it's as if the sunlight was falling only on her. She has the look we used to call BCBG when I was a kid, bon chic bon genre, rich girl, good home, blue, white and beige, which she wears just the kind of casual way that makes her look fantastic. She's tall and slender, elegant figure, the perfect image of the kind of bitch the aristocracy turns out best. This femme fatale speaks incredibly slowly, she must have been smoking joints all day. The Hyena gives her an odd look.

'And you talked about it with her, when you thought she'd changed?'

'No. We weren't friends, actually. But I could tell by

looking at her. She looked different.'

'Yeah, it was obvious that she'd let her appearance go, these last months.'

'Perhaps she was depressed, heading for a breakdown? She wore a lot of black, but like Noir Kennedy, vintage gear, sort of I'm-giving-up-on-life black.'

'Yeah, that's right, she stopped wearing designer stuff. But before, she used to like it fine.'

'Yeah, before, she liked to dress cool.'

'Then after a bit, not to be bitchy, but she had a bit of a punky look, like when you listen to Manu Chao?'

The drop-dead beauty shrugs. 'Yeah, I think she wanted to be distinctive.'

These kids round the table, are actually pretty easy-going, compared to the ones I usually meet. They tease each other, they josh each other, but they're not aggressive. There's no obvious tyrant among them, and they haven't got that arrogant manner you generally find in rich little Parisians. When they talk about Valentine, I find they sound quite calm. Still, that kind of sex-mad girl isn't usually so popular nowadays. These kids are resigned to never really being part of the elite. They've all dropped out. They don't have that juvenile effervescence that their equivalents in a swanky suburb like Neuilly would have. They've already tasted failure. They have all seen in their parents' eyes the disappointment at having to enrol them in a private school for children who are not making the grade.

We go back to the car. The Hyena is concentrating on one precise point. 'The pretty girl, back there, I couldn't work out if she was a baby dyke, or whether I just found her so stunning I mistook my desires for realities.'

'Is that all you really care about? Come back to earth, she's way too pretty to be a dyke.'

I regret saying this the minute it's out of my mouth, because it seems particularly insulting, but she just stares at me for a couple of moments, then bursts out laughing.

'You know, your mind is like Jurassic Park live.'

'Well anyway, she's sixteen at the outside. You're interested in her?'

'I'm interested in *all* girls. That's simple, easy to remember, even you can do that. Right, now I'm off to see Antonella, the woman I sent to see the father. Are you coming, or do you want me to drop you off?'

'Whatever you like. Perhaps you want to keep your contact confidential.'

'Keep my what what? You really are weird. Lucky for you you met me, because on your own, where would you be?'

The Hyena slows down at a pedestrian crossing and with a nod of her head lets a pregnant woman go by.

'See that one's face? Don't tell me she couldn't have given it a bit of thought before reproducing... some people, nothing stops them.'

'Do you ever, when you're on a case like this, do you ever feel frightened, I mean of what you're going to find?'

'Yes. It's happened to me before.'

'And that doesn't upset you? You don't imagine that Valentine could be in the grip of some sadist who's torturing her? Or who's even killed her. And yet here we are, taking our time.'

'No, frankly, I think she's gone to see her mother. I think we're going to spend a few days messing about in Paris so we can say we did, then we go straight for the mother. Don't you think? If your mother had abandoned you, you'd want to go and see her, wouldn't you, see what she's like?'

'I don't know, mine didn't abandon me, on the contrary she calls me up all the time.'

'Well, anyway, OK, tomorrow when you go and see the parents, do me a favour and observe the father's reactions when you mention her real mother. And the stepmother's reactions too. The stepmother, a priori we're suspicious of her, right?'

'Why?'

'Basic principle. All stepmothers are suspect. Don't you know your fairy tales?'

I burst out laughing, and she looks at me sideways. It must be the first time I've laughed at one of her jokes. I ask, 'But why don't we just go straight to the mother right away?'

'Because we're allowing some time for Rafik to find out where she is.'

'Oh. You know Rafik?'

Rafik is the cornerstone of the Reldanch agency, the guy who runs our IT systems. Everything goes through him, so much so that it's difficult to ask him anything.

'Of course I know Rafik. How would I survive without Rafik?'

In the Buttes-Chaumont park in north Paris, there's a little sunshine and a lot of dogs. We wait, sitting on a bench, for the famous Antonella to arrive. She's a good twenty minutes late. The Hyena is in a chatty mood.

'Antonella is wicked, but funny. Everyone who met her when she first got to Paris knows she's only a shadow of her former self. She *was* a diva. She was working for the news-papers, Italian correspondent. In those days, if you were a journalist at that level, your address book filled up quickly, and if anything happened in town, it wasn't hard to get to the spot. I don't know when she started being an informer, I guess she had some relationship with a politician – her speciality was culture, but the two worlds often met. When I met her, she was consulted all the time and very protected. With all the internal in-fighting in the main parties, there was a huge demand for information for a few years. Antonella was in her element. But times change, the media empire collapsed, her protectors fell into disgrace. Now she does this and that. Same as everyone else, more or less, you'll say. She comes pretty expensive though. The other journalists will trade information, but Antonella has no problem about sources, she only wants cash. I asked her to get hold of the contents of all the computers in the apartment, she's got a sidekick who's good at that. Her own interest is that it allows her to peep around. You never know, she might pick up some interesting titbit of information, just by chance...'

'How did she manage to get into his apartment so easily?'

'All artists like to give interviews to the press.'

You can't miss her when she does turn up: she's wearing enormous fuchsia-pink après-ski boots. I suppose they must be the in thing, something which never ceases to surprise me. Without apologizing for being late, she throws a large envelope into the Hyena's bag. She has an attractive husky voice which doesn't fit her look of an ethereal slut.

'Wow, he comes on strong, your client. Still at his age, they're all more or less nymphomaniac.'

'Don't fish for compliments, Antonella, you know you just knock them out.'

'Ah, don't talk about the past. How are you?'

She hasn't said hello to me, not even a glance. Humiliating but I'm starting to get used to it. It's like when you're a teenager and you go out with the school prom queen, after a while being in the shadows is restful. We all start walking towards the park gates and the Hyena asks, 'Do you know the stuff he writes?'

'Domestic dramas among the bourgeoisie. Catholic, right-wing, but in a traditional way, not aggressive or racist or antisemitic. So nobody much is interested in him. He'd do better to write a blockbuster about the camps, if he wants to be taken seriously, that would make a change...'

'Is he successful?'

'Not so much now. He still has a bit of a profile. A little TV, state radio, does a few signing sessions in bookshops. He publishes a lot of articles here and there, wherever they'll let him, he's the right age and CV to get on the jury for literary prizes, and I couldn't quite see why he's so isolated. He's not very aggressive, that always reduces your credibility. Publishers have fallen into the habit of looking after him, I've been told he gets an advance of fifteen thousand per book. He doesn't sell more than five thousand. So you can see why he writes a lot.'

'He'll be disappointed when he sees there's no article.'

'No, it's OK, I really was asked to put together a file for a book by this journalist on *The Times* who discovers every year that French culture doesn't have any international influence any more. Big deal, eh? I'll pick up on this one malicious and well-aimed remark he made about Sollers and his importance, and that'll do the trick. He'll be cross at having chatted to me for a couple of hours, making eyes at me all the time, and finding I've only included that one little jab, but basically he'll be glad he's quoted at all. If it wasn't for you, he wouldn't even get that.'

Antonella is flirting outrageously with the Hyena. I wonder whether they've slept together.

'Did he mention his daughter at all?'

'No. His father, yes, his mother a bit, his daughter not at all.'

'Protecting his privacy?'

'Men his age don't often talk about their children. They are their parents' children, but nobody's parents. Unless there's some drama, children aren't very good subjects for novels, at least for men. If his kid were to die, then yes, there might be a novel in it... then again, a father's grief isn't bestseller material. But if she comes back home now and slags him off for being an old fusspot, what's he going to do? He prefers to think of something else.'

CLAIRE

WHEN CLAIRE LETS HERSELF SLIDE BACK IN THE bath, plunging her head under the warm water, she can hear sounds from the flat below. As so often, the neighbours are having a row. Amplified by the water, the sounds become strange, muffled, low. Often, the husband is violent. Claire hears the woman yelp two or three words, then she hears him retorting from another room, before he finally goes striding through the flat, and that's when he hits her. She screams and protests, sometimes trying to run away from him. Then the scene is punctuated by some louder sounds than the others, hard to identify, not necessarily blows. Followed by silence. The first few times, Claire was afraid he'd killed her, but in time she realized that it was the calm after the row. You wouldn't think, to look at them, that they were that kind of couple. Him, she often sees in the lift, he's an examining magistrate. Reddish face, rather puffy, a nose swollen by alcohol, but always well-dressed, polite, and smelling of aftershave. He was probably good-looking in his youth. He still acts the gentleman towards women. He has two children, a boy and a girl, two years apart. When Claire moved in with François, she used to see them often, playing with the concierge's little girl on the pavement out in front.

They're big now, no more scooters and marbles until they have children of their own. She never hears them intervene when their father raises his hand against their mother. Like all people this kind of thing doesn't happen to, Claire is sure, or so she thinks every time she meets someone from that family in the lift, that she would never have put up with what the woman downstairs endures. If only for her two daughters' sake, she'd have found the courage to leave, to pack her bags, whatever it cost, she'd have protected them from a violent father. Christophe had never laid a finger on Claire, nor on his daughters, come to that.

He left her just before the older girl's sixth birthday. Claire had loved him unreservedly and obstinately for ten years. He'd come into her life when she was twenty-two, one New Year's Eve at a friend's house. She'd felt his eyes on her, trying to locate her wherever she was in the room, and then his large figure had kept appearing within a few feet from her, following her round from group to group. A mild form of stalking, which he hadn't tried to conceal. He wanted her. It attracted Claire. She waited. That evening he was wearing a black sweater and three-day stubble, which suited him. She was young, still unsurprised that life revolved round her, pursuing her and offering her the choicest gifts. After spending a few nights with him, she'd begged him to shave. Claire's face was burning, her fine skin irritated and painful. He was her first serious boyfriend. She had met Christophe the same year her mother had marched her off to a dietician – and it had worked, she had lost weight, had to buy new clothes, and had become attractive again. She managed to stay slim for two years, but after the birth of the older girl,

Mathilde, she'd put on five kilos and never succeeeded in losing them. It was distressing, but it hadn't dragged her down into the depths of depression, as it would have done before she had given birth. Something had happened to her with motherhood, it had given her calm and confidence. The presence of this baby in her life had transformed the way she looked at things.

Before Mathilde, there had been holidays abroad: Egypt, New York, Ireland, Sweden, friends, dinner parties, evenings at the cinema, their first flat, family parties, and plenty of long mornings in bed. Then there'd been the enchantment of declaring her pregnancy, decisions to take together, the nursery to be furnished, the first scan, thinking of a name. Her parents had completely changed their attitude when she'd told them the news. Claire had a sister three years younger, who had always been her mother's favourite. Claire had been the child who was a bit too fat, a bit too placid, never managing to engage her parents' attention. When they divorced, she had been twelve years old, and once more, her mother had devoted herself to her little sister, everything revolved round her. Claire didn't get up to any pranks, she didn't worry her mother. And she wasn't as pretty. She couldn't do anything without attracting blame. Nobody around her had taken the trouble to notice that she had been deeply upset by the divorce. It's true that she hadn't done anything outrageous to alert anyone. She had just started putting on a few kilos, slowly, and become more withdrawn. In her childhood bedroom, for years she had secretly pinned the holiday postcards sent by her mother next to the ones from her father, so that the blue hills of the Vosges were up against the mountains of Peru, the Mediterranean jostled the Pacific. With a little Sellotape to stick them together. That was back when the children of divorced parents used to have to explain to their school-friends what it was like to have two homes, in the days when that was still unusual. Her sister Aline hadn't needed a year's mourning in order to start boasting in the playground of two lots of Christmas and birthday presents and all the special permissions to be absent or to extract more pocket money through parental guilt or bargaining: 'Mummy said yes,' or 'Daddy promised me.' Claire often wished she could strangle her sister. But once she was pregnant with Mathilde, every-thing changed. Both parents got into the habit of calling her up all the time, and she had to schedule their visits so that they didn't coincide too often. The day of the birth, they had both been with her in her hospital room, without their new partners, and she had seen the joy on their faces: shared emotion, the first grandchild. And it had lasted until the birth of the second daughter, Elisabeth. Then, wouldn't you know, Aline had become pregnant just afterwards, from some one-night stand, not that that made the coming child less welcome. On the contrary, as usual, she had managed to spoil everything, demanding the maximum of attention. One day, Aline had turned up at her mother's house, declaring firmly that she couldn't go through with it, she wanted an abortion at six months. Next day she turned up at her father's, saying she would have the baby but give it up for adoption, she couldn't take care of a child on her own. A week later, heavily pregnant, she was snivelling in her mother's kitchen, drinking her fifth beer and chain-smoking, claiming that she was sure the baby would be stillborn, and of course that she would never get over it. Poor little dead baby, she spent the whole evening torturing her mother. And it worked. She got all their attention. The parents started telephoning each other every day, telling each other what they'd had to endure from her, and making frantic efforts to rescue their daughter from the brink of madness. Aline had always done whatever she liked, and her tactics were spectacularly successful. She had given birth to her son. It *would* be a son, of course. For three months, she'd gone into ecstasies over the bliss of motherhood, then her figure had come back, she'd put on a dress, left the baby with her mother, and continued her life as before: plenty of affairs, too much alcohol, and hefty overdrafts.

Mathilde was just five then, the age when children stop being little angels and become little people, they're not quite so cute, adults find them less entrancing. Her grandmother went on looking after her with pleasure, but her real pride and joy was Thibaut, the first male child. The adorable, extraordinary, reckless, wilful, insufferable Thibaut. Claire was already in therapy at that stage: she was getting the feeling that at last she could take control of her life and would be capable of going forward alone, without her parents' support. She had everything she wanted. A husband, two daughters, a very nice apartment. She'd spent ages studying interior design magazines, so that within the limits of their budget, their flat would look stylish. So that Christophe would be proud to invite his colleagues back, and be happy himself to return home in the evenings. She had thought how grateful she was for what life had given her in the nine years with him, every time she found herself chatting to a friend whose husband was unfaithful, or having problems with his career, or being difficult to live with. She had thought how grateful she was, every time she met former schoolfriends who still had no children and thought they could fill their lives with something else. As if you could do without that kind of love and not miss out on what life was all about. In return, she tried her best to take care of everything properly, writing herself long to-do lists that she never completely dealt with. She saw to all the family medical appointments, sorted out clothes for the different seasons, organized their holidays, supervised the children's homework, thought of interesting activities for them, had plates that matched the tablecloth, found a good dentist, arranged fun birthday parties, paid the bills, drove the children to the swimming pool, bought new shirts for her husband before the old ones wore out, recruited a cleaning woman, located the best car insurance. She had never imagined that Christophe would underestimate the happiness they enjoyed, and his good fortune in having a wife like her at home. A wife who would help his children grow up, who wasn't a big spender, who was always cheerful and took care of everything without complaint.

One Friday evening, he had rung up at eight o'clock to warn her he had to work over the whole weekend and wouldn't be home. Mathilde was watching *Buffy the Vampire Slayer* on television and the little one was in the bath surrounded by Barbie dolls. A lump had suddenly formed in Claire's throat. The previous times, no doubts had occurred to her, but a list had been building up, in her reason's blind spot, of all the occasions recently when he had got home at two in the morning, of the conferences in the provinces, and of the meetings at weekends. And that evening, despite her unwillingness to understand, the pieces had come together. There'd been a lot of absences recently. He didn't call home all weekend and on the Monday night when he got in, he wasn't his usual self. Claire had started talking, an unconscious mechanism. Her mouth opened and words spilled out endlessly, because she sensed that as soon as she paused, he'd say what he had to say. It had worked before, she knew that without admitting it to herself. She just had to play for time for him to give up trying and say nothing. But that evening, almost as soon as the girls were in bed, he'd interrupted her. 'I've met someone, another woman. And I'm moving out.' It was ridiculous. She wanted to wipe out the words. It was a cliché. It couldn't happen to them, it wasn't *like* them. Before believing he was capable of leaving her, she was angry with him for saying the words. Their love would never again be intact. It would take her a few more years to admit that he had not said something he would later regret. Her great perfect love, he'd smashed it to pieces. And then, rapidly, she'd lost everything.

Her mother's pained tone when she telephoned, and the awful feeling that apart from her, everyone else had suspected it. The humiliating pity of other people. The ten years when she had been convinced that everyone she met was impressed by her happy marriage. And perhaps even jealous, since many people were unlucky in love, or had no children, or had to bring them up as single parents. Having to endure their so-called understanding, their self-satisfied pity, and their humiliating encouragement. People had all been very quick to expect her to get over it. As if their story had been one you put behind you, a love like any other. For a long time, Claire had hoped that life would prove them all wrong, that

Christophe would come back and she'd be able to show them all what kind of love they had. A rock-solid love, invincible, a couple that nothing could separate. She had never been angry with him, not once. She had waited for him. Nothing that happened after he left could satisfy her, she just wanted her old life back, she didn't want to take any aspect of the new situation seriously on board. Her friends' unwelcome remarks, the hints uttered in falsely friendly tones to the effect that she should have realized long ago that he was unfaithful, that he was tired of her, and that he'd taken the right decision.

She'd distanced herself from her former girlfriends. She didn't want to be thought of as 'a single mother' of her two daughters, or as 'unattached', still less as 'remaking her life'. She had nothing in common with all those losers, so they were wrong thinking she was like them. Even her relations with the girls were affected. At heart, she thought that the children ought to have made Christophe come back home. She felt they weren't trying hard enough. They could have fallen ill, refused to see their father, been hostile to his new partners, failed to enjoy holidays with him, they could have insisted, taken their mother's side, and found a way to get what she wanted for all of them: their old life back. Instead of which they'd grown up, immersed themselves in things at school. Mathilde had become coquettish, by nine years old she was wanting nail varnish, brand label clothes and lip gloss. Other things didn't seem to matter to her. Elisabeth had begun learning the piano and liked gym. They didn't apparently realize that all three of them had been badly hurt, cheated of the life they were owed.

And now as they were growing up, Claire started feeling

that her daughters were judging her. Not saying anything openly. But perhaps behind her back, when they were alone. As time went by, they looked more shifty. They seemed to be scornful of their mother. This woman abandoned by her husband, obliged to count her pennies, living on a derisory sum of alimony, since she hadn't even managed the divorce successfully, having failed to select a ruthless lawyer, who would have got the maximum for her. At the end of every session, the therapist would explain to Claire that if her daughters listened to her less, it was simply because they were growing up, they weren't judging her. There too she wanted her old life back: to be the idol of her children, the centre of their world. She wanted to feel their soft little bodies and their arms round her neck. For them to be little girls again, when she had always known how to make them happy and when she had had an answer for everything.

Claire had also become distanced from her mother, who scarcely four months after the break-up was saying, 'Come on, sweetie, get over it. And anyway between ourselves, he wasn't God's gift was he, your man, I know he's the girls' father, but let's not kid ourselves, he was pretty much a philistine and very selfish.' Claire hadn't been able to hang up on her, or tell her how hurtful these words were. Long knives plunged into her heart. To realize that, for other people, their love hadn't been stunning, her good fortune hadn't been amazing. Just an ordinary couple, an ordinary break-up, life, like everyone else. She was shattered, flayed alive, and her shrink prescribed a course of anti-depressants. She lost fifteen kilos. Her weight started to obsess her, as it had in the past, and the transformation had been enough to make her feel better. Claire wanted people to think she was just fine. In the end, what she really felt didn't matter. She was watching for signs of how other people saw her, interpreting their looks; and if she could convince herself that they thought she was on top of things and lucky in life, she felt better.

She'd found a part-time job as secretary in an upmarket sports club, the girls were doing well at school, and she paraded them as if they were living proof that she was well-balanced; she brandished them in the world's face, they were her Grade A in the great exam of wordly success. Women whom their husbands have left for a younger model after the age of fifty will often say, 'I wish he'd gone earlier, then I could have rebuilt my life.' They don't know what they're saying. There's nothing worse than being left before you're even thirty-five. You're being left for what you are, nothing to do with age, and it deprives the children of a whole life with both parents, it means being left lying on your back like some stupid insect that'll never be able to right itself again.

The only female friends Claire could tolerate now were unmarried women her own age with no children. These were the only ones on whom she could look down, the only ones she could meet without fearing that the comparison would be unfavourable to her. But even women like that ended up making her feel nervous. Elise, her best friend for the last two years, was forty. Poor thing, she claimed she didn't miss having children. Claire listened to her lying through her teeth, with the maternal patience of one who knows that the other dare not admit her sorrows. What it could be like, living your life as a woman without giving birth, without that basic centre around which all life is organized, Claire preferred not even to think about it, and she listened to Elise's rants without reacting, displaying considerable benevolence. But even Elise wasn't unfortunate enough to her taste. Last heard of, she was planning to go off sailing the world for several months with her latest lover, a chancer ten years younger than her, who was obviously using his older mistress to help pay the bills on his boat. And Elise was convinced that this was the call of love, she'd decided to give notice at work, let her apartment, and go to sea. In her head, over and over, Claire mentally rehearsed all the points against this decision, for her friend's own good. She realized that she was obsessing about it and admitted as much on the therapist's couch, acknowledging that there was some jealousy at the bottom of this anxiety. Forty wasn't even too old for Elise to get pregnant. She didn't want Elise to suffer. Just that she should remain in a situation slightly less desirable than her own.

And then, after all, François had come along. Encountered in a first-class compartment of the TGV, on the way back from Lyon, where she had dropped Elisabeth off for a pony-riding holiday. Claire had been reading a book by Paul Morand, which she found boring, but since she had nothing else with her, she had opened it and tried to find some interest in it. The man sitting next to her had hesitated for a while before speaking to her. At first, the only thing that she'd found attractive about him was that he was interested in her. He'd managed to extract the number of her mobile from her before saying goodbye at the station, and had called next day with a pressing invitaton to have dinner.

She found him on the plump side, a bit old for her, with tired features: his stumpy reddish hands had something of the peasant about them. More full of himself than charismatic. But she had liked it when he paid her compliments throughout the three-hour train journey, even if she was well aware of something a bit pathetic about the situation: chatting up your neighbour on a train wasn't exactly high romance. He had said he was a writer, and had repeated his name on the message he left on her voicemail. When she had googled him though, her feelings had changed. Inwardly, she had mocked herself: 'All it took was three good reviews and you find he's worth seeing after all... at your age, acting like a groupie, you ought to be ashamed of yourself.' Then she had called Lucette, her manicurist, who was a great reader – she and Lucette had become quite friendly, the manicurist stayed for a cup of tea after doing her nails and they gossiped about this and that. Lucette had a son and a daughter, but neither father had recognized the children or even stayed round long enough to see them. She had money problems, a family that gobbled up all she earned, and what with everything it was entirely relaxing to be friends with her, especially since she had a sense of humour and was quite witty. Lucette read a lot, trying to drown her sorrows by escaping into books. When she heard the name of this new man on the horizon, she'd reacted very satisfactorily: '*Mata Hari in My Dreams* – fabulous novel, haven't you read it? Oh, I'll lend you it if you like. You actually met him? No!' Her reaction had made Claire feel like accepting the dinner date.

During which she had been rather bored, although she appreciated the impressive place he took her to, a fancy seafood restaurant, grand surroundings, good wine, huge bill. It had been quite easy to keep to 'not on our first date'. She had let him hold her hand in the taxi going home, inwardly convinced that this wasn't going to come to anything. When he wasn't talking about himself, he was ranting about literary prizes, how journalists could publish terrible books but still get good reviews from all their colleagues, about authors who were translated without deserving it, and other examples of unjustified success. But François had been persistent: next day he called her about going to the theatre to see a play based on a novel by some friend of his.

She'd accepted, thinking she might back out at the last minute. Nevertheless, in her local bookshop, Claire had found a paperback of *Mata Hari in My Dreams*, with on the cover a detail of a Botticelli painting, not all that exciting. And that afternoon, lying fully dressed on her bed, she'd fallen in love. She'd slipped into his power, as she read page after page, description after description. An almost painful desire had taken shape deep inside her, a desire to belong to the man whose hand had written those lines, a desire to be the object of his gaze, to be penetrated by his lucidity, taken limb from limb, exhibited, seen, re-transcribed. The writing had authority. Every sentence became erotic because it had been framed by the power of the man who desired her. She'd never before read a novel thinking physically about the novelist who'd written it. Some particularly aggressive pages aimed at women had triggered in her a wild sexual desire.

She spent the whole afternoon on the bed reading. It was more thrilling than really sleeping with him. Her daughters had hardly got in before she left them alone and made a dash by metro to the Virgin Megastore that stayed open until midnight, to find two more novels by him, one hardback, one in paperback. Locating books with this man's name on the cover, in that immense shop, had been the final touch, propelling her into an insane erotic trance. She had hardly slept, plunging into their pages with the feeling that she was truly alive, a sensation she had long forgotten. She even liked the bits that seemed rather puerile, like the way the narrator always had the best lines, even in situations where it was clear he wasn't very successful. François always had to twist the scene so that it came down to the level of his narrator's character, then he could dominate it. But even that she ended up liking, the childish side, the suggestion of fragility, an aspect of him that she could protect. His novels whispered, to a corner of her heart, that she had met a man she could love.

In practice, when they had actually gone to bed together a few days later, it wasn't like in his books. François was a lot older than Christophe.

Say what you like about pornography, it had had the merit of telling men of his age that you don't make love lying flat out on your partner without even looking up from time to time to see how she is reacting. François wasn't a bad lover but he was from a different age. He rubbed the parts of his body he thought relevant up against her, giving the impression of taking advantage of what she let him do. But then Claire wasn't a woman who expected to enjoy sex. It sometimes happened, perhaps inadvertently. She didn't find it all that interesting. All the same, a little sensuality, a minimum of foreplay, wouldn't have come amiss. She had always secretly thought it must be the same for everyone and that other women were like her. They were playing with words when they talked about orgasms. Except for sickos of course. But normal women, women like her, liked the climax, feeling that their partner was having pleasure and that they were making that possible. In fact, it replaced orgasm as far as she was concerned, her liking for another person's skin, penis, pleasure. That, she thought, was woman's true enjoyment of sex. This sharing.

So François writhed about on top of her for a couple of minutes, came, seemed happy, declared that for a first time it had been great and they'd do better – he had no doubt she wanted him. For all that he was an older man, he was sure of himself: she loved him, she wanted him. Upon which, he had gone to sleep and started snoring. Dissatisfied, Claire had thought about sex with Christophe, her memory of it, the perfect chemistry between them: her own body offered up, belonging, married, and deeply happy to be so. The experience of their complementarity in their flesh. She remembered his hands, the perfect size of his hands holding her hips, the playful authority with which he moved her, stretched her, searched for her womb which seemed to be opened like a flower warm and dark, and endless, and he filled it entirely. But then you could make love like that, and he could walk out on you two days later. Claire never told herself the story in its chronological order, tracing its progression didn't interest her, she retained only a chaotic memory of it. What had come in her mind to stand for sex with Christophe, once and for all, had taken place in the early years of their relationship. They'd hardly had time to start again after Mathilde's birth, and then there had been Elisabeth, and for months Christophe hadn't tried to touch her.

That first night with François had been the worst. She'd thought of going home without waking him up. The girls were staying over with her mother, she could have had a nice peaceful morning. But she wasn't familiar with the part of town where he lived, she was afraid of not finding a taxi. And anyway she didn't want to hurt him, even leaving a note he would have found a hostile act. She composed in her head scraps of the novel he would write if she behaved badly towards him. And this habit, which she had fallen into on their first date, would ever after determine her attitude towards him. She always tried to behave like a good heroine. As time went by, she came to understand that she would never be a character in her husband's novels. She wasn't a part of his fictional imagination, in fact that was something he made a point of honour. Which had disappointed her, like so many things. Life passes, a series of capitulations.

She had continued to see François, then had moved in with him, and in the early days there had been a state of grace. Sexually, he had surprised her. He was hardly very sophisticated in bed, but was much more inspired from the day – very soon, he'd asked her this after a week – when he had suggested tying her up. Claire had agreed at once, without betraying the disgust this had provoked in her. It must be something old couples did to spice up their sex, otherwise why would you do something like that? But that was before. Because once she was standing, gagged, with her little panties round her knees, her arms raised and tied by the wrists to the highest bar in the bookcase, she had discovered that at such moments she forgot to wonder if she was too fat or not beautiful enough, if her partner was feeling good, if she wasn't making too much noise, because the only thing that interested her was her sex, between her legs pulsing away like a furious hammer. She had begged, groaned and waited. And radically changed her ideas about sex. For a while there had been a time of ecstasy. It was obvious, everyone remarked on it. She had flowered. Her girlfriends found she looked fantastic. It had been a revelation, the cement binding them together as a couple. Or at any rate the cement of the plinth. Because after a while, of course, the games were less frequent and then they forgot to play them.

It was difficult being in a couple, with three daughters. A lot of the time they weren't alone. Claire's friends told her to beware. Her mother had mentioned it straight away: 'Valentine will do all she can to get you away from her father.' It had seemed inappropriate to her. You couldn't put these two kinds of love on the same level. She remembered very well the women her father had had, women whose age never varied as her father turned into an old man and Claire was more and more likely to be the same age as them. Very young women who sleep with old men always have something a bit weird about them. Girls who were less and less interesting, who knew less and less how to dress well. But the old man was happy enough with them. And in any case, her father seemed to be senile in the end, his girlfriends could have crapped on the table and he would have said 'Oh poopy doo' and found it charming. He did what he could with the means left to him. And, in fact, seemed happy.

Her father's girlfriends had come one after another to his house, and every one of them had behaved as if she was the first and last, the one and only. A procession of beautiful bitches. Exactly what Claire didn't want to be for Valentine. Neither hostile, nor intrusive, nor unfair. A respectful and open-minded adult. But the kid had behaved abominably towards her. Claire had set about neutralizing her with kindness, submerging her with tact, affection and under-standing. Valentine had decreed from the start that Claire was plain stupid. And had never changed her opinion. Most of the time, she simply refused to speak to her. 'Just leave me alone please' were the words Claire heard most often. But the teenager had always been perfectly well-behaved with Mathilde and Elisabeth. It was as if the three girls had estab-lished a tacit non-aggression pact.

Claire had hoped to convince herself that it would all work out with a bit of good will. Then one day Valentine had brought her a short story to read, one that she had written. Claire ought to have realized that it wasn't just to ask her opinion. It was the story of an 'unspeakable Jewish woman' – Claire, being a Protestant, had felt reassured at first, thinking it couldn't possibly relate to her – who was of unimaginable lubricity, crawling through the house on all fours asking to be spanked. There were long descriptions of the parcels of flesh on her great thighs shaking under every blow. How did Valentine know so much about their sex life? It was a mystery. They had never done anything when the children were in the house. Claire hadn't dared tell anyone about the teenager's story. But its extreme obscenity had demoralized her. Valentine frightens her now. And has done, in fact for some time. It's terrible to admit it, but it's nicer now that she isn't there.

She gets out of the bath. The comforting warmth of the

fluffy grey bath towel hanging over the radiator. The steam on the mirror. The bathroom's a mess, the girls showered before her and they've left all the things they used lying around. They have a bathroom next to their bedroom, but in hers the bath is bigger and the shelves are laden with beauty products that they shamelessly plunder. She keeps telling herself in vain that it's not aimed at her, but it always makes her think that her daughters are attacking her, 'you're old and ugly, let us use the lovely bathroom with all this stuff that smells good, your time is over'. The therapist gives her to understand that it's her own aggressivity that she's imagining as coming from other people.

It hadn't got better over time. Valentine had refused to sit at the same table to eat and if she was obliged to, she became unbearable. François didn't know how to handle it. He thought it would blow over. Basically, he thought it was fairly normal for his daughter not to like her stepmother. Jacqueline Galtan had taken her daughter-in-law's side. She thought Valentine needed taking in hand. The teenager had become physically violent. The first time she had slapped Claire they were alone in the kitchen. Valentine was drinking a Coke while getting an ice cream out of the fridge, and Claire had mildly pointed out that that was a lot of calories. 'Oh, don't worry, I don't want to be a whore like you when I'm your age.' Tears had immediately sprung to Claire's eyes. Vulgarity wasn't part of her mode of communicating. But she found the strength to answer back for once. 'Where'd you get that idea, sweetheart? Think your family's so rich, I must be after your papa's money?' And Valentine had slapped her face. 'Stupid cow, you don't go out to work, you just sit around doing nothing, so don't start getting on my tits as well.' The exchange was meaningless. It was the terror that mattered. Claire had told François about the scene. And he'd had a long discussion with Jacqueline. The upshot was they decided the teenager needed help. It remained to choose the right institution. Valentine's grandfather, who had always been opposed to her being sent to a boarding school or even seen by a psychiatrist, had died a few months earlier. Claire felt sorry about it, she would have much preferred it if things had worked out better. But they couldn't let the teenager go on running wild. And then the child had disappeared.

The interview with the detective didn't go well. Since she's left, Claire has had a bad feeling in her stomach, like when you've broken a valuable ornament or missed a date with someone, without being able to warn them you had let them down. A feeling of wrongdoing.

She hadn't imagined it would be like that. Jacqueline had announced to them that she'd hired a private investigator and it had seemed like a good idea. The police would complicate your life. They're so used to people going missing, they don't rush to pull out all the stops. And then if there was a lot of publicity, you never knew where it might end. François would hate it.

It's pretty obvious where Valentine has gone. François doesn't realize it, but he's changed since his daughter has disappeared. He's aged ten years in a few days. You think that's a figure of speech when you hear other people say it. But the expression exactly describes what's happened. He's aged ten years. The face of a mature man has turned into the face of an old man. He is so attached to his daughter.

He reacted badly when the detective came round. 'I can't tell you much. What good would it do for me to tell you about Valentine's life? I'm glad you feel able to take advantage of our family sorrow to extract a king's ransom from us, but with respect… if I don't know where to find her, I doubt you will manage it.' The detective was looking round the room, she didn't seem offended. Her eyes were doing a search. She sat hunched up on the sofa and seemed to have difficulty finding questions to ask. François couldn't refuse when she asked if she could have a little time on her own in Valentine's room. He just sat on the sofa heaving angry sighs. He wanted her out of the house. Claire couldn't understand the strength of his reaction. She went to sit in front of the TV, preferring not to say anything. After a while, he came to see her, beside himself. 'And she's ugly, what's more, the woman. That's all we need, eh? Doesn't surprise me, coming from my mother. Anything she can do to get up my nose. Never misses a trick.' The private eye didn't stay long in Valentine's room. When she'd left, everything was in place, so if she poked about – which she certainly must have – she took care not to disturb anything.

François hadn't mentioned the violence, or the insults. They should have, perhaps. Valentine had simply taken away their breath, their appetite, their desire to laugh, their words. And he had refused to mention Vanessa. His first marriage. All Claire knows about it is what Jacqueline has told her, or what she's gathered from reading the novels he wrote in the years afterwards. She well understands his silence. She doesn't like talking about her first marriage either. She hates people not taking it seriously. But it's stupid not to have told the detective that Vanessa lives in Barcelona. It would save her some time. That's probably where Valentine has gone, to see her. And in spite of the warnings from the adults around her, the teenager will have wanted to go and check for herself whether her mother really doesn't want to know about her. You can't blame her for that. But if François were to find out that Claire had taken it on herself to phone Vanessa to warn her, he'd hit the roof. Especially since if she told him that much, she'd have to confess that she had telephoned her once before. At the beginning of their affair. To meet her. To see what she was like. Vanessa is not a good person. She's as negative and poisonous as Jacqueline's portrait of her. All the same, Claire thought she ought to be warned.

RAFIK'S RIGHT HAND MOVES FROM THE MOUSE to the silvery Thermos cup of scalding-hot coffee, his eyes still fixed to the screen. He's converting the pirated data into a form I might have some chance of understanding. I stay sitting alongside him, not daring to complain that all this is taking a long time.

Rafik arrived at Reldanch in the mid 1990s and was installed at first in a cupboard up on the fourth floor, in front of a computer with an enormous tower. Jean-Marc says his internet connection was through a dial-up phone line and it made a crackling noise that they could hear at regular intervals. Two years later, he was settling himself into a small suite of rooms that had become vacant on the ground floor, so as to have room for his machines and the staff he hired; then he took over the lodge of the concierge, who was let go and never replaced. In his lair, always darkened, the keyboards rattle away, the ventilators make a deafening background noise, and the people there nearly all wear headphones. It would never occur to them to open the shutters, they say it's to keep burglars away, but given the thick bars they've fixed on the windows, even a highly-motivated gang of Chechens would give up in disgust. Especially since the place is hardly

ever empty, because Rafik's teammates are not the sort to
leave their work stations and go home to sleep. They're ruth-
lessly competitive – they must always be telling themselves
that if they leave this power hub for too long at a time they'll
lose their position in the race. Rafik's domain has become the
heart, lungs, eyes and brains of the whole outfit.

When he arrived, everyone was thrilled that he could
access bank accounts, phone bills, ID data or legal records so
easily. Then Rafik convinced the boss that we should link up
with a firm of lawyers specialized in checking internet data.
The older staff said he was crazy: it could only be of concern
to a handful of obsessive VIPs to check how often their
names came up on the internet. But Rafik got his way, and
he had his service up and running exactly a year before all
the chatlines, blogs and other social media exploded, making
his sector the most productive of all our activity. They comb
the internet. Our partner lawyers send out emails so aggressive that the site hosts put up very little resistance. If by any
chance they play hard to get, you just knock out the page in
question. Basta. When you see Rafik's team in action, you
quickly understand that any ethical sermon about censorship
shows a failure to grasp what modern times are all about: any
virtual content can be eliminated, and is intrinsically capable
of being rewritten, cut or manipulated. Our customers soon
started giving each other Reldanch's address. More and more
often, they pay our team to outwit the competition.

It was Rafik too who went to tell our former boss that
keeping tabs on teenagers would generate a lot of income, we
should specialize in that before other people got in on the act.
He was the first to bring a bugged telephone into the office

and to realize that its chief function wouldn't be for adultery cases. In those days, the divorce laws hadn't yet changed, but when they did, they'd make *in flagrante* redundant and at a stroke wipe out a big percentage of our clients. Rafik loves technology and he can predict where it's going to go. He was right. Mobile phones became extensions of teenagers' bodies. And their parents don't see why they shouldn't use them to know in real time what the kids are doing or saying, what messages they're sending and receiving, and where it's all going on. The growth in turnover was exponential. Reldanch was one of the first firms to handle this trade. In some ways it was because of Rafik's intuition that I was hired.

That morning, when I arrived, weighed down by the three-kilo hard disk in my handbag, I expected it would be like every time I have a request for the ground floor: they'd make me wait half an hour without even offering me a chair to sit on. In Rafik's team, being nice or welcoming is equivalent to displaying weakness. Their department keeps the whole firm afloat. Us, the people from upstairs, we're just a herd of dinosaurs, tolerated but in the way. But today, Rafik jumped up as soon as he saw me – before this, I don't think he's even troubled to say hello, it surprised me that he should be capable of recognizing me so easily. He acted as if we were old friends. I felt the team looking me up and down, one by one, without any benevolence, conveying a disagreeable mixture of envy and hostility.

Rafik asked me to sit on his right, at the end of the open-plan office. I therefore cleverly deduced that he'd been contacted by the Hyena and that she had been telling the truth. She does know him, and well. I like getting this privileged treatment, but I'm surprised by the immediate ill will it has provoked towards me. I can feel the distrustful and hostile looks piercing my back.

I've never liked his team. Their little barbed remarks, their special language we don't understand, their unwillingness to speak, which comes more from a superiority complex than from shyness. I don't like the false jollity of the coloured gear they wear or the kind of glasses they choose. I don't like their twisted sense of humour. Their systematically racist remarks which you have to treat as deeply ironic so as to not be (horrors) politically correct, they're incapable of seeing anyone black, or Chinese, or Indian or Arab without making some reference to race. In Rafik's team in general they're free marketeers, they're happily pro-American, and see themselves becoming pro-Chinese, and they say all this in the tone of guys who aren't afraid to stand out from the crowd, aren't afraid to broadcast their opinions. Always on the side of whoever's in power, they like to think they're the subversive avant-garde. It perplexes me to think about the kind of France they seem to have dreamed up, in which collectivism and Bolshevism are the mothers of every vice. A relentlessly vegetarian France, full of interracial orgies, where every woman is ready to sodomize her neighbour, brandishing a Sandinista flag. As for having the courage to say out loud what no one else dares say, these young guys can't even pronounce the word 'overtime' after spending three sleepless nights on the ground floor, and when someone tells them off, the gleam of hate behind their eyes has no chance of ever being fanned into the flames of rebellion, until the day pyromania gets on to the school syllabus. They're against strikers, against demonstrators, against artists, and foreigners, against old people, public employees, and scroungers – but it doesn't bother them to collect housing or unemployment benefit whenever they can. Rafik talks dismissively to them, pays them badly, never thanks them, never congratulates them. Rafik treats them as they want to be treated , they respect him, and in return their work is impeccable. They have total scorn for anyone who doesn't work on their level, and we have ended up agreeing with them that we belong to the past.

Rafik is tapping furiously at his keyboard, you'd think he was launching a rocket. He mutters, 'Don't worry, just a few minutes', which being interpreted means 'you're just going to have to twiddle your thumbs alongside me all day long if we have to'. I want to be outside, I want to be back home, surfing the internet, I want to go and see a good film in a real cinema. I couldn't care less about what was on the computers of this family I don't know, who seemed perfectly odious when I went to see them. Their apartment put me off for a start. Too big, too clean, too grand. I'd vaguely prepared some questions: who she saw, where she went, her mother. Everything about François Galtan put me off: his snapped replies, his way of avoiding looking at me as if it was purgatory to have me in his house for five minutes, his whole attitude shouted, 'Get out, you're incapable of finding my daughter.' The stepmother was less unpleasant, but in her politeness I sensed a class disdain that was even more humiliating. When she ended up admitting that she didn't get on too well with the kid, François Galtan rolled his eyes: 'You're her stepmother, God in heaven, when have the daughters of a first marriage ever got on with their stepmothers?' I didn't find out anything about the child's biological mother, they claim not to have had any news of her for over ten years. They were lying, but I didn't have the energy to insist. I just had one idea in my head. Get out of there as fast as possible.

Rafik gets up, and starts connecting various cables to the machine alongside his, then switches it on so that I can see what he's seeing. He speaks to me in an undertone, a hypnotic sound, typical of people who are doing two things at once. 'To find the mother, I've got someone outside on the job, my team was all busy, it'll be faster and I'd rather it stayed between us. We'll have her details by tonight, I think.'

I agree, trying to look like the Queen of Cool. This is what it's like then, to be part of the privileged few: do sweet FA yourself, and let other people run round for you. I concentrate on the internet trawl which Rafik is now reading off aloud, as long lists scroll down on both screens. He starts with François Galtan's computer. I keep to myself the thought that comes to mind: we really don't care what the father's hard disk tells us. He's a pompous prick, but it's hardly likely he's got his daughter locked in the cellar, and even if he was that kind of man, I doubt he'd boast about it on the internet. Rafik explains that what's coming up are the searches the father does online.

A whole string of As with a yellow comma come up, I click on one of them and find I'm on the sales page for his last novel, *The Great Pyramid of Paris*. 'What the hell's he doing on Amazon, looking at his own book thirty times a day?'

Behind us, a technician I hadn't noticed enlightens me,

not unhappy to reveal he's overheard everything we've been whispering. 'He's looking up his ranking in sales figures, it changes every hour.'

I glance back over my shoulder, surprised to find he could put together a whole sentence without the words 'firewall' or 'router'.

'I've got a pal who published an essay once. The sales rankings drove him crazy. He started placing orders for his own book. One a day. He tried not to, but if he saw his book slipping, he couldn't bear it. He'd ordered fifty copies before his mother hauled him off on holiday to the Caribbean, to a bungalow without an internet connection.'

'Well, Galtan can't be ordering many of his, he's about seventy-seven thousandth. Not so good, is it? Perhaps we should buy a few. Poor guy, he's already lost his daughter.'

Rafik and the other kid burst out laughing, as if I'd displayed the most hilarious sense of humour. The assistant is laughing because I'm sitting at Rafik's right hand and Rafik is laughing because I've been sent by the Hyena. That must be it. A virtuous circle. Apart from this, the father looks up the book review pages of *Le Figaro*, *Les Echos*, *Bibliobs*, *L'Express* bestseller list, *Livres-Hebdo* and the kind of blog that rabbits on with great seriousness about Literature with a capital L. Galtan posts various shame-making contributions under different identities. It's quite easy to track him: 'She's full of shit, she can go fuck herself in her big ass' was his obliging comment on one colleague. Completely self-confident, eh, a man who's not bitter, oh no, no personal hang-ups. The comments had all been posted *after* his daughter disappeared. Someone who doesn't let himself be easily distracted then.

I look through his inboxes. He has three addresses: one for activity as an author, almost entirely devoted to his press agent, whom he bombards with slightly flirtatious and falsely jocular messages: 'I wonder why I haven't been invited to the radio programme *From the Bookshop*, since I understand it's about literature, and I happen to write books... I'm also asking myself if you're wearing that red dress that makes you look so fetching.' One wonders whether perhaps he'd like to be able to control himself and slow it down, but he sends her ten emails a day. If the girl has gaps in her press listings, he immediately jumps on them: he tells her what's out there, in any form of media, relating to novels. His second address is personal, for close friends and family. I can't find any mention here of his young daughter's disappearance. He simply tells people regularly that he's 'feeling terrible' and cries off various parties, anniversaries or dinners. The third is a secret one, devoted to his mistresses, and he keeps every message. You can reconstitute for the last two years the clumsy and rather brief sequence of his consecutive mistresses, in order of breaking it off. He's a coward. When he dumps one of them – and he only does so when he's sure of a new one, no gaps between adulteries – he just stops answering, and there are plenty of messages from the rejected women, not even opened but saved to their files. Rafik is tackling the Word documents, versions of his CV, sketches for blurbs on the back of his books, the first few lines of a text about 'Women', an official letter to the telephone company that hasn't cancelled his contract, and a few notes about Paris brothels of the last century. The fast succession of pages on the screen makes me feel sick, I want to take a break.

'The only interesting thing is he doesn't mention his daughter at all.'

'That's normal, he's a man, men don't like to moan.' He explains this to me as if I have never had the good fortune to observe at close quarters how life is lived by men, that little-known species of human being of whom we all know that they go through life standing tall and dignified, strong and silent. Rafik is opening the hard disk of the stepmother, and I get the impression now that I'm being punished. She is passionately interested in new recipes for roast duck, or beef, or lemon tart. She posts on mumsnets: pathetic little blogs about the books her daughters are reading. I'm already on automatic pilot when I move on to the emails. She sends a terrifying number of them. And she is soon talking about Valentine. 'It's terrible to see her empty room.' Yes, we didn't expect her to announce right away that she's contemplating turning it into a dressing room for herself. 'I hug my own daughters, praying never to be in this ghastly situation of not knowing where they are.' After thirty seconds' attention, I can already feel the sirens of total boredom calling me, but then if we go back a bit, just before the disappearance, it gets more interesting. 'It's begun again. And in the kitchen again. She pushed me against the sink, shouting the most awful things, I'd just advised her to be a bit more careful what she eats, she called me all the names under the sun. Now I'm afraid when I hear her come into the house. She goes to her room without a word to me, but I know she's there, and I'm afraid any minute she's going to come out and hit me. I'm afraid at night before I go to sleep, I think, What if she got hold of a knife and came and cut my throat. François keeps telling me not to worry, she'll get over it, but he's never seen her when she gets in a rage. She's unrecognizable, she's a monster.'

Rafik is silent, tense, opens all the emails one by one, and I'm sitting upright, my eyes riveted to the screen. Several sensations go through me, happiness at finding something, but also a certain pleasure in imagining that bitch in her beige body-warmer who looked down on me in her sitting room this morning, squirming against the kitchen sink, terrorized by her stepdaughter. 'This morning Valentine slapped my face before she went to school. I know you'll say I should tell François and that I shouldn't stay here in the house with her. I spent all day crying.'

Rafik asks me at the same time as he reads: 'What was she like, the stepmother?'

'Well slappable.'

His fingers leave the keyboard for a moment and he turns to me. 'If it was her bloke who was hitting her, you'd think that appalling, but when her stepdaughter does it, it's funny, is that it?'

'No. Believe me, if her husband did it, I'd still think it was a good idea.'

Rafik hesitates, then smiles knowingly. I see I've scored some brownie points.

'Doesn't surprise me to hear you're working with *her* then.'

I resist telling him that I grew up with a stepmother too, and it puts me pretty much on the side of any little wankerette who punches hers on the nose. Rafik discovers several exchanges between Claire and Madame Galtan senior, with links to private psychiatric clinics: Switzerland, England, Canada, the States. They searched far and wide. Claire assures the grandmother that she'll press the case with the father, who seems resistant to the idea of having his little girl locked away. He's in denial, understandably, and luckily the two women are taking care of everything. Rafik holds out his hand towards me, as if I should congratulate myself about something. Still in an undertone, he tells me as he opens the last hard disk, 'I'll leave you to work out the detail on your own, but it opens up a few avenues.'

'If Valentine suspected something of all this, you can see why she'd run away.'

'And we can see why you were hired. For that kind of place, you need to build up a dossier, it's like getting into a top-level university.'

'We've already got a dossier on her, believe me.'

'Apparently it's quite a read.'

'Well, she doesn't do animals, but frankly that seems to be the only limit.'

It's already dark by the time we meet in a little bar in the Goutte d'Or district, not far from the office. It's Ramadan and the place is crowded. An entirely male clientele. Smells of coffee, mint tea and spicy food come from the back room. We've picked a little corner to the left of the counter. The Chibani manager seems to know the Hyena well – someone else who's a friend of hers. Rafik explains that he can't get over it.

'You have to go back more than two months to find anything like normal mobile phone activity, calls or texts. Nearly three months. I've never seen anything like it...

Fifteen years old, she stops any internet access and doesn't use her mobile – how do you explain that? Even if you were depressed, really, really depressed, it wouldn't stop you checking your emails now and then, would it? Is she on drugs? Hardly – we'd find her trail all over the web, twenty-four seven, if she was. A love affair? Without a mobile? Can you imagine teenagers in love without texting?'

The Hyena is less bothered.

'Could be she's joined some sect we haven't heard of. A sect that doesn't text during Ramadan perhaps.'

'Three months with no mobile, no email, no tweets, nothing. Not the slightest post to a blog. You seem too calm. You must have some idea you're keeping to yourself, yes?'

I'm sitting opposite them, and nobody expects me to say anything. My ego has been trampled on more times than an old fag end in the gutter. I'm getting used to it. I can appreciate the restful aspect of the situation. For instance, it means I avoid saying something stupid. No one asks anything of me. Not even to pay for my drink. I've got a slight headache after spending the whole day in front of a computer screen.

Rafik is still worrying away at the puzzle. '… That's unless she's watching such hardcore porn on the internet that her father preferred to cough up to have it all wiped off, and after that they strictly forbade her to go online…'

'That doesn't explain why she hasn't sent any emails.'

'And you're absolutely sure? Never seen her in an internet café, or using a friend's mobile? Never?'

This question was in fact addressed to me, but by the time I wake up they've moved on. The Hyena just has one idea.

'And when will you get some info on the mother, Rafik?'

'Tomorrow sometime. Nothing's come up under her name yet: social security, tax return, bank account. But it'll come up, I'm not worried. We can do like we did today. I'll take Lucie through it and then in the evening...'

'No, tomorrow, we're working together: a concert by that band, Panic Up Yours, in Bourges. We're going to the setting-up session. I don't suppose you listen to them, Rafik, you prefer Rihanna and Lady Gaga?'

This time I butt in. 'Great to hear I'm supposed to be on the road tomorrow.'

'What's the matter with you, Derrick, you got other plans?' She appeals to Rafik with a big laugh. 'I've rarely met anyone so reluctant to do anything.'

'Would it be too much to keep me in the loop? It's my time you're asking for, after all.'

'No problem, Derrick, next time I'll send you a fax.'

I roll my eyes with a big sigh, meaning I'm fed up with being called Derrick and being treated like mud. She appeals to Rafik again.

'See that? She's crazy about me. They all are. It's a bit of a problem actually. It's like I'm always telling you, Rafik. The thing about testosterone, it isn't the quantity, it's the quality. See with me, they're all like bitches on heat, they don't realize what's happening. They just fall in love with me.'

Next day the Hyena is waiting downstairs for me. Today she's driving a metallic grey four-by-four, no idea where she got this monster. We drive through Paris slowly, and in this vehicle it feels like being in a carriage, you sit really high up, makes you feel like waving to the pedestrians like the Pope or the Queen of England. France Gall is singing 'Si maman, si, si, maman si', a song I haven't heard for ages. It makes these amazingly clear images flit across my eyes, ones I'd completely forgotten, of Sunday mornings sitting in the back of my parents' car, when we went to see our grandparents for the weekend, and we listened to this programme called *Stop or Play It Again*. Then Michel Berger starts singing 'Si tu crois un jour que tu m'aimes' and I realize it's not the radio. The Hyena drives in silence, absorbed in her thoughts; she drives sitting far back, arms out straight.

'Won't we be there a bit early for the concert?'

'I know one of the organizers, so I called to know when they'd be setting up the sound system. I thought that in a provincial town, where they don't know anyone, just before they go on stage would be the best time to catch them.'

'You know what you want to ask them?'

'What do you think I'm going to talk to them about? The situation in Israel? Carbon taxes?'

'I wish you'd stop treating me as if I'm retarded.'

'Well, change the kind of question you ask, that would help.'

'Is it true that Cro-Mag started calling you the Hyena?'

'No. I was already called that when I started working. It's because I've got a big clit.'

I roll my eyes. I really don't like this kind of talk. I get the impression that she's insisting on drawing my attention the whole time to her genitals. We take some time to filter on to the motorway and I try to show some interest in what we're doing.

'Have you found out a lot about the group?'

'Saw their Facebook page. Rich kids, rebels, they look like a milder version of White Power.'

'*Mild*? White Power?'

'I dug around a bit, they're making up their stupid spiel. Bunch of wankers really, I think. They're from posh families, but they'd like to have been born working-class. They'll get over it when they join daddy's firm.'

'So racism doesn't shock you?'

'I'm old, you know. When I see white kids who need to say, I'm white and proud of it, I just think in my day it would never have come to mind to say we were proud to be white. If we did think it, we felt sorry for everyone else, full stop.'

'They may not be card-carrying members of a party, but it doesn't stop them being political, does it?'

'If you don't have any links to politics, your group won't get noticed by anyone, just you and your pals rehearsing in a cellar... it's sort of like being a poet in a way. You can't blame people for wanting to write poetry, can you?'

'You don't take them too seriously, I gather.'

'Look, they're about seventeen. On their website, they call themselves far right, and where do they play? In a venue run by dykes. That's how I know one of the organizers. So what with one thing and another, no, I don't think I can be bothered to give them a lecture on morals.'

That's all she ever says, honestly. Dyke, dyke, dyke, I've never heard this word so often as in the last few days. As if I could care. As far as I'm concerned, she can be lesbian, or nympho, or celibate, the end result's the same. I have to put up with her, and I couldn't care less what kind of sex she has when she leaves me. She carries on.

'The extreme right isn't what it used to be… They'd have been better off calling themselves the Asshole Whingers' Social Club, you'd have a better idea what they're like. Valentine, now, you've never seen her hanging about with fascists, or religious groups, or anything remotely political?'

'Yeah, course I did, she ran this shooting gallery at a festival run by Friends of Palestine, should've told you.'

'Well, maybe she'd spotted you and she kept it under wraps.'

'It's true I did lose sight of her now and then. But do you really think she ran away to dress up as Joan of Arc and make Hitler salutes? Why would she hide to do that? It's not as if she was scared of making a fool of herself.'

'Could be a problem for her father. No respectable novelist wants to see his daughter going round with swastikas tattooed on her forehead, it could make him look bad at dinner parties.'

The motorway's not too busy. Industrial zone. Hangars with big advertising hoardings on top, and car parks in front, like a long commercial corridor. I'd forgotten that I like travelling by car, getting out of Paris and seeing the tarmac rolling past under the windscreen. Quite soon we're driving through fields and forests.

We get to Bourges in no time. I recognize the cold and the winter light. The trees are still bare, the landscape is flat with its chequerboard of fields, brown and yellow, and a lowering sky; all the outlines are clear. The bleakness of rural France. I get flashbacks to my childhood again, walking along with a satchel on my back, waiting for the school bus, losing my gloves, riding my bike on waste ground.

We park in a square courtyard covered with graffiti. A gigantic clown's head is painted over the door of a circus school. It's five o'clock and already dark. I follow the Hyena into a concert venue, which is empty; none of the technicians takes any notice of us. We pass a staircase to the right of the stage, go along a corridor, and the Hyena turns to me, asks me if I'm ready, then whispers some advice. 'Stay behind me. Whatever happens don't smile, keep your eyes fixed above their heads, don't say anything, don't move, OK?'

I nod yes, not because I feel as ready as all that, but it's not the moment to say I need a bit of preparation. I think to myself that she could have been briefing me during the three hours' drive. She goes into the dressing room without knocking. A square room with no windows, yellow-painted walls, mirrors with light bulbs festooned round them, shower rooms to the side. The place is full of cigarette smoke, which doesn't entirely mask the smell of young animals. I stay leaning against the door, hands in pockets, for a while, and despite my instructions, I find a smile creeping on to my lips, one way to disguise my unease.

There are a whole lot of them in here, all of the male sex, they must think we're part of the staff from the venue, and don't pay us any attention at first. I feel physically afraid being here. I tell myself to be reasonable as I sneak a look at them, they're just kids. But they're big kids, very tattooed, lots of piercings, half-naked and fit. They're used to each other and they make a lot of noise. I concentrate on my breathing, trying to control it, starting from the principle that as long as my heartbeats stay at the same rate I won't be sending out any signals that the animals facing me can interpret as fear. There are seven of them, I've hardly had time to count them before the Hyena, standing in the middle of the room, barks a shout. Out of place, but effective. As if she was a coach, calling her team to order under the showers. The more I shrink into myself, the more she seems to me to be expanding. Usually I think she looks thin and delicate, but now for the first time I realize that she's strong, she has the shoulders of a swimmer. She's exaggerating. But oddly it suits her. I expect her to start thumping her chest like Tarzan and yelling, 'I'll take on the lot of you.' Instead of which, she looks round them, one by one, until they fall silent and before they have time to start ribbing her, she addresses a short dark boy. The best-looking in my opinion. It's as if she has picked him out.

'I need to talk to one of you. I'm conducting an investigation into Valentine's disappearance.'

A tall jokey-looking blond guy, who looks like he's the oldest, answers back. 'And you're what? A cop? You've got ID?'

He has bad teeth, which gives him a proletarian appearance the other boys don't have. Not yet, or perhaps ever. They smell of soap underneath the stink of young males. The Hyena thrusts her hands in her pockets and smiles.

'No, kiddo. The police will only come into it when the girl's found cut up into little pieces. We just want a quiet chat.'

The little dark one she homed in on first treats her condescendingly, but does answer her, which immediately gives her legitimacy. 'What makes you think we know this Valentine?'

He has delicate features. He might or might not be good-looking later on, but right now he's stunning. In spite of the piercings and his menacing expression, he has something angelic about him. Whatever life is going to land on him, and however much he tries to hide it, it's obvious that he doesn't have a clue, which is why he's so utterly charming. He wrinkles his nose when he wants to look like Joe Cool. I'm surprised by the silence she's managed to create. She's a tamer of heavyweights. There's something about her, her way of planting herself in the middle of the room, looking them straight in the face, something in her smile and her calm behaviour, that is slightly worrying. It's not exactly that she looks frightening, but her eyes are a little too bright, her good humour has this edge to it. I think again of Cro-Mag and the dozens of times he's told me about their outings together. Yes, now that I'm leaning up against this door with my arms folded, watching her act, I begin to understand how fascinating it can be. And unhealthy. It's the pleasure she takes in it that bothers me most. She has a gift for suggesting that things might get worse, and that she would be only too pleased if they did. She addresses the dark-haired boy with a certain gentleness, beneath which she doesn't try to conceal a note of pure madness.

'Because I've heard about you. A lot of things about you.'

Bursts of laughter, shouts, they all come back to life as if by an invisible signal, like a flock of birds suddenly flying up in the air in unison. They protest, call to each other, laugh, start shifting their feet. The Hyena doesn't take her eyes off the dark youth, she takes a step towards him, changes her tone, becomes more menacing.

'Afraid to leave your pals for five minutes, are you? Will you wet your pants if you let go their hand? I've got three questions for you. Think that's too difficult?'

'No. But I've got nothing to say. I don't know her.'

'Oh yes, you do. You know her all right. You know her very well, in fact. Do you think I've driven all this way from Paris without finding out a thing or two?'

She's like a snake, her words hiss and coil. He looks round at his mates, but the atmosphere has changed. They're still sort of laughing, but their hearts aren't in it now. I don't know how it happens, or why one of these great gangling lads doesn't just take her by the collar and sling her out. The kid would be best advised simply to refuse to answer, but he's too young to realize that. He gets up with an exaggerated swagger. He's already acting towards her as he must when his headmaster calls him out at school, and in fact I bet he hasn't often been kicked out of his lycée. He's saving face in front of the others; he goes to the door and boldly declares, 'Well, if you really want to have a private interview with me, madame, I won't oblige you to go down on bended knee. Hey gang, if I'm not back in fifteen minutes, call the cops!'

She stands aside to let him go first, and eyes his ass as he walks; he hasn't gone a hundred yards before she says, 'Well, fuck me, kid, you gave in pretty quickly there. Do you always let someone unpick you from the gang as fast as that?'

He turns round, surprised at her tone. I think his instinct had told him there was something a bit louche about this woman, but he preferred to listen to his reason, telling himself he had nothing to fear from some old hag who's looking for a missing girl. She pushes him forward, just a pat on the back to get him going, saying, 'Don't worry, this won't take long.'

We're in the little courtyard outside the big hall. Away from prying eyes. It's quite dark now. Behind the railings, some kids are already queuing up waiting to come in, I see one who can't be more than fourteen drinking vodka, holding the bottle in both hands like a bear cub. He'll enjoy the concert all right. The Hyena sits on a low wall, elbows on knees, and invites the boy to sit beside her, patting the wall with her hand. 'You knew Valentine had disappeared?'

'I did hear something about it. But I haven't seen her for months. She hasn't been in touch.'

'So what did you think when you heard she hadn't come home?'

'Nothing. I felt sorry for her, in case something nasty might have happened to her. But well, nothing. Didn't think anything, really. I don't know what you've been told, but honestly, the last time I saw her was, oh, about four months ago.'

'And what was that like, the last time you saw her?'

'It was at a concert. She was tanked up. As usual. But after that, well, we went our different ways. She started going round with... well, I dunno really, some people from her family, Arabs... immigrants.'

'I see. And that's when you went your different ways.'

'She got kind of grotty, I dunno what she was into altogether. I didn't talk to her about it. She's on her own, Valentine. I don't know what you've heard about her, but she's always been like, strange. In the end, we couldn't take any more, we were fed up with the way she carried on. And she didn't want to see us either. She dropped us, and we were relieved. Even before that, frankly. I don't know why you want to ask me about her. She came to our gigs. But we didn't see that much of her. We weren't interested in her. Not as a friend, not as a girlfriend, nothing. Really, we just wanted her to piss off.'

'But she came to your practice sessions, didn't she?'

'We didn't ask her to, she just kept hanging round us all the time. Valentine, see, she's pretty randy. I'd be surprised if she's changed. Once a slut… but it's got nothing to do with me, right?'

'No, and then what?'

'Then nothing. We couldn't stop her following us round, but we're not into that kind of girl, none of us, we're not like that.'

The Hyena rubs her forehead as if suddenly overcome with fatigue, she gives a sigh as if she's not getting anywhere, and then she says very softly: 'I told you this would take five minutes. And I'd be happy for it to take five minutes. But what I'm hearing is a little boy giving me a load of bullshit. And that bugs me, your trying to cover up. That really bugs me. Because I don't want you to miss your concert. Just tell me what really happened, I'm simply trying to understand the state of mind she was in when she disappeared… I'm not judging you. Just tell me what happened.'

'Nothing. Nothing happened, I haven't seen her for months, I keep telling you, you're on the wrong track.'

He's spoken rather too loudly, as if on the point of losing control. Wallop! Not an ordinary slap with the flat of the hand, a brutal blow, using the edge of her palm, and the death's-head ring makes a long red scratch on his cheek. I didn't see it coming. I don't think he did either. He staggers, she grabs him by the scruff of the neck. If this was a film, it'd be like when someone turns into a werewolf, but too fast and a bit exaggerated. She's become a different person, her voice has changed, the pupils of her eyes have changed, her whole face is transformed by a vicious, but still contained, anger. Her features are drawn. She's not at all pretty now. She's metamorphosed. And you can tell she's got plenty in reserve. This is just for starters.

The boy puts his hand to his cheek. The mark has gone red. He's more shocked than hurt, opens his mouth to protest indignantly, when he sees her face and doesn't even try to hide his terror. He turns to me to be a witness. I'm petrified too. If I dared, I'd intervene, thinking, What will his parents do to us, when he goes running home to mummy to tell her about this? But I'm rooted to the spot, my legs won't move, my mind is frozen.

The Hyena stands up, and from her fragile-looking body she summons phenomenal strength, grabs his collar, hoicks him upright, then throws him to the ground. For a micro-second, he flies through the air. Then she is kneeling astride his chest, he moves his arm to try to push her away, but it would better for him to be completely passive, the slightest resistance enrages her, and he gets three more slaps. She turns him over easily on to his stomach, his arm twisted behind him. She presses his face in the dust to stop him crying out. Lying on top of him, she speaks into his ear: 'Listen, you little shit, I just told you; we're not going to spend all night here. You've got your gig, I want to be back on the road, it would be simplest if you make it snappy. You keep me waiting another five minutes and you're going to get fisted. You know how much it'll hurt? Want to try it?'

This really doesn't seem necessary to me. The kid probably doesn't know anything, but even if he has something to say, surely we could have got it from him some other way. I ought to run off and get help. But I'm afraid of her and her reaction. She moves the kid's knees apart with her leg, and gives him an impatient tap on the head.

'Come on, pull 'em down, I'm going to rip you open. Just relax, you'll love it.'

His lips in the dust, he tries to speak, she lets him lift his neck, his mouth is full of dirt, and his eyes are full of tears. He's trembling with rage or fear.

'She stuck to us for months, we didn't want her around, she was just this fat lush, we wanted her to leave us alone. She was keen on me, one night she bombarded me with texts saying she had to see me. We were all a bit high, so I told her to come out to play, she sneaked away from home, she turned up half naked, like Paris Hilton or someone. We were in our van. And we all screwed her in this parking lot in town, but look, she was *willing*, she didn't tell us to stop, she was knocking back beer after beer, and she'd do anything you wanted. Then we left her there. But we all pissed on her before we left, she didn't even notice, she was lying on her back, not a stitch on. Next day, she turned up to a practice session, like we were just going say 'Hi' and carry on talking to her. As if. So we chucked her out. Then she vanished, she went off, tagged along with someone else maybe, I dunno what she did then. We didn't ask. I swear that's the truth.'

'Oh, when you're telling the truth, I can tell, don't you worry. What's all that about some cousins she was seeing?'

'That was before the parking lot. She said she'd discovered

this other side of her family, and they were these Algerians, but they were cool with her going to see them. I don't know anything else about them, I didn't talk much to her, I swear it, I don't know anything else.'

'Like I just said, when you don't tell lies, I believe you. No need to be scared.'

As he's been speaking, she's gradually relaxed the pressure, letting him recover, he stays for a moment on his stomach, then sits up. Around us, nobody has heard a thing. At any rate, nobody has intervened. In the distance, behind us, we can hear the voices of people starting to arrive for the concert.

The kid stays sitting on the ground, staring up at her, trying to be defiant, but he just looks pitiful. Standing in front of him, the Hyena dusts off her knees carefully, before holding out her hand to help him up.

'Sorry about the roughing up. But you were pretty slow off the mark. Don't look like that, you'll see worse. Better if I knock you about a bit and then don't tell anyone. Because what if I was to go and inform the cops, or tell the parents? Any idea of the shit you'd be in then? It'd be a lot worse than a few quick clips round the ear outside the hall, wouldn't it? Go on, off with you now...'

He takes a few paces backwards, she snaps her fingers and warns him: 'Listen, we won't breathe a word about this, but you do the same, you hear me! We've just had a little chat, right? You go to the gents, you clean yourself up, and we'll forget you tried to fob me off with lies. OK? Or the next time I get my hands on you, you little scumbag, it won't be empty threats, I'll slit you right open. Agreed?'

She's called the last words to his back, as he runs away. She takes out a cigarette from her jean jacket, the packet is crushed and the cigarette bent in half. She acts as if she's completely calm again, but her hands are still shaking and her face hasn't completely recovered, her features still have a haggard look. The worst thing was the way she enjoyed it, visibly enjoyed it, when she was lying on top of him. She zips up her jacket, puts her hands in her pockets, and heads for the car park.

'It won't be difficult to make this generation toe the line. They're made of papier mâché.'

She has asked me to drive on the way back. I start the car without a word. I feel sick. We're stuck in the courtyard for a long time: in front of the entry gates, four kids are kicking a fifth who's lying on the ground, and a crowd has gathered round them. We'd have to run over them to get the four-by-four out of there. I look up at the sky, full moon. I feel like crying. Police siren, sound of a van skidding roughly to a halt, any numbers of uniformed cops jump out waving their guns and super-charged, they shout even louder than the kids. At first I thought they were coming for us, and my blood drained into my feet, my heart stopped, I felt petrified, but no, they were there for the fight. They were even more violent than the kids who were drunk, they got all the young-sters to kneel down in the middle of the road, hands on heads. Someone from the concert venue recognizes the Hyena and comes over to her side of the car with a smile.

'That you? See all that commotion? We're trying to get the cops to cool down. Then we'll have to see how to deal with the kids. Don't you want to stay for the concert? It"ll all calm down in a while...'

'I just had something to say to one of the boys in the band, no time to hang about, sorry.'

He passes her a spliff, she takes a couple of puffs and gives it back, he glances at me, I indicate I'm not interested. A few yards from us, the flashing police lights are illuminating the street, the kids are protesting, furious that the cops want to go inside, others are raging because they won't let them out, and a few who are already smashed decide to take a leak, staggering about. The guy from the admin looks on from a distance, visibly fed up.

'These youth concerts, we've really had it up to here. Christ, we're not in the business for this kind of thing.'

The Hyena laughs, completely in control of herself now.

'The kids aren't very together, are they... but what would you do, turn it into a jazz club?'

'You can laugh, but the more it goes on, the more I appreciate country-and-western. Or an organ-grinder.'

He gives a sad little laugh.

The Hyena asks, 'Is it just this band's fans that are specially stupid?'

'No, put up a reggae sound system here and it'd be the same. It's out in the sticks, Bourges. Not like Paris. Nowadays, the kids turn up, but all they're interested in is drinking. The band, they don't see much of the band, they're already wasted before the concert starts, they don't even go into the hall. They've got their tickets, nothing to do with money. They just couldn't give a toss, they do their heads in, they vomit, they piss all over the place.'

This time he gives a full-throated laugh, scaring himself by what he just said. The Hyena declares pompously, 'The cops are being too rough. They shouldn't act like that.'

'You can't even talk to them when they turn up, you can't get near. They've already flipped, you saw them just now. Getting the kids on their knees in the road, with an accident black spot round the corner... I dunno, that's not what I'd do in a million years. Sure you don't want to stay for the concert? We'd have time for a beer. Or if you want something to eat. The band didn't touch anything, I think they get really choked if people start fighting before their gig.'

'No, no time. It'd make us too late getting back to Paris.'

The guy says he has to get on, and asks someone to let us out through the back entrance. My hands are gripping the wheel, I still feel sick and my throat's dry. We drive for a long time in silence. Then she declares that I'm a good driver. And pushes her seat back. I shouldn't be so affected by the scene she caused. I'd been warned, she's well known for that: getting what she wants by force. I feel grubby as well, after hearing what the boy ended up saying.

The Hyena knows I'm upset, I get the feeling she's angry with me for that. I'm afraid of her. She borrows my mobile and talks to Rafik without paying me a scrap of attention for nearly half an hour. Then she cuts the call, looks for some music on her iPod, chooses Fever Ray, puts her feet up on the dash and looks at the road.

'How long are you going to sulk at me?'

'I'm not sulking, I'm concentrating on the road.'

'Come on, spit it out.'

I want to cry. She speaks to me as if she's really annoyed.

I'm afraid she'll get into a mood and start hitting *me*. The creature I saw emerging in the courtyard of the concert venue might come out any minute. The cab of the four-by-four seems tiny. She gives a long sigh.

'Hey ho. Give me patience... I wonder what the hell you're doing in this job.'

I don't reply. She sits up, full of indignation.

'All right, OK, I hit him! Just a little tap. He could take a little beating up, couldn't he? It didn't hurt him, for God's sake. It's not as if I'd... torn him limb from limb or suspended him from a hook. That's life, isn't it? You don't think that little kid is made from sugar and spice and all things nice, do you? When he and his pals all stood there and pissed on that girl, do you think they worried if she'd get a good night's sleep afterwards? That's life. What goes around comes around.'

'Yeah, OK. It's obvious I'm not cut out for this job. I don't want to go on doing it. I didn't ask to do a full-scale investigation, I was perfectly happy just checking on teenagers outside their schools, Deucené insisted...'

My tears prevent me carrying on. Alongside me, the Hyena looks at me with a strained expression, but seeing I'm starting to sob, she laughs.

'OK, just stop on the hard shoulder, I'll drive. What do you want me to say? Yes, I gave him a hiding, just a little one, so he'd tell us what really happened. I swear to you that right now, he's less bothered about it than you are... I'm sure he's playing away fine at his concert, the little toerag. It made him see sense. I gave him a little mandala to realign his chakras, that's the way it works. Come on, signal and pull over, you can't drive when you're crying your eyes out, it isn't safe. I don't *believe* it, how you can react like that. I don't *believe* it.'

I stop on the hard shoulder, and she gets down to go round and sit in the driving seat, while I slide across into hers. Then she comes back and opens the door on my side. It's an attack of nerves. I can't stop crying. She pulls me gently out of the car.

'Look, I'm sorry. I never thought you'd… take it so badly. I'm really sorry. Come on, calm down.'

She puts her arms round me and I'd like to push her away because she disgusts me, and because she's a lesbian, and I don't want her to think she attracts me or whatever. But her body is large and warm, her arms are round me, it's not like a seduction, more like being hugged by a solid reassuring statue. I let my head fall on her shoulder, she strokes my hair and I go on weeping.

'How can anyone be that sensitive?… I shouldn't have taken you with me. You've got a problem with violence? You were abused as a child? Your parents beat you? You were raped? What's the matter then? PMT? Listen, Lucie, I can't do anything about it; that's how you get people to talk. If not, they just give you nothing but bullshit. Nothing works like a bit of violence to get you somewhere.'

She takes over at the wheel. My eyes are puffy and I have a sudden urge to go to sleep. She keeps on talking, driving too fast.

'That's how it is, that's the real world. I didn't invent it. There is no dignity, there is no gentleness. All the people who were good and honourable, all the nice guys, have been wiped out. And not yesterday either. All that's left is people like me, scum of the earth. People like you, what can I say, you're just not going to make it. Do you hear what I'm saying? Even to teach primary school these days, you need to be tougher than you are.'

She is taking me seriously for the first time since we met. I like it. I make a silent promise to cry from time to time. She shoots me a few sidelong glances, to see if I'm on the mend.

'Did you hear, just now? Rafik is making progress. He's getting the mother's address, she lives in Barcelona. Great, I love going there. She's changed her name, she's married an architect. They're loaded. And the story with the cousins, that's intriguing. Better take a look at them before we leave Paris. We'll take the four-by-four to Barcelona, OK?'

'Why not go by plane?'

'Because I can't stand airports. Going through all that security, all the stupid pricks with suitcases on wheels who go ahead of you, the stupid pricks in uniform, the stupid families, the stupid people who pat you down… Not being able to smoke or go anywhere once you've checked in, having to show your passport a million times, sitting in some stuffy little departure lounge without knowing when they'll let you out, having to take your shoes off every five hundred metres. For-get it. Pity though. Cos I really like the plane itself and looking at clouds out of the window.'

I wonder whether she wants to drive to Spain so that she can cross the frontier with guns. I prefer not to go there and change the subject. 'Do you think Valentine ran away because of what happened in the parking lot?'

'No, I don't think so. She doesn't see those boys any more.

I think that bit's true. Something else must have happened.'

'But they raped her.'

'Did you see that gang of little shits? Would you get in touch with them at night to go and have a few beers?'

'No. Unless he was lying, and he'd been OK with her before, so she didn't suspect what was going to happen.'

'Yeah, you're right, it could be. But anyway that's not a reason to run away. If all the teenage girls who got themselves raped ran away there wouldn't be many left at home. When I was young, I thought being a lesbian was the most difficult thing in the world, but really you, the straight women, you eat shit as well. They tell you so often it's good that you end up saying yum yum, but you eat it, Christ, you don't half eat it.'

'And we're not going to tell Valentine's parents?'

'No, I don't see that it's any of their business.'

Headlights on full beam, we're about the only car on the motorway. Speed cameras flash at us at regular intervals. You can't see the landscape now, it's plunged in darkness. I watch the black night go past, leaning my shoulder against the window.

'Tell me something. When we go and see Valentine's real mother, are you going to jump up and down on her if she refuses to talk?'

She bursts out laughing and doesn't reply.

Once she's dropped me off at my place, I can't get to sleep. I've noted Valentine's mother's maiden name, and I google it. Up come an Algerian football team, the words of a German pop song, a security firm in Nantes, an article in *El Watan* about a village that's been destroyed. Perhaps in this family, nobody has a page in their real name. I'm discouraged, as well as tired out and on edge. My tiny living room is lit only by the blue glow on the computer screen, and I soon feel sick from scrolling down all these pages. I'm internet-seasick. I'm working automatically, concentrating and absent. Old friends. A link that could be to an aunt of Valentine's. Lycée in a northern suburb of Paris, Aulnay-sous-Bois, law school, but dropped out, according to the dates. That figures, she must be about forty. Link to her Facebook page, date of birth. The surname is spelled differently there, which explains why I got off on a false start. I note the names of the children. I find a MySpace page for a son, called Tedj. He started one but he didn't keep it up long, almost empty and long since abandoned. The kid had 34 friends. I go to each of them in turn, and end up finding a Facebook link to a girl cousin. Then another cousin, the virtual family's getting bigger. I've got hold of a thread. They leave lots of messages for each other. Someone called Nadja posts hundreds of photos, she's documenting her family's whole life. I do Apple key +F Valentine, systematically, on every new page. I'm not thinking too much about what I'm doing and then bingo, three mentions, I'm on to it. I get a rush of adrenaline, my nerves are jumping. Valentine, in the middle of a family photo, everyone round a table. Taken two months before she disappeared. I look at the faces round her. A little guy with glasses who's laughing, a fat hulk, two little girls wearing headscarves, a cool guy in a Lacoste T-shirt, a sensible-looking girl-cousin, and some others who look more saucy. I recognize Nadja, the original cousin, she's in the photo, and I've been looking at her for two hours now from every angle. She's beautiful, but not in a friendly way. You wouldn't want to cross her. And her brother Yacine. Who doesn't like to be photographed, but she didn't give him the option. Valentine only appears in one series.

I call Rafik. I am only mildly surprised that he replies at 4 a.m.

'If I have a Facebook page can you find me the address?'

'That's what I'm paid to do, kiddo.'

YACINE

HE NODS TO THE YOUTHS HANGING AROUND at the bottom of his tower block. Short silence as he passes. Good, bit of breathing space. He knows once his back is turned they'll start talking again, but to his face they keep their big traps shut. He has his reputation. Knife man. Guns, yes, fascinate them all, but with guns in a fight, you'll miss your target two times out of three. Got to be a crack shot to make it worthwhile. But a knife, if you can handle it, you score every time. Just got to be able to take it, as well as dish it out. And be motivated by a philosophy, some idea bigger than you are. Be someone who's ready to pitch in. They all want to challenge him, but he's too strong for them to risk it. They're stoned out of their minds anyway, can't stand up straight, no backbone. Nobody speaks to him. See if he cares. Just because he was born here doesn't mean he's got to be like the rest of them. Layabouts. And he couldn't care less about their cheap hiphop. He listens to the same music his father used to. Funk, soul. Real music. When the blacks weren't yet eating shit from the backsides of the whites, and flexing their abdos for any TV camera. In the stairwell, some young kids are messing about with a dog. He motions them to get out of the way. The ankle-biters push off without answering back. They're scared of him. What are they there for anyway? To get mauled by a pitbull? It'd be all over the front pages, because this estate, if ever you see anything about it in the papers, it's because someone's been killed. He wonders what the fuck their mothers are doing all this time. Painting their faces again, even though they've no idea about makeup. If they really want to look like trash, they should make an effort, learn to do it properly. But even that's beyond them, they can't even get the slap right. Too much to ask, eh, to wipe their kids' behinds, or work out how to look beautiful. They can't do a fucking thing. And the ones who ponce about in headscarves are no better than the rest. They can parade all they want at the school gates, the Darth Vader brigade, they'll never be the true faithful. Back home, they're just bitches, layabouts, know-nothings. No surprises, then, if their kids turn into the riffraff he meets every day. His own mother has never let them hang about all day on the stairs. His home wasn't like that. No man around, but she'd take out a belt and nobody batted an eyelid. Now that he's a man, if anyone gets out the belt, it's him.

In the hall, he holds his breath. A smell of cumin, stale cigarette smoke and piss. Animals. They talk about Allah all day long, but they live like animals. And that's just the adults. And not only the ones who drink. All of them. Incapable of holding in long enough to find a corner to piss in. Worse than dogs. If it was up to him, he'd soon show them. All of them. How to behave. He'd chop the balls off the first guy he caught pissing in the lifts. That'd teach them.

School's a waste of time. His mother wants him to keep going, she says she doesn't want any problems with the family allowance, or some busybody social worker turning up at the door. One time, his older brother got into trouble at school and his mother had to go and see his teacher and the headmistress. She let him have it when they got back home, she hammered him so hard his shoulder was put out. Then she left him lying there on the floor in the living room. She looked at her other son and her two daughters: next time I have to go up there and spend ten minutes being conde-scended to by those creeps because one of you's in trouble, I'll kill the lot of you and put a bullet in my own head, is that clear? And they obey. They respect their mother. Yacine understands where she's coming from. She doesn't want to sit in an office up at the school, and have those stuck-up bastards read her a lecture. She doesn't insist the kids get good grades. She doesn't look at their school reports. She doesn't mind if they repeat a year. She just asks them to keep their mouths shut, and to keep attending until they're sixteen. No funny tricks. She doesn't want trouble. She's right. But he doesn't listen to anything they say at school. That culture's not for his people. You can't force it into their heads. It's education for kids who were born French. Nothing to do with him. He has this aunt who went on studying, she thinks she's the cat's pyjamas because she got to teach at a university, and she's writing a thesis. She can show off as much as she wants. What planet's she on? She imagines they'll forget she's an Arab, because she copies their culture. Yeah, sure, Laïla, sure, all your colleagues treat you just like one of themselves. In your dreams, sister. To Yacine, it seems worse than being the neighbourhood whore or the local crack dealer. It isn't even as if she makes any dough. She drives a Renault Clio, and she doesn't live any better than the rest of the family. She has to watch what she puts in her supermarket trolley, and she can't afford country holidays.

He doesn't listen at school. Education, he gets it his own way. He doesn't listen, but he hears all right, through the pathetic racket in the classroom, with everyone shouting at once. He hears the whore up at the blackboard, who's stammering something about violence coming from 'fear of the other'. Bullshit. They're not afraid of anyone, that's the whole problem. He doesn't play up in class. He just contents himself with staring at her, sometimes her eyes meet his. She really likes him, she'd like to get him on her side. She'd like him to join in, she thinks she's got something to offer him. As if. What she really wants is for him to screw her, he can guess that from the way she looks at him, when he stares back at her without smiling, she'd like him to come up at the end of the class and ask for private coaching in literature. That'd really turn her on. But he doesn't go with just any slut. No way, he's not like that. He stands up straight. No one can take that away from him. His dignity.

When he gets home, he can tell immediately that the sounds are not the usual ones. His mother isn't in the kitchen, where she's always to be found at this time of day. His sister isn't yelling from her bedroom where she watches TV, 'I can smell from here you've been smoking!' She's really pissed off with him about that. She says good Muslims don't smoke. Where did she get that idea? Nadja thinks you have to keep making a constant effort, that's the only way to stay on the straight and narrow. If you let yourself go, you'll slip back. They've been as close as that since they were little. His other sister's left home, married. The flat seems bigger now she's gone. Raouda used to be a good cook, looked after the housekeeping too, and that helped their mother out. But she took up too much space. Talking all the time, listening to stupid radio shows.

When he gets home, as a rule, his face changes. He relaxes. Takes off the mask. But today, something's not the same as usual. He rearranges his expression before going into the living room.

This dark woman with short hair is sitting on the couch. Legs apart. Like a guy. Not like a tart, like she's *really* a man, no kidding. Good-looking for her age. That's because of her skin, the grain of her skin catches the light, looks luminous. And her nose is delicate. She's got big eyes. Serious-looking. She doesn't smile at him when he comes in, she looks him straight in the eye, just long enough to let him know she's not going to be apologetic about anything. He sees that his mother's offered her coffee, the empty cup's on the low table. His mother explains.

'She's looking for your cousin Valentine. She's run away. Did you know that?'

'No.'

Nadja gets up, and puts her hand on his shoulder as she goes past. Everyone says they look like each other. She's exactly his height. He'd have looked good too if he'd been a girl. His sister's beautiful. Her beauty is grave and majestic. Not like those silly little girls who only wear headscarves because it's today's fashion, and then behave like sluts when they're waiting for the bus. Modern Islam, a stupid idea invented by Muslims in France. Nadja started wearing the veil before he'd started growing a beard. For two years, she'd pinched his cheek when they were alone: 'Think it'll grow one day, or will you always be a baby?' Now she asks him: 'Want a coffee?' and goes into the kitchen. From the way both women are acting, he knows that the stranger must have behaved correctly. They don't need to wait for him if they want to kick someone out. Even if she looks slightly daunting, this woman. Not fat, but capable of a bit of strong-arming. Sturdy shoulders, straight back. A plain-clothes cop, perhaps. She hasn't bothered to smile when she looks at him. Makes a nice change. The French are so hypocritical. Nation of shopkeepers. They always start by being smarmy, when what they really want is to shaft you.

'I'm looking for Valentine. I work for a private detective agency. She went missing a week or so back. I saw on the internet that she'd got in touch with her mother's family recently... so I took the liberty of calling to see you, to ask whether she had... mentioned anything that might give me some clues to follow up.'

You can tell she's making an effort, all the same. Trying to talk politely, so that they won't be insulted. And that in itself is insulting. Well, anyway, do what she likes, there's no way we can get on, her sort of people and our sort of people. Only the kind of French who live in cloud cuckoo land could imagine it's still possible to understand each other. The ones who never see any rats. In the places they live, the way they live. No meeting possible. No forgiveness. No argument.

The people who don't like them are absolutely right. The day Yacine has something to say, he'll have his knife on him. For now it's a cold war. When things get bloody, he'll be there. And war's like football: they'll be world champions. Yacine takes the coffee his sister holds out to him, pulls over a chair and sits down face to face with the newcomer. His mother speaks, neither friendly nor aggressive, just going over what she's already said, spontaneously, so that Yacine can see the line to take.

'We haven't seen her since Christmas. You haven't seen her either, have you? No, like I said. She wants to know where Louisa is. Well, we'd like to know that too.'

His mother loves her sister, Louisa. He knows that she misses Louisa, that they were close when they were young. Of all her sisters, even though they never see each other now, she's still her favourite. That was why, when Valentine turned up, his mother was happy. Louisa's daughter! She didn't look much like her mother, but still, it was a bit of her coming back, a corner of her life reappearing. Since Louisa's changed her name to Vanessa, she's thought herself too grand for them. Apparently she lives in some palace now, in Barcelona. The high life. Vice often pays. She's always used her brains to find herself a place in the sun, and she'd rather fall out with her entire family than see that bunch of losers turn up on her doorstep to dirty her carpets. One of these days, Sheitan in person will come and tell her he likes her style, but till then she's right to act the way she does. The more you give your family, the more they hate you. But parents, that's different. And Vanessa *never* speaks to hers any more. What astonishes Yacine is that his mother, who's so proud, and upstanding and intransigent, can regret the loss of her sister, when Louisa isn't even bothered to know whether her own parents are all right. No phone calls, nothing. Of course she abandoned her daughter too. Though the daughter's got a cushy life, you have to say, but still. He'd asked Valentine if it was true she'd never heard from her, no, nothing, not a thing. In their house too, any photos of Louisa have been burnt or carefully cut out from the family snaps. Because of the evil eye. Because for ages, whenever a kid was ill or some slacker lost his job, it was 'Louisa putting the evil eye on them'. With Nadja, on the quiet, they would laugh together. Yeah, right, Vanessa lives in a posh district, she's treated like a princess, she goes to the hammam with Jews, and eats fancy food off porcelain dishes, but when she's awake in her bed, she envies her family. That same bunch of losers. Of course she does, logical, that's the way it's got to be. But in fact he's never seen Louisa. Even his mother no longer has any photos of her. He knows what it cost her, the day she had to bring them all out, so that they could be burnt in front of the whole family. But she did it, without cheating. That's the way his mother is, straight, honest. Never does anything behind your back, everything's always up front with her. Good deeds don't often get rewarded, and his mother's probably the one in their family who's had to take the most godawful jobs, cleaning up other people's shit, and she's seen hard times, like when his father went off, and the kind of bad stuff you get from people when they see you're trying to behave correctly. More correctly than them. Because when they see someone decent, they feel threatened. But anyway her children are all OK. Not one of them goes round moaning, 'Oh, it's society's fault I have to deal shit, French society forced me to drink wine, society turned me into a piece of rubbish hanging about in the stinking stairwell.' They stand up straight. Yacine's responsible for his own actions. He knows where Louisa is. He doesn't know her address, but he knows she's in Barcelona. His cousin told him, that big slob, Radia's son. How he found out was nobody's business. He'd been mighty interested in Valentine, and pissed off because she only had eyes for Yacine.

When this girl had turned up, one Sunday, his cousin'd been like one of those old-fashioned cartoons, the wolf with his tongue hanging out and dollar signs whizzing round in his eyes. Knocked sideways. Nobody said a thing while she was there, but you could see what all the younger members of the family were thinking: she's loaded! Even her way of sitting on a chair looked like a million dollars. She immediately took to Yacine. She picked him out from all the others milling round her. He'd taken her back home. He felt sorry for her. Valentine was rolling in it, you could tell by her handbag, her cute haircut, her top-of-the-range Nike trainers... but Yacine had recognized from the start that the little princess was unhappy. He didn't distrust her for long, because she was too vulnerable. Completely nuts, ready to do anything, and totally lacking in self-esteem. He'd have liked to do something to help her, but she was beyond help. Living in this flat in central Paris, 200 square metres, where her bedroom was bigger than their living room, and having pocket money like it grew on trees. He'd never seen her without a few banknotes on her. But Valentine had nowhere to put her feet on this earth. She was a lost soul, floating somewhere in the stratosphere. Her father couldn't give a toss about his daughter, her stepmother wanted her out of the way, her grandmother couldn't stomach her any more, and her bitch of a mother had even forgotten the date of her birthday. At first Yacine had been wary, because she was like no one else he'd ever known. But she tamed him. Valentine laughed non-stop. She contradicted herself all the time, with comical carelessness. From a distance, you'd think she was totally frivolous. But close to, it was more complicated. Getting to know her, he'd discovered for the first time in his life that there's such a thing as the misery of the rich. He wasn't going to shed tears over her lot, but he finally worked out why she was sad. Valentine just didn't have anything much. Socially, yeah, she'd probably do better than his family, the world was her oyster. Even if she didn't do anything but mess about or get into trouble. Wealth is a thick mattress, it breaks any fall, and lets you bounce back. Where he is, it's another matter. The walls close in on you, month after month, the registered letter, always the same, you won't make it, you'll never make it. You take up too much space. You want too much all the time. You're always too hungry.

Crisis, what crisis? This is all he's ever known. So he's hardly going to take fright at it now. How could they have any less than they have now? Cut off the hot water? OK, go ahead, we'll manage, like we've always managed. All the same. Valentine was worse off than he was. Buy all you want, you'll never fill that big hole eating up your heart. If he compared Nadja and Valentine, he saw a queen and a dropout. Valentine made an effort when she saw him, but however much she watched what she said, he could always second-guess her. All over the place and damaged. And that darkness inside her was waiting to burst out. He'd come very close.

He'd slept with her. Almost at once. He'd never told Nadja. He'd hardly pulled out before he was already regretting it. But he'd started again. Often. The animal in him was straining at the leash. She drew him to her. Every millimetre of her skin was screaming for him to come into her. Yacine knew she would sleep with anyone. He ought to have been disgusted. But he doubted it was the same for her with anyone else like it was with him. The first time, she'd started putting on an act, the easy lay who knows all the little tricks. Playing the good-time girl, I'm so emancipated, suggesting porn-star positions, and making too much noise. But it had all changed very fast. She hadn't been expecting that either. They had frozen, arms round each other, drenched in sweat, astonished, on the edge of an abyss, and looked at each other, wondering what was happening to them. Surprised by the violence of what they'd started. Not the usual kind of teenage brutality, with a bit of violent fighting and clumsy sodomy. Not that kind of thing at all. Unspeaking, beyond words. A magnetic path from which they couldn't escape. At that moment he saw her transfigured: a black virgin. Deep inside her, a blood-red heart opening up to swallow him. It was like a hammer blow, invisible and of phenomenal force, sending him into a darkness filled with whispers. They were in a clammy intensity, a dark and overgrown jungle. When their skins touched they reached a different level of sensuality. Valentine was transformed: a goddess of destruction, holy and terrifying. He was altered too. And that frightened him.

But not her. Straight away afterwards, all she did was keep quiet for a moment, while her prosaic partner regained possession of his body. Her wings came off. It didn't mean more than that to her. She was without any sense of the sacred that might allow her to fear the forces they were unleashing. She was too trivial to be distressed. She was just a teenage girl again. With her dopey way of talking. Giggling about nothing, with something fragile and flaky at the back of her eyes. Just a girl. Attractive, annoying. Normal. He didn't like the power he had glimpsed. It freaked him out. And what attracted him most was precisely what made him want to run away. A huge force, that he was the only one to be summoning up. He never let himself go to sleep alongside her: he thought she was quite capable of putting a knife in his guts.

No good could ever come of it for them. She was full of all the fancy ways of a French girl who thinks she's liberated. As if liberation meant letting yourself be screwed like a whore by some guy who wants nothing to do with you when you're dressed again. Yacine is used to girls, he often talks to them, they don't scare him. Valentine wasn't the first to run past him her little number about sexual freedom, the right of girls to like it and not to feel defiled if someone touches them up, and so on and so forth. It would have pleased him if it had been true, he'd have liked to meet a woman who really didn't care and came out of it OK. Not one of those who makes believe, who takes it up the ass, and then when she can't sit down makes up some story about how she's happier standing up. It would be nice if the world was like that. But walls are walls. The mouse can always pretend she gets on fine with the cat, but the day he bites her in the neck, she'll be on the ground and he'll have a good meal. It's like the tarmac all round them, it's concrete, you can't escape it and nobody cares whether you like it or not. There's an order in this world.

He'd stopped seeing her. He'd fucked her one more time, in an alley, anyone could have seen them, from behind, like a whore. It hadn't succeeded in making things sordid enough for him to be free of that image of her. It had been fantastic, yet again. When she turned round to look him in the eye, there was no more to be done. They both knew they'd crossed the frontiers. She was a divinity. Too attractive. Pleasure in abjection. To touch her made him too feverish. He had no desire to learn any more about this stranger inside him, the one who emerged every time he touched her.

Just after he had come, making her take it up the back, she had stayed with her forehead against the wall. He'd walked away without saying anything. When she called to him, he'd said it was over, she must forget him, give him up. He didn't want her to come near him again. Ever. She hadn't insisted. She'd disappeared from his life.

He had missed her, missed not seeing her any more. He even missed her silliness. When she got angry, she was like a furious kitten. But he breathes more easily now he doesn't see her. It's a danger avoided.

His mother and Nadja are still talking away with the detective. He's surprised how friendly they're being. This private eye's good at her job. They don't usually chat like that. Especially since they hardly know Valentine, in fact. They're going on about how happy she was to discover she had a family, how she liked meeting her grandparents, her false shyness. Yacine says nothing. He gets up to make some coffee, and offers one to the woman, who accepts at once; he wonders if she's going to camp there. She's carrying out her plan, saying 'Oh really?' and 'Are you sure about that?' to get the conversation going again, you can see that mentally she's registering every word.

In the kitchen, he heats up some water. A spoonful of instant coffee in both glasses. The detective appears, stops at the kitchen door and asks· 'Can I have five minutes with you on your own?' He gestures towards a chair with his head. She acts like a cop, Clint Eastwood style. She must have seen his films when she was young and considered him a good role model. Yacine wonders what kind of man shacks up with a woman like this. Must have brass-lined balls, her guy. Yeah, she's good-looking. But too masculine. Could be a turn-on, but you can't imagine yourself coming home at night and asking her what's for supper. You're be scared she'd punch you on the jaw. Yacine looks at the floor, hands clasped between his knees, unmoving. She says nothing. He breaks the silence.

'I didn't say anything in there, because I've got nothing to say.'

'But I know that Valentine was in love with you, I think you saw each other without anyone else knowing, and what I'd like is if you'd tell me, just quickly, what happened.'

How does she know this? She was careful to keep her voice low so that they can't hear from the next room. He doesn't like what she said one bit. He keeps calm.

'You're wondering if I've locked her up in some cellar and

how much I want for her? Sorry, madame, wrong address. Try the Africans across the landing, maybe they've eaten her?'

She stares at him, glacially, then changes tactics and bursts out laughing. She can look after herself. Women as a rule find it hard not to convey that they find him attractive. Even when they try to play ice-queen, there's some giveaway glance or smile. They can't hide it. But not her. She's got the situation under control. She's unreachable. It makes her attractive. In spite of everything, he's glad he made her laugh.

'I don't know where you've dug up a story like that, I don't know any more than what they told you next door, and that's the truth.'

'Ah yes, but on the internet there are some pictures of the two of you... Photos, I wouldn't exactly call them compromising, but the way she's looking at you, I'd say that you know each other a lot better than you're telling me.'

He is silent. Nadja and her damned computer. Nadja and her craze for photos. He doesn't bother himself with what she gets up to on the internet. He'd forgotten the photos. The private eye isn't charming now, she's just a standard model cop. An unarmed cop. Out come the violins.

'And you don't think she might be in danger, and it would be better if I can find her?'

What he really ought to do is slash her ugly mug and have done with it. He clenches his teeth. He hates her. He has no desire to tell her what happened. She insists, still speaking in a low voice.

'If you like, we can go down for a walk, nobody else needs to know what we're talking about. I've got a deal to suggest.'

'You're threatening me? You'll make trouble for me if I don't cooperate, right?'

She leans across and speaks in such a quiet voice that her lips hardly move, she doesn't stop looking him in the eye, her face is expressionless.

'Your cousin Karim, for me it's not a problem to get them to reopen the file, discover it was a case of mistaken identity and he shouldn't have been charged. I can get him out in 48 hours. Interested?'

That waste of space. His cousin Karim. Shooting around on his scooter, when some other kids were chucking stones at the police. This one cop got hit on the head, bust a blood vessel, and was paralysed after that. OK, tough luck, but come on, it's his job, he should have been wearing riot gear and a helmet. What kind of cop goes round in the middle of a riot without head protection? Practically professional misconduct. They arrested everyone in sight, of course. Karim hung about, because he's stupid, and he thought just because he hadn't done anything, no reason to rush off. And they got hold of him, among others. They formally identified him – as if you have time to photograph one out of about fifty guys milling round the place. He didn't get done for the stone that hit the cop, by chance they pinned that on another couple of cretins. Apparently those two weren't even down there when it happened. They were fetched out of their homes. But between what people say and what really happened, they don't bother to distinguish. Karim's been charged with attacks on public property, supposedly setting fire to a dustbin during the riot. As if he had nothing better to do. He could cop it hard though. Be made an example. Actually, Yacine has never liked his cousin. He's stingy, cowardly and fat, he likes football, porn movies and fancy cars. Not much to be done with him. But he's family. The bitch. She's really worked hard on her little file, before turning up at the door with her foundation-covered face. Yacine resists. But he knows she's got him.

'If he gets out like that, everyone will say it's a deal, gotta be something behind it.'

'Up to you. If you tell me the truth, he'll be out in a week. I give you my word.'

She empties her coffee cup, throwing back her head to catch the last drop. She really does act like a man.

'You know perfectly well what happens to little girls all alone in the big city. It isn't as if you were up to anything criminal. I've got to find her. And I need to know what she was doing in the weeks before she took off. I think you had a relationship. I want to know what she told you, the kind of things she was interested in. And don't forget that if I don't solve this case quickly, one of these days it'll be the police knocking at your door. I found you through the internet, and they'll soon turn up the same photos. All they're interested in is getting your name down on a charge sheet, so they can say to their boss, "Right, sir, I've got it sorted." The truth never got anyone promotion.'

She's playing superwoman now, but getting more angry, and Yacine wonders if she practises this for hours in front of the mirror because she does it very well. For a bitch. She stands up.

'OK, I'll walk to the metro with you.'

'I came by car.'

'All right then, I'll walk you to the car.'

He knows already that she's right. It's in his interest to talk to her. Whereas from the pigs, he can expect nothing but trouble.

BARCELONA

THE HYENA FOUND VALENTINE'S MOTHER'S precise address before Rafik did. The night we've just spent watching the tarmac flash by has hardly lessened my irritation: for once I'd had a lead to follow up. As dawn breaks, just before we reach Barcelona, we pass some enormous and intriguing white globes: a nuclear power station gleaming in the already blazing sunshine. A spaghetti junction of motorways, and we're slipping into the city. The resounding blue of the sky, a uniform backdrop, magnifies everything it covers. I didn't sleep much, I'm bizarrely wakeful, with the glucose from the Red Bull plus caffeine circulating in my jangled nerves, on a platform of dulled calm. Electricity on my nerve ends. The blinding light hurts my eyes. I feel well, actually, although I'm on the edge of a strange and worrying abyss. The absurd happiness of seeing the first palm trees, and the façades of the buildings covered with useless florid detail, the balconies bright with every colour of the rainbow. At the first red light, the Hyena operates the central locking.

'Watch out, they have very cunning thieves here.'

'Worse than in Paris?'

'Much. They're cutting-edge delinquent in this town. They can empty a car at the speed of light, very nifty, very effective.'

She wants a coffee and stops when she finds somewhere to park. Her features are drawn with fatigue, but a joyful expression, such as I haven't seen on her before, lights up her face. She says cheerfully, 'Nice here, eh? Come on, we can go to a bar, have a fag, that'll revive us.'

For the first few hours of the drive, the Hyena gave me a long description of Yacine, his sister Nadja, and how much she liked their mother, whom she would gladly save, if she had the time, from the 'shipwreck of heterocentrism'. Gradually we're getting a picture of Valentine, but without yet being able to describe her clearly. The Hyena is interested in this little teenager, I think she's touched by the way the kid bounces all the time from one side to the other, without finding her place, but without getting tired. She's a valiant little pinball.

When you get away from Paris, you realize what a grey, noisy, depressing and morbid city it is. As we sit on this café terrace, the wind on our skin hasn't the same texture. We proceed slowly to our hotel.

A tiny room, very expensive. The tap water that I splash on my face has an unpleasant smell. I check that the television works, then crash on to the bed and go to sleep. Less than half an hour later, the earth shakes, the walls vibrate, and I just have time to realize I've got a headache before I see from my window a whole lot of workmen, naked to the waist, attacking the façade with pneumatic drills. I lie there under the sheets, can't get my brain in gear. A knock at my door, the Hyena bursts in, she's beside herself. I immediately imagine the drills being confiscated – the poor men don't know what's coming to them.

'I'm out of here. They've got a fucking nerve, saying they don't have any quieter rooms. In reception, they said nobody but us complains, that people don't come to Barcelona to spend all day in their hotel rooms. I'm off, I need my sleep. I'm going to a girlfriend's place. Are you coming, or do you want to stay here?'

I grab my things and follow her without thinking. On the way she works out how to get some advantage from the fiasco. 'I'll make out some false hotel bills, that'll bring us out ahead.'

'Whose place are we going to?

'Some French women who live here. We'll be fine over there.'

The streets have now been invaded by scooters. Buzzing insects coming at you from all directions. Crash helmets, flipflops, summer clothes, graceful bodies on two cylinders. The city has become a vast cauldron of noise. People sound their horns all the time, while gigantic machines are digging up the roads, exposing the town's entrails, taking the din to new levels. It seems to be a local custom.

The blonde woman who takes us in is built like a lumberjack in exile from her forest. Solid and slightly gaunt. She has poor skin, and very fine hair receding from her forehead, her nose is prominent and her bluish-grey eyes are bulging. She serves us coffee so strong it's practically all grounds. The Hyena monopolizes a joint as soon as she has sat down.

'Good thing you're here… when they started to knock down the hotel wall, I was on the point of murdering one of them.'

'Touch a hair of their heads? Building workers in Barcelona?

Don't even think about it. It's their religion here. Barcelona's the noisiest city in Europe. They're always knocking everything down all the time. You see them working on building sites at midnight on Saturdays. Nothing stops them. Cranes – they're the opium of the masses for the Catalans. They dig up the pavements just to see what's underneath. You wouldn't believe. They'd kill their father and mother, just to be able to put up a new building.'

These two are old friends. I don't dare say that I want to go to bed. I drop off on the couch. When the noise around me forces me to come out of it, the heat is stifling in the room, and the curtains aren't effective enough to filter the blinding sunlight. The house has filled with people, and I've had a lot of painful dreams that I can't quite remember. There are a dozen or so girls scattered throughout the rooms. Hoarse voices. The blonde, now with a cigarette in her mouth, is hanging up some black garments.

'Sleep OK? Want anything? A coffee? Or I can show you your room.'

'A coffee, yes, I'd love one. Where's the Hyena?'

'Telephoning out on the terrace.'

She drops the clothes she's hanging up and leaves them there on the ground, not bothering to come back to them. She goes off to make me a coffee, but forgets me on the way, to take a draw on a joint passed to her by a little blonde punkette in a shiny skirt, Fairy Tinkerbell in the city. I'm sorry now I didn't stay at the hotel. Going on to the terrace, I pass a girl with a red Mohican, naked to the waist, tattooed, with a leather skirt and big boots, snorting a line from the wall. It's like a scene from *Mad Max*.

I find the Hyena sitting cross-legged on a battered wicker armchair. She's changed into shorts and is speaking in Spanish to a dark androgynous girl with a shaved head. She doesn't sound the same when she speaks another language. She's being remarkably amiable.

'Have they shown you where you're sleeping?'

Just then another blonde flings herself at the Hyena with a great shout. She's wearing a shabby evening dress, held together down the back by a row of safety pins. I don't know what to do with myself. I wonder whether all these women are lesbians. What a weird idea, to assemble together by sexual orientation.

Leaning against a wall, a girl in combats and and a man's white tank top is is also standing back, and looks at me with a smile. 'You don't speak Spanish?'

'No.'

'And you don't know anyone here?'

'No.'

'Come along, I'll show you your room.'

This flat is arranged either side of a long corridor. She opens the door of a tiny boxroom without a window. There's just enough space for a bed and a wardrobe. I fall asleep immediately.

When I wake up, I've no idea of the time, but I'm so hungry it must be late. Coming out of the bedroom, I see that night has fallen. The flat has now been invaded by fauna of both sexes. Party noise, exactly what I hate most. People have been drinking, and they're talking loudly. I don't mind at all that I can't understand a word they're shouting. In the living room, a group is dancing in semi-darkness. I recognize the Hyena among them. I wouldn't have thought she liked dancing. She's moving her body slowly, eyes shut. She's graceful. Doesn't seem like herself. She looks very young at that moment. I don't dare interrupt her. I try my luck in the kitchen where the girl in combats and tank top is toasting bread and sprinkling it liberally with olive oil, lemon and coarse salt.

'Want some?'

I take the plate she holds out to me and lean against the sink.

'So what brings you to Barcelona?'

'Work. You speak good French.'

'I lived in Paris for five years. You from there?'

'Yes.'

'The French think they're so great, don't they? Can't see why. Nothing interesting's happened there for twenty years. But I like Parisian women. They're good to look at. Want a Coke or some beer?'

She opens the fridge, acting as if she's at home here. A thick leather bracelet round her wrist accentuates the delicacy of her joints. When she smiles, it reveals a gap between her front teeth. Two parallel lines frame her lips. She has delicate skin. She conveys an impression of fragility combined with great capacity for endurance.

'And you and your friend the Hyena are going to squat here, are you?'

'She's not my girlfriend, we're working together.'

She smiles, tipping her head back to swallow the beer. 'Don't worry, anyone can tell right away that you're not one of us.'

'Oh really? How can you tell?'

I don't say to her that it would never cross my mind to

say to a woman who likes other women that 'anyone can tell'. She might take it badly and I'd understand if she did. In the next room, someone has turned up the sound and the surrounding noise gets louder. She says her name is Zoska, and disappears. I sit down next to the fridge, on my own amid all the noise, smoking the joint she left me and hoping it'll help me to go back to sleep. I get up to go and tell the Hyena I'm going to bed, although I don't get the feeling she's bothered about me.

In the living room, at first I think I must be seeing things. A mass of naked bodies, scattered in groups, is writhing about all over the room. On the floor, on the couch, under the table. The spectacle is so startling that I find it hard to work out what it consists of. One girl on all fours, clad only in her big boots and her little round red-lensed glasses, with an axe tattooed on her back, is being had by another girl who has short hair and a muscular body. This one is pinning the first girl's neck to the ground, while her hand and part of her arm has vanished inside her.

The woman who was wearing the evening gown has pulled it up to the waist and the demonic Fairy Tinkerbell is leaning over her. A string of saliva leads from her lips to the blonde's face. Her hand is moving between her thighs. The evening-dress girl lifts her pelvis and cries out: from her shaved pubis flows a transparent stream that doesn't look like urine, then they roll around together saying things that make them both scream with laughter. Two fully dressed girls are standing near them, talking, and one of them plants a hearty slap on Fairy Tinkerbell's buttock, without interrupting her conversation.

One girl standing up, whom I can only see in profile, is pulling on white latex gloves and putting some gel on them. With the other hand, she's holding the shoulder of a slight brunette, and with her knees is pushing her legs apart. Behind her, a dark girl pulls her head back by the hair. Across the room, I recognize Zoska, with her back to me, leaning over a bare-chested man who has muscular shoulders and taut abdominals, with chicano tattoos on his arms. A swallow on his chest. He has large, almond-shaped eyes and cupid-bow lips. She slowly traces a line on the top of his shoulder. A thick red scratch mark appears. He turns his face towards her, with a faraway ecstatic expression. He reaches up with his mouth, she kisses him voluptuously, then raises herself up and traces another line under the first. Another boy watches, glass in hand. Zoska looks up, turns to him and beckons. The blonde whose flat it is joins them, she's holding hands with a dark-haired girl with pale skin, and gives her a long lingering kiss, then stands back and gives her a loud slap on the face, then another. Suddenly the Hyena is by my side. I'm relieved to find she's still fully dressed, before I realize that she too has a latex glove on her hand.

'Maybe you'd be more comfortable in your room, Lucie.'

'Oh don't worry about me, I'm not ten years old, you know. I've been around.'

She looks at me disbelievingly, then shrugs and plunges back into the middle of the scene. The woman with the orange Mohican says something to her and gets her to kneel down.

I turn round abruptly and leave the room. In my bedroom, I shut the door firmly behind me and try, like people do in films, to block it with a chair. I can't work out exactly whether I'm angry, disgusted or terrorized. I'm still holding the joint in my hand; it's gone out. I light it again and lie on the bed. I'm furious because I feel I've been forced to witness something that has nothing to do with me. But not so disturbed as not to admit that at the same time I'm fascinated. Nothing will persuade me to come out of the room I've barricaded myself into, but there's nothing either to stop me contemplating in the quiet of my room the images I've just registered.

VANESSA

VANESSA WAKES UP IN THE MIDDLE OF THE night. On her pillow is a bundle of feathers, a tiny hooked claw, a beak, and some round white internal organs. It takes a moment to realize that Bel-Ami, the cat, has just vomited there. A pestilential smell makes itself felt. Vanessa opens the window before pulling off the pillowslip and putting it in the washing machine. From a chair, Bel-Ami watches her movements with suspicion. She takes him on her knees, and strokes him under his chin, something she knows he can't resist. Wide awake now, she knows she'll find it hard to get back to sleep. Too many things are chasing round in her head and disturbing her, she lies down again, hoping at least to be able to close her eyes before dawn.

The sun is beating down on the Plaza Real; they're on a restaurant terrace. White cloths on the tables, waiters in black aprons. Two young Romanian girls go from table to table, less than five minutes later a tourist notices that his wallet's gone, he shouts and jumps up, but it's too late. The staff will pretend to sympathize, directing him to the nearest police station, where tourists are queuing up to report thefts. Vanessa, dark glasses, chin in hand, is talking, without looking at her interlocutor, about a well-known young French actress.

'She sleeps with all my exes. The lot. But some of them, you know, I wonder what I ever saw in them. Nothing puts her off. Funny.'

Sitting back in his chair, he widens his eyes, but tries to look cool. He's calculating that once he's slept with her, he'll just have to let the actress know, and she'll throw herself at him like a starving castaway. The prospect of this double hit makes him feel dizzy.

Vanessa looks at him out of the corner of her eye. What string of circumstances has brought her to this point? Into this situation which she would still like to think ambiguous, yet in this little man's eyes she can read that he's perfectly sure of himself, and already plucking up the courage to hold her hand. As a precautionary measure, she puts one hand under the table, while the other is occupied by a cigarette, and out of danger. Whenever did she think it a good idea to have a date with this guy? She must have been bored out of her skull. If a woman's pulling power is measured by the quality of her would-be lovers, she's in trouble. He punctuates his speeches with a strident and unattractive little laugh. He hasn't stopped talking since he got here. About himself. Without giving away anything personal – he must be afraid of letting drop something about his wife and children. He's a French musician, who's had some recent success, but he hasn't often had much chance to play away. Now he's explaining the difference between modern art and contemporary art, kindly assuming from the start that she's an imbecile. He's telling her about his tours, and every five minutes he assures her that he isn't impressed by all this sudden fame, but that's all he talks about. He claims he couldn't care less about meeting celebrities, but he's constantly name-dropping.

She met him at a dinner party with some French friends, he was spending a few days in Barcelona because he wanted to work with flamenco musicians. He shadowed her all evening, and because she wasn't keen to talk to anyone else in particular, she allowed him to. Then he got her email address out of their hostess, claiming he wanted to invite her to the premiere of an Almodóvar film, followed by dinner with Javier Bardem. If it hadn't been for what turned out to be a lie about the dinner, she'd have sent him packing directly. As it was, she'd had the evening from hell, sitting on a hard seat. When she found out that the dinner was nonexistent, she walked out on him as soon as the credits rolled, saying she had a plane to catch next morning.

But he hadn't given up. When had she given in to some morbid urge and allowed herself to be drawn back in? At first she'd found it rather touching to see his naive way of strolling into town, like a cowboy. People who've recently acquired celebrity status go mad with joy, dazzled by their good luck, and they think they've made it now, everything's going to be OK. They're as happy as baby turtles, waddling clumsily over the sand, convinced they'll reach the sea, while up in the sky the cunning raptors are circling. The pathetic pride with which he boasted to her about his thirty-square-metre apartment he's just bought near the Gare de l'Est in Paris. He calls it his bachelor pad.

Why hadn't she just made a break for it? Her failure to do so bothers her. Only women who are ugly or fat or old allow themselves to be lulled into acquiescence by someone else's intensity of desire. Never sleep with anyone beneath you, that's the first rule of respect for your femininity.

He talks a lot about the money he's making, while repeating that it's no big deal. He's against consumer society, lives very modestly himself. He's a dropout with a rich daddy, she worked that one out in three questions. Brought up in big houses in exclusive districts, went to top schools before realizing he didn't have the strength of character to keep up the family tradition of success. So he decided to be an artist and a rebel, and to live off the monthly allowance from his papa, he thinks himself amazing for managing on it, and he likes living in downmarket districts, because he will always be superior to them, and knows he can get out any time he likes. When he's fed up with his children seeing the prostitutes hanging around downstairs in his block of flats, he'll change his tune and pick up the keys to one of the apartments his family owns. But for now, he's pretending his weakness of resolve is a subversive choice.

She can do without artists' company. Sportsmen or politicians, yes, they can impress her. But artists – invariably pseuds. And top of the list without hesitation, she'd put writers. Been there, done that. What they offer with one generous hand is grabbed back a hundredfold with the other, the rapacious, mean, and unscrupulous hand. The hand that writes, betrays, crucifies, pins down. The one that sacrifices you. She was married for three years to a novelist. He's put her in every novel he's written since then. And he'd be mighty indignant if she dared complain of the treatment he inflicts on her.

She is really so bored right now... if only this little man had managed to display one or two qualities, she might have convinced herself that he was worth a try. He has a nice name, Alexandre, quite trendy, she would like to whisper it. And he's taken care over dressing. He's a bit weedy and awkward with his premature paunch and narrow shoulders, but his suit is handmade, otherwise it wouldn't hang so well on him. He has a nice voice, but no idea how to turn a compliment. He's gobbling up his paella, with greasy lips and the grin of a little boy who thinks he's found out something all by himself. 'You're incredibly beautiful!' Oh really. Nobody else had ever noticed such a thing before he came along, of course. He orders coffee. Shifts on his chair, he must already be thinking about the hotel room and how to go about it. His sausage-like fingers grip his liqueur glass, and he goes on boasting, without noticing that the woman he's talking to is ill at ease. She's considered lying, thinking up some excuse, so as to let him down gently. But she opts for brutality: the sun's beating down, the parasol no longer protects them from the heat. She feels dozy. He deserves to be dropped right now, no kid gloves, because he hasn't inspired any dream in her and isn't even aware of it, because he's been excited since yesterday at the thought of sleeping with her, when he doesn't even know how to make her laugh. She feels him panting with impatience. She picks up her jacket and her bag. He looks up with a start, a little apprehensive because he thinks now he's going to leave with her, the screwing point has arrived, here we go.

'Shall we go for a walk?'

Already on her feet, she doesn't look at him.

'Thanks very much for the lunch. But I have to go home now.'

'Right now?'

She's already turned her back on him, he has to wave his short arms to attract the waiter, fumbling in his pockets, cursing away, he can't believe this is happening to him, she was on the end of his line, hooked, he'd practically landed her.

What a pain.

She walks along one of the little alleyways running up from a corner of the plaza. Narrow, high-walled, cool, smelling of dishwater, echoing with building works, past scaffolding and the iron shutters of closed shops. Past a dark bar with a brightly painted façade. She turns into a cobbled street, narrow and shady. She's hurrying to get away, she doesn't want him to catch her up, he's capable of making a scene. She'd like to stay downtown for a while, but she wouldn't feel easy. She reaches La Laietana, and stops the first available taxi. She has to repeat her address three times before the driver understands.

She lives high up, in the northern part of the city. Old elegant houses, more or less well-kept. A few white modern buildings give the streets a phoney Californian atmosphere. You don't meet anyone except domestic staff, Cuban or South American, wearing black dresses and white aprons, emptying the dustbins, doing the shopping, taking or fetching children. There are a lot of private schools round here, bilingual in English or French. Just before five o'clock, the traffic's blocked by the school run, huge shiny vehicles, parents picking up their kids.

Vanessa asks the driver to drop her off a few streets before hers, and he agrees with relief. At this time of day, to take her to the end of the cul-de-sac where she lives could take a good thirty minutes. Walking up the steep slope, she keeps her head back, watching out for birds in the trees. Green parakeets have invaded the territory, they seem to get on with the local pigeons. She likes to see them just as much as before, but having only birds to look at, she's spotted other smaller ones: there are little black birds with bright blue fronts, and brown ones with orange necks. Bel-Ami probably spends all day lurking, hoping to catch one of them.

She greets the parking valet of the restaurant in Contessa Street. She doesn't say hello to many people, she only rarely sees any of the neighbours, and the ones she meets don't seem very friendly. If she were still in France, she'd think they'd got her down as ethnic. But here, and that was one of the reasons she was so keen to come, she looks just like the natives. She just dresses better, that's all. Here she's a Parisienne. Nobody looks knowing when she says her name is Vanessa.

There was a long list of reasons why she'd been glad to come and live in Barcelona with Camille. After two years, she's changed her mind, but Camille says they must wait another year for the crisis to blow over and then they'll leave Europe. He wants them to relocate to Shanghai, he's trying to land a long-term contract there. He says it's like going to New York in the 1960s, that's where it's all happening now, she'll love the French quarter, the food, the city. When he first mentioned it she was keen, and ready for any amount of travel. Now she's not so sure. She'd like them to go back to Paris. In those early months in Barcelona, she'd been enchanted, she'd combed the design shops to furnish their vast house, found a cleaner who could teach her Spanish – she never stops talking and asking questions, Vanessa has had to make rapid progress to keep on good terms with her. She had taken the metro every day, got off at random, with her camera, insatiable for the special light of the city. Barcelona is a town full of little corners, hidden squares, tucked-away streets. She spent hours every evening on her computer, sorting her photographs, framing or altering them. For those first months, it had been enough.

Camille's always away, he does his best to be home at weekends but it isn't always possible and he's rarely as much as ten days running in his office, down by the sea. The scheme he's working on hasn't been cancelled, but half of the architectural practice has been let go, and those who are still there have to adjust. That means abandoning large-scale projects and spending more time on eco-friendly log cabins heated with solar panels. So she's often alone, and her circumstances mean she spends a lot of time thinking how her life was in France.

She's not really cut out for Catalonia. It's impossible to find a good manicurist here. When she arrived, she liked the hairdressers, who knew all about straightening. But in the end she'd like to find a hairdresser who can actually give her a decent cut. The fitness classes are all organized for the third age. What they call Pilates consists of a sort of gymnastics using a stretch band, the kind of thing they did in France in the eighties. At the sports club she's joined, which people told her was one of the smartest in Spain, the women are all practically a hundred years old. They must have been eating the wrong things for years and never used any beauty creams. They don't mind going in for plastic surgery. But at their stage of decomposition, the burqa is the only solution. She thought she was coming to the most Californian city in Europe, and instead she finds herself surrounded by badly made-over peasants, strangers to elegance, who shout into their mobile phones, and have no idea about makeup. Even the young Russian women at her club are not drop-dead beauties. But the worst thing about the whole region is the men. OK, she can make allowances for their being short. She's known men who were seductive even if they weren't tall, all the more seductive in fact because they tried to make up for it. And OK, they have this weird taste for glasses with fancy frames. She could have lived with that. Plus, after twenty years, they start losing their hair. All right. But it begins to pile up. And when you consider that they're not seductive, or good talkers, or skilled at flirting, that by forty they've got pot bellies... well, in the end it adds up to a lot. Luckily there are the South Americans, Basques and Andalusians, without whom she'd have died of boredom.

When she arrived here, the sensation of being a Parisienne who can look down in amusement on the locals had enchanted her. Never before in her life had she had the happiness of being racist. Of being born somewhere else, in a country less touched by misfortune, where you get a better education. The joys of condescension. As racist as a real Frenchwoman. Legitimately. The most fortunate of the Catalans, from the oldest family, would always be a hick in the eyes of a girl born in the shadow of the Eiffel Tower. How good it had made her feel, observing wealthy people here and picking up, point by point, everything that betrayed their lack of sophistication, culture, luxury or taste. But in the end, she'd rather be in

France. It was always the same old story, you had to choose between loving or being loved. Better to be afraid of making a mistake in your French or a lapse of taste in Paris, than to feel at ease here.

Camille says she exaggerates, she's prejudiced. Of course he finds Catalonia fantastic; he's never here. He laughs like anything at home, when she tells him her conclusions of the week. 'When I think about it, all this stuff about Catalan autonomy, it's a bit like if me and my friends from our council estate in Sarcelles had decided that France has been oppressing us since our grandparents arrived there, so we absolutely need subsidies to teach us how to talk our native dialect. It would be great, we could write a whole grammar book, the four of us, and we'd decide we were going to talk Sarcellish, a mixture of North African and bad French, we could put in thirty or so backslang words, and then we'd ask for all the road signs to be translated into Sarcellish. Then we could live off the grants for "linguistic normalization". But of course we'd send our kids to private school, to make sure they learnt a real language.' Camille advises her to keep her opinions to herself, he says anti-Catalanism is something only the extreme right goes in for, and outside their living room it wouldn't amuse anyone. He tries to make her understand that it's because of forty years of Francoist oppression. But come on, Franco executed communists, and that didn't give the people round here a burning desire to join the reds. Franco had this vision of a Spain living off tourism and real estate, and since his death nobody has shown any sign of changing that. The Americans were allies of the dictatorship, weren't they? And Vanessa doesn't get the impression anyone minds learning *their* language. She's had enough of this backwater, she'd like to move.

She'd have preferred to live in San Sebastian. Camille says that with her gift for getting up people's noses, their house would have been bombed already. But respect, eh, the Basques are different. When she says that, Camille raises his eyebrows. He pretends to be shocked, but really he admires her toughness: 'You're not French for nothing, are you, you want to see bloodshed before you think any cause is worth it.' She likes the way he treats her as a Frenchwoman, and he's intelligent enough to know that. But if you're looking for a one hundred per cent Frenchman, well, that's him: a family tree that goes back to the Merovingians or something. His family is so important that they can trace ancestors from times you didn't know existed – his family owns actual chateaux, and here he is married to her, without listening to his mother or his colleagues at work. He married her, he doesn't want children, he loves her, he treats her like a princess. He's as brilliant as she's beautiful. With the same straightforward self-confidence. They don't tell each other stories, they know that there was some luck on both sides at first, for him being born where he was, in a place where getting a good education was automatic, and for her being born with the right face and body. And they both know, too, how much effort it's cost each of them to make the most of what they'd been given. There were other pretty girls where she grew up. But she's the only one who's managed to have a decent standard of living, ever since she was of an age to work things out for herself. The only one who gets to celebrate family occasions in a chateau. And probably the only one heading for forty with a body more perfect than when she was twenty, and a face that no syringe or scalpel has yet come near, unmarked, faultless, unlined. Camille, for his part, has left no stone unturned to get on, to improve, not one sleepless night did he spare himself, no language was he too lazy to learn, no risk did he refuse to take because he was scared. He's thrown himself into his work, and never sat back on his laurels. Vanessa meanwhile has never missed a chance to learn something, to learn what kind of clothes to wear in the circles she wants to move in, how to hold yourself as if you've done classical ballet all your childhood, how to sit down when you really are a princess, what make of handbag to carry if you want people to think you're rich. Learning to look like something different from what she is. Swallowing all kinds of humiliation and never complaining.

Her mother always told her that love doesn't exist, it's just an invention to get girls into bed. In her other affairs, she has always been well aware who was doing the loving and who was being loved. She usually managed to be in the second category. Less exciting, but more profitable. With Camille it's more complicated. Who's loving and who's loved? They've been married three years. She has hardly ever cheated on him. Not that that means anything, but still. And every time he comes back, he seems just as much in love as ever. The lover and the loved in their relationship seem to be more evenly balanced than usual. But for some time now, she's been feeling so sad, things don't have the same taste any more. Before, she was sure she was giving him the best present in the world just by being his wife. Now that her self-examination has revealed some cracks, she doesn't have such confidence. A doubt has crept in: what if his mother was right? What if she is just a pretty little girl from a North African family, a well-packaged bundle of losing cards? But always an imitation, never the real thing. Lacking authenticity, the real luxury of never having been poor, the luxury of being what you seem, someone who never cares, ever, what things cost, someone that life would never dare lay a finger on, for fear of making a scratch on the beautiful bodywork of happiness. To be rich is to have confidence. Even if it's misplaced. To feel protected. One's body. Never in danger. Protected by the house, by the name, by history, by the police even. The accessories can be bought and worn, you can make believe with them. But memories can't be changed. What Vanessa knows about herself she can't tear out of her mind.

Camille, after experiencing the problems in his practice, has become more fragile. He won't tell her exactly how much money he's lost since the crisis started, he avoids the subject. In the papers they say it's over, that the worst is behind them, but Camille isn't the same these days. Both of them have lost a little of their gloss. There are plenty of things they haven't dared say to each other in recent months.

A year ago, building works had started in the house next door. An indescribable din, all day long, never an hour's peace and quiet. They're knocking everything down with sledgehammers. It's as if it's never-ending. Life was telling her something, very loudly. Before that, everything about the new house had made her feel physically happy. The size of the rooms, the furniture she'd chosen, the parquet floors, the big terrace. That was until the works began next door. Demolition, going on endlessly. Camille had given her a sound-proofing helmet. It made things better but she could only stand it for five minutes, after that she felt she was living inside a goldfish bowl. It was because of her reaction to the building works that she had realized she wasn't feeling the same as usual. She was reflecting too much about her past. Vanessa has always had some aim in mind, her attention has been entirely concentrated on what's going to happen next. But for some time now, by contrast, the wounds she thought were buried deep under her skin have started to make noises under the smooth surface, and terrible rages have started to trouble her. A jumble of past events is tormenting her, and she'd like to get rid of it, but she's caught fast by it.

When she catches sight of them, down below her house, at first she thinks they must be girls from the design studio, come out to have a smoke in the sun. They often do that. Then she remembers that it's been closed down. The site hasn't found a new taker, the To Let sign has been set crookedly on the terrace for months now. As she comes up level with them, she looks them over – at the dinner parties she goes to, people tell atrocious stories about women being tortured for hours in their own homes by vicious Albanians who've broken into their houses, so she's wary. One of them's a bit taller than the other, she's wearing baggy jeans low-slung on her hips, which are remarkably slender. She has big boots, rather shabby and well worn, and her mirror-glasses date from two summers ago, but they suit her. The other one is stockier, ordinary-looking. Vanessa is used to people staring at her with that astonished insistence, people notice her and can't take their eyes off her. She really is a striking beauty.

But when the taller one gets up and comes towards her, Vanessa understands who she is.

Lying on his back on the couch, Bel-Ami is watching what's going on round him, head thrown back. The detective unhesitatingly makes towards the cat, who doesn't run off, although he's normally very snappy. When she touches him, her gestures are incredibly gentle, she crouches down beside him, scratching him under the chin and making him purr.

'What a beautiful cat. What's his name?'

'Bel-Ami. I found him in the gutter in the middle of August. He was a little alleycat, you'd never think he was going to turn into this, well, sublime creature.'

The detective stands upright and accepts the offer of coffee. Quite an impressive specimen, but she's let herself go. No makeup, no decent haircut, she's wearing practical clothes that don't display her at her best. The smaller one, Lucie, isn't good-looking at all. And she hasn't tried hard either. She gets good marks for that. In Vanessa's book, compiled over time, plain women who don't try to disguise it are less pathetic than ugly ones who put on the slap and dress as if they were raving beauties. Women's magazines and the cosmetics industry get blamed for a lot of things, but they're not often accused of the real damage they do: they make a nation of puddings imagine that with a bit of effort anyone can look like what they are not. Nothing is more pitiful than a plain woman in an eye-catching dress, or a fat one trying to show off her good points. In this respect, true, men's views do not coincide with Vanessa's. They have their own criteria, nothing to do with good taste. They'd always prefer someone with greasy skin and a figure she's let go, as long as she's well-presented, rather than a perfectly passable girl without makeup. Luckily, fashion is dictated by the kind of men who don't listen to what women think. The tall one is a real beauty, for all she has the stance of an all-in wrestler, she has a feline power: one wants to watch her move.

Vanessa puts the coffee on the table and opens the doors on to the terrace, then excuses herself to consult her voicemail: nobody has left her a message, but she needs some time to think. She didn't want to turn her mind earlier to what she would do when this happened. In fact, she has scrupulously avoided thinking about it. She was expecting a man, just one of him. When the word 'masculine' passed through her mind, she looked at the taller detective, put two and two together, and came up with: lesbian. Short nails, the air of a plumber's mate, very pleased with herself. Lesbian. She remembers a phrase from Arno, the Belgian singer, that she heard on the radio: 'Lesbian, yeah, may not look too hot, but don't we have fun!' She herself had never considered that lesbians didn't look good, she's known too many of them. Perverted perhaps, but that's not the same thing. Vanessa stands up the way she would if she were facing a man, making her body move gracefully through space in order to disturb the person in front of her, and mark her domination. She wants to impress the tall one. Women who are disturbed hide it better than men. And it's more exciting.

The detective remarks, 'You don't seem surprised to see us.'

'Claire Galtan warned me.'

'You know each other?'

'Not really.'

They've met only once, at Claire's insistence. François has never forgotten Vanessa, and his new wife must have imagined that meeting her absent rival would make her lose her power. It had been a long time ago. Poor woman. Big bust and skinny legs, she looked a bit like a chick in a cartoon: a huge pair of boobs perched on top of tall boots. Very fine skin, but her oval face was already a bit puffy. She had a rather fetching short-sighted expression, which made her look cowlike and affectionate. Vanessa felt slightly sorry for François. Ending up marrying something like that. Hardly surprising if he was still having difficulty moving on. He had once thought himself so handsome... I bet he doesn't take her out often, his lawful wedded.

It was Claire who, on that occasion, had warned her that Valentine wanted to find out where her 'real' mother was. She had explained that since she had two daughters herself, and they were what she cared about most in the world, she understood why the teenager wanted to see her 'real' mother again, inviting Vanessa to rethink her decision.

'*My* decision?'

'François explained to me what happened, but I thought, perhaps with time...'

It had been during the winter sales, they'd met at Angelina's. For a hot chocolate. Vanessa made a sign to her to stop right there. 'Does François know you've come to meet me?'

'No, I thought I'd only tell him if you...'

'Do you realize how furious he'll be? If he finds out I've told you the way things really happened, you know that you'll never think of him again the same way?'

She had no intention of telling, on the contrary, the other

woman could be left to worry about that. Work out who you've married, what kind of a pathetic bastard your husband is.

Claire had finally admitted that she'd found Vanessa's whereabouts after coming across the report of her latest marriage, carefully clipped from a newspaper and filed away by François. She had said, 'If I could find out, Valentine could do the same any time. It wasn't difficult, I telephoned your husband's office and left him a message... which obviously he passed on to you.'

She had felt no joy at the thought that François was still interested in her. Disgust simply. And Claire paid for it. Because she was there, because she wouldn't tell, because she was the kind of woman one felt like giving a good shaking to.

Since then, Vanessa hadn't heard a word from her. Until a fortnight ago, when Claire had called in tears, to warn her that Valentine had disappeared. 'What business is it of yours? You've got a nerve, crying about my daughter as if she was your own.' And she'd hung up. Which hadn't stopped Claire, masochistic Claire, from calling a second time, to say they'd hired a detective, 'from the best agency in Paris' – people with money always need to console themselves with the idea that they've shelled out more than common mortals – and that Vanessa would surely be getting a visit from them, although no one in the Galtan household had taken the liberty of giving them her address.

'Look, sweetie, I've already had the cops round, I told them all I know, I'll do the same with your fucking detective. So just tell your dickhead of a husband and his bitch of a mother that if they'd looked after my daughter properly, she'd still be tucked up in her bed, and not out on the fucking streets like some little waif and stray.' Straight out of the high-rise slums of Seine-Saint-Denis. A way of talking she'd spent a long time suppressing, but it could rise to the surface when she needed it. People who live in the smart districts of Paris aren't used to being spoken to like that. And they don't like it. That's why they spend so much money taking holidays in Russia, Romania or Thailand, unlike what people think, it's not just to have sex with under-age teenagers on the quiet. The French need to see poor people who don't insult them. They know that if they got into an armoured bus to gawp at the living conditions of the poor in their own outer suburbs, the bus would be torched. It distresses them, all that poverty: they can feel sorry, give away a few coins and old clothes. The trouble with homegrown poor people is that they can be nasty. It makes Christian charity complicated.

The little investigator is concentrating on her coffee cup. The big one – the best in Paris then, Vanessa supposes with amusement – looks round before saying suddenly, 'Valentine came to see you, didn't she?'

'The police have already been round.'

'Can you tell me what you told them?'

'Yes. But I can also tell you the truth. Valentine did come to Barcelona. But I don't think she's here any longer. Would you like some more coffee?'

'Yes, please.'

'Black, no sugar?'

'Yes, could you give me a double shot?... I thought I'd have a few while we were waiting for you, but there aren't any bars round here.'

'Shall we go on to the terrace, the workmen don't seem to

be making much noise today.'

'No, they've had a balcony collapse on the front of the house. We spent a long time watching them. We were there two hours. A big balcony, I think it'll take them all day, moving the rubble: it came down on top of all the building materials, their planks and machines.'

Alone in the kitchen, Vanessa takes her time. She hadn't planned to say anything. She keeps telling herself she's got nothing to feel guilty about, nothing to hide. She doesn't know where the kid's gone, she hardly knows her. It hadn't been her choice not to know her own child, she doesn't have to justify herself. The big detective has heard the story from François's family's point of view, obviously. And the other one, the one who says nothing, the one who looks like a petrified deer. They've already made their minds up, like everyone else. Nobody needs to hear Vanessa's version to condemn her.

When she comes back with the coffee, the detective is on the terrace, leaning on the stone balustrade, looking at the huge mobile-phone mast on top of the hill facing them.

'That must be a powerful transmitter. You're not afraid of the radio waves?'

'No. When we first got here, I thought it spoiled the view, but in the end I quite like it. It's practical, wherever I am in the city I know where my house is. And then you have the sea opposite.'

'Well, I suppose there's that about it...'

'I'm sorry, I didn't catch your name.'

Play for time. Again. Talk about something else, anything

that lets her avoid deciding what she's going to say, what she's not going to say, what this woman may pick up about things that are better hidden.

'People call me the Hyena.'

'The Hyena! Because you're a creature who's cruel, fast and ruthless?'

The taller woman hesitates for a moment, then smiles for the first time since she got there. That's another male strategy: because she's playing cold and inaccessible, the slightest sign of relaxing, a smile for instance, takes on special value and makes you want to provoke others.

'No. I was lucky. This idiot called me that when I was just starting out. He could have christened me Garfield... it would've been less serious, but it would have stuck just the same.'

She looks round her. In the gardens down below, there are trees with pink blossom, and clumps of white flowers, and a huge shiny aluminium pipe stuck on to the façade of an old stone-built house which had been beautiful before that addition. Roses in pots lined up under the balustrade to protect them from the powerful winds that sweep across the region all winter. One plant that looks dead straggles along the cracked walls; a few huge buds have appeared in the last few days along its bare branches.

'You must be glad to have got away from Paris.'

'The vegetation's nicer here, yes. But I'm not a great one for botany.'

Vanessa has made a litre of coffee in a green Thermos, and fills the cups to the brim. The little one, Lucie, has huddled into a corner again. You tend to forget she's there.

'So Valentine came to Barcelona to see you?'

'Yes, she came to see me.'

'And you don't know where she is now?'

'No idea. She disappeared.'

'And you hadn't ever seen her again, before this time?'

'No. I presume the Galtans told you their version of what happened.'

'No. They don't say anything about you. Just that you left when the baby was a year old. If you want to talk about it, that's more or less what we're here for.'

She does want to talk about it, yes. When she opens her mouth she's even surprised to find out how much she wants to talk about it.

'I met François when I was eighteen. He was thirteen years older than me, he was already a well-known writer, he was in love with me, and I liked that... But his mother didn't. His friends were more welcoming. They all used to talk to me about couscous, the East and belly dancing. It was the early nineties, for girls like me the hangover was beginning. We'd grown up thinking things would be fine, that France was a mature place, that we just had to go to the city for people not to hassle us about our origins. I'd already changed my first name, after the model Vanessa Demouy, and I'd say I was Lebanese. But they could spot it. If you knew the number of references to tagines and gazelle horns I had to put up with at dinner parties. The left-wing ones were the worst, they were afraid we'd forget our roots. But like any girl my age, that's exactly what I did want to do, forget where my parents were from. I got pregnant early on, I was glad, I could already see myself as the little wife, staying at home while he wrote his stuff. I liked François fine. But even his more open-minded friends, who understood he was sleeping with me, told him to watch out. That I might go back to the desert with the baby. What the hell did they think I'd do there? Is there a Carita salon over there? Anyway... I didn't like being pregnant, I didn't like being so fat, I wanted it to be over as soon as possible. It was François's mother who wanted to call the baby Valentine. She tried to move heaven and earth hoping to persuade her son to 'get rid of it', but she turned up the first day in the maternity ward. François was relieved, he'd been worried his mother would quarrel with him for good. But she fell in love with the little girl. I wasn't too bad at looking after the baby, as good as anyone else, I guess. But the old bat was always round at our place. I wasn't doing this right, I didn't know that, and so on. François just chickened out of the arguments, he took care not to be home, leaving me with Jacqueline, she had her own keys. I spent whole days at the park or the swimming pool or with my sisters. Anything, to stop her catching up with us.'

Vanessa pauses. She's spinning a bit of a yarn, of course. She has a right to, the Galtans have been spreading their own lies for long enough. She forgets to make it clear that she got pregnant immediately, and on purpose. François hadn't wanted to marry her. Because of his mother. So she presented him with a child. She was very young, she didn't know the ways of the world, she thought Galtan was a good catch. She's making it up about the park and the swimming pool. In fact she had the blues after Valentine was born. The child got in the way of her life. She'd left her with the grandmother. More and more often. She hadn't suspected anything. Jacqueline was only too happy to take the child. She's just massaging the facts slightly, it's always pleasant to be a little economical with the truth if you can make yourself look a bit better.

'And then I met someone. Just when I was least expecting it, that's life, I guess. This guy was good for nothing, he was a rich kid, but way off the rails, same age as me, face like an angel, and all he ever did was tinker with his Harley-Davidson and listen to Led Zeppelin. Face of an angel, character of a bastard. Classic.'

It had been the first time she'd really fallen for a man. She'd always had the advantage before. She had always slept for profit before, her mother had warned her that sex was only for pigs, and women got nothing out of it at all. On that point she had been wrong. Guillaume was a strictly cash payer. They were like in *Goodfellas*, when he went off somewhere he asked her how much she wanted and she showed him with her thumb and finger how thick the pile of notes should be. When he touched her it was like an electric shock. She'd walked out on François just like that. Without the least hesitation. She hadn't hurt him, she'd killed him. The morning she came back to pick up her things, she'd been missing for five days. She'd come home at dawn, high on coke. He was up, white-faced. If she'd snapped her fingers, he'd have opened his arms wide and taken her back at once. She was the love of his life, as she realized at that moment. She felt as if she was stabbing a sword into his heart. But it was inescapable. Love or be loved. And at that moment, she was in love. She thought it was the greatest thing in the world. And when François, still in shock, had asked her when she would come back to see Valentine, she'd said she'd telephone. She could see from his eyes that he couldn't believe she wouldn't even give him some explanation. She'd packed her bag, she wanted to get out of the house before he collapsed. A bitch, yes, she's been a real bitch. But she paid for it later all right. Paid for what she'd done.

'I'd have liked to take Valentine with me, but the way we lived, I couldn't. I wasn't thinking baby clothes. I wasn't yet twenty. I thought I had the right to my grand passion. But then when I tried to see Valentine again, I couldn't, they'd changed the locks and the concierge where the grandmother lived had been told not to let me in. People told me I should lodge a complaint. But I was living in one room, knee-deep in coke and stolen goods. How could I go to the cops?'

Guillaume had been in love with her, but he was incapable of fidelity. He always had to play the field. It made her ill. He liked making her cry, because those were the times he could see she was crazy about him. And then he'd comfort her, divinely. It quickly got to be a pattern. First I humiliate you, then I go off and cheat on you, than I come back and we make up. Coke and his prick, two addictions that went together. She'd never have left him, the dramas were part of their story. It was only by the amount it hurt that she knew how much she loved him. Pain and then relief. People who don't understand why some girls stay with a guy who hits them around don't know anything about women. It gets you behind your knees, deep in your guts, and you give in. You'd die for it. But then one day he hadn't come back. A bank hold-up. It was only at the trial that she found out that he too was married, with a kid, he hadn't said anything. His wife wasn't the kind to give way gracefully. Only one of them could have visiting rights.

'I really did want to see my daughter again. I left Guillaume's place, I squatted with a girlfriend. François was expecting me to come crawling to him, begging to be taken back. But after what I'd experienced with Guillaume, I couldn't bear him to touch me. He took it very badly and since all he had left of me was the child... he just let his mother take charge. She'd been longing to anyway. Like a fool, I went round all the friends we'd had as a couple. Well, people I thought were my friends, I thought they'd help, talk to him, tell him I was perfectly capable, he could safely leave her with me. But they all testified against me. The whole lot of them. Not one of them refused to sign papers saying I was a nutcase, a threat, a nuisance, a drug addict and a thief. Anything the grandmother invented, they put their names to.'

She hadn't thought that leaving her daughter for three months would have had such lasting consequences. Valentine was just a baby, she didn't recognize anyone yet, and anyway she'd never breastfed her. Vanessa hadn't thought she was doing something really serious. But when she came back to see the people she knew when she was with François, they all avoided her, they were embarrassed. Galtan had some power in those days. He wrote a column in a newspaper. Enough for all of them to side with him, given the choice. The stronger party. And they did. Unanimously. They said horrible things about her, in black and white. They wrote, they signed, they photocopied their ID cards. They hadn't forgotten their own roots, oh no, or which way the wind was blowing. Even the ones she'd trusted. The lawyer she'd been allocated knew her case was lost in advance. Signed and sealed. And she had lost.

She could only see one good thing emerging from it: a girl her age was a lot more attractive to men without a kid round her neck.

'I was entitled to one visit every fortnight, at the grand-mother's house. It was like I was on probation. The old girl suggested right off that she could buy me a flat, in my name, somewhere a long way from Paris, making sure her name didn't show anywhere on the contract – and in exchange I'd give up any right to visit or to go to court. I didn't say yes at first. She put pressure on me every time I came to see Valentine. She'd be out, she'd forgotten to tell me. She'd keep Valentine up without a nap, to make sure she would grizzle all the time I was there. So I changed my mind. I got this flat, a fair size, eighty square metres, in the centre of Mont-pellier. That seemed far enough away for them to feel safe, I wouldn't bother them. I signed all these papers, that didn't have any legal force. Except that if ever one day I wanted to reopen the affair, there it would be, down in black and white, that in exchange for a flat, I'd agreed to disappear from my daughter's life. I know I could have gone back to the tribunal. I could have said I'd changed, that I'd been manipulated. But I never did it. They'd convinced me that it was the best thing for Valentine, and I ended up believing them.'

The old granny had loved the baby, you couldn't deny that. She couldn't stand it when Vanessa came to visit her. She'd had to fight to get a decent apartment, the old witch had wanted to fob her off with a bedsit in Marseille, getting on her high horse at the idea that Vanessa stood up for herself. So she'd decided to make the Galtans disappear from her life, she'd have a place of her own. She'd move town and change her life. She could always have more children if she wanted to one day. She was still young, she saw her sisters having a kid every year, it wasn't anything special having kids. If babies were paid for by the kilo, the women in her family would be dining at the Ritz.

The detective listens, drinking her coffee, expressionless. Vanessa feels like hitting her, to make her show some reaction.

'Well, I have to say, I'm over it all now. At first I thought I'd never be able to see a woman with her baby and not feel the pain. But no. The school run, taking them to the pool, birthday parties, coughs, colds, measles, homework, doing the laundry – women who need a child can't be getting what they want from a man.'

The detective's face still doesn't give anything away. Usually people take that kind of remark badly. You can call women bitches and whores and nobody will say a thing. But if you attack mothers, they get up on this soapbox and shake with anger. That's one good thing about lesbians, they don't play the shocked matron. The little detective, though, is looking at her with a sad expression. Vanessa knows she's talking too much. Like every time lately when she's had someone to talk to. A sort of verbal incontinence.

'I spent less than six months away from Paris. I'd never lived in the provinces, but I realized right away I wasn't cut out for that. I sold the flat in the south. I invested the money. Until 13 September 2001. When the Twin Towers came down, within forty-eight hours I was at the bank selling all my shares. The banker was in despair. But I couldn't afford to find myself with nothing.'

She'd had the feeling, back then, that she had a small

fortune. But today, that's just a modest nest egg. Things panned out OK, though, for a new flat, another marriage. That's what guys are for, aren't they? No need to make a mystery out of that. A duplex in Joinville. She spent all the money she got from selling that one. She has had a lot of expenses, and never felt like taking a job. Her second husband wasn't the worst, but he paid for the others. He had a ready fist. When they quarrelled, it soon got nasty, he would end up clocking her one, aiming for her eye. She knew all the buttons to press to get him going. She'd cottoned on pretty quickly. It was the early days of the internet, and she kept all his emails. The ones where he apologized for hitting her. So when the divorce went through, bingo, she hit the jackpot. You could say she'd learned her lesson well.

After the second marriage, there had been Claude. She was back on coke, she had a serious habit. To get hold of the stuff without paying, she had continued to have a social life. New friends, in advertising, finance. That was how she'd met Claude, or rather he'd met her. He was over seventy and retired when she first got to know him. They came face to face at a charity event, and he fell for her. When she realized that he was coming on to her, she was irritated at first that a man of his age could imagine that a girl of her age... but Claude knew how to handle it. When she moved in with him, people called her a gold-digger. It was true that he'd won her over with presents. What's so bad about that? When an affair's over, what else do you have left? It was the first time she'd met someone like him. The Galtans were nouveaux riches, their money was the wealth of the cunning peasant who'd gambled at the right moment and then invested his earnings.

The grandmother might give herself all the airs she liked, she still had mud on her clogs. But Claude was another story. He didn't impress her by the money he spent going after her. It was his classiness that dazzled her. The first time she set foot in his house, she knew she'd stay there. Everything was so beautiful. He put her on a pedestal and never took her down. He could make anything he saw interesting. Even the ugly. He put her together again. And just for her to be there made him happy. Not proud. Happy.

He was patient with her. He knew her through and through. She didn't hide things from him. Sometimes when she turned to look at him, she was amazed to see how old he was, it gave her a shock, a moment of repulsion. But she didn't want to be anywhere else. Everyone looked at her askance, such a young girl with an old man, they knew what the attraction was all right. It was weird, certainly, to touch someone as old as that, his skin. Death was already at work on it. But she had to do it from time to time, and it could go on for hours, because he could hardly get it up, the sex was mostly in his head. She'd got used to it. Someone that age is still 'a man' but really it's something else. A third sex, neither man nor woman. He liked her to undress in front of him. Of course she had been looking for a substitute father, she didn't see that as a problem, because she needed one, and he carried out the role perfectly. Claude had taught her things. He was very disdainful about other people. Their opinions mattered very little to him. She had told him about Valentine. She's often thought about Claude since the kid turned up again. She wished he could be there, so that she could ask his advice. With him she'd understood there could be love outside passion, a stronger link than the kind made by compulsion. A peaceful understanding. Claude knew what she felt for Valentine, or rather what she didn't feel. He told her not to worry. That women had been having children they didn't care for afterwards since the world began. That to get sentimental over it was the kind of thing scullery-maids did. He said she was lucky, because there's nothing like having children to drive you crazy. One morning she'd woken up to find him lying still in bed beside her. Claude normally slept very little. He was never there in the morning. She would usually find him in his study. She'd jumped out of bed, horrified. She knew. His own children turned up the same day. When they realized that he had never secretly married her, or even left her anything in his will, they breathed sighs of relief. They sent her packing before the day was out. Two daughters and a son, three great stupid caterpillars. You should have seen them that day, going round the house, putting her things in cardboard boxes. They had arguments over every item. They had her out of the house in three hours. Watching them, she thought about what Claude had said about children. Three shameless grabbers, bustling about in his study, his cupboards. She knew he'd been right. That's family for you. And that's what people make this big fuss about.

She had never understood how he could have left her in that situation. He must have thought about it after all. Perhaps he thought she was cleverer than she was. She should have made sure of all the presents he'd given her, and any other objects she liked, before calling the doctor. She'd found herself on the pavement, without a credit card and with nowhere to go. Three cardboard boxes, one suitcase and one very good coat she'd managed to snatch away from the heirs. If you're happy somewhere, you're only a temporary resident. You can be chucked out any time.

They're getting to the point now. Vanessa picks up the tray, offers to make some more coffee to play for a little more time. The detective is smoking cigarette after cigarette. She asks, 'So how did things go with Valentine when she turned up?'

'I can't say I even recognized her, there are so many teenagers like that round here, I wasn't paying attention. Only it was a bit weird because it was raining, and she was just standing there in her little anorak, under a doorway. That was why I noticed her, she looked like a drowned cat. She didn't dare speak to me, the first time she saw me. She left a note in the letter box, just a sheet of paper folded in four. Good thing it's always me that picks up the mail.'

'What did she write?'

'I am Valentine. Your daughter. I didn't dare come up to you. I'll be in the same place same time tomorrow. Come and fetch me if you want to talk.'

'You kept the paper?'

'No, I tore it up. I was thinking about Camille. I've never told him I had a daughter. And if you don't want to get caught out after telling a lie, the best thing is not to leave any evidence. So I tore it up and threw it away. I waited till the evening and I went to take out the rubbish myself, to the big bin downstairs. It's usually the help who does that.'

'And you went to see her the next day?'

'I didn't sleep all night. I didn't know what to do.'

'You didn't want to see her?'

'No. I'd got used to not thinking about her. And then

there's Camille. He doesn't want children. Suits me perfectly. How was I going to tell him one fine morning that this fifteen-year-old came knocking at the door and – oops! – I'd forgotten to tell him about her?'

'You'd never said anything to him? But Paris is a small world. Nobody ever thought to tell Camille about...'

'No, Camille's an architect, he doesn't see many French people, just his colleagues. It could have happened, yeah, but I got away with it.'

'So, next day, you went to talk to her?'

She's not being allowed to fight the way she wants, Vanessa can feel the leash, the collar being pulled in a series of short sharp tugs to get her to go in the right direction.

'I did go downstairs, yes. I took her to the seaside, by car. I thought it would be best to see each other in the car first, that way I wouldn't have to wonder how to play it, I'd just be driving, that would be all. Half an hour to get to the beach, then an hour walking on the beach. And then I'd have dropped her off wherever she wanted to go. I'd prepared things to say, I thought she'd ask me right away "Why did you leave me?" and "What have you been doing all this time?" But no. She talked a lot. About her school, about the music she liked. On the beach I bought her an ice cream. I asked her why she didn't watch her weight a bit better, she said it was "genetic". Her father's thin, I'm thin, I didn't know what to say. She gave me news of the family, because she'd met my brothers and sisters... That took up a bit of time, there are a lot of them. But after that, we didn't really know what to talk about. I would say the weather was nice here in Barcelona, she told me she'd often gone windsurfing in Brittany, I said

it rains a lot in Brittany, but I liked the crêpes and the cider...
And then I said I had to go home. She asked if she could
come and have a shower in the house, and I realized she had
nowhere to go. I had my bank card with me, so I took out
500 euros in cash, because I didn't want Camille to find a
hotel bill on my statement, and I took Valentine to a hotel.
Not far from the port, up towards the town. I paid for two
nights and left her the rest of the cash, I said I'd come back
but I couldn't stay just then.'

'And when you did get back, she'd disappeared.'

'Not straight away. She stayed for a week. I would go and
find her in the late morning. We'd have lunch together. I'd
asked Valentine to say she was my niece if we met anyone, or
even Camille, you never know...'

'How did she take that?'

'She didn't say anything. We acted as if it was normal.
Actually, she didn't talk as much as the first day. She's rather
reserved. And very badly dressed. I suggested we could go
round the shops together, get her some things, but she didn't
want to. I'd pick her up at the hotel, we'd find a restaurant
with a terrace and have lunch. I was getting used to her. I
thought I was going to have to talk to Camille.'

'Did she tell you what she was doing the rest of the time?'

'She said she had found some other girls, Spanish, and
they were fun. She said they went to Barceloneta Beach, the
area by the harbour.'

'Did she seem happy?'

'She didn't complain. I just had lunch with her every
day for a week, it's rather a short time to really know... She
seemed glad to see me, and to be here. She didn't open up to

me that much really. I thought we had plenty of time to get used to each other.'

'And when the police came to ask you questions, you didn't tell them anything.'

'No, she'd asked me not to. I had said to her that she'd have to go back to her father's eventually, and she said yes, she knew that. I promised not to say anything to anyone. I thought that was the least I could do, keep my word. In fact, I was starting to like having her around. I wondered how I was going to bring it up with Camille. I needed a bit of time.'

Valentine's arrival had awakened a torrent of wild and destructive thoughts. About a series of failures, humiliations and hasty decisions. When Vanessa had settled in Barcelona, if anyone had asked, she could have replied sincerely, she'd say she was lucky, well-balanced, blossoming. Life had been outrageously good to her and she felt she had known how to ride the wave. But seeing her daughter every day, tête-à-tête, had modified her own view of herself. Not just by making her realize her age, with cruel sharpness, making her unquestionably one of the ones who will soon be on the way out. It was above all the vision of her own trajectory that she'd been forced to confront. Surviving, making the best of it, ruthless: all the words she's applied to herself were losing their ability to convince. She was just a poor girl who'd drifted from one mediocre marriage to another, collecting her derisory capital, like a little squirrel collecting nuts, putting all her effort into that. It was when she looked at Valentine, and wondered how to describe her own life story to her, that it had all changed. And she dared not touch her. She was incapable of physical affection, she wanted to make the gestures but she couldn't manage it. Vanessa wasn't the woman she'd always imagined herself to be. And Valentine had made her realize that.

'And François Galtan has never tried to contact you?'

'No, he's too afraid of hearing my voice. His mother didn't call either. You've been hired to do that, basically. To avoid them having to have anything to do with me. I thought Valentine would have gone back home to them. That it would teach them a lesson. Well, one day I came to pick her up at the hotel, and she'd gone.'

Vanessa tells herself again that she hasn't done anything wrong. She'd paid another two nights in advance, and left a note saying she'd come back. She'd gone on paying, and returned to the hotel every day. Then she cleared the room. She hadn't been worried at that stage, just rather cross. It was only later that she began to be troubled by the images of that afternoon. Her hands picking up clothes and putting them in a bag. Intimate objects. Some hair conditioner, the bottom half of a bikini, very large size by the way, a paperback of a Japanese novel, *Kafka on the Shore*, with a picture of a cat on the cover. A pack of fortune-telling cards. Vanessa thought her daughter'd never told her she did that sort of thing. Some red socks with holes in. A packet of cigarette papers. A little blue pottery scarab by the bedside table, a soft green scarf she hadn't seen before, that smelled of a sweet scent. A pair of yellow high-sided Converses. It was as if she was stripping the room of its intimacy, effacing Valentine's presence, as she packed her stuff into the little orange rucksack she'd been carrying the day she arrived. It was such a small bag that it had reassured her in the middle of her panic, the kind of bag you take just for a weekend. She'd packed the things carefully inside. She'd stayed for a short while, leaning out of the window, it was a nice view, on to a little square with a church. A decapitated angel was sculpted on the façade, alongside a Virgin and Child.

And then she had closed the door and given back the magnetic card to reception. These images are engraved on her mind, a long take in a film. Vanessa didn't cry after that. It just remained like an imprint.

The Hyena, sitting opposite her, insists, without trying to rush her, 'And you kept her things?'

'I spent the afternoon down at Barceloneta Beach, I went into all the bars, I asked if they had seen a plump little French girl, about sixteen, called Valentine. That night I called Camille, I said I was dining with some girlfriends. And I went on looking. I combed the beach as far as Poblenou. I didn't know what to do with the bag, to hide it somewhere would put me in an awkward situation. In Paris, I'd have thought of someone I could leave it with, but here... I dumped it in a dustbin.'

That was the clearest image of all. She was exhausted, after walking all day. A little after midnight, she'd pressed the lever of a big municipal rubbish bin. The orange bag, once inside, was too deep down to be visible. That's the image, exactly. Engraved on her eyes. Even if basically she thinks Valentine is all right. She tries to stop herself thinking that it's possible someone has done exactly the same thing with her daughter's body. Chucked it in a ditch, into a river, off a cliff. Just another little news item.

The detective asks, 'Do you remember what happened the day before she disappeared?'

'Yes. And the days before that. Not many of them. I don't think we talked about anything in particular.'

'She didn't seem out of the ordinary that day?'

'No, not at all.'

'And you didn't report it to the police.'

'No. Are you going to do that now, for me?'

'It wouldn't help us much. Do you think she's still round here somewhere?'

'I don't know what happened. I don't think all her gear was at the hotel. I get the feeling she must have taken more stuff with her. But I'm not sure. She always dressed the same way. Not very feminine.'

'And you still haven't told your husband?'

'It's too late now. Perhaps if I'd told him at the beginning. But after four years with him, I'd be surprised if he just took it calmly, gave me a kiss and changed the subject. You know he's ...'

She has the words 'a good catch' on the tip of her tongue. That is exactly what she's thinking but she'd prefer to put it differently. Because Camille is a good catch. Her age doesn't bother him, she knows that she's not the sort of beauty that fades quickly. She's got another good ten years ahead of her. But no need to say that. People mock mutton dressed as lamb. Vanessa only mocks women who do it without being able to carry it off. She thinks that she needn't worry about her age if she really wants to start over, but she's happy with Camille, and doesn't want it to stop. And that's why she threw the backpack into a grey rubbish bin by the sea, before getting into a taxi, and coming home to him, and not saying a word.

WE GO BACK DOWN TO THE CAR IN SILENCE.
I check the time on my mobile: we stayed three hours at
Valentine's mother's place. There were times I wanted to
shake her, to hurry her up a bit.

The Hyena stops, in the middle of the pavement, and
looks round, puzzled.

'This is where we left the car.'

'You must be wrong.'

All the streets look alike in this goddam residential area.
Trees everywhere, nice houses, all more or less dilapidated,
and no obvious landmarks.

'Could someone have stolen the car?'

'If I was a thief, I wouldn't choose ours. There are plenty
of top-of-the-range cars around here.' The Hyena spots a little
triangular sticker on the edge of the pavement. She kneels
down to unstick it.

'They've towed it.'

'You're joking! We paid a fortune when we got here. Three
euros an hour, in case you think I've forgotten...'

'Yeah, for two hours, but we were much longer.'

'Must be a mistake.'

'I did warn you when we got here. Daylight robbery's a

fine art here. *Benvingut*, darling.'

'They tow away a car for overstaying by one hour? When we'd already paid for two?'

'Ones with foreign plates, yeah. They know we'll come running to reclaim it. Come on, let's look for a taxi. Don't look at me like that, you're not going to let me go and do it on my own, are you? Anyway, your bag's in the boot, yeah?'

I had thrown together some things when I left the flat that morning, swearing I'd never ever spend another night in that sink of depravity and vice. At five in the morning, they were still making a huge racket and all night I didn't dare cross the corridor to go and have a pee.

The Hyena goes down the street without hesitation. All round us, nothing moves, not a person, not a car. I wonder where we're going to find this famous taxi.

'Do you know the district? Or where you're going?'

'You heard what she said, opposite the big mast it's the sea, so the city's in between. We're going into town. So it's this way.'

For want of any better idea of the direction to take, I follow her.

'She's pretty sinister, the mother, eh?'

'Sinister? Not what struck me most about her. Did you see her hands? And her legs? And the fragrance? Even her elbows are beautiful, did you notice? She had superb elbows. And the way she breathes, you can see the majesty going right into her lungs. It makes you want to be air. I just loved her voice... no, the grain in her voice, as if there was sand in it. You can imagine her singing when she comes. But actually no, I don't even want to think about it, it's too much. I don't know if you noticed how she holds her coffee cup to drink. The way she puts her fingers round the handle, the grace of her wrist. You didn't look? Unforgettable. I've hardly ever seen such a fantastic creature close up.'

'Excuse me. I was thinking about what she *said*, not the way she looked.'

'No problem, Sherlock. You can concentrate on the investigation and I'll just enjoy the décor.'

'Do you think something terrible has happened to Valentine?'

'I'd incline to think she's just split. Our Vanessa, the more you might want her in your bed, the more she's really bad news as a mother.'

'Leaving all her stuff behind?'

'Leaving pointless items. A book you've finished reading, some cards, an old scarf... you said the kid has an iPod, right? Well, no iPod in the hotel room. And I bet she took a few pairs of knickers with her. She didn't just bring a swimsuit.'

'So your instinct tells you she took off of her own accord.'

'My instincts, at the time, were occupied with something else. But common sense advises me she ran out and slammed the door. That cat's better cared for than the kid. I like animals fine, that's not the problem. They'll pollute the planet less than some dumb little teenager... but still, when it's your daughter, when you did a deal over her for some rotten apartment, when she comes back to see you, it would be the least you could do, take her home for a glass of Coke, wouldn't it?'

'Do you think the mother's lying about anything?'

'About anything that interests us, no.'

'So what happens next?'

'We go to the car pound.'

She guides us on to a road where there's some traffic. She raises her hand and stops a taxi. A black and yellow cab. The Hyena spends some time talking to the driver. From the top of a street running downhill, looking out over the whole city, you can see the sea. It brings a rush of calm. I ask myself why certain landscapes give so much pleasure.

The Hyena settles back in her seat. 'He doesn't even need his GPS, he knows the way blindfold: he says round here the car pound is one of the few things that works properly.'

'I'll need to find a hotel afterwards.'

'We'll go on and take a look at the one Valentine stayed in. It might be OK. You could take a room there. You don't have to, you know, you can come back to Staff's and stay with me.'

Staff must be the blonde Frenchwoman who took us in. I don't even answer, I look out of the window.

She asks: 'You didn't sleep well?'

'I'm not used to orgies. And before you say anything, whether it's women only or mixed, doesn't matter, just not my scene at all. I was a bit uncomfortable, yes.'

'Sorry, I didn't want you to feel awkward... I didn't think it would be so, er, full on... I hope you didn't feel, well, threatened?'

'No, it just seemed childish to me.'

'Childish? Oh. Is that what you call it? Pity you don't work in a nursery school, the kids would soon learn to like school, eh?'

She loses some of her good humour when, after queuing for

half an hour behind two French couples who have trouble proving their cars belong to them, she finds that our bill comes to 215 euros. She changes tone, leans her elbows on the counter, and I don't know what she says, but it rises in a crescendo. On the face of the car pound official, there's a succession of expressions: polite refusal, annoyance, incredulity, anxiety, panic, and finally pure terror. He gives her a form without a word, and she walks away, muttering various curses and threats. I follow her. We cross a huge parking lot, far larger and fuller than the car park of a provincial shopping mall the Saturday before Christmas. She carries on for a couple of hundred metres in silence, then turns to me.

'So this time, you aren't too shocked? I don't exactly have the car's papers. Well I do, but they're not in my name. It's a borrowed car. I was afraid that might cause problems, so I thought the best strategy would be for the guy to want to get rid of me as fast as possible. It worked. I promise you, I don't like that approach any more than you do, but really nothing makes people get the picture better than scaring them a bit.'

'At two hundred and fifteen euros, you can't be the only one who gets angry.'

'That's better, you're catching on. It makes a change when you don't moan.'

We go straight to the hotel where Valentine stayed. The Hyena is now bringing out an aspect of her personality that she hadn't shown me before: she's very good at dealing with young men. At first sight, the youth in reception has no intention of giving us any information, he's polite but firm, and extremely busy. I expect her to grab him by the collar and give him a little 'mandala to realign his chakras', instead of which she lays on for him a feast of smiles, good humour and friendly insistence. And it works. He interrupts what he's doing, calls the manager, a chambermaid, a waiter and even the night porter. I listen from a distance, a blur of syllables, trying to interpret their body language. I like not understanding what's going on, it makes my bubble more airtight, and it's less upsetting that people aren't paying me any attention. Sometimes she turns to me, and sums up in a sentence or two. That's enough for me.

There's a big staff turnover, many of the people who work here hadn't been hired a week ago. Can't pay very well. As for the others, well, one tourist's much like another, and no, they don't remember the girl who stayed a week. Luckily, the mother left more of an impression on them. The manager remembers Vanessa. He must even have been quite keen on her, because he asks his staff to try and remember. One chambermaid now recalls Valentine: she didn't leave her room much, it was hard to get in to make the bed. The kid was there almost all day long and wanted to bribe the staff so that she could get room service, which was never possible. The kitchen worker snaps his fingers, yes, in turn it's coming back to him. She was always first down for the buffet breakfast, she could put away as many as seven croissants at a sitting, he'd started to keep an eye on her. And apart from that? I watch the tourists walking past, Germans, Japanese, French, Americans, all coming up to the counter. I imagine being Valentine in this hall which is a bit too grand, and full of adult couples or families. She must have felt lonely.

'Do you want to take a room here? You can take advantage of it, no building works, I asked. And they'll offer us a reduced price.'

'No, absolutely no way.'

'Ah, oh well.'

In the street she asks me, 'So where do you want to go?'

'Just a normal hotel. I don't like this one, it's depressing. I bet the rooms are cold.'

'The Argentinian chambermaid was quite clear about it: Valentine only went out for about two hours a day. She must have spent her evenings, her mornings, and most of the afternoons all on her own here. All the stuff about "new girlfriends" and Barceloneta Beach was just made up.'

'Meaning she was just waiting for her mother the whole time. Sad.'

I don't dare say what's going through my head: it must mean she could have followed anyone who'd deign to spend a bit of time with her. I can easily imagine what it must be like, a whole week in a strange town, with nobody to talk to. Waiting in her hotel room for the night to come. I say, 'That was a really shitty day, I feel grubby, I hate this.'

'God, you are negative, aren't you? Is that why you don't have a boyfriend? You turn them off in less than two days.'

'Nothing to do with it. I've only been a very short time without a partner.'

Except that's not true. It hasn't ever happened to me before to be on my own for so long. It's the job. I don't even like telling potential boyfriends where I work. It seems hard to explain how I spend my life. And it's hard to see how I can start a relationship when one night in two I'm stuck waiting under some kid's window to see they don't make a run for it, and following them if they do.

The Hyena insists: 'And you're over thirty-five. For you straight girls, that's your sell-by date.'

'Oh, it's much better for lesbians, is it?'

'Like everything else. Old dykes are just brilliant, they have lovely skin, they stay young-looking, they haven't been ground down by a putrid life. With us, thirty-five isn't even the beginning, just the prologue. The peak is when you hit fifty.'

'So you have a regular girlfriend then?'

'I'd love to. Fidelity is my utopia. But I'm too attractive to the girls, I can't do that to them. So what about this one as a hotel?'

I hadn't realized we were walking with a destination in mind. She's brought me to a nice little guest house, I look at the rates and find it dear, but I think it's the same everywhere here. She seems to read my mind.

'You won't find better value. And it's very respectable. I'll leave you here, or do you want to come and have dinner with us?'

'No thanks. I think I'm… familiar enough with your habits now. I'll be fine.'

'As you like. But well, we're meeting on the beach. On the sand, the atmosphere will probably be calmer.'

I doubt if the sand will be enough to damp down their ardour and I'm getting ready to reply that I feel sleepy, then I picture myself in my hotel room, all alone in front of the TV, and I realize no, I'd like to have a drink and see the sea. The day's left a nasty taste in my mouth. And her reflections on my unattached state, my thirty-five years and my negativity have just finished me off. The kind of little sentence, quickly said, that stabs through you like an arrow, letting out a black tide.

'Can you wait? I'll just take my stuff upstairs then I'll come with you.'

She seems surprised. Pleasantly surprised. Makes a sign to say 'take your time'.

The group is easy to spot from a distance, sitting on the grass, just above the beach. About fifteen of them, listening to some old techno on a red Discman, patched up with Sellotape and wired to some small speakers that look like they were retrieved from a dustbin.

Around them, people are walking their dogs, families are playing ball, couples lying on the sand are kissing or smoking. Some groups of young Englishmen are drinking beer. None of them comes within ten metres of where we are.

I nod briefly to the ones I recognize and sit in my little corner. I realize quickly that I've installed myself right by the spot for lines of speed, which they come up to take, two by two, off a magazine. They are discreet, but not too bothered. I glance anxiously at the families and strollers round about. No one is paying any attention.

The girls aren't at all inhibited between themselves about yesterday's goings-on. They congratulate each other, pat each other on the back, kiss each other on the neck or put an arm around a shoulder.

There are a few boys in the group who weren't there yesterday. They're sweet-looking, and they too are happy to kiss each other.

The Frenchwoman from the flat, Staff, greets me, as she comes to take a line. She asks me if I slept well, whether I'd like some. I say no. She stays near me for a few minutes, but can't find anything to say to me. I see her again, yesterday giving that resounding slap to her girlfriend. In the end, I'm regretting running away so fast, I'd like to know what they did later. I look at the beach a few metres below us.

'So, it seems you're a private eye!'

Zoska has crouched down beside me.

'I didn't see you.'

'I just got here.'

She yawns, offers me a spliff, which I refuse. She's wearing the same camouflage trousers as before and a black and white T-shirt, very tight-fitting, with Big Sexy Noise written on it. I notice on her forearm a few parallel scars. Her hands are large and white, with elegant fingers.

'You didn't say you were here on an investigation.'

'I prefer to be discreet.'

'So I noticed. But other people aren't. You're going after someone then?'

'A little girl of fifteen.'

'Fifteen? Not so little then. It's the average age of the population in this town. And it needs two of you, does it?'

I check that the Hyena is fairly far away from us, and pretend to be someone who's completely on top of her work.

'It's more practical. A case can take a long time. Sometimes you have to be up all night, other times be in two places.'

'And you've been doing this a long time?'

'Two years.'

'It's a bit like being a cop in the end, isn't it, your job?'

'Not state employed, not so well paid. But yeah, a bit like it.'

'And you're happy in your work?'

'It's not a vocation. Let's say I wouldn't do it if it wasn't for the money. What about you, what are you doing here?'

'Waitressing. Six euros an hour, on my feet all the time, and these days the customers think they can cut back on tips because of the crisis... so, did you make any progress today?'

'No, not much.'

She sits up, looks around. I'd like to find a subject to keep our conversation going, because at least when she's there, I don't have to put on a front. But I can't think of anything. She starts to walk off, then throws over her shoulder: 'I'm going to have a smoke on the beach if you want to join me.'

At that precise moment, something happens, a slight tear inside my chest, or at the back of my neck or maybe a catch in the throat. The way she turns her head, the way she looks straight at me. An invitation, on the edge of being hidden, to which I respond violently. I stand up to follow her. Nothing's happened. Nothing's changed, but a cord has been stretched somewhere, and it's feverishly trying to attach itself to something and make contact.

Around us, the beach is a scene of devastation. Empty beer cans, crisp wrappers, McDonald's cartons, crushed plastic water bottles, fag-ends and greasy papers. The waves are even pushing a Tampax tube on to the sands.

'Is the beach always in this state?'

'Since the fine weather arrived, yes. In high summer it's worse.'

'Have you lived in Barcelona long?'

'Too long, I want to get away. But for now, there isn't a city that appeals to me. Everyone's off to Berlin, because you can get cheap flats there. But it's so grey. And with artists everywhere. In the end you get really fed up of people talking about their installations.'

'Do you speak Spanish as well as you do French?'

'No. I was a long time in France. That's where I ended up first from Poland. For us, France meant… affluence. Even your post offices are heated. You can't switch on the TV without seeing someone holding a book, it's like that's all you have to do, read, read, read. It takes time to find that it's just a con, you French people don't really have any more education than the birds in the trees. And you don't speak a word of Spanish, do you?'

'No.'

'That might be a problem with your case. If you need someone to translate, call me. I've got a motorbike as well, it's practical for getting around. How are you going about your search?'

At this point I hear myself answering very seriously, 'Me? Well, I let the city do its work. Transmit its energy. I try not to think too much, I just walk round. You need patience. We know she's here. We have to let her come to us.'

She doesn't comment. I carry on, as if it's just a detail, 'Still, give me your mobile number. It might be a good thing to have a translator.'

'Well, you know the Hyena does speak Spanish fluently.'

'Yeah, but we're not always together on the job.'

'I tell you, the age she is, if she starts again this evening,

I bet she'll find it hard to get up in the morning. Seems she really got going last night.'

'I wouldn't know. I stayed in my room, I'm not too...'

'Keen on group sex? Me neither. Shall we go back to the others?'

'Yes, I think I'd like to try a line. Would that be OK?'

'Oh, you'll see, it's hard *not* to take drugs here.'

Actually I loathe coke, and speed, because of the comedown afterwards. But I need some reason to stay with her. Zoska prepares me a line of speed, and leaves me to take it and goes to talk to the others. After my second line, and my third beer, communicating without being understood doesn't bother me any more. The Hyena is sitting off to the side against a tree, with her arms round a brunette I hadn't seen in the group before. At regular intervals, their lips seek each other and they stay there not moving, their two bodies pressed together. Nobody pays them the slightest attention. I turn my head and my eyes meet Zoska's a few metres away. She looks at me for a moment with intensity, without smiling, then turns towards a little blonde sitting opposite her. I remember her yesterday leaning over an arm on which she was tracing lines with a scalpel. A bite of fear in my guts is mixed with a sudden burst of desire.

THE HYENA

AT THE OTHER END OF THE BEACH, THE TALL
silhouette of a new building juts into the sky, grey, shaped like
a shark's fin, probably a hotel. The temperature has plunged in
the night and it's on the cool side for bathing, but an old man
is coming out of the water: skinny legs and a bulging belly.
He seems lost inside his bermuda shorts, all alone as he steps
over the waves. Further down, some little girls who ought to
be at school are playing with a dog that's gripping a deflated
balloon in its jaws. Techno music is blaring out full volume
from the beachside bars, the kind of music that goes with
the drugs on sale round here, synthetic and stimulating. The
Hyena goes back up the Paseo Maritimo, a street bristling
with concrete, subsidized sculptures, and in-your-face palm
trees. The seafront is entirely lined with junk buildings, but
despite all their efforts to fuck up the landscape, the sea is
blue and it's still beautiful.

From the outside, the bar where she's arranged to rendezvous with Lucie looks like a tiny neighbourhood café, like
there used to be in France in the 1970s. It seems even smaller
inside, because it's bulging with customers and thick with
smoke. The counter, facing the door, is laden with oily foods
in stainless steel containers, like in canteens. The clientele

is fluid and voluble, there are few places to sit down, most people are standing, a mixture of local working class, Latin Americans, kids still up after a night out, and old rogues who've seen it all. She looks around for Lucie, and spots her under the plasma screen on the wall, the improbable and only high-tech feature of the place, installed for the football. Lucie isn't alone. The Hyena was expecting to find her looking grumpy because she's a bit late, and her little colleague is inclined to moan all the time, before rolling her eyes to indicate that as far as she's concerned, the incident's over. But she's neither alone nor sulking. She's already drinking a beer, sitting at a table with Zoska, a pretty little brunette who doesn't smile much and of whom the Hyena has previously only taken casual notice.

'What are you two up to then?'

'Zoska's offered to help me, with translating... and since she was free today...'

'And she's translating what? The menu?'

'No. We've been searching the whole district this morning. We've been on our feet the whole time.'

Lucie has never, since they've been working together, taken the slightest initiative on her own. And suddenly she seems to have woken up. The Hyena looks her over suspiciously: right, she's come to Barcelona, so what's happened, she's taken to doing lines of coke the minute she gets up?

'What do you mean, *searching*?'

'With her photo. We did all the bars and restaurants on the beach, the Chinese massage parlours, the Pakistani drinks sellers, the blacks who hire the deckchairs. One by one, from Poblenou to here. We're done in.'

What a weird idea. As if you looked for people by walking round the town with a little photograph in your hand. From what damaged section of her brain did this concept emerge? The Hyena stretches her legs out under the table, and says to herself OK, it suits her fine not to have Lucie trailing round with her today, and if it'll keep her busy all afternoon as well, why not encourage her?

'I don't know what to say... It's true anything can happen. You might just come across someone who saw her.'

'Yeah, that's just what I thought. Seeing as we've got absolutely no clues, thought we might as well try our luck. At her age, you'd expect her to be round the beach, wouldn't you?'

'Yeah, sure. Except the beach is pretty big, and the idea even...'

'You never know. Since it was here her mother came to fetch her, I thought it would be the logical place to start.'

'Logical? Not sure I'd go that far, but, yes. You certainly have to start somewhere.'

Lucie is relieved that the Hyena can't be bothered to criticize her pathetic methods more openly. She stretches out her hand towards Zoska's tobacco, asks, 'May I?' with a brief glance, and at that precise moment everything becomes clear. The Hyena frowns and looks at one of them, then the other. Suddenly, she tries to remember why she's never made a pass at the Polish girl. Who is in fact just the kind to attract her. Lucie gets up to go to the toilet. The Hyena waits for her to be out of earshot.

'It's OK, is it, not too much of a drag, this mission?'

'No, it's fine. But I don't know whether it's getting anywhere, actually.'

'Yes, you do know. You'd have more chance of spotting her if you sat in this bar all day, waiting for her to go past. So that's what you're up to now, you're picking up straight girls, right?'

No reaction, no smile, no glowering either. Superb. Her eyes are clear, you could probably spend a lifetime wondering what's going on in that little head.

She counter-attacks, disdainfully. 'Why, are *you* interested? You were after her yourself, perhaps?'

'Ah, no, not at all.'

She's against the concept, that's all. In the end, it's true, she's developed a strange affection for Lucie. Her determined apathy forces respect. But she's an outstanding example of a dimwit, and the Hyena sees no great urgency in allowing her to bring down the level of the elite. In the bar, flamenco music is playing, a few clients are swaying, holding their beers. Zoska checks a text message on her iPhone. Pretty, not flaky, elegant, feline. The Hyena adds, 'I didn't know Lucie was interested in girls.'

'She's not interested in girls, she's interested in me. That surprise you?'

'It depresses me. It ought to be off limits for you to let her.'

Another cool look, very cutting this time. Really, she has no idea how she didn't spot her earlier. They've met a dozen times at parties, here and there. And she's never paid Zoska any attention. A pity she doesn't have time now to turn the situation to her advantage. Lucie comes to sit down: overnight she's discovered a passion for the enquiry.

'Once we've done this district, we should look for places

where there are lots of men. Young ones. Valentine likes kind of laddish hang-outs: beer and tattoos, that's where we have the best chance to pick up her trail.'

'Well, since you're such a good team, perhaps I'll leave you to it this afternoon. I've got a few things to do myself. I'll let you do your search in peace, OK? But if you do pick up her trail, don't forget to call me, will you?'

Lucie's in such a good mood that she bursts out laughing in an open and musical way that the Hyena has never heard before. You can tell that they're into each other. Sitting side by side. The electricity of the body. They show it in silence, touching hands is enough, sensing their mutual warmth occupies them entirely.

'Aren't you going to eat with us?'

'No, actually I'm in a hurry. I'll take the chance to get on.'

They're delighted, she's leaving them alone to waste time any way they want. The other day, in among the dykes, Lucie was so ill at ease she was practically going to the bathroom every five minutes to splash her face. Sometimes people adapt quickly. Straight women are all alike: they'll tell you, 'no, that's not my scene at all', when you haven't asked them for anything, then before you know it they're down between your legs and into your pussy before you have time to react. Makes a change for them from the hairy monsters, poor things.

A huge advertising hoarding, with a bank's logo in yellow lettering on a red background, covers the main façade of the cathedral. The Hyena goes past the trestle tables covered with candles shaped like various saints, and the rosaries, medallions and religious images being sold at the bottom of the steps. Five euros to go in, you have to pay in the morning, but it's free for the tourists in the afternoon. She came an hour early, to have some time to look around. It feels like going inside the gigantic skeleton of a dinosaur. The stone pillars are the monster's ribs. The place makes her stand up straighter. Flat screens are fixed to every pillar. A progression of moving images, their prosaic nature clashing with the solemnity of the place. The flickering candles at the feet of the altars have been replaced by trays of electric nightlights. Few people come to pray there at times when you have to pay to get in, the nave is left to the tourists who take photos before they even have time to look at anything. Who do they think they're going to show all that to when they get home? It's a frenzy of desire to broadcast, but without any receivers.

The Hyena sits down. She likes churches. You can't hear the traffic, the sound is different from outside, rather like in luxury shops. Her thoughts are disjointed. Her mind's become like some kind of rock festival: groups that have nothing in common with each other occupy the stage, one after another, in complete and utter anarchy. This is the chaos that comes before taking decisions: she's familiar with this tension, but that doesn't mean it's any more bearable. And the girl she spent the night with has dislocated her wrist, keeping her hand tightly clenched, neither in or out, but locking it, and rolling over all the time. Her hand's a wreck.

She gets up and walks round the cathedral, finding herself in an inner cloister open to the sky, with some geese round a pond. A palm tree in the centre is so tall that it has to be held by wires to the portal of an archway. The Chapel of Las Almas del Purgatorio. A woman is standing with her head bowed, in front of the crucifix. It's still a shock, when you haven't been used to it since childhood, to see this guy in agony, his eyes half-shut, his head hanging down and eyeballs rolling up. Wounds on show, blood streaming. Out of the corner of her eye, the Hyena observes the woman praying alongside her. She's wearing flat, round-toed shoes, a shapeless but complicated dress, not just a grey cotton sack, something more subtle, shaped like a trapeze. The language you speak shapes your lips: Spanish women's lips are made larger by the vowels and stronger by the accents. They make you want to kiss them.

The Hyena looks up at Christ on the cross. It would be so restful to believe. Confession. Forgiveness. To be able to atone for your sins. Redemption. All that admirable folklore. She is not a believer. She's alone with her shit. She forces herself not to forget. It's a matter of pride rather than of remorse.

She killed him twenty-five years ago. She waited for him to come out of his workplace. She meant to talk to him, to give him a scare. She followed him without his seeing her, he didn't know her at all. She was furious with herself for feeling so foolish, furious for not preparing what she wanted to say to him. She couldn't go home without doing anything. Behind the station, in those days, it was a kind of wasteland. He set off walking up a deserted street: on one side, a fence ran along the edge of a big building site. It was too late for anyone to be working there now. She caught up with him, grabbed him by the arm, and forced her face into a fierce expression. He just looked her up and down, without expecting it was anything to do with him personally. He was a grown man, he wasn't going to be scared of a slip of a girl of sixteen. Seen close up, he was an image of France in the early 1980s, a France still deep in ideas of decency, authority and moral attitudes. He gestured to her to push off. He didn't say a word, but his body language said 'stop pestering me'. And that was when she hit him with her schoolbag, aiming at his head. She'd taken a good swing at it. It could have been a grotesque and clumsy gesture. She might have missed him. In the bag was a little glass bottle of Orangina, bought at lunchtime, which she hadn't had time to drink yet. She put all her strength behind the blow. He staggered, felt for the wall with the flat of his hand, didn't reach it, and pitched the other way. She ran away. She left no trace of herself behind, neither on his body nor on the frozen ground.

She'd arrived home where her mother was ironing in the living room, in front of the television. She'd gone straight to her bedroom: 'I've got homework to do', like any other evening. Most normal days she'd lie down in the darkened room and listen to records. At dinnertime when her father called her to come to the table, he'd switch on the light in the corridor and a white ray of light would appear under the door, she'd just have time to jump up before he came in to say, 'Supper's ready, come and eat.' That day, she hadn't closed the shutters to put her music on. There was a little blood on her US Army surplus schoolbag, a dark stain about the size of a large plum. She didn't know at that stage that the man was dead. She didn't panic. She'd taken out her school things, her geography and maths textbooks, her Clairefontaine exercise books with dog-eared corners, her ink-stained red pencil case, her set square, and an old packet of dried-up tobacco.

Her notebook was covered with stickers, her mother said she couldn't be working seriously with such scruffy things, it was a perpetual subject of argument, among others.

She'd slipped into the bathroom alongside her bedroom, picked up the big bottle of bleach, and filled the washbasin with warm water. Her mother would be thinking she was washing her hands or wouldn't even hear her, because of the TV quiz show she was watching with the sound turned up loud, so she could hear it while going to and fro to put away the ironed clothes. She dabbed some bleach on to the dark stain, then used the water in the basin to dilute it and plunged the bag in. Her hands under water rubbed at the fabric. Then she left it to soak. Basically, she didn't imagine she would escape the consequences of what she'd done, she thought she would have to answer for it, it was just a matter of keeping the dizziness at bay by doing something. When they caught up with her, she could confess that she'd tried to make the stain disappear, but it wouldn't greatly change the seriousness of what she'd done. She was waiting for the telephone to ring at any moment, or for someone to come to the door, for the outside world to enter her universe and shatter it.

Their evening meal had taken place normally, and anyway she never spoke much. At table, the conversation was confined to the grown-ups' concerns. Even when her sister was still living at home, they'd wait until after the meal to yell at each other in their rooms. Her parents would be talking about things that happened at work. So-and-so has been promoted unfairly, this woman in our office is an alcoholic, the union rep made a comment that was out of order. Her mother worked in a bank, her father was a head salesman at a furniture store.

After supper, before watching a film on TV, her mother had gone to the bathroom. When she heard her mother say, 'Why does this place stink of bleach?' her heart had stopped; fear gripped her in the gut. Here we go: now the troubles will start. But her bag had simply turned white. Her mother was furious. 'What on earth's got into you? How do you think that's going to be dry by tomorrow? It'll have to be rinsed, or it'll go into holes. And then dried on a radiator. Do you think that's why we send you to school, to go with a bag looking like nothing on earth and smelling of bleach? You don't know you're alive, my girl, one of these days you'll see, you'll be surprised when you find out what real life's like.' There was no stain at all on the bag, just the shadows of the names of rock groups she'd written on the canvas with felt pens. Not a drop of blood. The bag had been rinsed, stretched out on the radiator, her mother was in a foul mood because she'd missed the beginning of the film. The bag ended up a sort of beige colour, with no visible trace of any stain.

Next day, she spent the whole time with her eyes riveted on the classroom door, waiting for Loraine to appear. Or a policeman. Overnight, the whole thing had got bigger. The realization of what she'd done. The idea that he could be dead. She reran the scene in her head, wondering if someone might have seen her without her noticing in the heat of the moment. What was beyond doubt for her, in those days, was that a culprit would always be found out. The smell of bleach permeated the whole classroom, and the other pupils looked at her, laughing, pulling faces and holding their noses.

That night, she found her parents both at home. She had put her nearly-white bag on the dark brown sofa in the sitting room, which was immediately filled with the smell of bleach. Her parents had hugged her tightly, an unaccustomed warmth coming from them, an intense and annoying contact. They had heard from one of the other parents who lived in their street. They didn't know how to tell her. It was her father who finally stammered out, 'Loraine's dad is dead.'

They hadn't wanted to come straight out with it at first: 'he was murdered'. They wondered if she wanted to call her friend, would that be the right thing to do, what did she think? As a rule, they knew exactly what to do and how you set about it. In normal social life, how many times you should let the phone ring, what time of day you should or shouldn't telephone people, what sort of gift you take if you are a guest, what you should wear on special occasions. But that day they were at a complete loss: what do the rules say if the body of the father of your daughter's best friend is found lying lifeless in the street? She knew she would have to own up. The sentences were there, all ready, in her head, but she was incapable of pronouncing them. Her bag was in her line of sight. How long would it be before they made the connection? She would have to tell them, but her lips remained sealed.

She hadn't called Loraine. She was convinced that Loraine knew. She thought Loraine would say something, end up by cracking, and give her away. It was for Loraine that she'd done it.

Overnight, everything familiar seemed now to have taken on a new savour, and for several weeks, she had felt she was in a state of expectation and tension that illuminated everything around her. The wind on her cheek, how blissful. Walking through the streets after school, deciding to do most of the journey on foot. The way the people looked so smart first thing in the morning, smelling of perfume and aftershave, watches on their wrists, the women's faces newly made up, the smell of their hairspray. Sitting in a coffee bar, opening a newspaper and ordering a cappuccino. The mosaic of the latest record sleeves, displayed in the window of the music store opposite the bus stop where she waited every evening. The grating sound of the garage door when her parents left for work, just as she was getting up in the morning. The step at the bottom of the cellar stairs that always creaked the same way when her father went down to fetch something for her mother. She knew where the town prison was, they often went past it in the car. That building was waiting for her.

In school, everyone talked of nothing else, the papers were full of it too. It lasted three days, then there was less, then nothing, very quickly. Every morning, arriving at the school gates, she checked from people's faces that no one knew, and every morning, she felt a certain relief without really being at ease. Life went on, as normal, but nothing was the same as before. Nobody was thinking about her. Loraine was absent for a fortnight, without getting in touch. And when she did come back, it was clear that she suspected nothing. Like everyone else. She looked thinner, paler, her eyes had circles under them. So she had shed tears. A group formed round her, sympathetic and curious teenagers, attracted by the smell of drama. Normally, nobody paid much attention to Loraine. She was taking advantage of the situation to have her fifteen minutes of fame, appealing to the older pupils, feeling for once part of the school. But between the two of them there were no knowing looks, no reproaches or guilty complicity.

Life had resumed its course. It was as stupid as that. A few months later, one night, lying in bed with the light still on, reading a novel without taking it in properly, she was struck for the first time in days by the obvious fact that nobody would ever know. Justice wasn't always done. Impunity. Before, it had been a word that didn't mean anything to her, now it filled all her mental space. It was something to be envisaged: impunity. The man falling backwards, herself running away. Justice was something exceptional, an unusual break in the banality of bloody events.

She'd finished her school year, and done well in all her subjects. Between herself and the world, an impassable gulf had become fixed. She did all that was required of her with remarkable efficiency. She'd always been a rather borderline pupil before, the kind over whom the staff meeting at the end of year hesitates: 'Should we make her repeat a year, or let her go up?' By applying herself just a little more, she'd improved her grades. She did her homework carefully, reassured to be sitting in her bedroom, crouched over her exercise books. This tranquillity, which had always seemed so bland before, had transmuted into comfort. She didn't try to go round with gangs of boys at school, or make passes at the girls. She no longer spent all her free time with Loraine. She didn't feel like going out at weekends, she didn't want to be tempted by the idea of drinking, with the risk of breaking down. Her parents rewarded her. They told each other with a knowing air that her teenage rebellion was over. They sent her on a language course abroad. She wasn't afraid any more to look like a swot. The immoral aspect of all this did not escape her, on the contrary it fascinated her. That's what happens when you do something bad: you get a reward. Anything else is just romantic rubbish and hypocritical naivety. She was subject to bursts of maniacal joy, during which she thought of herself as part of an elite: those who have *done it*. She got crazes for history books: China in the twentieth century fascinated her for a whole year. Then pell-mell Chile, Spain, Germany, Korea, France, the USSR, Turkey. Sometimes she went further back in time: the history of the United States, the Spanish Inquisition, the Wars of Religion, colonialism. Who gets rewarded, who gets punished, which dog eats dog. Who wins and gets to write the history books. Who decides what counts as evil. Serial killers, bandits, terrorists, were of less interest. They were people rather like herself: amateurs. She preferred more serious historical cases: when the crime was massive, openly committed, not denied. Truly rewarded.

Outside novels, she'd never heard of any criminals shedding tears, asking sincerely for forgiveness. Their stories were always the same: the guilty person only remembers the humiliation, the wound or the terror that governed *his* decision to kill. What was done to *him*. Then comes a gap in the story. And he goes straight on, to talk about the unjust treatment inflicted on *him*, when the law seeks to make him pay. What, me? But I've done nothing wrong! The space in the real world in which he killed, tortured or massacred only exists for the victim – if the victim survives, that is. The ones who express remorse are always just hoping for some mercy from the court. Anyone who claims to regret their crime is lying. The killer doesn't even remember it. There is no link left between the act perpetrated and the individual responsible for it. All he thinks of is the aggression of others towards him, when he's charged with the offence. It's as simple as that. Victims, of course, have good memories. They cling to the injustice someone committed towards them, to justify any act of barbarity that they will commit in turn. But the murderer has no need to make an effort. It has become detached from him. It was never really him anyway.

She had understood how it worked. *Not* forgetting demanded a constant effort. Not to focus on the offences committed by her victim. Or the stupidity of the people who hadn't caught her. Or the icy loneliness that had overcome her afterwards. Not to focus on her own pain, banish it somewhere to the very edge of consciousness. It was a matter of pride. She would not let human nature do its work, but put up a barrier between herself and the forgetting of what she had been. She refused to be like others of her kind, an amnesiac predator whining about her lot.

Loraine had arrived in the fourth form at high school – the Collège Albert Camus – halfway through the year. Fair-haired and well-built, she wore an off-white sleeveless pullover, a sheepskin jacket and heavy shoes. She carried her schoolbooks in a rectangular bag, made of maroon leather, different from the other children's satchels. She wore her hair in two plaits. She didn't try to make friends with people, she looked scornful of her schoolmates. But her arrogance had no real basis. She was neither particularly pretty nor rich, she was only so-so at sports, and her grades were nothing to write home about. But her parents had bourgeois aspirations.

They lived in the same kind of house as everyone else, they had the same boring middle-class jobs, drove the same kind of car, and wore the same chainstore clothes. But they thought themselves a cut above the others, with a couple of dozen books on their shelves and a smattering of English. They considered themselves educated because they listened to classical music and sometimes watched films with subtitles. They were snobs.

Then there had been the incident in the history-geography lesson. The class was taken by a supply teacher, who couldn't hold the pupils' attention for more than few minutes: he found public speaking difficult. He would hardly have started the lesson before the class broke down in chaos. It was the ferocity of children in a group, raging because authority wasn't being exercised with full force. He would lose control, throw temper tantrums and punish four pupils at random, like throwing a few glasses of water to put out a fire. That day, he had picked on Loraine: three hours' detention, on the pretext that she had been laughing loudly. She wasn't at all the kind of girl who would join in the laughter. He'd picked on her because she wouldn't dare to protest. She looked completely devastated and changed colour. So much so that the whole class turned and looked at her, the noise was suspended for a few seconds. The teacher was looking pleased with himself.

'You stupid prick! You know fine well she hasn't done anything, but you don't dare punish the ones who were really shouting.'

She didn't know why she had felt like defending Loraine. She rarely spoke up in class. All the other pupils knew she was into girls, for them it was as if she was somehow grubby, the whole time. The group excluded her, but without bullying her. She didn't fit the good victim profile. She liked a fight. And she put sufficient passion into it that any attackers enjoyed it less than she did. Since primary school, she'd worked out her strategy: start every new school year by attacking in public a boy who was enough of a show-off to attract notice, but not dangerous enough to be a really serious enemy. After that they were more likely to call her 'the nutter' than 'the dyke', and leave her in peace. In return for which she tried not to be conspicuous for the rest of the year. But that day, she'd abandoned her low-profile approach, and other pupils had taken up the cry.

'She's right, sir! You've given her three hours and she was the only girl who didn't laugh!'

After that, they'd been told they'd all be kept in, but they weren't too angry, as they left the room, because of the fun they had had hearing their teacher called 'stupid prick' several times, in a class that had finally fallen silent.

On the way out, she'd caught up with Loraine in the corridor. 'Don't look so sad, that's life, we all get kept in now and then.'

The other girl nodded without replying, then instead of going to her next class, she had run frantically out of the building. And had thrown up on the grass.

'Did you eat something in the canteen to make you sick? Oh, no, you don't go to canteen, do you. Want to go to the sick room? I'll come with you. Was it the detention? Will you get into trouble? We're all being kept in, your folks can't blame you for it.'

That was how it had begun, trying to defend her, and that was how it would end. Until then, she had always fallen for the same kind of girl: the prettiest in the school, as long as she was up for it. She liked beauty with a bit of edge. She had a weakness for vulgar, precocious girls who didn't mind going behind the bike sheds for a snog with another girl. It was their brothers who were a problem, as a rule. Loraine wasn't at all that type. But it had happened all the same, after the detention business. She'd fallen in love. She had sought out the new girl's company. And Loraine had reluctantly accepted, like a wary animal.

One very hot day, Loraine came to school wearing a black woollen sweater: its sleeves were too long, hanging down over her wrists. They were on their own near the bike sheds.

'Wow, your face is really red! Good thing you can't see it. Why don't you wear a T-shirt like everyone else? Think it's cool to be sweaty, or what?'

But instead of smiling vaguely, and putting on a superior and absent-minded expression as she usually did, Loraine had pulled up her sleeves, challenging her to look. Her forearms were black and yellow, covered with bruises and scars, her elbows were raw. It made no sense. Those bare, mutilated arms and the rest of her body. This proud, rather stuck-up girl, always fussing that this or that was clean and up to scratch. It didn't fit. With her quiet behaviour, her straight back, her delicate lips and finely shaped nose, the care she took of her things. Her arms were from a social worker's casebook, grafted on to a fragile body. Some children at the school showed off the marks from being belted, or turned up with a black eye, or burns from an iron, others pretended they'd hurt themselves falling off a swing, and some took pride in telling you the gory details of the abuse they'd suffered. Yes, of course it happened to other kids. But they were expecting it, it was well known, or not surprising. Loraine had pulled down her sleeves in silence. She'd thought that was the end of the revelations, but the teenager now pulled up her sweater. Her torso was like her arms: marked, bruised, scarred, all over. Loraine said in a neutral voice, 'He takes care to keep off my face or hands. Once I put my hands up to protect myself, and the next day the teacher asked me what had happened. After that, he's taken to tying my wrists above my head before he starts.'

'Your *dad*?'

'He's sick. He can't stop himself. But the rest of time, he's normal.'

'Normal has to be full-time, or it doesn't count.'

What a let-down. She'd fallen madly in love with a princess, who'd turned out to be a poor kid being abused in secret by a crazy father. She'd asked a few more questions to be polite, but was wondering all the time how to put an end to this outburst of confidences.

'Is he like that often?'

'If it isn't me, it's my mother who gets it, and that's worse. And when it's not my mother, it's my little sister. We try hard to make it us, so that it's not her. She's only five.'

'Why don't you run away?'

'He's not like it all the time. Mostly, we're fine, all of us. It's, well, it's complicated.'

She'd already seen Loraine's mother. Loraine's mother looked classy. She wasn't the only one who'd like to think:

I'm a cut above this run-down area. But she was more elegant than the others. She had a way of getting out of a car, of closing the door behind her daughter; with her gentleness and tact, she impressed. And this woman, who wore her hair in such a neat bob, who went round in smart suits and trimly knotted silk scarves, this woman was a battered wife? Like poor old Madame Tunard down the road? Like the fat alcoholic woman opposite? Battered? Like some ordinary woman round here? And she couldn't get away because it was 'too complicated'? Everything looked different now. That was why Loraine never invited her home. Why she didn't hang about after class. Why it was so important to get good grades. Why she had odd, touchy reactions. Everything that had made her seem so mysteriously uninterested in everything around her, her air of seeming to float above the mediocre world below – for all this, there was a simple, banal explanation. She was an abused child, living too far from the kind of district where the social workers called and lifted up kids' T-shirts to check for bruises. That was why she never came to the swimming pool, never wore shorts for games. Why she never cheeked the teachers, or horsed around in the playground, no physical contact. Obviously with her body like that, she wouldn't want to tangle with the boys.

And that evening, going home, she'd sworn to herself that that was the end of it, her obsession with Loraine was finished. Over, all that time of riding her bike to school instead of taking the bus, so that she could catch her up at the corner, of knowing where she was in the school buildings without even needing to look, of reading a book she'd mentioned so that they could talk about it, even when the books were totally boring, about people who lived five hundred years ago in some other country. It was over, listening to the slightest things she said, as if she had to learn all the nuances of a language foreign to her, so that in conversation she too would be able to sound condescending, use words like 'naff' and know what it meant, even while realizing in some shamed corner of her mind that it invariably referred to the habits of her own family. Over, having to be willing to listen to records by male singers who couldn't have a drink without crying, or take drugs without moaning about it, and who were always being abandoned. That evening, she'd vowed that it was all over with Loraine. She was going to get back to her normal self.

But that's not how it worked out. An invisible hand had swooped down to pluck her up as she was about to run away, and had set her back on the rails of her destiny, making sure she'd see it through to the end. Insidiously, admiration had gained the upper hand. It must take enormous willpower to go through what Loraine was going through without anyone else suspecting. Most of the time, they acted as if it wasn't happening. Loraine would choose moments when they were alone to show her her bruised body, or just to talk about it.

'But doesn't your mother have any relations? Her parents aren't living? Couldn't you run away to some uncle?'

Because Loraine's mother didn't go out to work, she had no friends. No exit that way. They often moved house. The mother was isolated. But still she was an adult, wasn't she, couldn't she just pick up her car keys, take her two daughters, and go back to her family?

'My mother won't let me say anything. She says nobody

would understand. My grandmother, for instance, she adores my father, it would kill her if she found out. Everyone adores my father. When he's OK, he's always got a kind word for people, he's interesting. Nobody would understand. He just can't help it, you see. He cries afterwards, all night. He's in pain too. He does it because he's too sensitive. He can go mad over the slightest thing.'

'Yeah, but when he gets going, it's against you, he doesn't hit himself, and I don't hear you telling me he has a go at the people at work.'

Loraine wouldn't listen. She didn't like others to interfere in her life, where there was much pain but no way out. She just wanted someone to lend an ear and confirm her diagnosis: 'Nothing to be done.'

'Most of the time, you know, he's in a good mood, he's funny, he jokes. But if we don't laugh, that can trigger it – or if we laugh too much. Or if the dinner's too cold. Or if he spills orange juice on a shirt he meant to wear next day. And he's off. You can see it coming. But you can't predict why it'll start. For instance, one day I can come home with only twelve out of twenty in French, and he'll just shrug his shoulders and say I must try harder next time. But next day I can have fourteen, and he says how come I didn't do better, and if he doesn't like my answer, off he goes again. Or say my mother cooks the pasta too long, she panics, she has tears in her eyes, and he'll make fun of her, "Oh it doesn't matter, the pasta's fine like that." Then the next day, he might see her wiping down the table with the sponge we use to do the dishes, and he'll haul her into his study and beat her up, because he's decided we have to have two sponges, one for the dishes, one for the table. But you can't predict the rules we're supposed to follow, see, they change, and we don't know when we're going to get something wrong. The problem with my father is he wants us all to be perfect, we're supposed to know instinctively how we should be, without him having to tell us all the time.'

It took place in his study, the room nobody else in the family could enter without being asked. Loraine was being beaten up so that she would get better grades at school. She went into morbid detail when she talked about it.

'If you could see his face, going round the chair and shouting at my mother to stay outside, and as long as I don't cry, he goes on hitting me, he seems to be proud of me if I can stand it for a long time without crying, or screaming, but it makes him mad and he can't stop. He gags my mother, I've seen him through the keyhole, one day he's going to throttle her.'

Loraine liked her to fall into the trap and plead with her for hours to do something to make it stop. She liked to reply no, to point after point, it was a game she took pleasure in. Stubbornness.

She had a life outside her passion for Loraine, because of all the evenings and weekends when she could go round with other people. She was friends with the boys and she had girlfriends outside school. She was streetwise, nowadays she knew she could always get what she wanted from girls. When the two of them met up again after the holidays, in the first year of the upper school, the *lycée*, everything seemed to be likely to drive them apart. The *lycée* was in the town centre, and it was full of much more exotic and surprising creatures than Loraine. For the first time in her life, she wasn't the only girl who was into girls. There were four of them in the top class, always going round together. The first time she saw them in the yard, it had been a shock, like when she'd first heard the word 'dyke', pronounced by an uncle talking about a woman he'd met in Paris. She'd been ten years old. She knew she was one, even before she knew there was a word to describe her state, and it was odd to find that it really did exist, that it wasn't just something she'd invented for herself, to be in love with this girl or that in silence. She had never seen the woman, who was a friend of her mother's, but the howls of laughter that had greeted the uncle's remark had taught her that it was about as highly valued as having been born with a big red nose. It was before the word became associated with the word 'pervert': that came a year later when a primary school teacher had found her french-kissing a schoolfriend in the toilets. 'Little perverts!' It was getting complicated. And it was wicked as well as grotesque. Luckily it was exciting too, because you had to be highly motivated not to be persuaded to forget the whole thing. Her old lady hadn't said a word, after the headmistress had telephoned her. They didn't talk about things like that. Her mother thought it would pass, all girls go through a phase. So when she saw these tall girls from the top form, with their short hair, unsmiling faces, always with a cigarette in the corner of their mouths, wearing leather jackets like boys, a separate gang in the schoolyard, she'd had several epiphanies. She wasn't the only girl in the entire region to be 'that way'. There was a 'look' for what she was, a way of being recognized immediately. The chatter in the school playground didn't come to a halt when these four girls appeared, nobody threw stones at them in the street. At a stroke, a whole lot of interesting perspectives opened up.

She and Loraine met in front of the hot chocolate machine at school. The four other girls were smoking a few feet away from them. Loraine rolled her eyes, looking disgusted. 'How ugly they are. At least you don't look like that.' Loraine had lost her superior airs. She'd become old-fashioned, with her Clarks shoes and her plaits, her paperback books, and her scornful look at other people. She was trying to reduce things to her measure. Sensing that she was losing her grip, Loraine had counter-attacked. 'Can I talk to you for a few minutes?' and then with a worried but determined expression, and clasping a copy of Boris Vian's *Heartsnatcher* tightly to her, she said, 'I've had enough, he's gone too far, you're right, I'm going to run away. Will you come with me?' The Hyena had been waiting for this to happen all the previous year, but now she just felt like saying, no, you sort yourself out, I'm fine here, can't you see I've got plenty of new friends and there are girls everywhere that I need to get to know? But Loraine, realizing that this wasn't enough to restore her domination, had moved her lips close, slipped her hand under the Hyena's sweater and up her back, whispering, 'I love you,' and it had worked. Their skin had touched and it was worth all the troubles in the world. After that, she had learned her lesson: always take the first exit when it appears in an affair. As soon as you get bored or tired, get out fast.

Loraine had no intention of running away, she would have been too scared to leave her mother and sister behind to pay the price for her action, but right now she needed to imagine she was going to do it. She had never been so openly anxious for company, for someone to talk to. And it had been nice. That and the sweet excitement of her skin, her tiny warm tongue, her active fingers always wanting to go further, letting herself go, more and more. Loraine was playing at being a girl seduced against her will, but losing all desire to resist. So with Loraine, in the quiet alleys of public gardens, or in the cinema, sweater pulled up to her shoulders, her sex being fingered, she was being pleasured to ecstatic levels. None of the others must know. And then one grey morning in February, after the half-term break, Loraine came in looking shattered. She was getting beaten less, but her little sister was getting it now.

'I've thought about it. The only thing I can do to protect my sister is to set her an example. And the only example I can give her is to run away.'

Loraine was much unhappier than before. Her little sister's screams hurt her more than when she was receiving the blows herself.

She didn't say anything to Loraine but her mind was made up. She was going to seek him out and threaten to denounce him.

When he had realized he was being followed, he'd turned round and stared at her at length. Not afraid in the least, just looking scornful and annoyed. She was furious with herself, for wanting to give up at that point. To surrender, and realize she couldn't do anything, submit to the authority of things being the way they are, so that nothing will ever change. She had charged at him like a wild beast. When she came level with him, she had hit out. Not to avenge her girlfriend whom he'd been torturing. A sudden desire had surged up inside her. To fell him. To force him to reckon with her. To get her out of this anguish, whatever the cost.

It must have been at that time that her way of thinking was transformed: through expecting always to be unmasked, she became capable of observing the slightest gesture, of analysing every sound. Something inside her must have been released. She paid such attention to what was happening around her that, little by little, she learnt to read between the lines when facing other people. She could spot those who were concealing something. She could recognize a lie. It even happened sometimes, with painful flashes of knowledge, that she simply guessed truths that had been covered up. It was like a kind of lucid madness, gradually extending its range. The sound of blood, other people's blood, started to reach her. The drives, hidden thoughts, secrets that had never been whispered. She found it easier and easier to judge people. Their ferocity. Their weaknesses. Which had nothing to do with what was on the surface. She didn't like it. The whole folklore thing about being 'clairvoyant', muttering over candles, smelling of patchouli. As the years passed, her senses became spontaneously more sophisticated. When she heard on TV that some girl was missing, she knew instinctively whether the girl was alive or dead. When someone told her about some incident, she could see the place, visualize what had happened. More pragmatically, she was a good listener, to whom people could tell their troubles of the heart; she knew, and was rarely mistaken, who was deceiving whom, who was lying, who was two-timing, and who would come back shamefaced after cutting a dash somewhere else.

She had got through her further studies effortlessly. She fascinated people. Nothing is less exciting than getting what you want too easily, especially if you think you don't deserve it. When she finished university, everything seemed flat. The depressive stage had kicked in. She didn't want to study any more, she wasn't interested in getting a good job. Success would have brought a bitter taste. She'd gone to Paris. For the first few years, she worked at the postal sorting office near the Louvre, and by filling in for other people, she ended up working full-time. She preferred the night shift: going to work at eight and walking back home as the city woke up. She had an attic room opposite the Gare d'Austerlitz. She didn't particularly enjoy her new life. She wasn't surprising herself or rebelling. She was as if in suspense, a state that suited her. It seemed to her entirely desirable for a whole life to go past in this peaceful solitude, without anything happening, exciting or sad. Nothing but a succession of nights standing up emptying sacks and sorting envelopes by size, reclassifying postcards from the wrong boxes, throwing packets with accuracy into the big metal bins. Her colleagues weren't very different from herself: pale, silent, rather absent-minded. A team of about twenty people, in a huge hangar with very high ceilings, impossible to heat in winter. A beehive in slow motion. In the post office hierarchy, the people on the night sorting shift thought they were looked down on, outsiders. She felt at home among them. A team of ghosts. A new rule had banned any alcohol in the building during the breaks. They didn't laugh a lot. They drank packet soups, and didn't have the guts to complain or to be vindictive. They didn't talk much, or only about their kids, holidays, food, programmes on daytime TV, or how to look after houseplants. Things that didn't concern her. Nobody took much notice of her.

But after a year, she'd been assigned the task of training a new recruit, a dark-haired boy who never stopped talking, who complained because he was missing rock concerts that interested him, or going out with his pals. His name was Arnaud. She didn't really want to start chatting to him, but the nights were long, with nobody else near, they were thrown together. He'd succeeded in hauling her out of her torpor, insidiously, he'd get her to listen to a tape, buy a record. He took pains over his appearance, he was good-looking with full lips and big brown eyes. He deserved to be gay, poor boy, instead of which he had a string of affairs with straight girls his own age, each more pathetic than the last. She hadn't managed to stop herself taking an interest in him. Because of her conversations with him, one afternoon she'd left her flat and walked over to the Place Jussieu to look at some second-hand records, and spotted the dark-haired salesgirl: an upfront dyke, condescending and raffish-looking. Impossible not to keep going back. Life had started to reassert itself, without her realizing it. The girl's name was Elise. She listened to Siouxsie and the Banshees all the time, and liked Chinese films. The depression blew clean away. Elise was like a blazing coal, a tiny body that allowed itself to be lifted and turned as much as one liked. Her behind was like a baby's. Her back was tattooed all over. Elise liked Philip K. Dick and went round clutching Valerio Evangelisti's first novel, which she was reading for the third time. She would describe how her mother had died after endless suffering, with that coolness of youth, when one is still running too fast for emotion to catch up. Her wrists were scarred by razor blades. Elise's charm was all the more overwhelming because she wasn't free, she was the kind of girl who loves duplicity, the kind of girl you can never trust, one who was excited by the idea of betrayal. She lived in a bedsit, on the sixth floor without a lift, near the Place de l'Horloge. Elise had other girlfriends and introduced them to her. She'd have liked to get off with them all. And it was mutual. One evening she'd called in to work saying she was sick, a second night she said she had a problem, the third night she didn't call at all, and assumed they'd realize she was quitting her job.

She'd started in the debt-collecting racket by chance. This guy she hardly knew had agreed to go and pressure a porn film producer to pay an actress right away. He'd asked her to go along with him. The job had immediately pleased her. Some people fall for heroin first shot, some people fall for coke at the first sniff, what she'd fallen for was the adrenaline. Her number was passed round, she took on missions the way other girls might have offered a quickie: regularly but not the whole time. She'd become the Hyena. An outfit had offered her a full-time job, she'd accepted. Not a great job, but quite well paid. In a detective agency, getting creditors to pay up is pretty much the equivalent of cleaning lavatories. She wasn't unhappy to play the dyke the way heteros expected: brutal, marginal, ready to cut the balls off anyone who crossed her. The first years, she quite enjoyed it.

She wasn't in the business to make friends. She didn't want peer-group recognition, she had no intention of being understood or sympathized with. But the first man she worked with as a regular partner, Cro-Mag, was OK. When he gave up, she didn't enjoy working with other people. Her colleagues were heavy-handed, too highly motivated, cut-price sadists who thought they were tough. Something had kept her hanging on for a while: the chase itself. She'd developed a taste for it early on: one day when she was doing her act, a gipsy hiding in the corner of a room had pinned her to the ground, he'd put a knife against her throat and hadn't needed to say a word to indicate that it wasn't a good moment to threaten anyone. For a tenth of a second, his breath had invaded her space, they had exchanged looks, nothing in his eyes gave any hint of his humanity. She had come very close to death – he would have slit her throat like that of a chicken, without a pang. She had not felt afraid. Not at the time. Instead, she had replied to him on the same wavelength, as if she were digging her hands into his guts, a geyser of cold, still, intense hatred. It had been a moment suspended in time. A shard of life. And for the next few days, she had had the sensation of being aware of every cell in her body, every particle in the air. Reinvigorated. She didn't care which side she was playing for. She didn't even care whether she got the best of it. What had hooked her was the precise moment: two wills fighting full tilt. She would have liked it to happen with a girl, to see if it was even better. Everything was always better with girls.

But she hadn't stayed much longer in debt collecting. Too many rules, too much timekeeping, paperwork, trivial internal quarrels, egos squabbling in a teacup. She'd taken on fewer missions, plugged the gaps in her income by selling grass, then moved on to dealing in coke. Because of her former contacts in debt recovery, she was naturally contacted by the French intelligence services. A good-looker and fast talker, she had very long legs, a powerful motorbike, and the best suppliers in town... Within a year, her network was set up: politicians, sportsmen, doctors, actors, journalists, officials, hairdressers, prostitutes, traders, drivers. Apart from sex, nothing unites people like drugs. It wasn't hard in the circumstances to get hold of various pieces of private information about the wife of a minister, the son of a left-wing singer, the neighbour of a captain of industry. Cocaine was the ideal vehicle to get her into every kind of milieu, and even those who weren't users were willing to see her, there was always someone close to them who might be interested in the service she provided. Her appearance and her business fended off curious questions. No one asked what she was up to, why she was so interested in everyone's affairs. Her androgynous looks were an advantage: the man of the house was always a little turned on by the thought that she might make a pass at the lady of the house before leaving the family sitting room. People didn't enquire too closely into her life. But she did enquire closely into theirs, and knew who to pass her findings on to. The more information she delivered, the more protected her own racket became; the better able she was to carry it on with impunity, the better she could inform, and the more she was appreciated and introduced to new circles. She ran all over Paris, with wads of cash the size of Big Macs in one pocket and sachets of coke in the other. When she ran out of supplies, the narcotics squad helped her out. It was hard work – people siphoned the stuff up like crazy, she'd hardly got to a new address before she was being called back for more. It was well paid too. Those were the days: wherever she arrived, people were pleased to see her, even if she turned up five hours late.

Waugheirt had moved her on to a higher level. Still passing intelligence. He had a dark comb-over on his bald head, and his long fingers, bristling with hairs, made his hands look like impatient spiders. He wore a wedding ring. She found it hard to believe that a woman could be in such deep shit that she'd want to share her life with him. He spoke slowly, like in films from the Far East, you had time to think of a hundred other things while he was explaining something. Waugheirt was ugly, yes, but he gave an impression of intelligence, deep concentration, an impression reinforced by his voice, which was amazingly deep and throaty. He said he'd spotted her and observed her at work. It was time for her to give up dealing, he said, give up the amateurism and the info picked up in exchange for trivial favours, small-time protection rackets or perks, flats belonging to the Paris city council, freebies. He thought she should work – without official cover – on more ambitious projects. Full-time, at the going rate. Which was quite a lot. Thinking to refuse the offer, she'd replied that Paris wasn't short of double agents ready to do anything to get on the right side of French intelligence. 'People aren't that complicated. You just have to hint that someone in power's behind you, and all they want is to go and brown-nose. So why me?'

'You're just a small-time dealer. How long can you go on doing this? You're getting on for thirty, right? Someone younger will come along one day soon, and take your place in your "in" circles. You're happy with what you can make from it for now. But everything could change if you're willing to make the break.'

Waugheirt had taken his wallet from his inside pocket, glanced at the bill, paid for the two coffees, leaving a small tip, but a tip all the same. Before standing up, he had added, soberly, 'Why you persist in playing below your real level is your own business. I've got contacts. Everywhere else, to get a quarter the information you bring in calls for three times the work. And that's not taking into account this disconcerting gift you have for knowing *where* to look.'

She'd shrugged her shoulders, unconvinced by his argument. 'But it's no big deal.'

'That's exactly what I'm talking about. Your "no big deal", my dear child, is incredibly hard for common mortals. A gift isn't to be trifled with. It's an order to go on a mission. I advise you to take it on, while there's still time.'

He'd stood up and left her there. For a moment she'd felt like in *Star Wars* when Luke Skywalker gets his lungs blasted.

It was logical. You want some information. You have three contacts in town, you think a bit, you concentrate, you relax, you ask questions, and that's it. She was just a bit faster on the draw than the other people doing this kind of job, that's all. On the ball people don't often have to go through their neighbours' dustbins. But the conversation had hit home: in fact, yes, for three months now, she'd found nothing out about anyone. She knew what he was talking about. It was her old history that was undoing her brain... She knew. Even if she carefully avoided being aware of it. She knew she had one GPS too many in her head that never stopped working.

And often she got things wrong. Between a right and a wrong intuition there was no difference. They felt the same.

She'd assumed it would come more into focus. But time had shown her that no, the more she tried to refine her talent, the less use she would be able to make of it. In the end, that was what had made the difference between an exceptional agent and herself.

But she'd gone back to see Waugheirt, and he'd become her boss. He'd begun by giving her files on people's networks. Easy: compile a dossier on someone without their noticing. She hadn't had to try too hard. People liked to talk to her. She'd changed milieu. It was goodbye to the districts of Paris where the pavements were thronged with people, goodbye to smoke-filled bars frequented by prostitutes and addicts, goodbye to basements that were sordid but lived in, kitchens smelling of grease, and flea-infested bedsits. Now she only did trips to districts full of banks and town houses. She'd specialized in businessmen, politicians, industrialists... Waugheirt kept her at it, but he was a little disappointed. He had expected a more brilliant success. She didn't care, because now she was making three times as much money. Then a journalist from Ivory Coast had gone missing in the centre of Paris, nobody explained to her why it was urgent to find him fast, but they took it very seriously. It had taken her three days to locate the place he was hiding out, in Canada. Getting hold of him physically was someone else's job. Waugheirt had been so pleased that he patted her on the shoulder, the equivalent in his body language of a bear hug. It was as if someone had pointed out the zone to her on a map. Built-in compass. From then on, her name had become blue-chip. She'd started to play for high stakes, probably for the thrill of getting caught. Selling information commissioned by one person to someone else, or passing it to a third party. Selling false intelligence, playing a double game, making sure someone else would pay better. Protected. Always protected. It had lasted ten years. Of tightrope walking. The feverishness of the gambler. Raw emotion takes you close to disaster. Around her, accidental deaths started to become frequent, suicides, overdoses, unexpected fatalities from a minor infection, often after a stay in hospital. But as time passed, her talent was becoming worn out, following a curve inverse to that of her popularity.

She had become too well-known in her milieu. She couldn't turn up anywhere without people immediately knowing who she was. Even in the depths of Chechnya, a cub reporter could spot her at once. The Hyena's here. In the circumstances, it was hard to keep on being a good agent. And she realized that for her, it was over.

The evening she had met Lucie, she had only turned up to see the little brunette who hung around at Cro-Mag's bar, and who was playing sufficiently hard-to-get to make it exciting. She didn't feel she'd slipped so far down the rankings as to envisage seriously going after a missing kid. Still, it was a way to find out how Reldanch worked, pick up some information, keep in the loop... but on finding out what Lucie looked like physically, she'd felt rather depressed: typical bog-standard straight girl, a bit scruffy, but not enough to show character. No fun, full stop. And then she'd seen the photo of Valentine. A bombshell of emotion, stunning and irrational. Something in the kid's eyes had burst open her thoracic cavity. Nothing sexual, no, much more disturbing than that. A tailspin, out of control. Inexplicable but imperative. This little girl had called for her entire attention. She had to be found, it was impossible to define exactly what she had to be protected from, but the Hyena had immediately known that she had no choice, she had to get going. She had to see this kid. It was poorly paid work, not interesting, and she was teamed up with a dozy mollusc. On the trail of a little rich girl, indistinguishable from thousands of other mixed-up teenagers... but this one had called out to her. And yet the Hyena had understood almost at once that it would be no use. What was on the way was inevitable, but she had to go and take a closer look.

Now she goes back into the church, finds the agreed place, front pew facing another crucifix on the right of the main door. Juan's late. Always incapable of arriving on time at the rendezvous he's arranged himself. One of the strategies of this poor man's Anthony Blunt: he makes you wait, to make sure you need him enough to hang about for an hour. Juan is undeniably a genius, his memory above all is remarkable. His brain holds an encyclopedic amount of knowledge, he could beat anyone at Trivial Pursuit, but in the age of the internet, who cares if someone knows everything? Juan had arrived in Paris convinced he was going to have a brilliant career, and that his alpha-plus academic patter would wipe out his working-class origins. It had taken him a while to realize that the upper classes sense each other by smell, and spot intruders the same way. Try as he might to be invited to fashionable dinner parties, nobody had ever offered him the kind of work he'd dreamed of. Then he'd been run into by a smart alec from the secret services, who'd spotted him, and treated him well, in exchange for some gossip and a few nuggets of real information. Juan quickly realized he had become an informer, and the idea filled him with joy. He'd specialised in Zionist milieux. He'd been helped to find a suitable publisher, with whom he'd put out a book on the question. An attentive observer would have been surprised at the ease with which he managed to write articles in the newspapers and receive state grants. For a while, he'd published on subjects that interested his paymasters. His books got him entry to conferences, to book launches, to debates with specialists, and he wrote reports, not always very serious, on the chattering classes. He was well connected, so he provided good material. Informers are like prostitutes: made to believe they're protected, that they're irreplaceable and respected. But they can be quickly crossed off guest lists, nothing is sadder than a tart who's been around the block one too many times. So he'd served his turn, survived a few months longer by specializing in placing comments on the internet. On current affairs, or personalities who were to be protected or attacked, depending on the orders he received: he bombarded the internet with messages. Then, overnight, probably after some kind of administrative shakeout, he'd been dropped like a stone, and offered up to exposure. The kind of thing that didn't necessarily happen because one had made a mistake, it could just be because of a personnel reshuffle, different mood music, one's face didn't fit. So he had changed country. These days, he is an assiduous visitor to the Alliance Française, and passes on as best he can what the expats are up to in his neck of the woods. He must still be getting a few state grants for books yet to be written. By dint of playing the affable little Frenchman, politically active and turning up at all kinds of demos, he knows the city very well.

He arrives a good half-hour late, stops at the threshold of the chapel, looks round, then comes to sit near enough for them to hear each other but not for anyone to realize they're talking. Leaning forward, hands clasped, he's looking straight ahead, at the altar.

'There are a lot of French girls her age in Barcelona, not sure I've identified her.'

'You got me all the way here to say that?'

'Well, I've been told about a kid who could be her... but I'm not sure. She's been seen several times, talking to a sister of the Mission of Charity.'

'Sister of *what*?'

'Remember the Mother Teresa look? Sandals, blue and white habit? It's that lot, the Sisters of the Mission of Charity.'

'Valentine? I think you may be barking up the wrong tree, you know.'

'Well, it's all I've got. A Sister Elisabeth. I've been told about her and a little French girl who looks like your one.'

'Do they have a convent round here, these sisters?'

'Not in Barcelona anyway. I've been trying to find out what they're doing here. Perhaps they were taking part in an international seminar on emigration organized by Opus Dei last month. That's all I know.'

He's lying, without trying to hide it.

'Big help, what you've given me. Finding a nun in Barcelona...'

'These nuns go round in a group, they're not staying in a hotel, they must be being put up in a local convent. And there aren't that many left, come to that.'

He must have his reasons to send her chasing round all the convents in the region.

The Hyena leaves the cathedral, in the streets you hear all the languages in the world. There are too many people for the surface of the city centre. She has to walk a long way to find an internet café, they've got rarer now that everyone has a laptop. She sits in front of a computer with a keyboard that's been used so much that some of the keys are worn bare. She googles 'Barcelona convent' and orders a *cortado*.

An hour in the train to get to the foot of the mountain. She's opted for Montserrat. Because you should never pass up the chance to see a Black Virgin. Harsh sunlight. A range of giant stone mountains rising up from the ground stretches kilometres up into the sky.

To reach the summit, you have to take a funicular. The trip seems long and oppressive, because of the deep ravine that the train climbs through. Slightly disappointing when you get to the top: a burger bar, a souvenir shop, cobbled streets. Less impressive than it looked from down below. A determinedly contemporary effort has been made to desacralize any place where your soul might take wing. Naked emotion without the mediation of shops would probably get in the way of selling knick-knacks.

Most of the tourists have brought their children along, though it's hard to see what fun a kid of three years old could have in this kind of place. They are either crying or running wild under the indulgent eyes of their mummies. Children are the authorized vectors of their parents' anti-social behaviour. The adults roll their eyes, pretending to be unable to cope with the destructive vitality of their little ones, but it's easy to see they're happy to be able to get on everyone else's tits with impunity via their progeny. What hatred of the world can have driven them to duplicate themselves so much?

ELISABETH

STANDING IN THE COURTYARD, ELISABETH listens with half an ear to the little Indian woman describing in her precise but unattractive English the attack on the convent of the Sisters of Charity which she had witnessed one night in Sukananda. Hundreds of men, armed with axes, clubs and knives, sacked the order's building. The brothers and sisters had had time to take refuge a few kilometres away. Fundamentalist Hindus were demanding that the Christians get out of the region. Someone somewhere hadn't been properly bribed. Things like that didn't happen in Mother Teresa's day. The Albanian nun knew where to find the best protection.

It's the tenth time in two days that the Indian woman has repeated her story, including the most sordid details. At first, it was very moving. But in the end, the sisters are wishing above all that she'd cut it short. Around her, they all exhibit the same patient smile. The level of sincerity behind the grimace varies from one to another. Not all of them are dead from the neck up. But others are, frankly, a bit touched. The austere mode of life to which they have submitted doesn't rule out the ardent awakening of superior faith, but more often it encourages the most arid kind of idiocy. The day before yesterday, Elisabeth saw two of them praying that the doors of the truck into which they were supposed to be loading large refrigerators would get wider. On their knees in front of the trailer, fervently supplicating God, in his great goodness, to create a little extra space so that they could get the load in. You can get used to that, even, but it takes a lot of patience.

Elisabeth observes the figure approaching the group. She recognizes it from a distance. She never forgets a face. She interrupts the Indian woman with a gentle gesture, excusing herself in order to walk away unaccompanied. Her juniors are used to it. She has her privileges. She walks with little steps, bending over. An elderly woman, slightly built, radiant and energetic, her face framed in the blue and white coif of the Sisters of Charity. The resemblance is striking. It makes you think right away of the famous Albanian. A closer examination of her features immediately destroys the illusion, but the point has been made: at her approach, people are already disarmed.

The Hyena is exactly what Elisabeth has been expecting: a brazen invertebrate, the worst kind of person this age has produced. Abject beings, flaunting their lack of grace, and proud to live like animals. One doesn't even think of Satan on seeing her approach: he would choose a more impressive shape. Not this long, slim, flexible body, stupidly pleased with itself.

'Are you looking for anyone? I'm Sister Elisabeth.'

The Hyena shows neither surprise nor fear. Her encephalogram is too steady for her to demonstrate amazement.

'Sister Elisabeth? Did someone warn you I was coming?'

'Oh, you know... people come to see me.'

'Your headquarters isn't that easy to get to, is it? But it's worth the trip. Lovely place.'

'Very inspirational. Yes.'

'I'm looking for a French teenager, Valentine Galtan. I believe you've had some contact with her?'

'Valentine? Valentine ... what was the name?'

She deliberately uses the intonations of a little old lady, a bit deaf, but with her wits about her. People like that style. She's acquired more charisma with every line on her face. She's feared and respected, it's instinctive. She doesn't feel old in herself. In fact, she feels less old than she did ten years ago. She's had a new lease of life, she forgets to feel her body declining.

'Ah yes, yes. Valentine. A very young girl? Yes, I do remember her. A lively child, intelligent, but very lonely. Would you like to come with me, we could have a few quiet words.'

She points to a side path. Above it, the stone mountains rise vertically, hieratically. If you look up, their mass hides the sky. The Hyena follows her slowly. Something seems to be oppressing her.

'This is steep, are we going far up?'

'No, no, here we are. Do you suffer from vertigo?'

'Let's say I wouldn't like someone to give me a push.'

'What a strange idea! Do you feel guilty about something?'

'No, but you know how it is... A young girl, the Church, you immediately get ideas about satanic rituals, orgies, St Andrew's crosses, dirty photos, with some violent climax as a bonus. You might have a good reason to want me out of the way, mightn't you?'

Sister Elisabeth turns round and gives her a look heavy with reproach, but also laden with benevolence. Since she's taken the veil, this has always worked a treat. She can short-circuit aggression. The Hyena remains hermetic, too shameless to let herself be intimidated.

'Dear me, you must have a very dark idea of our evangelical mission. But let me reassure you. I am not at all familiar with the group practices you refer to...'

The lesbian seems to listen in silence. Her profile is classic, and when she stops showing off, you can see that she would have been a beautiful woman.

There aren't many tourists at this time of year. The two women sit down side by side on a small stone bench. Opposite are the clouds, almost within arm's reach. A bird swoops down into the void, hundreds of metres, then lands, with careless accuracy, on a little branch protruding from the rock.

Elisabeth could do with a cigarette. She gave it up, without difficulty, for the first years after taking the veil – sisters aren't permitted to smoke. But she's been feeling like it again, these last months. The worst thing is her dreams. She smokes in them every night. Next morning, she feels pierced with blind stabs, a terrible craving for nicotine. She gives in to temptation when she can manage it. That's not often. She's rarely alone. She shares her bedroom with an African woman just back from Boston. The sisters get moved around, to protect them from getting like the lesbian for instance. Relationships can quickly become too intense, the young ones aren't always hard-wired to resist. Turning her face up to the sun, the Hyena looks like a satisfied lizard. She speaks without turning her head, her eyes closed against the blinding light. 'Are you not allowed to smoke, among the sisters?'

'What do you think?'

It's a nasty coincidence, as if the other woman could read her thoughts. The lesbian offers her a cigarette. She accepts it. Nobody can see them here. A slight dizziness, then immediate relief at the first draw.

Sister Elisabeth pats the lesbian's hand reassuringly. She's surprised at the warm smoothness of her skin.

'But tell me, why are you looking for Valentine Galtan?'

'She's run away from home. Her father and her grandmother have called in a detective agency. So you have met her?'

'Yes, I've come across her. You know, these youngsters, they come to me hungry, I don't ask questions. She's a brave little thing.'

'Do you know where she is now?'

'No, I haven't the slightest idea. Valentine's path crossed mine. I told her not to be afraid, I could see she'd recover. And she went off, just as she'd come, without any explanation.'

'So why drag me all the way out here?'

'I didn't ask you to come, my child. You came here of your own accord.'

Elisabeth remembers the Hyena perfectly well. And the extremely unpleasant impression she had already made on her, long ago, in Oxford, in the early 1990s. Elisabeth was running a course in rapid reading and memory improvement. It was the first time she had been teaching for the US National

Education Agency. The purpose was to spot the most interesting pupils and report them to her hierarchy. They could be recruited and trained. It would be her speciality for some years. She had always had a good eye. She was never a good teacher, because mediocre pupils soon bored her. But she homed in quickly on elite individuals. They are rare. Good brains have been that way since childhood, so one can't expect miracles.

She remembers the Hyena, from that winter in Oxford, because the lesbian had taken a keen interest in the seminar on offer. Not because of her job as a hybrid detective, partly working in the private sector and partly for state secret services, but because a girl she was attached to had signed up to it. Elisabeth remembers this perverted presence, prowling round her new protegée. A brilliant pupil with exceptional potential. She, Elisabeth, had had the last word, and the girl had resisted the morbid temptation implicit in any relation with the degenerate element. But it had been a close-run thing. The Hyena – she already had the nickname in those days – had that haughty arrogance that disturbs young minds.

The daughter, wife and mother of military men, Elisabeth knows all about willpower. Having a backbone. Nothing makes it easier to convince other people than to be convinced yourself, and she had won that battle in a fierce struggle.

Her son had died, shortly beforehand. Not yet thirty, he liked driving fast cars. A fatal crash.

His death hadn't driven her into depression. She isn't that kind of woman. She has never known the intoxication of great sorrow. Death simply robbed her of everything that had any value for her. But the past will always be there. Nothing can change it. She doesn't believe in God, but she feels there is a journey to be made, and that you have to do it with your head held high. And not soften on the way. Right, left, atheists, believers, in the end they all speak the same language, they all end up in tears. She doesn't have any faith. At first she had thought it might come. She wasn't asking for a spectacular revelation. She wasn't one of those crazy erotomaniacs who need to brandish their devotion to God and their intimate relation with the deity as if they were boasting of masturbation. She isn't vain, she has no need to be distinguished by some extraordinary vision of a saint or the Virgin Mary. But she had expected that devotion would take possession of her in the same way that love and respect for her fatherland had. She was prepared for fervour. The loss of the son around whom she had organized her life had carved out a sublime emptiness inside her. She could have filled it with faith. Like a marriage of reason, when love grows out of the habit of sharing the life of your partner.

The first year she had been with the sisters, the silence inside her had been total. Invaluable calm. Then her critical faculties had returned. That was her character. In India, one day, she had been observing, along the room, a volunteer leaning over a patient who had just died, and had reflected how disagreeable was that way of exhibiting your delight at being a witness to other people's suffering without being able to do anything to relieve it. The young volunteer had an ecstatic smile on her lips, her hands were trembling with unhealthy excitement, as she pronounced the last prayer. You could see she was happy to be there, that she was feeling superior to anyone else, because she was sacrificing two months of her holiday to watch other people die. Everything in her demeanour pointed to the most shameless, the most inappropriate self-satisfaction. A charity based on pride and the will to do more and better than other people. Elisabeth had thought that the young ninny in tears would have been incapable of retaining her dignity if it had been her own child lying there, with maggots eating the wounds on its legs.

Their outfit hadn't been a hospital: they gave no medical care, because they had no resources. The number of beds was insufficient for all the sick people, and most of the bodies were groaning on mats on the floor. Until that particular day, Elisabeth had made no judgements, she had simply done as she was asked. Change dressings, clean infected wounds, bring the dying a bowl of rice, help them to eat. She was also there to send back accounts of everything she saw around her, and any information she could pick up, to certain superiors. They had not suggested that she take the veil out of vocation, but because they wanted information about Mother Teresa's succession. Although this service had been unofficially requested by a member of Opus Dei, Elisabeth had good reason to think that her information was also relayed at once to the secret services of her country. Considering the colossal sums of money transferred by the Missionaries of Charity, it was logical that someone wanted to make sure the exchanges could be traced. She had been carrying out her mission for some months without passing judgement on the people around her. Even the idiotic volunteer. But it had woken her critical antennae. The harsh relentless intelligence that let nothing escape it. And which made it hard to tolerate the presence of other human beings. Her eyes had opened again, her words had organized themselves into sentences: the placid stupidity of this sister, the excessive ego of that one, the tedious machinations of a third... and her own loneliness.

She scorned the prohibitions she had imposed on herself, the sickening but ecstatic poverty which encouraged only the develoment of crass stupidity, the constant proximity of the other missionary nuns, sometimes good women who had taken the chance to flee the poverty of their homeland, but more often simpletons whose brains, already not too impressive, had literally melted under the effect of the spiritual, material and emotional privations forced on them.

For a long time, she'd been forgotten. The people at the top had changed, the leaders of her country were only interested in undermining their own allies. No one came to ask her for information any more. She had not been too distressed. She had arranged to return to Europe, and there she had taken on new responsibilities and distinctions. Last year in London, a man had arrived, declaring he wanted to make a donation and asking to speak with her in private. He'd claimed to be high up in the secret services. She'd taken him for a crackpot. He was obsessed with the restoration of the Christian faith in Europe, and was convinced that wars needed to be waged on several fronts: against sects, against Islam, against Judaism, against capitalism. The more he went on, the harder it got to see who he thought his allies would be in this war, in which he seemed to be the only person involved. He was a young man, one of those saps who hadn't even been snatched from his mother to do his military service, but who was quite sure of his virility. Still, from the amount of information he conveyed, she had had to admit in the end that he really did have the contacts he was boasting about. He arranged for regular, discreet payments into an account in Sister Elisabeth's name. So that was the point they'd reached, in the country for which she had always considered she should be ready to die: they were using extroverted and unstable eccentrics for the top responsible jobs, they were letting the show be run by halfwits. When he had asked her to keep her eyes open, on the ground, to find a young man prepared to make the greatest of sacrifices, she had only half-listened. Then he had sent her off to Barcelona, officially to study the possibility – at a time of collapsing house prices and the influx of impoverished Christians from all over the world – of opening a convent; unofficially because he encouraged her to re-establish contact with old friends from Opus Dei. Because they weren't in her good books either.

Then Valentine had stumbled into her – literally– in the street. Having drunk too much, the teenager had tripped over the nun, as she knelt over an unconscious wretch lying in the gutter. The teenager had immediately clung on to her, a child with alcohol on her breath, a waif, staggering round, too young to be repulsive. A little bird intoxicated with wine. She had stammered out a few words about her grandfather and his faith. In spiritual terms, Valentine was about as aware as a pumpkin. But she was emotionally attached to memories of prayers in the family. And very quickly, before she had been asked anything, she had come out with 'I don't know how you manage it, loving your neighbour and going on your knees to try and clean people's wounds... because when I see the crap we live in, all I can think is I want to blow it sky-high.'

Recruit and train. Sister Elisabeth had her doubts though. This little girl was suspiciously docile, too easily led for new impressions to remain fixed firmly on her. There was some duplicity there, which made her hard to manoeuvre. She had quite a lively intelligence, but superficial and disorganized. Still, she had all the right attributes: poor relationship with her family, unstable personality, massively attention-seeking. From that point, things had got moving. Until she had been warned of the two private detectives arriving in Barcelona. Who have turned up a bit soon, before the teenager has been fully trained.

Consequently, Sister Elisabeth has been informed that it would be good if she could wrap up her report on Barcelona as soon as possible, so as to follow Valentine back to Paris. And the moment has arrived.

You never know exactly who you are working for. And you don't know for whose sake you die. Not a problem. Sister Elisabeth does what she has always done, what those humans she admires have always done, she obeys orders.

'No, really, I'm afraid I can't help you. I'm so sorry. The last time I saw Valentine, she mentioned some friends... squatters somewhere, I think? I tried to persuade her to go home, but...'

She doesn't have time to finish her sentence. A harsh animal cry escapes from the Hyena, who has closed her eyes in a grimace. She turns to face the nun, rage darkening her gaze. Her state of alarm is grotesque. The old woman shows neither surprise nor fear. She knows all about the brutality of the weak. Degenerates mistake this for strength: an emotional outburst. The lesbian snarls: 'Aren't you ashamed of yourself?'

Without replying, Sister Elisabeth looks her straight in the eye, simulating sincere astonishment, while thinking to herself, What right have *you* got to talk about shame, you poor pervert?

The Hyena replies out loud, as if she had read her thoughts. 'I can't lecture anyone about morality, but I don't ponce about in a little white sari and a holier-than-thou expression. I don't do deals on the backs of children.'

Sister Elisabeth feels the bite of cold sweat on her back. She has nothing but scorn for the kind of pathetic sentimentality behind that kind of remark – there's no way nations can be governed simply with good intentions – but she can't suppress a moment of panic at the thought that this lesbian really can read her mind. The Hyena hammers home her advantage: 'Yes, of course I can! What did you think? And you won't get away with it. I'm picking you up on my radar, like I've never picked anyone up before!'

'But what on earth has come over you, my child?'

Never admit anything. Block your thoughts. Matters mustn't be compromised by this stupid incident. A little bird perches a few feet from them and pecks at crumbs from a tourist's sandwiches. Sister Elisabeth spreads her hands as a sign of impotence. 'My child, what can you be imagining? What is there so terrible that could concern this little girl? Lord in heaven, perhaps I should have taken more care of her than I did. Do you want me to try and help you find her? I could ask around if you like, and let you know if I get any news?'

'Why *her*? Didn't you have anyone else from your own people? Couldn't you send your own children?'

'But I'm offering you my help, to get her home safe and sound... And I think I really want to help you. As I said, I'm sure it would be worth trying to find out something from these squatters...'

'Because she was all alone, wasn't she? Alone and easy to influence?'

WE AVOIDED THE SUBJECT BUT ZOSKA KNEW that what we were doing didn't make sense. After lunch, waving Valentine's photo, we checked the bars, the tobacconists, the record shops, the stores selling T-shirts and trainers. Then we had a coffee on a terrace, and after that we just strolled aimlessly, without asking ourselves whether it wasn't a bit odd to spend a day doing nothing in the middle of an investigation that was already more or less stalled.

Sticking close to Zoska, I'm electrified whenever her elbow brushes against mine. We eat ice creams on a bench in the sun, and I wonder whether I have ever lived such a sweet and perfect moment, as round as a bubble. Zoska says she doesn't want to stay in Barcelona, that the city has been ruined by tourism, that she's doing drugs too much here, and that everything's expensive. But for someone who wants to get away, she seems to me to be pretty pleased with the life here.

I really want to have sex with her. The side effects of the scene of that evening when we arrived here, which horrified me at the time, are disturbing now. Flashes of images, of sensations, running in a loop, are obsessing me, but pleasantly. The expression she had on her face, the slight smile on her lips, when she pulled on the gloves. I really want to have sex with her. As fiercely as I'm afraid of it at the same time.

Everything she does drives me crazy. She makes the things she's interested in seem important, even if they're super-boring at first. She's only got to look at a car she likes, and I want to know more about engine size.

I like the way she lets me know I'm attractive to her. It's peaceful. I don't bother my head wondering how we're going to get round to kissing, and if it'll be the way I want it. The pit of my stomach is the centre of my feelings, I can feel it reacting with fear, desire, impatience and excitement. I'm listening exclusively to it now. I'm in orbit round her gestures. Fascinated by her hands. Worried by the toughness of her gaze. I love the way her voice goes down a few semitones when she speaks in Spanish.

We end up on a square, in front of the gallery of contemporary art. A huge white building, with about thirty skateboarders on the space in front of it. A deafening noise. Kids sitting round the edges are drinking from beer cans sold by Pakistani vendors. Zoska spots something I can't see, asks me to wait a minute. She goes over to a group of teenagers, talks to them, takes them aside, and comes back a couple of minutes later. I put two and two together and gather she's dealing. That explains why she has this fancy motorbike, although she's only a part-time waitress getting six euros an hour. And why she moves from place to place so much, since her love of foreign languages isn't enough to explain her perpetual need to travel on.

In the Raval, the windows have posters up saying 'Respect the dignity of this district'. I ask Zoska if it's a protest about the horrible new buildings they're putting up in the city centre. Zoska says it's against prostitutes. My mistake makes her laugh. She glances into a bar, I imagine she doesn't see the clients she was expecting to find, and she turns to me. 'I'm worn out. I've parked a long way from here. I want to go back to my place before I have to go to work.'

'Yes, I'd better be going too.'

'Want me to give you a ride? It's further to your hotel than to my bike.'

Clinging to her as we speed along, I fling my head back. It's night-time. The sky's nothing like in Paris. Here, you can see the stars.

I'm aware of her back, her body against mine. To be able to clasp my hands round her belly, pretending to be afraid of falling off, makes me deliriously happy. Everything becomes interesting when you want someone. When it happens, you get this special kind of intoxication. It's been a long time. I tell myself it's as good as when I was fourteen. But that's wrong. Being fourteen was never as good as this. On the contrary, it was a tough, lonely sort of time, the worst moment of my life. I was never a little princess. My life was full of humiliations, brutal prohibitions, failures, and the inability to do things. I was scared of everything when I was fourteen, with nothing to protect me.

I gaze at the silver chain she wears round her neck. My entire body focuses on this detail. And I feel that even my ankles are enjoying looking at the metal links on her skin. Her profile when she turns her head to change lanes. Her way of turning round at a red light to ask if I'm OK. She likes me.

In front of the hotel, she takes back the helmet she lent

me. I ask her if we'll see each other tomorrow. She looks at me, moves slowly closer, and stands still, less than a pace away. We stay there like that, facing each other, for a long moment without touching. She comes nearer, I sway on my feet. Slide into her, between her lips. Under my skin, my libido is doing crazy somersaults. I'm high, on her. It lasts a long moment, just that kiss.

Then she leaves me there, saying we'll be in touch.

A pure high, without coming down. Like helium. A quiet bomb with a warhead that I need to explode on her.

At three in the morning, I'm not asleep when she finally texts me: 'Can I come to C U?'

The sun is flooding the grotty carpet with golden light. My tongue feels numb – after so much mucus contact with her I've picked up the remains of the coke. It's 8 a.m. by the hotel alarm clock, and I'm smoking by the window. Zoska's asleep, lying on her back. When she came to join me, in the middle of the night, she was a bit drunk, warmer and more expansive than in the day. I liked it that she was like that. Easy to make contact with. We made love until dawn made her roll on to her side, and close her eyes, leaving me unsleeping. It was all reflexes: I touch her and I feel inside my own body what I'm doing to her; she strokes me and it's in my own skin that I feel hers when I touch her, the limits have melted, we're wound round each other. I wake her up, sit astride her, clasp her to me, her whole body tells me to go ahead. She rakes me with her fingers, something is released, I'm soaking the sheets. It's a tempo quite different from anything I've ever known, unending, happening to a different rhythm.

When she leaves in the morning, I'm not sure if I'll see her again. I ask her this while she's doing up her trainers. 'What are you going to do today?' She turns to look at me over her shoulder and smiles. 'I keep forgetting you work for the police.' Then she gets up, picks up her jacket, kisses my shoulder, says I smell nice, and goes out. I tell myself that she's doing it on purpose, it's a ploy to make me come apart, a ridiculous manoeuvre. It works. I spend the morning with one eye on my mobile. I go down to rejoin the Hyena. Finding Valentine has frankly never been an obsession for me, but now it's become the outer edge of the outer edge of my worries. I arrive in the bar where she's waiting for me and she gives me a long hard stare.

'You look very well, that's odd. Have you been in the hotel beauty parlour or what?'

I make like I have no idea what she's talking about, ask her what she did yesterday, and pretend that we combed the whole city like lunatics. She's not listening, she frowns as if she is trying to resolve a particularly thorny problem.

'Very strange. You look much more, well, luminous, don't you?'

And as I say nothing, she starts to sing 'Like a virgin, touched for the very first time like a v-i-i-irgin'.

I ask again whether she's found anything new in our search, and she sighs. 'I'll spare you the details of what my day was like yesterday. Cutting it short: Valentine got pally with this nun. Don't look like that, I thought it was weird too. This said nun has advised me to go and have a look in some squat…'

'We've already checked out Nazis, Muslims, toffs from the

sixteenth arrondissement... so now it's the Church and the loony left. You are joking, aren't you?'

'Well, she's certainly getting around, she's touched all the bases.'

'Do you have any serious leads?'

'No. But I get the feeling someone's going to help us find her. We're not going to have to strain ourselves.'

'And this feeling's based on what?'

'Call it my instinct. Don't ask. Meanwhile our programme for today is, go and have a coffee in the central bookshop in Eixample.'

'Has someone tipped you off about this?'

'No, but I have met this bookseller. A redhead. She's playing hard to get. Really kills me.'

'And you met her where?'

'In a bar, last night, I don't know if you remember, but last night you seemed to want to stay in your hotel. Busy, apparently. So I went out on my own.'

'We're not being paid to pick up hard-to-get booksellers.'

'Well, no. As I recall it though, I haven't been paid. Are you coming, or do you have some other plan?'

So we find ourselves on the first floor of the bookshop, La Centrale. Wooden floors, low voices, white benches. Their hot chocolate's good, but I don't know what the heck we're doing here. The Hyena is hyped up. She's put on the table all the books she could find about Montserrat. I'm afraid she's decided to go and do some tourism. She flips through the pages, and sometimes stops reading to tell me it's this fantastic site, that aliens are known to have visited it, that flashing lights have been seen in the sky overhead, or that

Himmler in person went there in search of the Holy Grail. I glance absently at the photos and say yeah, it does look nice. Big rocky mountains. I don't know what else to say.

I'm thinking about Zoska's sunglasses, I'm thinking about the space between her shoulders, I'm thinking about the little half-moon tattoo over her navel. And the bracelet of plaited leather on her wrist. The bookseller comes over to us. She doesn't look that great to me.

'I really would like to learn Catalan. But I've never found someone to give me lessons.'

'There are free linguistic normalization classes, you know...'

'I can't possibly go to anything called normalization. But I saw this book downstairs about Montserrat, it looked very good. But it's in Catalan! Do you think you might be able to translate a few paragraphs for me?'

The bookseller, who has very short hair and such a strict expression that it's depressing, to me at least, puts her down. No, she doesn't know the book. Then she gets up and leaves us. The Hyena watches her walk away, then goes and leans on the counter, she looks more like she's trying to pick up the barista by the end. Two whole hours doing bloody nothing. I'm getting fed up.

'Are we going to hang around a long time like this, doing nothing?'

'It's quite simple. I'm not budging from here till you tell me everything you did yesterday.'

'I don't know what you're talking about. Shouldn't we be finding out about these leftie squatters?'

'What you don't understand is that we've moved into a

kind of Zen phase of the search. It works if you sit still. We don't go looking, but we'll find. Get it?' The Hyena crosses her legs and puts her elbows on the table. 'If we find our little Valentine, what will you do about Zoska? Are you going to have a serious relationship with her?'

'It's not at all what you think.'

'Oh really? Would you be freaked out if you had to tell people you're with another girl?'

'I can't see what's freaky about it. Excuse me, I don't live in the nineteenth century.'

'Oh really? So you'd tell your parents?'

'Of course.'

'OK. So I'm making a big fuss about something, when everyone else is cool with it.'

But I've had time to imagine being at home, sitting across the table from my father and announcing to him, casually, that I'm going to live with my new girlfriend. And what the neighbours will say, if they see me living with a girl, when my flat isn't big enough for two beds. The Hyena hasn't finished.

'But do you have room for you both, in Paris?'

'Oh come on, lay off it. We just spent a night together, it's not...'

'Aha! So you did. Now we're getting somewhere. You did spend the night together, then, I wasn't dreaming. Bitch, I almost didn't think so. But OK, now that you've chosen to confide in me, and let me say you couldn't have made a better choice – a word of warning right away. You don't know dykes. She'll turn up with her suitcases, asking for a spare key, before you've had time to remember the colour of her eyes. Because she can do her job anywhere. But apart from that, believe me, you're living the best moment of your life. Heterosexuality is as natural as the electric fence they put round a field of cows. From now on, big girl, welcome to the wide open spaces.'

And for the first time since we've met, this kind of stupid statement makes me want to smile.

VALENTINE

I'm plague, I'm cholera
Bird flu, the neutron bomb,
I'm a radioactive bitch
I'm a vicious little witch.
Aliens, humans all polluters
Universal contaminators

SITTING IN THE SHADE OF A TREE WITH gigantic pink flowers that look like velvet, Valentine closes the black Moleskine notebook she stole from the stationer's where she photocopied the false declaration of the theft of her identity papers. She's only half-satisfied with the last rhyme. She's in a little park. She yawns. An old man with a beard and a huge belly ventures towards her corner. He's wearing flipflops, so you can see his revolting feet, with their long yellow toenails split at the ends. Surprised to see her there, he mutters something in a language she'd be hard put to identify, German, Catalan, Turkish, then he retreats. She's relieved that he's gone away. Then a man comes past, pushing a child in a pram so hi-tech it could enter for the Paris–Dakar rally. Three teenage girls, her own age, walk towards her taking no notice, their wrists are laden with bracelets, they each hold a mobile and are chattering away. When she thinks she looked like that not so long ago. She's changed a lot. She is very attentive to her short biography. She looks back over it willingly, it's all she's got now. Her life. She remembers how the school terms followed one after another. Her old life. The Twilight phase, when you dream of this fantastic vampire, your hair's dyed red and your eyes are sore because you've rubbed them so hard to get the makeup off – she had to set her alarm an hour early, to have time to put on two sets of eyeliner and get them more or less symmetrical. Then there was the neo-metal phase, but people tell me that's for dummies, so I switch to the hardcore punk New York scene of the eighties, and my religion is Agnostic Front. Followed by the 'I'm just a bimbo' phase – that's the only way guys are going to like you – but I'm not really a slag, I can afford designer handbags. And I can feel cynical when I do a few lines of coke. All this past seems far away now. In the last year everything speeded up.

It had all begun with Carlito, more or less. It wasn't exactly a *coup de foudre*. It was in front of this club, Le Divan du Monde. She was hanging about at the door, on her own, hoping that one of the boys from Panic Up Yours, who were playing there that night, would come past and give her a backstage pass. She bombarded them with texts they never replied to. Sometimes she slept with them: in town they showed off as tough guys who could have anyone, but didn't give a shit – except that in fact when they were on their own, without their mates, and naked in bed, they were as soft as little puppies and hardly any more threatening in the sack. At first sight, Carlito and his gang had bothered her. They were coming out of an alternative bar and hanging about on the opposite pavement, vaguely harassing the crowd waiting for Panic Up Yours. They looked like anti-capitalist campaigners, just watching them you sensed a bad smell. They hadn't yet found the suckers they were looking for, but hadn't yet decided to split. Valentine was pretending to be reading texts on her mobile, and Carlito had crossed the street to ask her outright, 'Hey you, can you give me ten euros, please?'

'Ten euros? Inca bonnets too pricey, are they?'

She was sure that if he lifted a finger against her, the bouncers would leap on him. A little bourgeois girl like her and a big layabout like him, there'd always be someone to defend her.

Carlito had carried on in his loud voice, 'Oho, little miss smelly puss, we've got a sense of humour, have we?'

'Oh, leave me alone, get a life! Go find an anti-racist demo at Bastille or somewhere.'

He didn't impress her. Too fat. She didn't like guys with bellies. If, at that moment, an angel had come down and told her, *this man will change your life*, she'd have burst out laughing. He went a few steps away, but not far, she could feel him looking at her, while he went on doing his panhandling. There were fewer people around now. At the front of house, she humiliated herself pleading with one of the big dumb bouncers to let her in. The concert had started. She kept sending texts, still to no avail. She'd decided to beat it, feeling disgusted, she'd have to go past those three zombies to get to the metro, so she changed pavements, but it wasn't enough. Carlito had started following her.

'Go on, give me ten euros, I know you've got them, I so

want you to give me them. I love it when girls like you give me money, it really turns me on.'

They were both standing on the boulevard. And then this total wanker, wearing a grotty tracksuit tucked into cheap white socks, a wanker, yeah, but six foot tall, decided to get involved. 'Leave her alone, she's my girl,' – and he took her by the arm to pull her away. Bad scene. Obviously, Carlito was going to split, and leave her to sort it out with this half-witted giant. But no, he didn't push off, or even bother to argue, his arm had shot up, his fist clenched. One fierce punch. An uppercut to the jaw, like in wrestling matches where the opponents are mismatched; and the loser staggered backwards, obeying all the rules, almost in slow motion. Carlito had turned round to face the other guy's allies, with a twisted smile on his lips, and his own two sidekicks were already behind him, arms folded. You had to give them that, they relished a fight. Someone in the group growled, 'Look out! cops, cops coming,' the two protagonists threw looks of hate at each other, indicating, 'going 'cos we got to, but we'd really like to smash your face in'. And everyone dispersed, quickly but casually, hands in pockets. Without running or turning round, but taking oblique routes through the street, hugging the wall so as to turn the corner faster. And Valentine had fallen into step with Carlito. He seemed to think it natural that she should attach herself to him, and talked to her as if he knew her. 'See, if we hadn't been there, you'd really have been in the shit.' The two sidekicks laughed at everything he said, it didn't take long to see he was the boss. They stopped in front of a grungy bar near Pigalle, and Carlito had asked, as if it was a done deal, 'Right, those ten euros, going to shell them out now, buy us a beer?' They knew the manageress, it stank of grease inside, and Valentine disliked this kind of place, smelling of old people, poor people, and unhealthy fast food. She didn't say much, just took it all in. More pals of theirs had come to join them and a little gang had gathered round Carlito. It was sort of fun to be sitting at table with the kind of people she normally despised. Without actually calculating, Carlito arranged things so that she was sitting next to him, showing off that she was his little fun item of the day, and nobody else was about to contradict him. She watched everything around her, thinking this would make a good story afterwards to tell her real friends. It takes some time to learn other people's way of talking, and Valentine was too inexperienced to pick up everything that was going on. Carlito was cocksure and she liked that. At one point he'd turned to her, sniffed her neck and whispered in her ear, 'You smell of soap from a hundred metres. What's so dirty at home that you keep washing so often?' He looked her straight in the eyes, as if he were fucking her, standing up right there in the bar. He might not be a turn-on, but he knew how to talk to girls like her. He was still the leader of the gang, even when more people showed up. The one who talks more than anyone else, the one people listen to more, the one who makes everyone laugh. Whose judgement they all depend on. Their major source of entertainment tonight was a notorious left-wing activist who'd spent a few months in jail, suspected of having tampered with some railway containers. They all found his statements to the press hilarious. Carlito seemed to know them off by heart, and made constant fun of this indi-vidual he regarded as a political jester. In their conversation, there was no reference to her own world. She'd thought that these G20 protester types spent their time mocking the bosses, the rich, the powerful, and posh kids. She'd even tried to join in by making a clumsy joke about the president's wife. They looked at her without reacting, as if she'd made a reference to Montaigne. The Elysée Palace wasn't on their radar. Nothing to do with them. Valentine had always been told how lucky she was to be born into her family, that everyone wanted above all to have the kind of life she had. But in this scruffy crowd, nobody seemed worried that they couldn't afford an expensive lunch at Costes.

She had assumed Carlito would try to sleep with her that night. She would have agreed, if he had put a little pressure on. Valentine slept with as many men as she could. She thought you could improve in bed, like you could playing the piano: by practice. Carlito didn't really attract her, but she found it logical that the leader of the gang would get plenty of blowjobs from as many girls as possible. Otherwise how would he stay on top? She thought he would want to sleep with her, and like the others would be surprised how much he'd like it. Guys always ended up going nuts, either because they were hardwired to be grateful, or because she was good at it. She opted for the second solution. She had her own theory about sex. The key thing wasn't position, or little moans, any slag could do that. The key thing was to be able to talk, and there porn was no use at all, porn films were practically silent. You had to be not ashamed of talking dirty, but you also had to find just the right tone, so as not to sound ridiculous, which wasn't something granted to everyone. You had to work at your voice, so that it was sexy enough to be exciting, but upper-class enough to be arousing. 'Oh it's so big, please be gentle, your prick's so huge it's going to break my little cunt open, oh you're so big, you're going to blow me apart.' The ultimate hit was to persuade him that he was so good at fucking that he made her lose her mind. That never before had she been in such a state. You had to make a quick judgement. Would he prefer: 'Hit me, tear me open, baby, I'll be your whore, I'll do anything you want, you're so fantastic, you can do what you like with me.' Or was he more into little-girly talk: 'Oh, no, not so hard, you're hurting me, it's so big, gently please, oh no, no no, you're an animal, you're hurting me so much.'

Carlito hadn't tried anything that night, when he left her on the pavement. He'd merely stung her for another twenty euros for a taxi which he had suddenly remembered he had to take for some urgent reason. He'd promised to pay her back next day: 'What are you doing tomorrow night? Are you free? Want to meet up? Then I'll pay you back. Porte de Montreuil, outside the metro station? Wait for me, eight o'clock, OK? Sure? I don't like owing people money.' When she left him, she wasn't sure whether she'd go. But by not screwing her right away, he had created suspense. So she turned up next day. And so did he, half an hour late. He didn't pay back the twenty euros, instead tying himself in knots with a confused and convincing explanation, the upshot of which was that the simplest thing would be if she lent him another thirty, so that he owed her a round fifty, and he'd give it back next day without fail. 'Without fail.' That, she was to learn over time, was an expression covering everything he had no intention of doing. With the money she'd just lent him, he invited her to dinner in a downmarket pizzeria, in which he ordered bottle after bottle of wine. Carlito talked a lot and listened very little. At first, Valentine had found him amusing, by the end of the evening he fascinated her. He could do long riffs, whether on R & B, the African Football Cup, the Red Brigades, Japanese pornography, or surveillance technology. In the course of the conversation, she'd let drop that she was François Galtan's daughter – normally nobody recognized her father's name, but Carlito seemed to go mad, literally. He brought out his big guns, as if he had a chance to speak to the father through the daughter. He had his own particular way of arguing, she felt his brain was equipped with a pair of pincers that enabled him to pick up any subject and lift it, so that you saw it from an unaccustomed angle, then drop it with a crash to the ground when he'd decided to finish with it. Nobody else she knew was like him. He talked to her a lot about sex, but didn't try to seduce her. When the restaurant closed for the night, he'd negotiated a reduction of the bill with the owner, with an insistent bravado that paid off.

She got in the habit of going to meet him when he called. He didn't have a mobile of his own. He would borrow other people's, often without asking permission, and make a series of calls. He would give Valentine a rendezvous, never for a precise place, always by a metro station, and would turn up to fetch her up to an hour late, without apologizing. And then she would stay to listen to him. She didn't tell anyone about these meetings. None of her friends from her ordinary life would have understood what she was up to with this left-wing loudmouth. And Carlito wasn't in any hurry to introduce her to the people he hung out with. Sometimes, though, a girl called Magali, a redhead, with tribal tattooings right across her forehead, would come to fetch him. She would say as she arrived, 'Carlos, everyone's been waiting two hours for you, come on.' And then she would wait for him another couple of hours. Valentine liked knowing that he was making other people wait while he chatted with her. Or more accurately for the pleasure of having her as an audience.

For a few months, she'd kept her two worlds apart: on the one hand she was this arrogant posh teenager, who hung out with girlfriends covered in lip gloss and good-looking boys who pretended to be cynical punks, while naively expecting things to work out for them; and on the other hand there were her weird evenings, listening to a guy who thought that the only truth issued from the mouth of Karl Marx. There was her 'real' life and there was her vaguely shameful side interest, to which she was becoming addicted. Until one fine day, Carlito disappeared without warning. It was the summer of a financial crisis, and Valentine found herself to some surprise reading the newspapers, trying to imagine what Carlito would say about it. That summer wasn't much fun. She'd had a bad night with the boys from Panic Up Yours. She didn't care, but since then she'd felt a kind of vague shame inside, an angry cloud hovering over her head. It was true that she'd asked for it. Things had been bad at school too, she'd arsed around with a boy, and her father had been called in. He hadn't even wanted to talk about it, instead he'd enrolled her, without asking her opinion, into this crammer for retards. Things didn't go well with her girlfriends either, they were avoiding her more and more, saying she drank too much and got everyone into trouble.

She didn't want to make a big fuss, she wasn't the kind to start getting upset, but she felt she was living her life as if astride a wounded and furious bull in a corrida, clinging on to his horns and wishing he'd calm down. She had only to turn up somewhere for everything to go wrong. And yet she had sincerely thought she'd behaved well. But it was complicated. Her grandmother was always round at the house – and she could fly off the handle at the slightest thing. She'd always been that way; she couldn't explain anything without shouting. But it was tiring. Valentine couldn't relax in her bedroom for five minutes without the door bursting open, Western-fashion, and the old girl would come in to give her a lecture on Life. Five minutes later, she'd have calmed down and be baking cakes. But Valentine would still feel her bones shivering from the talking-to she'd received. Her stepmother tried to avoid her, but she was still there, she left bloodstained sanitary towels in the bathroom. A revolting smell, stale and pestilential. Her father was writing his novel, and wandered about the house with a vacant stare and wild look, to stop her talking to him, he was like this every time. And she missed Carlito, with all this chaos around her, more than she would have thought.

At the beginning of June, when she recognized Magali in the distance, at the Halles complex, she hadn't asked herself if it was taking a risk to be seen in public with such a conspicuously marginal punk, she rushed up to her.

'Do you recognize me? Have you seen Carlito?'

'He's gone on a trip. I thought he'd told you, he said he would.'

Magali hadn't pretended not to recognize her, or looked

sniffy about Valentine showing interest in someone who was *her* friend. It made a change for Valentine, who was being cold-shouldered from every direction. Carlito was on a trip, that meant he'd be back. And he had thought to tell her, so he had mentioned her to the people around him. She had taken such punishment, these last weeks, that she felt all at once that some dignity had been restored to her. Valentine had clung on to Magali in the most pathetic and wimpish way. But it worked. She'd followed her to a squat, a real one, full of punks and dogs, skinhead followers of RASH, with a smell of stale cigarettes and spicy food. And a grotty concert going on in the background. Even a month earlier, Valentine would have run a mile. Around her, people were drinking lukewarm wine out of cardboard cups, she was expecting someone to vomit over her at any moment. But she didn't have much choice. Everyone she knew had turned their backs on her. She stuck close to Magali, who had looked less than keen at first, but had finally let her tag along.

'Got any cash? We could buy some Es.'

As the evening wore on and as the drugs took effect, she'd warmed up. Magali was quite funny, in fact. Her brain operated like a steamroller. You didn't expect that, because of her delicate features, her porcelain skin and her baby doll lips. But when she got going, every time she said anything, it came out pow! But she expressed herself well, like she was top of the class. Valentine's grandfather would have said she was very articulate. Magali was a no-holds-barred feminist, but she only hung out with boys. Mostly ones who worshipped her, whom she got together in a group, reigning over them while pretending not to notice the effect she was having. Valentine found this quite a nice situation: a whole lot of disappointed rejected suitors who'd be there for her. She'd decided to go for this unkempt boy, a bit pretty-faced for her, but so drunk that he wouldn't remember. So the evening was turning out OK. She had kissed him in mid-sentence, to check whether he'd be up for it. Even better, it was like at a teenage party. He'd been surprised for a quarter of a second, then snogged her for real. Things were going well. Then a firm hand separated them. Magali, with a super-serious expression, made a sign to the boy to move off, clicking her fingers, like the gesture people make to their dogs when they're on heat, and turned on Valentine.

'You came here with me, so please act properly, don't let me down with this "I'm the local nympho" stuff. Behave yourself.'

'But it's none of your business!'

'I said, behave yourself, I'm fed up now, you've spoilt my evening. We're splitting, come on.'

Magali had decided they'd go and smoke a couple of spliffs at her place. A tiny room, twelve square metres, on a fifth floor with no lift, somewhere behind the Place Gambetta. They walked there. At first Valentine was sulking a bit.

'Don't treat me like I'm a whore!'

'I've never called you a whore. Were you working? Did you need to make some money? If that was it, I'd have respected you.'

'It's none of your business how I live my life.'

'That's all I wanted this afternoon, when you grabbed hold of me! Let you live your life. But you looked so lost, I decided to take you in hand.'

In the end, she'd spent the summer in Magali's company. She'd boycotted the family holiday. Her stepmother, only too pleased not to have her with them in Corsica, had pleaded in her favour. Let her stay in Paris. Magali was interested in things that at first sight were really boring: the meat industry, the situation in Venezuela, the stock market, the discography of Crass – but which she made highly attractive by systematically treating them dismissively. She despised a lot of people. People who paid rent. People who had a job. People who'd been to university. People who were afraid of prison. People who gave interviews to the press. People living in couples. People who could only speak one language. People who were cynical. People who weren't politicized. People without any morals. The good thing about her was that once she had decided she was on Valentine's side, she defended her, whatever she chose to tell her, with a bad faith that winched up her morale. Those boys had pissed on her? So what, they were impotent wimps, useless deadbeats. Her girlfriends wouldn't talk to her any more because they were ashamed of her at parties? Pathetic, uncool, bourgeois mummy's girls. Her grandmother thought she was too fat? Reactionary old fossil, she's just jealous. Her teachers had chucked her out of school because of her poor grades? Fascist bastards, regimented band of stupid pricks. Her father sulked all the time because she gave him grief? Egotistical, going through the male menopause, insensitive hypocrite. Whatever the subject, it was sorted out in two minutes: filthy rich, pathetic drips, piss artists. Valentine realized that if she reduced her circle to a small group of individuals, external judgements couldn't reach her. Her new friends thought her a laugh. They didn't have anything to blame her for. Magali didn't like going out, but she liked to have people back to her place. The entryphone buzzer started going at five o'clock and didn't stop. During these evenings, faces distinguished themselves. Valentine was being domesticated, she was becoming integrated into a close-knit group, where looking after each other wasn't undervalued. She was too exhausted to go on thinking this kind of thing was naff. She needed some TLC.

When classes started again in September, Valentine thought she would go back to her peaceful double life: evenings with Magali arguing hammer and tongs about post-colonialism, and daytime acting like a bimbo, exchanging lipsticks with girlfriends. She had always thought it best to say to people whatever she deemed judicious, in order to get what she wanted. She viewed herself as a manipulating little minx, without any sincere words or emotions. But it had hit her hard when she had to go back to school: duplicity didn't really suit her. She had found a place where she felt good. Not just a place to spend the summer holidays while waiting for her normal social activity to start again. She was honestly happy with Magali and her court of improbable subjects. She was changing. Part of her former self had detached itself in a block, without making a sound.

She didn't have a bad conscience about being a rich kid. Some of Magali's friends had tried to make her feel guilty along the lines of 'you can't understand, you were born with a silver spoon in your mouth, you don't know what it's like to be hard up and hungry', but Valentine had never tried to justify herself. They thought they were tough, lucid and angry. They were innocents. They couldn't even imagine the degree to which people from her background were indifferent to people like them, unless they wanted to write bad novels. If they had had to come face to face with the actual reality, they would have been gobsmacked. How much money there is swilling around in the circles she comes from, how many things are just taken for granted, including the self-esteem you get at birth as your inheritance. Not so much personal self-esteem – that's hard to acquire if you come from a family where the older generation has been too succcessful. But social esteem. If they knew, really knew, how people live up there, they'd explode with rage, they wouldn't even have the strength to discuss it.

Carlito had returned in October. Suntanned and spaced out, he didn't say where he'd been. The others seemed to know, she felt excluded. They talked a lot about the internet and the surveillance of everyone's words and actions that it made possible. Magali didn't have a computer in the house. She said you had to learn to live without one. That you would never be able to start a revolution if you left all your activities wide open to state snooping. The clandestine existence had to be worked for, by learning to live without the micro-technology of surveillance, without a landline or broadband connection, without being vulnerable to eavesdropping. The others didn't agree with her. They talked about Copyleft, resistance platforms, secret codes to access parallel networks. But nobody was going to share the codes. And one day Valentine brought her laptop along and asked Thibaut, the nerd of the group, to wipe out her entire virtual identity: her Facebook account, Twitter, her old MySpace, her old blog, her email inbox. Then she had thrown her mobile phone into the Seine, a grand gesture, full of panache. Thibaut had said it was a bit radical, especially for a girl with nothing particular to hide, no clandestine activity of any kind. She had replied that she needed this kind of experience in order to feel really alive. Valentine didn't really know what she meant by this, but it sounded good. Thibaut had done as he was asked. The amputation was unexpectedly painful. The panic of the first weeks had taken her by surprise, filling her with anguish. To learn to go without seemed at first like having lost the power of speech, her crutch and her best friend all at the same time. An attack of vertigo. Even if she didn't log on to the internet all that much in fact, it was always the first thing she did in the morning: she'd switch on her laptop, check her email and her bookmarked sites, glance at a few clips, with her MSN open permanently in one corner, then she'd google a few sites at random for a mosaic of news, images, novelties. It was worse than amputating a part of herself: she'd slammed the door shut on the best things the world had to offer. Valentine had stuck to her resolution out of pride, because her gesture had attracted welcome attention in Magali's circle, and she didn't want to look ridiculous. Then the withdrawal symptoms had stopped, as suddenly as they had begun. The odd hour snatched in an internet café helped her not to regress completely into the Stone Age and she could manage perfectly well without a mobile. It wouldn't hurt her grandmother not to be able to know every minute where she was. And the first time Valentine had said 'Don't bother, I don't do email' to a girl in class who asked for her address in order to send her a homework assignment, she had felt more mysterious and interesting than if she'd grown a pair of horns on her forehead.

She liked it, in the end. It was like giving up smoking pot: you got more energy and space in your brain. Magali had congratulated her. You can't at the same time want to start the revolution and be visible to the forces of order.

Other people in the group didn't agree: '... these are the last fun years on the internet! It's still possible to subvert it, and get into these, kind of, utopian spaces. We'd be daft to abandon this whole area completely, on the contrary, we should be trying to defend it and take it over.'

'Valentine's not abandoning anything, she just doesn't want people to know every minute where she is. That's quite different.'

'Utopian spaces – what on earth do you mean?'

'Well, it's completely free for a start. And you get instant communication.'

'Oh yeah? And Apple, and your ISP, they're your best pals, are they?'

Valentine couldn't care less about these conversations. All she knew was that what she did could trigger such heated discussions. Valentine was getting to be someone important. She liked that. A lot.

One day, it occurred to her, for the first time in her life, to go and see what her mother's family was like. Until then, she had modelled her behaviour on that of her father: she wasn't of mixed descent. She didn't look ethnic, she was just rather dark-complexioned. She didn't start sunbathing in May, she just took the sun well. She had her father's nose and nobody's eyes. Her mother didn't interest her. She'd always done as she was told, and had simply blanked Vanessa out. It was Magali who had changed things round, by regularly asking her questions, casually, about her mother. 'And you never wonder where she is? You don't know what she's doing?' 'So why does your gran hate her so much?' Her mother liked money, that was all she'd ever been told about her. Valentine had been taught to feel sufficiently ashamed of her mother to avoid the subject.

She'd decided to find her again. Partly out of curiosity, partly to shake off the rules that had been imposed on her. She had telephoned her mother's family, they had been glad to hear from her, you would think they thought about her every day. They had invited her round. In their IKEA-furnished sitting room, she had listened sceptically as they went on about the great importance of Allah in everything. They didn't see her mother any more. They didn't criticize her, but in this house too, her name was never spoken. She had regretted coming the moment she crossed the threshold. There were limits to her openness to other people. The maternal grandmother, who looked a hundred years old, sitting on the floor in the kitchen among the saucepans, mixing up her couscous, it had been a bit of shock, all the same, to think she was linked to these people by blood. The aunts were better, at least they looked as if they lived in the same century as she did. But she could summon up absolutely no interest in anything they said. Some of the boy cousins were cute, but too many of them looked dumb. As for the girl cousins, they were bimbos, either got up like MTV or like Mecca, narrow-minded, spiteful and stupidly vulgar. She had stayed through the meal until coffee, out of politeness, thinking that for once her father had been right, what good could it possibly do her to go poking about in her mother's relatives?

And then Yacine had walked in. The shock of his presence. A thunderbolt. Animal passion. And really cool, well dressed and elegant. An authoritarian air about him, lighting up when he smiled, which was rarely. Star quality right away. Sporty-looking. Taciturn. It changed the atmosphere at once when Yacine came into the room. She suddenly stopped asking herself what she was doing there. She didn't realize at first that he was interested too. He'd scarcely acknowledged her presence, and hadn't spoken a word to her. Just being able to look at him from time to time would have done, she wouldn't have thought of asking more. He was a young girl's dream. And then he had stood up and come over to her. 'I'll see you home if you like. You shouldn't take the RER on your own.'

'Oh, are you going to Paris?'

She would never know how she had managed to ask the question in a calm and detached voice, while inside her a thrilled monkey was climbing the bars of the cage, gibbering with joy.

He had left her at her door, in the old-fashioned way. He had telephoned a few hours later, on the landline, to ask if they could see each other next day. An overdose of magic. And it had gone on for a while: Yacine was Prince Fucking Charming, and a Rottweiler with it, capable of attacking anyone in the street who looked a bit too hard at Valentine, but with her he was gentle, never turning his strength against her. With him, it was like with nobody else. She had dropped her guard and believed in it for a moment.

What Yacine did best was to speak the language of anger. She adored it:

'... just open your eyes, and you'll see it's always, always, the fault of the same people. They need to be made to feel fear. When they go to sleep at night, they need to be shivering in their beds, to think what might hit them tomorrow. They need to be afraid, to be very afraid, like the poor buggers without anything. They need to be afraid for their jobs, afraid of seeing their kids get their throats cut in front of them, afraid of the police, afraid of prison, afraid of being ill. If fear could change sides, that's what would be good.'

There was a metallic pleasure in this kind of litany. The same kind of pleasure that came from being screwed up the ass without expecting it, it makes you grit your teeth, you don't come just at first, but it ends with a powerful nervous discharge. A total explosion. He was right, Valentine knew this in her guts, and that was enough. She distrusted her own intelligence, which would have driven her away from him. So she kept quiet, but her temples throbbed. He was right. He got your anger rising.

Then came the icy blade up against her throat. One day, he'd said to her that it was pointless for her to call him any more. It wasn't going to work. She hadn't had the courage to protest. Hiroshima. She hadn't argued. She hadn't been expecting it. It had been so easy between them. They hadn't had time to quarrel, get bored, clash with each other, nothing. She knew you can get over anything. You get thrown off course, then you pick yourself up. It was soon after that that she had chucked her mobile into the Seine.

She avoids thinking of all that now. An electric shock. A familiar one. Impotence is a narrow prison cell. You can't breathe properly there. It's like having your head in a plastic bag. It wakes her up from sleep. A bitter, physical anger: her blood's on fire, boiling in her veins as it flows through her. Life goes on as if nothing has happened.

She hadn't returned to see her mother's family after that. Their mean-spiritedness, their barely concealed material interest, their false declarations of affection. Their grubby stupidity. Her mother's ashamed of them. Like Valentine's ashamed of her. When she'd run away from home, her mother had preferred to pay for a hotel rather than take her in. Valentine hadn't said anything. She's used to acting as if she couldn't care less. She's good enough at it to be convincing. But still, all the same, my dear maman, wasn't that a bit over the top? Before meeting Vanessa, Valentine had imagined being able to tell her that the more time passed, the more she understood what had driven her to run away from her daughter and everything round her. But her mother had reacted almost with horror. How was she going to get rid of her daughter as soon as possible? She didn't even *pretend* to be anxious or concerned. Valentine had felt, with silent astonishment, a space in her chest tearing apart, like Saint Ursula in the picture by Caravaggio. Her grandfather had loved that painting: he'd taken her to Naples to see it. At the time she'd thought she couldn't care less and was only pretending to take an interest, but the truth is that she's been thinking of it ever since. It's stayed with her.

Her mother had been afraid of this little teenage butt being flaunted under the nose of her man. She's hooked a rich guy, she's taking good care of him. She knows nothing trumps youth. Old men are all paedophiles. As soon as their lawful has her back turned, they come and tell young girls how much they prefer their firm little arses. Valentine had pretended not to be disappointed when she met her mother. To be content just to have lunch with her. Content to try and avoid spending all day shut up in the hotel room planning the hours: go and buy an ice cream, thirty minutes; go to the bookshop Carlito talked about, and look at the covers of the books in the hope that someone would talk to her, one hour; go for a coffee, another half-hour. The worst was the evenings, the TV in her room didn't work properly, she waited until she fell asleep. Sometimes it took a long time.

Part of her advised her to be calm, not to complain, to play the good little girl while trying to soften Vanessa up, wear her down and wait for her to suggest Valentine come to live with her for a while. In Paris, things are too complicated. She's not stupid, she knows what they are trying to do is chain her up. Subdue her. They say it's because she's out of control. But she's not stupid. She watched her grandfather die, she saw them fussing around his deathbed. They didn't even bother to hide what they were after. How much? How much, for the old man's body? As if they were short of anything. Her mother's family, her father's family: all the same. How much could they get their hands on, how much could they grab and put in their pockets? None of them had actually told her he had managed to make sure that she would be the winner in the inheritance lottery. But she had understood. She's become an important person in her family. They've started keeping watch on her, she knows perfectly well what they're after: a solid leash to keep her tied up until she reaches her majority. So that they can get their hands on the only thing that interests them: some more money.

Valentine had been thinking of telling her mother about it, this was her trump card. The day she revealed that old Albert, by some cunning financial strategy, had left almost his entire fortune to his granddaughter, she would be sure that her mother would find room for her in her house. Her grandfather had had a lot of money.

Albert. They thought he was just a vegetable in hospital. How he suffered. He hadn't wanted to be kept hanging on, but nobody asked his opinion. And it had lasted a long time. He'd waited to be alone with her to talk to her, in his hoarse whisper. He said she ought to run away. Not to trust them. He knew them. His nearest and dearest, his family. Those were the only true ties, those of blood. She'd always been his favourite. He'd take her out every Wednesday when there was no school, he didn't want anyone else to come with them. It made Valentine's father laugh. 'Oh, he's getting a bit gaga with age, I dare say he'll take her to the Louvre, what fun for her.' He liked to take her for walks. He didn't say much. But he understood very well what she was up to, as she grew up. What was going on with the boys, for instance, he'd understood. He hadn't had to hire anyone to guess she was doing a bit of dealing. It didn't bother him. 'They're worthless, you're quite right not to bother with them.' And after his death, she was no longer anyone's favourite. He'd told her not to trust them. That they would be angry with her when she inherited everything. 'You'll see, at the top of the tree, you're always alone.' She doesn't know whether he was doing her a favour, or whether he was using her just to get his own back on them. She had told herself he was exaggerating. She still believed that her family loved her, she'd always been told she was lucky, she had people to take care of her. And the problems that had come were always of her own making. But the old man knew what kind of thing his family could do. When they put a private detective on her trail, Valentine realized that he'd been right.

One night, she had managed to lose the detective by jumping on the back of the scooter of some lone rider, and gone to talk to Carlito. When she told him about being tailed, she pretended to be cool about it, while really feeling ashamed. So these were the depths they'd fallen to: paying some woman to watch her from behind, noting everything she did.

He had been peremptory. 'You must stop seeing the others. Now I know about it, we can be careful when we arrange to meet. But keep away from Magali's, whatever you do.'

Valentine acted as if she was heartbroken but would be able to handle the situation. Except that in fact she didn't want to see Magali any more, or the friends who hung out with her. Things had gone wrong over Yacine, whom she'd introduced to Magali. Afterwards, Magali had made a big fuss: she'd shot her mouth off about Israel, and feminism, and his luxury tastes, etcetera etcetera. Valentine had said straight out to her, 'He doesn't give a shit, you know, he doesn't care what you think of him.' And soon after that, it had been the centrepiece of a small-scale showdown, she'd felt she was having to justify who she was seeing, in front of an impromptu jury. For heaven's sake, having a prison warder riveted to her back, seeing everything she did, to check she wasn't going astray, she already had that at home. Basta. The crux of the problem, as she vaguely realized, was jealousy. Jealousy on her part: she didn't like the smile that Magali – who hadn't spotted it, and couldn't therefore have prevented it, as per usual – had provoked in Yacine's eyes. She preferred just to give up on the whole gang. And frankly, she wasn't bothered: she'd been as far as she could go with them. That way they had of insisting she explain why she was going round with a boy who said things that were politically incorrect. You would have thought she was back at her grandmother's. All this holier-than-thou stuff, what's OK and what's not OK, what you can say and what you can't say. They draw this imaginary line, and you're on one side of it and everything on the other has to be criticized and corrected. Or eliminated. Whatever the colour of the chains, she didn't want to be bound by them.

Valentine had planned her escape. The day the detective had stopped in the metro to help some old biddy to her feet, she knew what to do. She'd made her getaway in broad daylight. The pathetic private eye, who tried to be discreet and who ate her croissant in the bar where Valentine had her coffee every morning: they must really take her for a complete sucker. It had been going on for a fortnight. A whole fortnight of distracting her follower, taking her all over the place, showing her some sights. Give them their money's worth. A little porn, that would keep them busy. She'd fixed up everything with Carlito. She'd gone to the station, taken a train to Perpignan, paying for her ticket with cash. He'd come to meet her, they'd crossed the Spanish frontier without difficulty, in a borrowed car.

She takes the bus now to the Oreneta park. Sister Elisabeth

has advised her not to hang about in the centre of Barcelona. They arrange to meet in parks where there are always plenty of people, so that they don't stand out, but sufficiently remote that they are unlikely to meet anyone significant. The nun is waiting for her, her little silhouette is reassuring. The brilliance of her smile when she recognizes Valentine. She gives her a brief hug and Valentine immediately feels comforted.

They walk up a slope between cactuses that look like big disjointed rag dolls. Further off is a eucalyptus the height of a building, leaning dangerously over an overhang. Behind them, the city stretches out to the sea. Sometimes they meet wild boars: fat bodies with eyes full of melancholy.

'Well, now, someone has come looking for you.'

'Oh really? Is my father here?'

'No, they've sent two detectives.'

'Oh.'

Her train of thought. There could be plenty of reasons to change direction, take a different path and move away from this current that both terrorizes her and attracts her. Just like when she decided to run away from home. It's scary. But you have to do it. In a way, she's been chosen.

'You think I should go back home now?'

'I can't take a decision for you.'

Elisabeth is like a boxer, fighting God's corner. She skips around you, testing, dancing, then she attacks, a knock-out punch. She has a notion of what dignity is, and it's linked to the idea that strength has to be worked for, deserved, acquired. Elisabeth isn't like other nuns. She has essential things to transmit. She's become her guide. She could have given Valentine the brush-off, been horrified by everything she stood for. On the contrary, she's helped her. Listened to her and understood her.

She even offered to put her up, for as long as necessary. She had first given her the keys to a little flat, like a cell, in a courtyard in the Poble Sec district. With no name on the letter box. Sister Elisabeth didn't come to fetch her, she said that a nun on her own in the city is too conspicuous. They would meet in the Oreneta park, in the northern part of town. They had long conversations. Sister Elisabeth knew how much Valentine needed her, needed her advice, needed her as a listener. Then she lent her the keys of a small isolated house at La Floresta. It flips her out a bit to sleep up there all alone, and the hot water doesn't work very well.

'I read in the papers that your father's going to get a decoration, he's going to be a Chevalier des Arts et Lettres.'

'Was it in the papers here?'

'No, Valentine, I read the French papers, because I pay attention to everything that concerns you.'

'That'll make him happy.'

'Don't you think you should make an effort to get on better with him?'

'Do you think this is the moment?'

'I can't take a decision for you.'

A dizzy flash, the whistle of a tiny bullet into the brain. Valentine talks of nothing else every day. At first she thought Sister Elisabeth wanted to dissuade her. But no, she too is disgusted, she too thinks passive acceptance is no longer the right thing. It does no good just going on putting up with things as they are. It's not human any more. Sister Elisabeth has warned her: standing out from the herd is never an easy thing to do. Alone, facing the crowd, she will have to work out how to play her part.

Around them, night is falling. Of the distant town you can only see tiny lamps, a valley of doll's houses. Aeroplanes' headlights flash on and off in the sky. A silence has risen in Valentine's throat.

Time to go home. She knows what she has to do.

Before they part at the bus stop, the nun, as she does every night, looks Valentine in the face for a long time. At the moment of farewell, she hugs her to her, something she doesn't usually do. They understand each other.

'You're so young, Valentine. And so full of light.'

'You'll help me?'

'I won't let you fall. You'll never walk alone, you know that.'

Next morning, as arranged, the nun is back in the empty living room in the little house. Today makes Valentine think of Wednesdays spent checking her homework, when she was small, with her grandfather. Irregular verbs. The 1914–18 war. Agreements with the perfect tense of 'avoir'. Chemical formulae. 'A little discipline please,' he would say with a frown, and he would make her organize her pencil case, copy her work out neatly, and he always insisted she wash her hands first and sit up straight on her chair. 'We're not in the monkey house here, are we.' Today, naturally, she sits up straight to listen, she articulates clearly when she repeats the words, her hands are on the table when she needs to concentrate. Her throat feels tight, there's anguish there, but she is learning to galvanize it into certainty. She feels tough inside. She likes it. She tries to connect to the reality of what's happening, but it's impossible. She still feels she's pretending, that it's a game of make-believe.

'You can pull out, you know. Until the last minute, you know you can pull out.'

They've become so close. There is respect and much affection between them. No need for excessive gestures or declarations. Sister Elisabeth will be watching over her. She understands her and accepts her just as she is. She gives her the kind of love you give a baby: unconditional.

And this old, wise woman, who has devoted her life to helping other people, does not try to dissuade her from what she has to do. Because she too is sick with disgust. Wherever she looks, she sees unhappiness, injustice and brutality. Just letting things happen is no longer an option. You have to intervene. Into this sordid reality. Stop things just going on the same old way, at all costs.

The first few days, Valentine had been tempted to giggle secretly when Sister Elisabeth started to talk about Jesus, the crusades and the importance of truth. If Jesus came back to earth, he'd be a freedom fighter, his disciples would be guerrilleros. Terrorists, the lot of them. They would be pursued, handcuffed, condemned to life in top-security jails. Always kept under surveillance. There wouldn't be any resurrection possible, there would only be arrest warrants, their pictures all over the media. And as many executions as necessary. If Jesus came back, he would have to speak out. He couldn't just have a quiet chat with the merchants. But he wouldn't be able, any more than the first time, to prove that he was a different kind of warrior. His miracles would be mocked, and his divine words printed on mugs to be sold in souvenir shops.

As time went on, Valentine had gradually lost her cynicism. She started to listen without feeling like mocking. Everything comes together. She's found the strength not to distrust her sincerity.

'Take these to help you keep going. Nothing to be ashamed of. It's as important as having weapons. And as important as faith. Everything has to work together.'

Some small round transparent pills. Made in China. It feels like swallowing a little pebble. Only one at a time, otherwise you wouldn't be able to sleep at all. Valentine feels her forehead being pulled forward, and her thoughts roll through it, implacable, linked, working in sequence. She is a war machine.

'In Paris, you'll be watched all the time. They won't want you to get in the way of their plans. They're on the lookout. You should go back on the internet, to show that you're normal, but don't ever try to contact me that way, not ever. I'll be there, don't worry. I'll show myself. You'll never be alone. And when you look down from your window and see a nun with a bunch of white roses, you'll know that's the sign. After she's seen you've seen her, she'll leave something for you in the flowerpot by the front door. It will be for the day after that, precisely.'

'How did you know there are flowers in front of the house?'

'I find these things out, Valentine, I find out. When you get home, you should say you want to go back to school. That running away has made you think a lot. Understand? Not a word to anyone. Don't leave any message behind you. They'd only twist it to make your action mean something different.'

The same instructions, several times. Sister Elisabeth makes her repeat: 'What will be going through your head when you walk into the house. Visualize the apartment, think of the smells, concentrate. What will you be thinking?'

'My grandmother, my father, my stepmother, her daughters: whatever happens, I'll say what they want to hear. No showing off, no tantrums. I have only one aim. I apologize when they're in the wrong. I smile if they insult me. When the police question me, or the youth magistrate, I'll say: my mother gave me enough money, so I took a cheap hotel room. I didn't do anything. I was feeling depressed. The meeting with my mother didn't work out, it devastated me. I'm glad to be back home. I realize it's important to get on with my school work. I thought a lot while I was on the run. I'm sorry I caused all this worry for the people who really love me.'

These pills are fantastic. She feels calm, euphoric, capable of concentrating without any effort.

Then it's the evening. Sister Elisabeth surrounds her with all her affection. She clasps her to her, and strokes her back.

'The simplest thing is to go home with the two detectives. That way no suspicions will be aroused. But watch out. They try to look more stupid than they are. Don't let your guard slip with them.'

'How will I find them?'

'What about going to see your friend Carlito? He's in town, isn't he? You know where he is?'

'We arranged that I'd call every day at the CNT bookshop at four o'clock. He's supposed to leave me a message if he can't be there.'

'Something tells me he'll warn them if you arrange to meet him. They can offer money, you know.'

Only three days ago, Valentine would have been revolted to think her best friend would betray her. But now it doesn't matter. Sister Elisabeth hugs her tightly, rocks her to and fro without a word, and they fall asleep on the sofa. Valentine's ready.

Carlito isn't hard to find. The next day she's drinking a beer with him in a scruffy bar in the Raval area. He doesn't suspect anything. He can't see the difference between the way she was a week ago and what she has become. He's too busy talking to pay her much attention. He's happy because he's having a torrid affair with a Chilean woman. As torrid affairs go, Valentine gets the feeling that the girl isn't that keen on him, but doesn't know how to get rid of him. None of that matters much any more.

And everything happens exactly the way Sister Elisabeth predicted: after a quarter of an hour, two silhouettes appear in the doorway. Valentine stares at Carlito, he still doesn't have a mobile, she wonders just when this son of a bitch alerted them. He plays the guy who has no idea what's happening. She wants to spit in his face. The taller one of the two comes up to Valentine.

'Can I have a word? Couple of minutes.'

Valentine picks up her bag and follows her.

'We've been looking for you for days. It's your choice: you can come back with us of your own accord, or we'll inform the police.'

'I'll come with you.'

'Do you want to tell your friend back there?'

'No, don't worry. I think he knows… Let's go.'

These two oldsters came by car. They're playing at Starsky and Hutch, only more decrepit and edgy. Their bags are already in the boot. As if they knew, as well, that it would be today. Valentine recognizes the younger one, the one who was following her in Paris. That ties things up neatly.

There's a white light inside her skull. One pill every morning. Not more. She mustn't let herself get high or lose the plot, but be wide awake. Carlito always used to say teenagers don't start drugs because they taste good, or because the kids are bored, or because they want to forget their problems, or because of their hormones, no, they get high to destroy their intelligence. Because if they kept it intact, just when it's at its peak, they wouldn't be able to bear the pain of the disgust they'd feel for their parents.

Valentine would like to be able to wipe out any remaining traces of Carlito. Traitor. Armchair terrorist. Where she's going, she won't need him.

She's not afraid. She knows she has to do what she has to do.

Valentine doesn't want to grow up to be like her father: a liar and a coward, who thinks of nothing but getting his prick inside the nearest cunt, but who plays the prude at the dinner table, as if he's a respectable gent. She doesn't want to grow up to be like her grandmother, brimful of nagging hate, talking of nothing but Christian charity, but really dying of loneliness and frustration. She doesn't want to grow up like her mother, obliged to marry someone and tell lies about who she is. She can't see any adults around her with a sense of direction. Any remains of dignity. They compromise all along the line, and tie themselves in knots to justify it. They say it's their choice. All the shit you have to eat, they just swallow it down without flinching. All they know is how to do what they're told. How to survive at any price. Well, she's going to slam the brakes on. This world they've built, she's going to introduce some order to it.

She had asked Carlito why he never took the step of moving to action. To cover up his cowardice, he'd spread his arms wide: 'That's a romantic temptation. But above all it's a way of getting people to notice you. What we ought to be working for is the revolution. Not some new spectacular act. This isn't the circus. The difficult thing isn't to die heroically, but to resist on the ground, with concrete results.' She had been disappointed. She'd wanted him to say something more flamboyant, like that he'd been waiting for this moment ever since he'd met her, that the two of them were going to do this really big thing. Magali had been even less enthusiastic. But with her at least, it was upfront: she believed in non-violence. Cue a boring lecture: 'What does terrorist violence achieve? Well, armed force is *their* thing. They achieve power by the use of force, they invent frontiers and fence us in by the use of force, they hang on to power by the monopoly of force. The whole idea of legitimate violence is a con. If you use violence, you'll always set up a new power, and it'll legitimize itself, just like the one before: by violence. The only thing that changes is the faces of the leaders. Because the new powers will never agree that violence by the people they oppress can be legitimate. So it all starts all over again. Back to square one, police, oppression, prison, torture. What I'm interested in is how to create a world where the leaders don't give themselves the right to exercise violence. I want to know how we can live differently from the way we are now.' Magali could hold forth about this for hours, but she was wrong. A political movement is only valid if it causes deaths. Otherwise it's just feminism: a hobby for kept women. You need violence. Otherwise nobody listens. Valentine has grown up in such luxury that she has no wish to turn her violence against the police. She can't be bothered with demos. Why fight battles with people who only earn the minimum wage? The cops are living in the same shitty world as the homeless. Kill a thousand of them, and another thousand will appear. Power has to be attacked at the top. Directly.

It will take at least ten hours to drive to Paris. The younger detective, sitting in the front passenger seat, turns round to Valentine and breaks the silence. 'I'm glad you're safe and sound. You probably think I'm out of order, but after thinking about you all this time, I'm glad you're OK. Everyone was so worried, you know. Can I ask you a question? Had you spotted me?'

'How could I possibly have missed you?'

'Do you want to call on your mother before we leave Barcelona?'

This is the taller one speaking. Valentine distrusts her. She may be playing the dozy elder citizen. But something in her piercing look is suspicious.

'No. Thanks. We've said all we had to say to each other.'

'She's worried about you, you know.'

'Oh yeah? Well, she hides it pretty well.'

The older one smiles before adding, 'Pity, I'd have quite liked to see her again. My name's the Hyena by the way.' Her eyes are looking for Valentine in the rear mirror. On the way out of town, a car hoots at them, the Hyena screeches to a halt, lowers her window and hurls abuse at the poor guy, who shrinks under the wheel, surprised by the violence of her reaction. She starts in Spanish and finishes in French. The younger one looks annoyed as they move off again.

'He won't understand if you swear at him in French.'

'So what! I think he got the message.'

Right, she's a maxi-monster, a psychopath. That's all she needed. The tension has gone up a notch in the car, the air is harder to breathe. Now that she's put everyone at ease, the Hyena seems to relax, but for an hour nobody says anything. Valentine says to herself that her grandmother throwing a tantrum by comparison is like Gandhi tickling you. Dying in a road accident because the car's being driven by a maniac, how dumb would *that* be? She feels that the Hyena is watching her non-stop in the rear mirror. She's playing a Johnny Cash CD. Prehistoric music. A fine rain has started to fall, as it gets dark. Valentine feels a wave of sadness run over her, starting in her shoulders, then spreading like an ink stain down her back, to take hold of her guts. She's on her own. The strength that Sister Elisabeth inculcated into her is already losing intensity. Every kilometre they drive makes what happened in Barcelona a bit vaguer, a bit less real.

The Hyena is off again: 'So, tell us then, what did you get up to all the time?'

'Nothing much. That's why I'm glad to be going home.'

'Yeah, sure, I can see you're bursting with joy. And why did you leave the hotel your mother took you to?'

'That hotel depressed me.'

'Was that a good reason to leave without telling her?'

'We didn't have anything left to say. She'd bought me lunch in every restaurant where she wasn't scared of meeting someone she knew. I was afraid we'd start going round them again.'

'So where did you sleep after that?'

'I had a bit of money, I went to another hotel.'

She'd like the trip to be over quickly now. Once they've crossed back into France, they listen to the radio. A debate about self-defence. Listeners with unbelievable provincial accents call in to talk about their experiences.

The Hyena wants to ask something. 'What about you, Valentine, have you ever been tempted to have a gun?'

She won't leave her alone. Valentine shrugs. 'No. All I want is to get home and sit the bac.'

'Oh really. The bac!' She takes this in, reflects, and obviously doesn't believe a word of it. 'Terrific plan. Aren't you afraid you'll miss the palm trees? Weather's not so nice in Paris, is it?'

Adults really have a pathetic sense of humour as a rule. They think they can win kids over by false complicity. She'll say as little as possible. The old detective is playing the kind of woman you can't put something across on, but if she really knew, she'd blow a fuse. Valentine wants to tear her eyes out. Concentrate on the objective. Luckily, after five minutes they forget her and start talking about the love affair of the little one, the plain one. Valentine doesn't bother listening, she's relieved to have been forgotten.

The mobile of the one called Lucie rings, she sits up and waves her hands in the air. 'It's your father!'

Then she goes into a string of yes, yes, yes, she rabbits on, with some pathetic traces of self-satisfaction in her voice, making Valentine feel like she's some kind of trophy. She's dreading the moment when the phone will be passed back to her. But her father is even more ill at ease.

'Are you OK, sweetheart? Sure? Oh, if you knew how worried we've been about you... I can't tell you how glad I am you're safe. I can't wait to see you. You're going to drive all night? You're sure you're OK?'

Is she OK? What a farce. She doesn't need to pretend, to make her voice sound choked, neutral, disconnected. The idea of going home makes her uneasy. It hadn't occurred to her when she was far away. That he hadn't even come in person to fetch her. She can't manage to be cross with him, she just feels sharply aware of her total worthlessness.

They stop north of Perpignan at a petrol station. They let her go to the toilet on her own. She needs to freshen up. Down some stairs. In the white neon light of the cloakroom, she looks different in the mirror. More serious, her face more delicate. Her features look drawn and there are slight circles under her eyes. It suits her, makes her look like someone who thinks a lot. She'd like to cry, but she can't.

The door slams, she jumps, her nerves can't stand the slightest jolt. The Hyena comes in, and stares at her in the mirror. She's terrifying. The idea flashes into her head that her family has paid someone to kill her. That would be too stupid. Valentine makes an effort, gripping the washbasin, her heart wants to jump out of her chest.

'You are a fucking idiot. A dirty, uneducated, pretentious,

fucking little idiot, way out of your depth.'

'Oh!... honestly, I'm sorry if you don't like me. But I thought you were being paid to take me home, not to do instant character analysis...' Valentine automatically gives a smart-alec answer, but she would really prefer to be able to seem humble and obedient, thinking that might calm this madwoman down.

'And what do *you* know about who's paying, or how much, or who to, or why? Eh? What have you grasped about what you're being made to do?'

'What I understand is, I need my dad, I need to go back to school now, and take better care of myself.'

'Be careful, little chick, anyone can tell that's been learnt off by heart. You'll have to try harder for it to sound sincere. Are you sure you're ready to go back?'

'I don't know what you're talking about.'

'For three hours I've been looking at your little face in the rear-view mirror. I've had time to think. What has she stuffed into your brain? What stories has she been telling you?'

'I'm really sorry, I don't know what you're talking about.'

Valentine has frozen. This madwoman scares her to death. She's never in her life had anyone speak to her as brutally as this, as close up as this. The woman's face isn't the same, it seems to be alight, hatred seeping from every pore. She could be in a horror film just like she is, no need for special effects, torn-off limbs, nothing. Just her ugly mug in close-up would be enough. The teenager's legs feel hollowed out, they can hardly hold her up. A little push would be enough to make her fall to her knees. Her thoughts are all on the ground, lying there inert. She's afraid.

The madwoman calms down, leans against the wall, facing Valentine. 'I feel like the huntsman in *Snow White*, the one who has to bring back her heart.'

'Look, honestly, I don't know what you're thinking, but I swear...'

'Shut up. You're lying. The huntsman, we all know the story, he lets her run away into the forest, and he takes a deer's heart back instead. Note that he doesn't take an axe when he returns to the castle, to cut the throat of the stepmother, or to attack the king who just let it all happen. Fairy tales are a good guide to real life. You don't fight your paymaster.'

'There's no need to get so worked up, just because you've got to take me home... I'm not going to stick up for my stepmother, but I'd be surprised if she asked you to rip my heart out.'

'Just who do you think she is, your Sister Elisabeth? You think she's interested in your case, why? You think every runaway kid that crosses her path, she takes them under her wing for a bit of brainwashing? You think just because she wears her little blue and white headdress, and because she has wrinkles that make her look kind, that she's a good *person*? You haven't had experience of enough rotten apples in your life already? What do you think her diary looks like, your precious new friend, Sister Elisabeth? What do you bet there's not too much about the infinite mercy of Jesus, sacrificing himself for our salvation? Who do you think she's working for, that Sister?'

Valentine takes this on the chin. She'd been warned: they'll lie to you. They'll try and make you have doubts. Sister Elisabeth had said: 'They'll know my name.' But she'd omitted to say: 'They'll sound like they're telling the truth, so convincingly that it will make you want to cry.' Valentine looks at the floor and says nothing. The less she says, the less she risks giving herself away. She blocks the inside of her brain, it's as if she had rolled into a ball, waiting for a disgusting big spider to go away. She'd like it if someone else came into these toilets to interrupt the confrontation, but nobody's there. The Hyena turns on a cold tap and lets it run over her wrists. She speaks to her reflection in the mirror.

'I've never had any morals, I have no passion for the good. I don't know whether it's age, getting tired, or your angelic little face... But I can't let you go back home without saying something to you. Do you understand? Have you ever heard the saying: you think you're dying for your principles and you're killing for a barrel of oil?'

'I don't know what you're talking about.'

'Get this into your head, that old woman is doing the same job as me. She may not have the stature of Mother Teresa, but she's the same kind of believer. With a fat bank account, and thinking poverty's fine for other people. Whatever she's said, tell yourself that what's at stake here can be counted in euros, or in the extra power someone's going to get. That's what we are. Total bitches, obeying orders, selected because we're good at working on people.'

Valentine wishes she'd leave her alone. She wants to speak to Sister Elisabeth, urgently. For a brief moment, like a freeze-frame, despite her struggles, the thought insinuates itself: what if this woman's telling the truth? But she's been warned: don't trust anyone. She closes her eyes and counts down. Get back to the hypnotized calm.

It doesn't work. Surely the Hyena is preaching untruth to find out the truth. Block it. Deny everything. Never admit anything. This is the first test. Valentine pronounces through her teeth in a cold and indifferent voice. 'All I know is I want to get back to my father.'

The Hyena has turned back into human shape, she floods the room by splashing water on her face. She wets her hair and combs it back. She holds out her hand to Valentine, smiling as if she was just talking about the cool night air. 'No hard feelings. Just a little injection of reality. Like when a vampire bites an innocent victim. Crunch! It's over. You know. After all that, it's true, you're old enough to make up your own mind. I'll let you think about it overnight.'

'Don't worry about me, I know perfectly well what I have to do.'

There, she couldn't keep her mouth shut. It was more than she could manage. The woman turns round, now she's neither angry nor relieved, she looks moved. And coming from her, perhaps that's worse than anything.

'Do you want a bottle of water, something to eat? You haven't eaten anything this evening. Some crisps, chocolate perhaps?'

In the car park there's a line of trucks looking like reassuring animals, their headlights out. Lucie, leaning up against the boot of the car, is whispering into her mobile, punctuating the conversation with happy little chuckles. She's pathetic, but she looks happy.

They get back on the road in silence. The poison is seeping into her thoughts, trying to make her weaken. Valentine is shaken. How is it possible that a few sentences down in those neon-lit toilets could make her have doubts? Sister Elisabeth. Their lovely understanding. 'Too good to be true.' The immediate love, as if the nun had recognized her own child. But it doesn't change anything. She's climbed up on the merry-go-round, her seat belt is fastened. To get down now, what could be more depressing? To wait for what? What could she possibly look forward to? Valentine sees again a photo Magali had shown her. The skeleton of an albatross on a rock, the fragile bones of its wings spreadeagled. It had eaten so many plastic bottletops, which looked like juicy morsels floating on the surface of the sea, that its stomach was full of multicoloured capsules. In ten years, or a hundred years, that's all that would remain. The bones, the feathers, the beak would all have turned into dust. But those absurd plastic bottletops, imitating food, won't even have lost their colours. Perhaps some other albatrosses will have eaten them.

Even if it's been taken for the wrong reasons, her decision is the right one.

They stop again after two more hours. Lucie stays in the car, pretending to be asleep but her mobile's in her hand, she's waiting for a text that doesn't come. Valentine sits with the other detective at a tall round table by the coffee machines; the strip lighting adds another ten years to the Hyena's age. She says, 'You have to be mentally confused to the highest degree to choose truth over lies, or virtue over vice, I know that. But I can't bring myself to leave you alone. Just tell me what you're going to do...'

'I'm going to go back to school. Really, I don't know what you're talking about.'

'But you've been looking very thoughtful these past two hours in the car.'

'I'm feeling nervous at getting back to my family.'

'Look, if you want, we don't have to go there. We won't go to your father's house. I'll take you anywhere you like.'

'Are you a paedophile or what?'

'If it makes you happy, no problem. I can take you, we've got the car. We can do whatever you want. But just cancel everything. Give me ten days, just ten days, and we can talk about it. Look, if you like, we can hitch a lift with a basketball team. We can say we're journalists. Think about it: twenty boys in a bus, plus the driver, the trainer, the physio. Or something else that appeals to you. For instance if you're into politics, we can go to Chiapas in Mexico, we'll wear ponchos and you can learn to shoot. Or Russia if you want? We can go to Russia and meet the rich boys and girls of a big country. Or we could tour the cathedrals of Europe, if religion's the new thing that turns you on. Whatever you like. But change your plans, don't go back to your father's house.'

'Why are you saying all this?'

'I know it's a heavy burden, I can see you, and I know it's heavy. It won't be like you think.'

She can be funny when she tries. And she really cares. Not so long ago, Valentine would have listened to her. But now she's had enough, she's trusted too many people in one life. She's tired of all their efforts, all of them. She can see the emptiness behind their eyes. They're clutching at straws. This private eye is clinging to her. Lucie is clinging to her mobile. They're all empty shells. Everyone. All the stuff this detective is suggesting is superficial, surface stuff. Rushing headlong into the unknown. Forgetting what's basic. She's consumed enough of that kind of thing. She doesn't want any more of those pleasures that leave you with a hangover. Valentine sighs. 'Don't worry about me. Really. You're being kind. But don't worry.'

On the parking lot, more trucks are asleep, like metal carcasses. The Hyena takes the wheel and wakes Lucie.

'Now we know. It's official. We're an endangered species.'

Valentine smiles. She's waiting. She's no longer troubled by any hesitation. She has no doubts.

PARIS

WE GOT TO PARIS AT DAWN. THE BUILDINGS, the sky, the pavements, all looked grey. The overalls of the municipal workers spraying the streets with water made green patches against the rest.

We found a parking space just opposite the Galtan residence. Valentine hadn't said much during the drive. The Hyena switched off the engine.

'I'm not coming up. I'll leave you here.'

She got out of the car and hauled her bag from the boot. Then she turned to the teenager. 'Sure you wouldn't like to come for a little trip round town with me first?' I thought she was making quite a fuss at saying goodbye – after all they hardly knew each other. I was amazed that she was just going to leave me there without asking what we'd do about the bonus. I thought she would call me later in the day. When my turn came, she gave me a hug. Visibly, fatigue had made her sentimental. I didn't think anything of it at the time. It was cold. I watched her walk away then disappear round the corner. Her long-limbed silhouette, seen from behind, had something touching about it.

When I turned to Valentine, I found she looked pale and drawn, and I put it down to the sleepless night, the built-up emotion and fatigue. In the lift, it suddenly gripped me: the feeling that I was making a big mistake. This time, I thought it must be because for me our return meant going back to the office, to those pointless assignments for the agency, and perhaps never seeing Zoska again. Every warning intuition I had that morning I decided to ignore.

I've rerun it so many times since. It was obvious that something was wrong. But I was tired, my mind was on other things, I didn't press the alarm button in the lift, I didn't say, 'Come on, let's get out of here.' The Galtans, unlike their usual behaviour, were being affable. There was coffee and plenty of croissants waiting for us. They were more awake than we were. Not the kind to make a huge fuss, either. But you sensed that they were genuinely relieved. Jacqueline, all in black like an old-fashioned widow, couldn't stop thanking me. She was as honeyed when you did what she wanted as she was aggressive if you crossed her. I didn't pay attention to Valentine, her fixed smile when her grandmother stroked her hair, repeating, 'Are you all right, little one, are you all right?' The father was ill at ease, he was having difficulty finding the right body language and words. The stepmother and her daughters came into the room a few minutes later. They must have discussed it beforehand and decided to let Valentine have a while alone with her birth family. At the time, the only thing on my mind was that it was going to be strange finding myself on my own again. And to wonder whether Zoska would forget me at once, or start texting me.

Then I left Valentine, without much emotion, since she had hardly said a word to me since the start of the journey. I patted her shoulder, repeating that I was glad she was OK and back at home. I don't remember her expression that moment. To tell the truth, I wasn't paying attention to her. I was glad to have the envelope stuffed with banknotes in my pocket, the old woman had slipped it to me with affected discretion, as if it was a tip for Christmas. I wondered again when the Hyena would come to collect her share.

I was feeling emotional and exhausted when I got home. A lot of things had happened, but as soon as I was inside the door it was as if I'd left only yesterday, nothing had changed. I called the office to say I wouldn't be in till the afternoon. Agathe was exasperated that I hadn't reported in more regularly, but impressed that the mission had succeeded. Deucené was relieved but distant, I think he was afraid I'd use this as a pretext to ask for a rise, he preferred prevention to cure, and not to get too matey with the staff. But he too was glad to be able to close the file. And to say that the agency had successfully completed its task. When he found out I'd been driving all night, he advised me to take the whole day off. I'd never known him be so magnanimous.

I installed Skype on my computer. And waited for Zoska to come online. She was sweeter than when I'd left. Enclosed in a frame on my laptop screen. It was frustrating to be with her without her being really there. I went to bed early. There was an underlying sadness, a kind of grey dust over all my thoughts when I emerged next day. I didn't see it as a premonition. I went downstairs at eleven. I walked to the office. I considered resigning. I thought about going to live in Barcelona. I would just have to take my courage in both hands and ask Zoska how she would react. But it seemed a bit premature to unveil my plans.

As I pushed open the door, I didn't know what to expect: we had spent seven days in Barcelona without my keeping my boss up to speed, and I hadn't yet written a word of my report. Deucené took the time to see me, a quarter of an hour, ten minutes of which he spent on the phone, signalling to me to hang on. Then he declared he was pleased, that he was expecting the file to be tied up by first thing tomorrow morning, and he hoped I'd gone easy on the expenses. I didn't try to explain that the family was going to cover all that.

I closed my office door. Jean-Marc came by for a coffee, his charcoal-grey suit looked good on him. I told him I'd fallen in love. I'd never before talked to him about my private life, but I was bursting to talk to someone. When he learnt that it was with a girl, he got interested in my story, so much so that suddenly I didn't want to say any more about it.

Rafik in person called me just before lunch, to ask if I'd like him to wait for me and go and eat something together. The high life, eh. But I didn't want to be there at all. I felt cold all the time. I was surprised to find myself missing the Hyena. I would have liked her to call.

I didn't put the report in next morning, because I still hadn't written a line of it. Or the next day. Agathe was being more polite towards me, she asked me for it in a respectful tone of which I didn't know she was capable. I'd gained status all of a sudden. I took no pleasure from it. I wanted Zoska to announce that she'd bought a ticket for Paris, or for her to ask me to come at once. But love by Skype seemed to satisfy her. I couldn't understand why the Hyena wasn't trying to reach me. I was disappointed that she could manage without me so easily. By the Monday, her silence was making me furious. I needed her help to finish my report. But I didn't know how to contact her.

That morning, I had all the same managed to write a few pages for the file. But I'd run out of inspiration and by lunchtime I was on the internet doing Tarot cards on the Vogue website, asking various questions about my relationship with Zoska and the importance she would have in my life. The cards were good if enigmatic, and I was concentrating hard when Jean-Marc came into my office without knocking. Ashen-faced, he was trying to keep his voice under control.

'There's been a bomb attack at the Palais-Royal. I'm going downstairs to look at the TV, do you want to come?'

'The Palais-Royal? Here, in Paris? Do they let Islamists in there?'

Like a stupid idiot, I had time to think it was rather nice being treated as if I was important, and I graciously followed him downstairs.

On the ground floor, a dozen people were standing looking at the flat-screen in the big hall. There was a funereal silence. Any desire to joke had been blocked in everyone's throat. It took time to understand what we were seeing. And an effort to convince yourself you were watching the news, live, not the trailer for some big-budget action movie. The TV commentators were talking in zombie-like voices, you could tell they'd closed down their brains, they were on automatic pilot but not sure what to say.

The smoke hadn't yet dispersed. The television cameras were being kept at a distance. The images they were taking on the spot only showed a thick black curtain. From the helicopters, it was different. In some places, the fires had died down. The weirdest thing was not so much what had been destroyed, but what had been displaced by the force of the explosion. What our brains found it hard to process was the stuff they could recognize. Grey tiles splashed with blood, the coloured sign for the metro station, intact but thrown a hundred metres from its original spot. A tree still standing. A bench on its side. A lamp post cut in half, lying flat. Part of some railings, their tips recently repainted gold. A fragment of sculpture from a façade, a chubby cherub with a big sword. One of the black-and-white Buren columns had landed, intact, in the top branches of a tree that had remained upright. The still-recognizable residue bore witness to the fact that the mass of black rubble surrounding them had indeed once been the Palais-Royal. Terror had spared these links with a ravaged normality.

In the room, the first remark was 'Some high-up in the government must have wanted to move a petrol pump, and oops, the Palais-Royal exploded.'

'Like Capri juice, but worse.'

They were trying to be clever, but their hearts weren't in it.

'But was there anyone inside?'

'Would there be, this time of day?'

'Can't see any bodies.'

'Wait for the smoke to clear... Then we'll know.'

'It doesn't necessarily have to be Al-Qaida, the Basque separatists said they were going to strike.'

'In Paris? You must be joking, the Basques aren't asking for the Ile-de-France to be independent.'

'Someone said there was an awards ceremony going on inside. Has anyone checked what it was?'

'What's the building anyway, a ministry?'

'No. It's the Palais-Royal. Keep up at the back.'

'Oh God, I've got a friend who lives opposite there, I must call her.'

'It's weird, looks like pictures of Haiti.'

'Or Chile.'

'What it makes me think of most, is the Twin Towers.'

It could have been anywhere on the globe, annihilated by a bomb or an earthquake or the attack of a malevolent giant. Life was starting again little by little, people were beginning to pass silly remarks. My legs had turned to jelly, my brain wasn't working.

On the screen, the area around the explosion was quite recognizable. A bizarrely familiar townscape. I felt like vomiting.

In the streets, we could hear the sirens of ambulances rushing past. We were within walking distance from where it had happened. We had to repeat it to ourselves several times to believe it. Like everyone else, I had often passed in front of the Palais-Royal, in the centre of Paris, opposite the Louvre, the seat of various bodies like the Constitutional Council, and the venue for investiture ceremonies attended by the great and the good. I'd never paid it much attention. I remembered that's where I had started smoking again, one sunny day, on the terrace of a café that had once existed there, with a boy I liked but whom I would leave for someone else. Right there, on that spot.

Rafik came to join me. He squeezed my shoulder, as if we

were brothers and I should know I could count on him, but must also prepare to be strong. At the time, I thought he was simply moved, and I wondered if he'd taken a shine to me, and how to let him know quickly that nothing of the kind was possible between us now. I've thought about his gesture since then, many times. Did he know, already? Who was in the know? And about what? Who had been manipulating me? Who had been protecting me? What really happened, and what role exactly did I have in it?

I called Zoska. Everyone in the room was telephoning someone. She'd heard already, people around her were talking of nothing else. I was repeating, 'It's just crazy, it's so incredible, I can't believe it.' And then Jean-Marc came to fetch me, and drew me aside. Rafik had a very odd expression on his face.

'Galtan was inside. He was getting his award as Chevalier of Arts and Letters.'

I didn't want to understand. I heard what he said all right. But I didn't want to believe it. I was already having enough trouble digesting the images on the screen, I wasn't going to be poisoned even further by this grotesque detail: François Galtan, the guy who two days before had been asking me if I took sugar in my coffee, François Galtan was in there under the rubble. A dark girl with long glossy hair, wearing a bright T-shirt and electric-blue trainers, had started to squeal, shaking her hands as if she'd been burnt. 'Come and see, look! look!' and we all went towards her screen without a word. Her excitement made you feel afraid. What on earth could be worth getting worked up about, after what we'd just seen?

'I'm plague, I'm cholera, bird flu, the bomb, I'm the shit in your eyes, I'm a radioactive bitch, I'm a vicious little witch. Aliens, humans all polluters, universal contaminators.'

It began like the kind of poem one reads in school, an insistent rap rhythm. Valentine was dressed all in white. She had heavy black eye makeup on. She was speaking calmly, facing the webcam. Sitting at the little desk in her bedroom. All eyes turned to me. I was drained. All my energy had been absorbed: I didn't want to believe this. Because of the amateur presentation, the document looked harmless in a way: just a girl doing something at home in front of her computer. So why were we watching this now?

'I vomit you all. What I'm about to do, I'm doing it on my own. If anyone claims responsibility for my act, they're pathetic bullshitters. I'm doing it just for fun. I hope you'll carry on the good work.'

Then Valentine stretched out her right arm to bring the camera down to the level of her navel, and showed a shiny metal cylinder, about fifteen centimetres long and three across – these measurements quickly became known and were compared to those of a mini-vibrator or a large tampon – then she unbuckled her belt with her left hand, pulled down her jeans, and stood up, she wasn't wearing panties, but nobody found this sexy, she had her pelvis toward the camera, and put one foot up on the desk, classic pornography angle, and inserted the tube right into her vagina, then zipped up her jeans again, gave a little wiggle, put the camera back in position and faced it, concluding in a serious voice, 'You want it? Come and get it.'

End of video. The film had gone online ten minutes before the explosion, under the pseudonym 'Little Girl'. From

François Galtan's iPhone, which Valentine had probably borrowed from him just before the ceremony. Some people say the metal detectors on the door picked it up, but the kid had proudly announced that she had had her clit pierced in Spain and nobody had thought fit to insist, she'd been told to go ahead inside and shut up. Or that's what was said afterwards, but nobody was around any more to confirm if it was true. The bomb wasn't a home-made production. It blew out buildings over a radius of four hundred metres. People often said later that it was a miniature prototype of an E-bomb that hadn't worked properly. It was supposed to cut out all electricity and radio and telephone connections for the whole city for several months. All they know, all they are sure of, is that Valentine certainly hadn't made this on her own with sugar, and that the bomb undoubtedly went off.

She had delivered her text very calmly, lighting a cigarette partway through, she knew it by heart. For someone who was about to do what she was going to do, she looked very relaxed. She kept her eyes fixed on the camera, her expression changed very little.

I turned to Rafik. 'This must be some ghastly coincidence. It's a fake, surely?'

Rafik didn't lift his eyes from the screen. That annoyed me. If I'd been alone, I'd have switched off at once. I'd have pretended I hadn't seen anything. But the entire world, at this moment, was looking at this video which was to beat all records for hits. And it wouldn't stay up for long. Less than five hours later, it had been withdrawn from all sites, the first example of censorship on a planetary scale. The Palais-Royal bombing, which would soon be christened 'Valentine's

massacre', no doubt to try and eliminate any political conno-
tations from the event, would go down in many ways as the
event that propelled us into the politics of the third millen-
nium. People would realize that the internet isn't as difficult
as all that to control, as long as governments have sufficient
motivation. And in the Valentine case, they would all be
agreed, from Poland to China, by way of Syria, Egypt or
Israel: it served no purpose to let this teenage girl spit out her
obscenities on the web. Fear of contagion? Perhaps.

Officially, the reason was respect for the victims' families.
For once they didn't need to plead paedophilia or women's
dignity to justify censorship. All the states in the world had
provided themselves with a legislative arsenal that fitted the
situation. Even Venezuela fell into line.

On the ground floor of our offices, people started to pick
up their stuff, slowly at first, then the group was seized by
panic. What if this bomb was radioactive? Rumours started
to circulate: it might cause acid rain, a vast electrical blackout,
huge-scale flooding. A minor exodus from the city took place
– a sort of improvised bank holiday weekend. Cars and trains
were full, some people even took to the roads on foot. Others
stayed put: those who were convinced that if this really was
an H-bomb it was pointless to run away, pessimists, alco-
holics, looters taking advantage of the situation, and a few
lost souls like me. It turned out to be a false alarm. The bomb
in the end had been 'clean'.

I have only a hazy memory of the exact order of events
that day, but soon I found myself alone on the ground floor
with Rafik and Jean-Marc. I was drinking whisky. The fact
that they stayed with me instead of fleeing inclines me to

think they knew better than they said what kind of explosion it was. But perhaps I'm fantasizing here and their pragmatism was the effect of shock, like mine. Jean-Marc was kneeling on the floor in front of me, like when you talk to a child. He was explaining things in a low voice and I wasn't listening. I interrupted: 'I've got to talk to the Hyena.'

He looked sorry for me when I said that. He'd just realized how totally unprepared I was for what was in store. I don't know whether they helped me, or whether they took advantage of it. I stood up.

'I must make a phone call.'

Jean-Marc caught me by the wrist, firmly, shaking his head. The office was empty, I couldn't think why everyone had left, I didn't ask myself the question.

The Parisians returned to their city next day. Tourism took off. The entire world came to see the Ground Zero of the City of Light, at the same time as making a trip to the Eiffel Tower.

Many people found this event terrific. Academics notably, people who'd never held a gun in their lives or spent a single night in custody, wrote superb articles on the question. Authors of all ages and every stripe used their ten little fingers to type out passionate declarations to the iconic nihilist. They'd done the thinking, she'd done the acting, a well-tried system. Other people condemned the little fool, with the innocent arrogance conferred by sitting in comfort. Some journalists who had done what they were told all their lives took her side. With enthusiasm. Some artists thought it was a good time to call for the decisive moment, the insurrection. Others on the contrary condemned an action with so little backup. Some people expressed their disgust at seeing this child insert the bomb. Her little declaration had been immediately taken up, turned into a rap chant, sung, changed, copied, recopied, translated. Her brief moment of glory. Morbid. Relatives of the victims were questioned by every kind of media, their distressed statements made the headlines. But they didn't grab all the public interest. *Everyone* thought they had been close to the drama. Millions of cybercitizens came online to say their piece about it. They weren't scared. It would take more than that to impress them. It was all the fault of video games, of divorce, of climate change; it was the fault of the president, of all the sugar in fast food, of the Jewish people, of asylum seekers. There were people who thought it a disgrace that the video could not be viewed any more, and others who thought that that was the least the authorities could do. Some people praised the concept but thought the place ill chosen, they would have done better. There were some who complained that it was always the 'children of' who get a lot of attention. Because overnight François Galtan became a world-famous author. Posterity took a broad view, and on all the online bookshops his novels became best-sellers.

The excitement might have been temporary and anecdotal, if it hadn't been repressed in such an exemplary way. All comments were first blocked then wiped. State security. The first judicial sentences were passed very quickly. A legal framework had long been in place for trials during a state of emergency, as soon as terrorism was involved. For posting a text in support of broadcasting the video online: ten years. One image shown a lot on TV was of this elderly writer entering Fleury prison under top security. Fifteen years he got. He looked more surprised than upset. He could hardly credit what was happening to him. He had simply mentioned the 'pretty little thing', and commented that children today have a lot to be angry about. What they wanted was examples, quickly, ones that were easily understood. A boy of sixteen, a cheeky-looking, baby-faced American: thirty years. He had put the video on a file-sharing site. Various laws were amended, initially intended to protect copyright, but beefed up and voted through as a matter of urgency: any agent of the state was empowered at any moment to proceed to the examination of any computer or telephone and to confiscate it if in doubt. The video was not to be circulated under any circumstances, nor was any insidious comment to be passed on what had happened. An appeal was made to the civic spirit of citizens. The desire to talk about it soon faded. Very few articles saw the light of day to complain that, several weeks after the drama, we still knew nothing about the nature of the bomb.

Surveillance cameras were installed in cybercafés. One after another, states adopted the most repressive laws. People whispered that some hackers had persisted, but getting on the discussion forums they organized was way past my competence.

Government-approved articles flooded the web. Any conspiracy theory was simply the fevered imagination of those benighted masses who try to impose a meaning on reality. The official version went out in every language. Valentine Galtan was a disturbed teenager, in a state of advanced mental confusion. She was a victim of drugs, sexual abuse, and under the influence of extreme leftist circles. I saw, to my stupefaction, photos from my file on her put out on the internet . A nymphomaniac, an addict, a mixed-up kid. Parents were warned in the current atmosphere to keep an eye out for any signs of distress shown by their children. To be watchful and firm: a little severity might save hundreds of lives.

Valentine's grandmother made statements of a stalwartness that impressed me. She refused to cave in, and went on declaring that her granddaughter couldn't possibly have acted alone.

Jacqueline Galtan died very soon after that, in hospital from the regrettable complications of a severe attack of flu. Valentine's mother, Vanessa, was questioned by the police, but her statements were not thought convincing. There were too many contradictions and grey areas in what she said. As far as I know, she's still in prison. They found out incidentally that she had been involved in some dodgy financial dealings, and this information was widely publicized. Yacine and his sister Nadja were suspected of complicity: they never confessed to it, but they too, as far as I know, have not been released from prison. Their mother died shortly afterwards, knocked down by a hit-and-run motorcylist. Several extreme-left activists were sought in vain. Except for a certain Charles Amocrana, aka Carlito, who committed suicide in his cell before the police had finished questioning him. I too am on the list of witnesses who have disappeared. But I don't have a political label.

In spite of the efficiency of the censorship, rumours have continued to circulate. They didn't think it worth trying to silence those who simply talked about the event; as long as they didn't do so in public, our governments remained magnanimous. It was said that the list of those receiving decorations that day was particularly remarkable. A journalist who had threatened to go public about some scandals relating to the private lives of certain top politicians. A minister about to lose a law case concerning various high-value financial dealings, and of whom it was said that he might reveal his sources. A stupid pop singer, who'd attracted anger on high by claiming that the president was a sex maniac who was spreading VD to all his contacts. (One wondered why he was getting a medal from the republic in that case.) People even mentioned some of the waitresses at the event, who were call girls involved in a high-class prostitution ring and planning to name names.

All these elements lead me to think that Rafik and Jean-Marc gave me the right advice that day: to go into hiding. Not to wait for the police to come and interrogate me. Even before we had understood how big this was getting, they had pointed out to me that the cops would never believe my version of events. If I declared I didn't know anything about it, I would infuriate them. Same thing, if I said that one fine day, while we were in Barcelona, the Hyena just decided to go into the town centre, and the merest chance had made her pick the very bar where Valentine was hanging out. And that yes, that had surprised me, but at the time I had just fallen in love and hadn't thought about it very much. Rafik said, 'That certainly won't go down well,' and Jean-Marc agreed, pouring me another whisky. If I said I had no idea how to contact the Hyena, except through this mate of mine who worked in a bar, Rafik said 'that will get you into deep trouble, believe me'. Rafik asked me to leave my mobile on the desk. I wanted to delete Zoska's number to protect her, but he pointed out that that was a pathetic precaution. It was about then that I came to my senses and realized that if I went into hiding I'd be putting her in danger, as well as other people I'd been in contact with.

Jean-Marc took me on his scooter to a house in Bougival, to which he had the keys. The journey lasted most of the night, many people were still trying to get out of Paris. I asked him to stop at a phone box, from which I called Zoska.

'I'm in big trouble. Can't tell you all about it on the phone. But you should know they may come looking for you as well. Is your mobile phone contract in your own name?'

'No, of course not. Where are you? Are you alone? How can I reach you?'

'I don't know.'

'Honey. Listen. Remember the name of the bar I told you I worked? Don't say it. I'll be there tonight. Call me in an hour, and get the number of a public phone box where I can reach you in the night. OK?'

Her calm manner reassured me. The place where Jean-Marc left me showed every sign of being a safe house: a basement without windows, furnished impersonally, like a hotel. Next day, Rafik brought me a false driving licence, with the photo off my CV from when I'd first arrived at Reldanch – it makes me look like an axolotl. My name now is Blanche Laure, and I wonder how he managed it so fast, when Paris was in turmoil.

I didn't feel afraid then. It was only later that fear struck. I asked him if my parents would be harassed, and he thought to reassure me: they wouldn't be kept long in custody, but it was essential that they shouldn't know where I was, because if so, they'd be made to talk. And indeed I think my parents spent only a week in prison... Later, I got Zoska to send them two postcards, saying 'see you soon, all well', signed with the first names of my two grandmothers. Hoping they'd understand. I wonder whether they're speaking again, telephoning each other if they ever got them.

Rafik gave me three thousand euros in cash, telling me to look out, it'll go quickly. Apparently Reldanch had a slush fund 'for cases like this'. Cases like this don't happen every day, though, and the fund policy isn't there to protect agents. I know no more on this point than about anything else: did he give me money from his own account? Had he been given the money to help me to disappear more effectively?

Jean-Marc came to say goodbye, and we drank instant coffee standing in the basement kitchenette. Rafik advised Argentina, he said it was a country used to receiving people who wanted to start again from scratch. Jean-Marc thought rather Poland. He didn't advise Sweden, too bureaucratic, I might be spotted quickly. Well anyway, I wasn't going to go to a country where it's cold all the time and hardly ever light. Everything was so well organized. At the time, I felt like weeping with gratitude. In the months that followed, I was more likely to ask myself who they were trying to cover for, and why it was so important to get rid of me. They'd seen others, people they were closer to, fall foul of the state without any protection. Were they trying to protect the agency, or the Hyena, or were they working for some third party, did their orders come from high up, same level, lower down, or off the map? I have never known the answer. And in the end, that was the worst thing. Worse than losing my whole identity. It's like a black hole, an area I mustn't get too close to: what really happened?

They left, asking me to leave the keys in the letter box which had no name on it, and not to stay longer than two days. I had to cling to the bed not to beg them to stay. And I didn't hold back out of dignity, but because I realized it wouldn't do any good.

Zoska called me as she had said. I hadn't told the others that I would venture out of the house, to the end of the street, just long enough to catch her call. I realized myself that it was dangerous, that there was nobody about in these residential streets. But I didn't have any choice. It was when I heard her voice that I started to cry. She told me my name was already being mentioned in the papers, on the radio, and that they were only naming *me* as the private investigator searching for Valentine, not the Hyena. Then she asked me where I was, and I said I wasn't supposed to say anything, so she said that would make it difficult for her to meet me. Again, I thought this was dangerous but I preferred to take the risk than to remain alone.

She asked me if I was far from the station at Bougival, and I didn't have the slightest idea. She didn't give me time to change my mind, she said she'd be there next morning from ten o'clock, with her motorbike, she'd have a helmet for me that would completely cover my face. She seemed to have this all worked out in her head. It reassured me.

Next day, Zoska trod out her cigarette as she saw me coming, gave me the helmet, and I climbed on behind her. I clung on to her back and off we went.

Since I had left Barcelona, she had been playing cat and mouse with me with great accuracy: I call you and say sweet things, I don't reply to your text messages, I promise I'll come and see you soon, I warn you I haven't time, I call you in the middle of the night and whisper torrid messages in your ear, I leave my mobile off all the next day. And it had worked very well with me, I became obsessed with my telephone. But this girl, whom I hardly knew, spent all night coming on her motorbike to pick me up, and took me to Brittany, to a house she had already rented. I was afraid this might be a bad idea. But in time I realized she had both the taste for and the experience of clandestinity. I could count on her to organize things properly.

We arrived in the afternoon, the keys were hidden under some logs. The back garden was bounded by two factory buildings without windows. I could go out there without being seen and enjoy daylight without ever opening the shutters on the road side. I did protest that Douarnenez seemed a bit too close for comfort compared to Rio de Janeiro or Moscow. But Zoska likes Brittany. She thought we'd stay there a couple of weeks, then take the ferry across to England, and fly somewhere from London. Her idea was Brazil. But she soon realized I was in no state to go anywhere. As soon as we reached the house, I collapsed.

The first three months I alternated between inertia, black rage, anguish, sadness and terror. The rats under my skin could find no way out. Every calm moment was just an interval before a fresh attack. The questions I kept asking myself got mixed up, contradicted each other, and wouldn't leave me alone until they'd tormented me for nights on end. What did the Hyena know? Who had Valentine met? What had happened? Was Rafik in the loop from the start? Did the grandmother suspect something? Could it have worked out differently if I'd paid a bit more attention to what was going on? What had the Hyena and Valentine said to each other during the journey back? Why was it those people who were present that particular day who had died? Who had commissioned this massacre? Who had provided Valentine with the bomb? What witness had we met that we hadn't identified as particularly dangerous?

For three long months, I remained obsessed with the day of the explosion. I was inside Valentine's belly, I was inside François Galtan's body, I was ripped apart by the impact, I was in the hands of the emergency services. I lost my identity. Everything I'd been before, and which I didn't value greatly. I had become dispersed into space.

All this time, Zoska was going to and fro, not always explaining what she was doing. She experimented on me with various kinds of 'look': I discovered she has a passion for hairdressing. I've been by turns ginger, platinum blonde, ash blonde, auburn. I've had my hair cut in a bob, then layered, crewcut, in spikes, and finally completely shaved when I couldn't bear to look at myself in the mirror. I never left the house, but I never looked the same for three days on end.

Zoska had decreed that to get me out of my depression, there's nothing like a macrobiotic diet. She thinks I look good slimmer. I catch a cold every time there's a draught and feel weaker. But I didn't argue. In any case, I had a phobia about going out. Not a reasoned fear, but violent nausea and vertigo every time I approached the door. Zoska also decided to take my wardrobe in hand, so for a while I looked like a rich Frenchwoman from the 1970s. I'm afraid this must correspond to her idea of the most intoxicating femininity.

One day, she declared that I was getting better and we should change our hideout. So we drove, in a car, to Seville. It was astonishing, I'd spent three months, cloistered, terrorized at the idea of taking a step outside, but after five minutes out of the house I felt fine. The further south we drove, the more light there was and the more I felt I'd left the worst behind me.

I'm still on the wanted list. My photo was broadcast everywhere for weeks. They somewhat exaggerated my importance in the affair. They speculated that I might have been kidnapped by a terrorist cell that's afraid of the evidence I might give. But unlike Magali Thalbo, my face quickly disappeared from the media. I get the impression that it suits everyone if I remain untraceable. I don't know why.

I'm living in a village which is invaded in the tourist season, Cantillana, a few kilometres outside Seville. I'm no longer afraid of being recognized: when I look in the mirror, I don't feel I look anything like myself. My expression is totally transformed.

We're still thinking about going to South America. A French woman who looks like me agreed to rent me her passport for the trip, but she's disappeared. Never mind, Zoska isn't in a hurry. She likes it here. Her business is going well. For a long time I was afraid she wouldn't come home one day. Either because she was fed up with having to be a nurse, or because she'd been caught and sent down for a few months.

Zoska is the best lover, friend, sister and accomplice anyone could wish for. She's the only person I've spoken to for months. I've never been very sociable and quite quickly I appreciated being able to do without the rest of the world. Her company is enough for me.

She brings me echoes from the outside world, what she hears, what she finds on the internet. According to various sources, the Hyena is in Chiapas, or in Gaza, she's in prison in Ukraine, she's died in Chicago, she's working in Saint-Jean-de-Luz. Some say she's even been sighted in a convent, in Mexico. I think she knew, when we brought Valentine back, what was going to happen. But I don't think she was truly involved. She knew, and she didn't like it. Because Valentine was special. When she finally joined us, I was surprised nobody had thought to tell us, about her, that she smelled good, that she had a lovely voice, that she had a sense of humour. When I was tailing her, I was seeing her from too far off. I didn't know her smell. I didn't know her smile. But Valentine had a special kind of strength. And I think the Hyena had glimpsed it. And she would have preferred things to turn out differently.

Zoska has several theories. The people who commissioned the attack are the manufacturers of the uterine bomb. The whole story was at bottom nothing but a mega advertisement to promote their precious gadget, and find markets for it worldwide. The people who commissioned the attack are the manufacturers of the X-ray detectors that you now see installed at the entrance to every public building. The people who commissioned the attack are in the government: it wants to be re-elected and to have its hands free. The people who commissioned the attack are top-level church dignitaries who wanted to destabilize the state, because they see it as too soft on rival sects. When I try to argue with her, she just clicks her tongue and says, 'You don't know the half of it.' Like me, she's chosen to make up a story for herself to believe, because she'll never know the truth.

Valentine did what she had to do. She was too young to be interested in the daily changes in the trees, or to watch the light on the water, to wonder about the destination of the boats in the distance, and to fill a life with those things. I was furious with her, a heavy unbearable pain hammered at me for months. For her or against her, it wasn't clear. I thought about the moment when we got back to Paris together, and her father put his arms round her. His awkwardness was touching. What did she think at that moment? Valentine did what she judged she had to do. Like everyone. I often think of all the things I should have said to her, and I listen to what she might have replied. I have told myself the story so often that in the end I've put together what I really know, inventing scenes that I didn't see, to make the story stand up, the way I imagine it happened. It was when the narrative started to get going that I began to feel better. Gradually I've come back to life. One day, I realized that I'd been awake for several hours and hadn't yet thought about Valentine. I felt like Noah at the moment the dove comes back with a little olive branch in its beak. The truth I'll never know. What remains is the story I'm telling myself, in a way that suits me, a story I can be satisfied with.